CORK CITY LIBRARY
Leabharlann Cathrach Chorcaí

www.corkcitylibrary.ie

Tel./Guthán (021) 4924900

This book is due for return on the last date stamped below.
Overdue fines: 10c per week plus postage.

D0493798

CLOSED
MONDAY

Claire
Rayner
Jubilee
The **Poppy** *Chronicles 1*

**HOUSE OF
STRATUS**

The right of Claire Rayner to be identified as the author of this work
has been asserted.

This edition published in 2001 by House of Stratus, an imprint of
House of Stratus Ltd, Thirsk Industrial Park, York Road, Thirsk,
North Yorkshire, YO7 3BX, UK.

www.houseofstratus.com

Typeset by House of Stratus.
Printed and bound in Great Britain by
Antony Rowe Ltd., Chippenham, Wiltshire.

A catalogue record for this book is available from the British Library
and the Library of Congress.

ISBN 1-84232-536-1

This is a fictional work and all characters are drawn from the author's imagination.
Any resemblances or similarities to persons either living or dead are
entirely coincidental.

FOR JAY

To welcome him to the world of words
with love

ACKNOWLEDGEMENTS

The author is grateful for the assistance given with research by: The London Library; the London Museum; the Victoria and Albert Museum; the General Post Office Archives; the Public Records Office; the Archivist, British Rail; the Meteorological Records Office; the Archive Department of *The Times*; the Imperial War Museum, London; Marylebone Public Libraries, and other sources too numerous to mention.

BOOK ONE

1

It started to rain about an hour after dinner and that helped. She could sit and watch the drops chasing each other down the panes and bet with herself on the winner. It wasn't the most exciting way to pass the time but it was better than sitting and staring at the dull street below, her sewing unheeded on her lap.

The rain should have cooled the air, but it hadn't. The heat still pressed down on her head like a thick blanket made of food smells, and she played with that thought in a desultory sort of fashion, imagining the smells being visible instead of just heavy in her nose. She saw the layer of cabbage in limp wedges of greyish green leaves separated from the pallor of the boiled potatoes, with slabs of beige fat-trimmed mutton and glutinous gravy, and on each side the dingy brown and yellow of oxtail soup and custard, and the image was so vivid in her mind's eye that it made her feel slightly sick and her forehead and upper lip became wet again with sweat. And she picked up her sewing, which was a new nightshirt for Harold, and mopped herself with it, not caring whether she made it grimy or not.

Somewhere in the house a clock chimed, and she lifted her head, listening for more signs of life, but there was nothing. Even the nursery floor was silent, quiet as the grave, she thought, and again imagination slid about her head unchecked and she saw the row of four beds in the big room that was the night nursery, each with its toy box at the foot and a dressing gown and slippers arranged on it, and each with a small brother lying stark and tidy and dead beneath the red counterpane. And then shook herself for being so wicked. They were boring and tiresome and made her life a misery in a great many ways, but they were but children and part of her own family after all. She had no right to wish them dead.

Not that she did. Again she sat and stared at the raindrops sliding erratically down the window and tried to decide what she did want. Not the boys dead – no, not that. Less boring and demanding perhaps, less adored by their mother and father – and then her face hardened, and she forced herself to fix her attention on to one particular raindrop that had seemed to find a barrier at which it sat, fat and sulky, in the middle of the pane while its competitors went skittering crazily down to the winning line of the sill. She would not think about that, she would not –

But of course she did. She couldn't help it. How could she do otherwise when once again here she sat wasting her life away while her brothers were having so much better a time of it? Even the baby Harold had more pleasure in this house than she did. But was it her fault she was a girl? She hadn't chosen to be a female. No one would ever choose that, not unless she were mad, and certainly wouldn't choose to be as plain and dull and dismal a female as Mildred Amberly. And she whispered to the raindrop, moving her lips with great deliberation to make the words clear, 'I am Mildred Amberly. I am plain and dull and useless and no one wants me, not even my parents, and I should have been a man,' and the raindrop seemed to fatten and lurch over the barrier and went running away down the pane to disappear into oblivion at the bottom. And Mildred laughed and rubbed the pane with her finger to see where it had gone and then yawned and looked out into the street again.

There was still nothing happening down there, and she gazed at the grey paving stones of Leinster Terrace and at the blank heavily curtained windows of the cream stucco-fronted houses on the other side, each in its big stolidity a mirror image of the one where she now sat at the first floor drawing-room window, and imagined something happening. A parade perhaps, a parade of circus animals, with clowns in floppy costumes and dead white faces and women in pink spangles and men on stilts in great crimson top hats and interminable striped trousers. The stilt men, she told herself dreamily, the stilt men would be laughing and smiling and smiling and laughing, and one of them would come and tap tap tap on the drawing-room windows across the street where the Frobishers and the Millars lived, and would break the glass and throw blue smoke bombs inside so that the silly people there all choked and coughed and cried out; and then one of the stilt men, a wonderful happy one with a face full of teeth that glinted in the light of the sun that was still setting in an orange glow behind the chimney pots, would come and break *her* window and pull her out, plucking her from this dreary room with its dreary overstuffed furniture and the dreary portrait of Papa over the fireplace and carry her away, laughing and teasing and laughing again at her until her own face was nothing but glinting teeth too as she smiled and teased and smiled back at him –

The image shivered, shattered and died as the rain stopped and she thought for a while about the possibility of opening the window to let in the damp air of the September evening and perhaps the smell of the park, rich and earthy and somehow threatening, even primitive, and then decided against it. First of all the windows, draped as they were in so many yards of Nottingham lace and heavy velvet drapes, would resist any attempt she might make to disturb them, and secondly it was absurd to imagine Hyde Park could ever be threatening and primitive. It would be lovely if it were, if walking along the Bayswater Road could be a risky occupation, if it were possible that great wild slavering beasts could jump out of the sooty thickets of shrubbery and carry her off.

It really was particularly bad this evening, the way her mind was running away with her, she thought, and picked up the sewing again and looked at it. The side seams were done, and the sleeves were in; all she had to do was complete the smocking down the front, and if she really tried she could perhaps finish it this evening before she went to bed. She ought to, really; Mama had bought enough flannel to make winter nightshirts for all the little boys, three each, and if she didn't get on with them the cold November nights would be here and Nanny Chewson would be wanting to know where they were, and sniffing and looking superior because, of course, once again, Miss Mildred had been wasting her time.

Yes, particularly bad this evening, she told herself again as she let the sewing drift back on to her lap. Really bad, and not just in her mind. Mama looking so pale she was almost green as her migraine clamped down on her and Papa shouting that he asked for little enough in this house, precious little, and why did a man have to beg for so simple a thing as a shirt ready when he came home from his business and an urgent City dinner to attend, and Basil and Claude sliding away as they had just after tea so that Mama kept asking her plaintively where they were, and she having to lie and say she thought they had gone to a lecture – oh, it had been a particularly bad day. She ought to be glad it was all so peaceful now.

But it had been bad in other ways too, and her face reddened as she remembered now.

She hadn't meant to eavesdrop. Not that she was above doing such a thing; when it suited her she listened and pried with a will and a clear conscience and a good deal of skill. But this evening she really hadn't meant to do it. She had gone up to Mama and Papa's room with a headache powder she had fetched from Cook, knowing that this time Mama's headache was a real one and not just another of her excuses to lie on her sofa and sleep, and, Mildred frequently suspected, restore herself with sherry. She had been feeling unusually benevolent towards Mama because Papa had been so particularly horrid about his wretched shirt, and had made Jenny, the parlour maid, cry till her nose ran and threaten to hand in her notice. Getting Mama a headache powder had been the least she could do to help. And there she had been, her hand on the very door of their room when Papa's thick voice had come booming out for anyone to hear. Only it had been she, Mildred, who had heard, and no one else. Which was perhaps a small comfort –

'I put it to him as straight I could. "The girl's no oil painting and I'm the first to admit it," I told him. "But she's a good-hearted soul, and has plenty of experience in the arts of running a decent man's house, helping her stepmama as she does. And she's young – twenty-eight, young, you know – and there'll be a handsome consideration, a decent sum settled on her, though, of course, with six sons to provide for as well – " and he understood, of course, he did. But he was as straight with me. "A man wants more to a wife than an income, sir," he said. "And with all due respect, your daughter isn't for me. I need some more comfort than just money, if you take my meaning, sir, and there it is." So there it is indeed, Maud. The girl's on our hands for life, if you ask me. I've done all *I* can to find her a husband and there's not one that shows a spark of interest that I'd touch with a barge pole. There's been one or two who'd take anything for a bit of ready cash, of course, but I'm not having that.'

He had snorted and coughed at the same time then, a particularly disagreeable noise at which he was an adept, and Mildred, her hand still on the doorknob, had almost been able to see him through the dark door panels, his belly pushing proudly over his black trousers and his shirt billowing over his chest as he stood there, legs braced apart and hands on hips while Mama struggled to fasten his studs and arrange his necktie. And had hated him as cordially as she ever had, almost finding enough strength in her hatred to push the door open to rush in and hit him with both fists and scream at him, 'I don't want you to find me a husband, I don't want to have to live with a creature like you, not now, not ever. I hate you and I hate your husbands and I hate, I hate, I hate, I hate – '

But of course she hadn't moved. She had just stood there and heard Mama bleating softly, 'Oh, Edward, poor dear Mildred, she does try, you know, and she means so well, it seems so cruel, and the boys so handsome especially darling Harold with his eyelashes so long – '

'So you put it clearly to her, Maud – ' Her father's voice again, thicker than ever, though a little muted. He was at his dressing table now, sleeking back his thinning grey hair with the pair of silver brushes her own mother had had engraved for him the year before she died, admiring his red face and his rows of chins as he stared at his horrible self – and Mildred had taken a sharp little breath in through her nose and squinted at the door, and twisted up her mouth, making herself even more hideous than she was, just to show him. Not that he needed showing –

' – you put it clearly to her. She's as plain as the cat, plainer, and she needs to make more of an effort if she doesn't want to spend the rest of her days a sour old maid. She's no conversation, no spark of life about her, makes no effort to please a man – haven't I brought them here till I'm blue? This one, old Masters' son, he was the last there was – and even he won't have her. Not two brass farthings to call his own, son of a useless fool as he is, and even he won't have her – she made no effort, you see, not an atom, to please him, sat there all through dinner like a long drink of cold water, which is all she is and so I tell you, and there's an end to it. I'm done with trying. I've done all a father can decently be asked to do – now, my coat. No, woman, not that one! I'm to dine at Guildhall, remember. If I've told you once I've told you till I'm blue. Guildhall! Lord Mayor, all the Aldermen – if I'm not one of 'em this time next year I'll be a Dutchman. And if I go looking the way you'd turn me out, a Dutchman is all I'd have the hopes of being. Give it here, woman – '

Mildred had stayed no longer, turning and running down the big staircase, holding her cream serge skirt in both hands almost up to her knees so that she could move as quickly as possible, and had only stopped when she reached Mama's small sitting room and had thrown herself into it and on to the sofa to catch her breath.

She had sat there very straight, feeling her face hot and her eyes wide and dry with fury; he had been trying to sell her all through the City, that was what it was, as well as among all his shopkeeper friends in horrible Kilburn and Acton and Lewisham and Camberwell, where he had all his hateful shops. He had sat there in his chop houses and his shop back rooms and his banks and all those other places where he spent so much of his life, offering her to men to be taken off his hands for a consideration. She had always known that the men he brought to dinner from time to time, and who were always made to sit next to her, had been paraded as possible husbands for her. Ever since first Eugenie Frobisher and then Charlotte Millar had married, just after their eighteenth birthdays, she had known everyone thought it was time she was off their hands too. With six boys to educate and set up in life, Papa was fond of saying loudly, a man had his work cut out to do all a father should, and he would stand there at his ornate fireplace in the drawing room and look round at his substantial furniture and substantial curtains and substantial house, clearly pleased with his substantial self. Until he looked at Mildred, sitting straight backed and with her eyes lowered, silent and unresponsive on the sofa as yet another dinner guest tried to make small talk with her and totally failed.

And how could it be otherwise? Mildred asked herself passionately now. How could it be otherwise? They were always so dreary and so unappealing, with their half-bald heads and their droopy moustaches and wet eyes and their weedy bodies and –

And who am I, she had thought then, catching sight of herself in the mirror in Mama's little sitting room, who am I to complain about a man's looks? With a face and figure like mine, who am I to complain at the sort of men he tries to sell me to?

Her image had stared back at her, blankly, and she had looked again, trying to see what others saw when they looked at her. A long face, sallow and thin, with a nose to match, long and a little oddly shaped, twisting slightly as it meandered across on its way to her mouth. And such a mouth – long and a little curly too, like her nose, so that she looked always as though she was despondent. And perhaps I am, she thought, staring at her image, and who wouldn't be? Brown hair, so ordinary in its brownness it looked like dust, straight and with so little life to it that there was no shine at all, and such stupid eyes, so pale a brown that they looked almost yellow in some lights, and straight fierce eyebrows and a long chin.

At least, she thought then, I don't have awful spots, like poor old Basil. Not that it matters to Basil. A boy – it doesn't matter what boys look like. Oh, God, I wish I was a boy and had a boy's body. Not this great long thin thing that has nothing to it that would please any man. And she had run her hands across her bodice, feeling even through the thick cream serge the touch of her own fingers as they brushed across her nipples, and knowing that however sensitive they seemed to be, the breasts they crowned weren't breasts at all, really. Flat-chested and bony hipped, with skinny legs that had nothing of the voluptuous about them at all, that was Mildred Amberly. Was it any wonder her father wanted to get her off his hands so eagerly? And any wonder that no one would take her, even after ten years or more of her father's efforts?

Particularly bad tonight, she told herself again, sitting there in the drawing room after dinner and remembering the afternoon's misery as the sun sagged wearily at the end of the street and let the dark come hissing in from the East. Papa going off in a huff and Mama so miserable over dinner, and the little boys fighting and fussing when Nanny Chewson brought them down for dessert. Oh, a particularly bad night. And the worst thing about it is it will be no better tomorrow or the day after that or any other day. Just for ever and ever like this, with Mama and me helping her and being in the way, and Papa looking at me and despising me because I'm only a girl and not one of his precious boys, and no use as a girl even – and she took a sharp little breath in through her nose and got to her feet.

Why she looked again into the street she didn't know. Perhaps there had been a hint of movement that had caught her eye? Whatever it was, she found herself half kneeling on the window seat and staring down into the dimness below. They had gaslight in Leinster Terrace now – had done ever since Papa had made a fuss and demanded the service be added to this important district where important people lived, and clearly the lamplighter had passed while she had been sitting there thinking, for there was a pool of soft yellow gaslight spilling over the paving stones, and in it stood the foreshortened figure of a boy.

An odd-looking boy, Mildred thought, staring at him. He had thick curly hair, the thickest she could ever remember seeing, so curly that even from this height, a storey above the street, she could see its springiness, almost feel it beneath her fingers. The boy looked up then, and for a moment it seemed he had heard her thoughts, had even felt her imagination's hand on his head, for he was staring at her.

But he was not; he was checking the number of the house with whatever was on a piece of paper he held in his hand, and she could see him more clearly now and found him even more exotic. A tanned skin, dirty but still a rich soft colour, and eyes so dark and lustrous that she felt he could see her, even here hidden behind her curtains, and she shrank back. But he didn't see her, for he looked again at his paper and then, to her amazement, ran quickly up the steps of the house.

Amazement, because there was no doubt the boy with the thick hair and the rich dark eyes was a street arab. His clothes were several sizes too big for him, his boots were battered and all too painfully oversized, and he was exceedingly dirty. What was such a one doing at the front door of Edward Amberly, Esquire, hardware merchant and would-be Alderman of the City of London? Even at the kitchen door, down in the area below, he would have been out of place. Cook or Freddy, the all-purpose man who doubled as butler, valet for Papa, and boot boy, would have sent him packing very quickly. Yet here he was, running up their front steps like any gentleman and ringing the bell.

For she heard it pealing through the house, and stood there with her amazement dissolving into excitement. Something was happening to improve this particularly bad evening; a street arab was ringing at their door, and so sterile and dismal was life for Mildred Amberly on that evening of 17 September 1893, that the event constituted an adventure. And she threw her sewing on to the window seat and ran to the door and out to the head of the stairs to meet it.

2

'It's all right, Freddy,' she said swiftly as she reached the hall-way with its black and white squares glowing in the puddles of dark blues and golds and greens that were thrown on to them by the gaslight on the other side of the stained glass of the front door. 'I'll deal with it, whatever it is.'

Freddy stood and blinked at her, his hand on the green baize door that led to the servants' part of the house and then shrugged slightly and went away, but this time she wasn't angered by his unspoken contempt. The fact that the senior servants despised her as a dreary old maid, just as her father did, rankled sometimes. But not tonight; tonight she was filled with a sort of reckless anger that was more exciting than dist-ressing. Tonight she'd do what she wanted, and to the devil with whatever anyone thought of her. And she whispered the words aloud as she struggled with the door fastening, feeling daring and outrageous to be using such language, she, a well-bred woman. 'To the devil with you,' she whispered and then pulled the door open and stood there staring at the boy on the front step.

At close quarters he looked even more exotic. His eyes, those dark and lustrous eyes, were sharp and knowing and he looked up at her and then, with a swift flick of his eyelids, beyond her into the hallway, and almost as though she were inside his head she saw what he saw; the rich mahogany furniture, the big paintings in their heavily gilded frames, the thick red turkey carpet, the gleam and glitter of brass stair rods and doorknobs, a place that breathed money, and, suddenly prudent, she pulled the door partly closed behind her.

'Well, young man? What do you want?'

'More'n you can give us, lady, and that's no error,' the boy said perkily. His voice was husky, pitched deliberately low and she thought – he's very young. No more than fourteen or fifteen. Basil and Claude had sounded like that when their voices were breaking, and that thought made her relax. Just a child, that was all he was, no one at all exciting or threatening. Her spirits, which had been so suddenly high, sagged again.

'We don't give to beggars at the door,' she said sharply, and she stepped back to go inside and close the door on him and at once his dirty face reddened furiously.

'Who are you callin' a schnorrer?' he demanded. 'I don't go beggin' and don't you never say I do! I ain't no schnorrer!'

She blinked. 'No *what*?'

He laughed then, a bubble of sound that she liked and she stood uncertainly, not sure whether to go in and slam the door as she had meant to, or stay where she was, and he grinned and said, 'Cor, you're an ignorant lot here up West, ain't yer? Schnorrer, lady, schnorrer. Beggar, scrounger, on the old ear'ole. I ain't one o' *them*. I earn my living straight, I do. Work dealt with, commissions executed, confidential trans-actions undertaken. You name it, I'll do it. That's why I'm 'ere. Commission executed, that's what this is. You Miss – ' and he peered. ' – Amberly? Eh? Miss M Amberly, are yer?'

'Who are you?' All her caution was up in arms again, and she stood there with one hand behind her, holding the heavy door close to her back, ready to push it open and spring back inside at the first hint of trouble from this boy. Young as he was, he was well muscled, and tall for his apparent age; not a person to try to deal with if he became threatening. For the first time she wished she had let Freddy answer the doorbell after all.

'Eh? Oh, I'm Ruby Blackman,' the boy said. 'Not that that's got anythin' to do with anythin' – '

'Ruby?' She spluttered with sudden laughter. 'A girl's name!'

' 'Ere up West, it might be. Where I comes from it ain't,' the boy said with dignity. 'Reuben, then, if yer must know. And it ain't got no connection with the matter in 'and anyway. Are you this 'ere Miss Amberly? If you ain't, I'm wasting my time.'

The fear was ebbing away now; to be afraid of a boy called Ruby seemed too absurd. 'You're not wasting your time. I am she. What do you want?'

'At last!' the boy said with exaggerated patience. 'All right, then. This 'ere's for you, an' I'm to wait, so sharp about it. I got more to do than 'ang round 'ere.' And he reached importantly into the pocket of his waistcoat, a vivid if singularly dirty affair of deep green satin stripes, and produced a large turnip watch which he looked at, frowned, and then twirled on its chain so that it slipped neatly back into its hiding place. 'Much better things.'

She looked down at the folded paper he had thrust into her hand and then, frowning, stepped forwards slightly so that the light from the lamp post just beyond the house could fall on it. And then felt a sudden lurch of fear as she recognized Basil's rather childlike scrawl.

'Dear Mildred,' he had written. 'This messenger will bring you to me and Claude. Take a four-wheeler, not a hansom, it must be a four-wheeler, and come at once with the messenger. *Bring money.*' This was underlined in several thick scrawls. 'Don't tell anyone what you're doing. This is urgent. I am relying on you. *At once.*' And again the thick underlinings before the scrawl of Basil's signature, the one he'd been practising for some months now. She recognized it with no trouble at all; this was a genuine message from Basil; there could be no doubt of it.

13

'But this is ridiculous.' She said it aloud, staring at the note and then at the boy Ruby. 'Things like this only happen in silly story books.'

'Up West maybe they do,' the boy said sapiently. 'Down East, anythin' can 'appen and usually does. We got better things to do than read stories. We *do* 'em, we don't read 'em.' And again he produced that bubble of laughter.

'Where are they? The – the people who sent this?'

'It's true then? You're 'is sister, that tall fella? A right droopy devil 'e is – an' the other one. Not safe out without their mothers, those two. Or nurses as the case might be.' And again he peered over her shoulder to look into the house through the narrow aperture left by the front door.

'Where is – where are they?' She made no move to block his view now; he was no would-be robber. His curiosity was just that, a simple and clearly lively interest in everything he saw.

'I ain't at liberty to divulge,' he said with great dignity and then flicked a glance at her. 'Which is bleedin' silly, on account of yer goin' to see the place anyway. Down Flower and Dean Street, Spitalfields.'

'*Where?*'

'Spitalfields. Other side o' Aldgate Pump. Honestly, 'ow narrer can a person be? Ain't you lived in London long, then?'

'All my life,' she said, stung. 'Here in this house – '

'Poor cow – ' the boy said, staring at her and then grinned, showing rather uneven dirty teeth. 'I mean, got all the trimmings, ain't yer? Fancy ken like this, carpets all over the place, lights and all – probably got privies inside 'n' everythin', eh? But never done no living, eh? Not like down East. That's livin' *if* you like – the Whitechapel Road or Shoreditch High Street of a Saturday evenin', oh, you should see it! Tarts togged up to the nines and the fellas – well, you wouldn't credit the way some of 'em looks! An' you've never bin down there – ' He shook his head, pityingly. 'Just shows yer, don't it? You can seem to 'ave it all and 'ave nothin' at all, really. Never been down East – sad, that's what it is, sad. Real sad – '

She was scarlet with mortification. Bad enough everyone here in her own home pitied and despised her; to have this street urchin doing so was more than anyone could be expected to bear and she opened her mouth to say something blistering but he forestalled her, putting out both hands towards her, palms upwards, in an oddly appealing gesture.

'Not that I means to blame you, lady. I mean, you can't 'elp it if you got a rotten life, can yer? It's different for those creeps of fellas down at Lizah's – they can do what they like, or thinks they can. But you, bein' a female – well, it's not right, is it? Are yer comin', then?'

'To – what was it you said?' It was simpler and perhaps less shaming to ignore all he had said about the narrowness of her life of which she was too painfully aware already. 'Lizah's? Who is she?'

The boy tipped up his chin and stared at her again and then roared with laughter, so loudly and with such gusto that Mildred threw a nervous glance over her shoulder to see if anyone had heard and would come investigating.

'Who's she? Oh, that's rich, that is, really rich an' ripe. Wait'll I get back an' tells 'em all that one – who's she? Listen, you come an' see for yerself.' He sobered then and gazed at her solemnly. 'You'd better. They wants yer, these fellas, they really does. If they're what you say, your brothers an' all, it's my advice to you to come and 'elp 'em out. They got problems, and that's the truth of it. An' I've spent enough time gettin' 'ere as it is. Omnibuses ain't what they ought to be. But we're goin' back in a four-wheeler, they said. So, you go and get your necessaries an' I'll whistle up a cab – ' and he turned to go.

'Wait a moment – ' She stood uncertainly staring down at him. He had reached the pavement now and was looking back up to where she stood poised on the top step, and she looked at the rough curly hair and the deep dark eyes and tried to think rationally.

To go with so odd a person as this merely because Basil had sent her a note telling her to do so – it had to be the most foolhardy thing anyone could possibly do. Basil hadn't said why she was to do it, or anything at all except to come; and for a moment she remembered all the tales she had read in those long dull evenings alone in the drawing room when Papa was at those interminable City dinners of his and Mama was yet again in her room sleeping off her day's sherried exertions, tales in which just such messages came to ladies, just such as she, alone in their houses, and who suffered extraordinary experiences as a result of obeying them –

But this wasn't happening in one of Mr Arthur Conan Doyle's stories in *The Strand* magazine. This was happening in real life, here in her own boring Leinster Terrace, and she lifted her chin and took a deep breath in through her nostrils, trying to convince herself even more of the reality of what she was experiencing. She smelled the wet earth and greenery from Hyde Park and the soft reek of burning coal from chimneys already belching grey smoke, even though it was still September and the weather warm, and horses and the rain-settled dust and a pungent whiff of dirt and food that was probably the boy who was still standing impatiently looking up at her, and remembered all at the same time the dreadfulness of the day and what Papa had said about her, and how the long empty days of her life stretched ahead of her and thought – why not? Even if it is a dangerous thing to do, why not? Whatever happens, it will be better than sitting here putting smocking stitches in Harold's nightshirt, better than knowing how useless and ugly they all think me, better than –

'I shall be as soon as I can. Don't fetch the cab here, I prefer not to be – it will be better to find one in Bayswater Road. I shall be quick.' And she turned and went back, not looking again at the boy, knowing he would wait there for her.

It wasn't until she re-emerged, her straw hat with the blue feathers firmly pinned to the bun on the top of her head and her blue jacket buttoned over her cream serge day dress, that she thought again about where she might be going with this odd youth, and was glad that she hadn't troubled to change into an evening gown at dinner time; there was no need if Papa was not to dine, and she had been grateful for that. Now she was grateful again, feeling certain that evening wear would have been quite excessive for where she was about to go.

'This way,' she said curtly to the boy as she reached his side beneath the lamp post and she began to walk hurriedly along, glad that there was a drift of fallen leaves on the paving stones to muffle her footsteps. No one had seen her re-enter the house or leave it, and there had been no sound from anyone as she closed the door softly behind her, but she was suddenly afraid someone would come running after her to stop her, Mama perhaps, or the hateful Freddy, or even the four little boys from the nursery, chasing after her in their nightshirts down the street towards the traffic of the Bayswater Road.

She pulled her wandering thoughts together, and said a little breathlessly over her shoulder, 'We should be able to find a cab at Lancaster Gate. They're always there for hire, during the day time at any rate,' and then caught her breath in alarm again, for she realized now just how dark it had become. The sun had fully set and the sky was a deep indigo above the serried lamps that threw their soft glow down on to the pavements, and she shivered slightly and tucked her elbows even more firmly into her sides.

There were indeed cabs at Lancaster Gate, the drivers leaning nonchalantly against the gateposts of the Park entrance waiting for fares, and she hung back, alarmed again. To call on one of those rough-looking men by herself? It was a terrifying thought for someone who only ever rode in cabs with her parents, and then only in such vehicles as had been carefully chosen by Freddy, and brought to the front door, but the boy Ruby had no such qualms.

' 'Ere, you, cabbie!' he called loudly and swung himself up onto the step of the first cab in the row as the horse between its shafts lifted its head from its plaited straw nosebag and whinnied softly in surprise. 'Take us East, will yer?' And he opened the door and hopped inside with all the energy of an eager hare, and then leaned down to reach out a grimy hand for Mildred, who still hung back.

'Get yer filthy hide out o' my cab, you!' roared one of the men who detached himself from the knot by the gateway and came lurching towards them. 'I don't ply for hire for the likes o' you – '

'The lady's payin',' Ruby said loftily. 'Come on, Miss Amberly! We ain't got all night, y'know! You've gotta wait an' come back 'ere. There'll be two other young gentlemen to come wiv 'er, too. Now, will yer get a move on? Fare both ways – you don't get that every evenin' and don't you pretend as you does. There's more flies on that pathetic object you calls your nag than there is on me, mate – '

The man stopped and stared at Mildred and then at Ruby, now sitting comfortably ensconced in the corner of the cab, his feet in their highly regrettable boots sprawling and then back at Mildred again.

'You goin' wiv '*im*?'

'Yes,' she said after a moment and lifted her chin and stepped forwards, ashamed now of her timidity and the man spat, aiming at the ground at her feet and she stopped and looked at him sharply, at the expression of scorn on his face, and her temper swelled and grew and blossomed. 'Ruby!' she cried loudly. 'That cab is not fit for my use. Leave it at once and select another.'

The boy leaned forwards and poked his head out of the cab door and stared at her and then slowly grinned and she raised her brows at him, and immediately he jumped out of the cab and pulled on the front of his hair with an exaggerated gesture of subservience.

'Yes, Miss Amberly, at once Miss Amberly, anythin' you says, Miss Amberly!' he chirruped and ran along the line of cabs, peering and prodding at the horses so that they stamped and blew chaff from their nosebags and the cab drivers by the gate watched and laughed.

'I'll take yer,' the first cabman growled but Mildred swept past him to the cab that Ruby had now chosen and climbed in and settled herself, and the driver of the new cab came across and settled himself on the driving seat and then leaned down to speak to her, grinning all over his heavy face.

'Where to, then?'

'Flower and Dean Street, my man!' Ruby said loftily. 'On the corner o' Brick Lane past Aldgate. And sharp about it, wait to return 'n' all – now move!'

'Right *sir*,' the driver said and whipped up his horse and with a lurch and a loud rattling of harness the cab moved away and Mildred sat and stared out at the familiar Bayswater Road swinging past, the houses and railings seeming to dip and dive with every movement of the wheels, and tried to think what she was doing and why she was doing it. To be sitting in a cab with a dirty boy with a girl's name going to the notorious East End of London in a four-wheeler, after dark – it was unheard of, incredible, a dreadfully wicked thing to do.

But, a corner of her mind whispered to the scandalized and aghast part of her, but it *is* living. It isn't sitting in the drawing room waiting to die of ugliness. Even if all this turns out to be some dreadful disaster, it will be better than that. Anything would be better than that.

3

Down Oxford Street they went, past the rich shop windows piled high with the pickings of the world, through to Holborn and the silent offices and on to the shuttered brooding City, and all the way the boy Ruby chattered about all that he saw, commenting disparagingly on the quality of the shops they passed, comparing them unfavourably with the glories of his precious Whitechapel Road and Shoreditch High Street; but she didn't listen to him. She sat tucked firmly into the corner of the musty cab with its smell of old leather and horse and dust and tried to convince herself that all this was really happening. That it wasn't one of her silly daydreams, the images with which she filled her mind and made her dismal life tolerable.

This was real; no doubt, she told herself, and firmly pinched her own hand between a sharp thumb and forefinger and winced at the pain. This was *real* – and dangerous; and her spirits sagged again and she wanted to lean forwards and cry to the man in the box, whipping up his bored horse, that there had been a mistake. He was to turn round and take her back to safety. But Ruby chattered on and somehow it would have been more alarming to see him turn on her with those dark eyes full of scorn than to go on. So she sat and held her hands tightly twisted on her lap so that her kid gloves strained under the pressure and tried not to think of all the awful things that were about to happen to her.

The cab swayed and lurched onwards, leaving the City behind, moving always eastwards, and now the nature of the passing scene changed. The rich heavy buildings of the West End gave way to more ramshackle edifices with peeling paint and battered brickwork, and the people on the streets changed too. In Oxford Street there had been a few well-dressed strollers gazing at the brightly lit shop windows and restaurants, showing in every languid movement their self assurance and their wealth, and in the City there had been hardly a soul to be seen apart from a few fast-walking people leaving their offices late and hurrying home to snug suburban houses in Kilburn and Acton. But here the streets shimmered with activity, and almost against her will Mildred found herself leaning out of her corner to stare out of the grimy window at them.

Ruby stopped seeming so exotic, suddenly. Everywhere she looked there were people just like him, glossy and darkly curled about the head, large-eyed and expressive about the face, and as they passed little knots of men talking and gesticulating and clusters of women in heavily trimmed gowns and pelisses in the most vivid colours the new aniline dyes could create – purples and fuchsias and rich crimsons and shrieking greens and blues – Ruby's odd clothes faded to insignificance. And she opened her eyes wide and stared and stared as though to collect and store up every image she could find.

'See what I mean?' Ruby said, smugly, in her ear. 'It's a bit of all right, ain't it? Real life, that's what all this is – and this is just the start of it. Up there –' and he pointed vaguely ahead '– up there the streets goes on and on, as far as the London 'Ospital an' beyond, an' all the way there's lights and there's people and there's life. Real *life*. Not like up West where yer all dead and buried, only not got round to stinkin' of it yet –'

'Yes,' she murmured. 'Yes –' not really aware she had spoken, and went on staring and, satisfied, Ruby leaned back in his own corner and watched her, well pleased with the effect all that she saw was having on her. He looked proprietorial and content, as though he personally owned the streets and was graciously sharing them with an admirer.

'Left 'ere!' he bawled suddenly, leaning forward and rapping on the roof of the cab. 'Left, yer great ninny – I told you – Flower and Dean Street! You goes left into Thrawl Street and then right, you bleedin' great schmuck! Everyone knows that. That's it – round 'ere – '

He was leaning out of the cab window now, waving and shouting, and all Mildred's fascination with what she had been watching shrivelled and died in a puff of terror and she shrank back into her corner again, clutching her reticule close against her chest and staring wide-eyed out of the cab over Ruby's shoulder.

The street they were in was a narrow one, flanked by even narrower houses with blank-eyed windows, roughly curtained, behind which shadows seemed to move to and fro, barely seen in the light thrown by the row of meagre gas lamps which straggled along the length of the small thoroughfare. The pavements were almost as full as those of the main road; not with gesticulating men and glittering women but chiefly with children and Mildred's eyes widened as she looked at them as they came in a great pack running alongside the cab, which had slowed to a walk. Thin, tousled, often filthy, some of them seemed to be wearing only one skimpy garment, and some were barefoot. But there were others, sleek and well fed and bright-eyed who made her mouth curl as she looked at them. She thought of the children at home, of small Harold, still, at four years old, with the round soft belly of the infant, and of Samuel and Thomas and Wilfred, gangling their way through the years from six to twelve, and tried to see them as contemporaries of this collection and quite failed. They, with their long pale faces and lank pale hair and dull pale eyes, were as like those capering creatures as cats were like goldfish; they could have belonged to a different species of creation altogether.

The cab stopped and juddered as the horse reared back, alarmed by the way several of the children leapt for its bridle and the man in the cab roared and swore and the children roared and swore back and laughed shrilly, clearly enjoying themselves hugely, and Ruby jumped down, and leaving Mildred to fend for herself as best she could, went tearing into the scrum of children, his fists flailing.

'On your way!' he bawled. 'Sling yer bleedin' 'ooks, the lot of yer – 'ere, Mo – you come 'ere. This 'ere lady – ' and now he looked over his shoulder to check that Mildred had left the cab. 'This 'ere lady'll give yer sixpence to watch that no one bothers this 'ere cabbie, right? You won't get a bleedin' farthin' if the cabbie tells me there's been any trouble. You understand? Now, the rest of you, 'op it – ' and he looked up at the cabbie on his box and shouted, 'Right Guv. 'E'll see you're all right. Tougher'n he looks – ' and Mildred looked at the diminutive creature who now stood at the horse's head, importantly holding its bridle, and could have wept, for he was so small and so dirty and so unkempt of hair that all that could be seen of his face was the glint of his eyes. But he seemed to be in command of the whole situation, for the rest of the children fell back to a respectful distance and stood and stared at him and his charge, and he glared ferociously back at them as the cabbie sat on his box and uneasily stuffed a small clay pipe with shag tobacco.

'Come on,' Ruby said and went hopping away to the side of the street and down towards the corner; and she looked over her shoulder at the cluster of watching little hooligans and then at his retreating back and for want of anything else she could better do hurried after him.

'Where are we going?' she panted, for he was going at a fast rate, and he peered back at her and laughed.

'Told yer – Lizah's place – '

'Who is she? You still haven't told me. And what are my brothers doing here? And – '

'Questions, questions, all you bleedin' women's the same,' Ruby said, in a high good humour. 'Wait and find out, and save your breath for the stairs – ' and he turned sharply and went plunging on into the darkest doorway Mildred had ever seen. 'Come on!' he shouted again, and his voice came echoing back to her as she stood hesitating on the doorstep. 'Come *on!*' And she heard his footsteps go clattering away over bare boards and disappear.

Behind her the grey street was menacing in its quietness, for the children had stopped shouting and were just standing and staring after her, and the horse was standing still, its head bent and making none of the whinnying and stamping noises that would have comforted her. And suddenly alarmed, she went plunging into the dark house after Ruby.

Once inside she had to stand still for a while until her eyes became accustomed to the dimness, and then she could see a narrow corridor stretching ahead of her, and a flight of stairs going upwards on her left. But he hadn't gone upstairs, of that she was sure, for the sound of his footsteps had disappeared downwards, and she moved forwards gingerly and called, 'Ruby?' in a rather thin voice and then more loudly, 'Ruby!' and this time he answered.

'Dahn the cellar steps!' His voice came up to her thinly from below. 'Along to the end o' the passage, on yer left – go careful; third step down's a bit busted-like.'

She picked her way forwards, still finding it more alarming to consider going back than onwards, feeling with her hand along the damp and peeling wall and then, as the wall seemed to disappear caught her breath in gratitude as a light appeared ahead of her.

'Cor, don't you creep around!' Ruby called disgustedly. 'Down here – come on then, we ain't got all night. Mind that third step, for Gawd's sake – '

The staircase, now she could see, wasn't so bad and she picked her way down it, wrinkling her nose a little. The air

smelled cold and damp and rich with cats, but there were other
smells too, heavy and musky and not altogether unpleasant
even though they were unfamiliar, and again the fear that had
started to rise in her belly subsided to a low mutter.

Ruby was at the foot of the staircase with an oil lamp held
in one hand and he took her elbow as she reached the stone
flagged floor and propelled her forwards.

'Come on, ducks,' he said. 'You're doing all right – bit dark
here, so watch it – ' and blindly she followed him until at last
he pushed open a door and she stood blinking in the great rush
of light and warmth that came at her, and also a great increase
in the heavy smells she had been so aware of on the staircase.

She knew what it was now, and had to open her mouth to
breathe, finding it too powerful to let into her nose. Male
sweat, great waves of it, the sort of smell she had sometimes
been aware of when she passed her father on the stairs, or
which Freddy left wafting behind him as he carried the great
scuttles of coal up the stairs in the winter. A horrid smell, one
she hated. And yet –

And yet here it didn't seem so unpleasant. She stood
hovering in the doorway as Ruby went swaggering in and
tentatively closed her mouth and went on breathing and
somehow it wasn't so bad after all. There was a sort of
excitement in it, an immediacy, something that made her blood
seem to ring a little in her ears, and she blinked and to her own
amazement stepped forwards of her own volition, needing no
Ruby to urge her. And stood in the middle of the room in which
she found herself, staring round in amazement.

A big room with a stone floor and in the centre of it a sort
of raised dais, with ropes slung round it. Against the walls
hooks with towels on them and balls and spring-laden
equipment that looked totally foreign yet far from alarming,
and skipping ropes and punchballs – and she blinked again
and knew where she was. A gymnasium; she had seen pictures
of just such equipment in Gamage's catalogue, and could

remember the boxing displays at the City of London School through which she had been forced to sit when Basil and Claude had been pupils there. Basil had always enjoyed pugilism, she remembered now, even though he had shown precious little skill at it; and she almost smiled as she remembered his lugubrious look when he had been helped out of the ring after one such display at the school, his cheek bruising rapidly from a well-placed blow by his opponent.

She lifted her eyes and looked further, and saw people. A man in a pair of old trousers and a voluminous shirt was in close colloquy with a man who stood close to him with a dressing gown over his bare shoulders and his arms dangling, each ending in a heavily gloved fist, and two or three others were standing nearby, obviously listening. There was another man on the far side of the big room, lying on his back and kicking a large ball in the air from foot to foot, and she stared, puzzled. It seemed very childish behaviour for a man of that size, which was considerable. On the other side of him, there were three other men, each working with one of the chest expanders that hung against the wall, and she averted her eyes hurriedly as she realized that one of them was wearing no more than a very skimpy pair of drawers, even shorter than those of her brothers' underwear, which she knew so well since she had all the mending of them.

The man seemed to become aware of her presence at the same moment she did of his and sat down hurriedly, reaching for a towel, and she turned away just as a door she had not before noticed, tucked as it was into the far corner of the room, flew open and Ruby stuck out his head.

'In 'ere,' he called peremptorily and at once she picked up her skirts in both her gloved hands and hurried round the central boxing ring and into the room.

And stood at the threshold staring at the sight of her two brothers, sitting side by side on a bench and looking quite extraordinarily miserable.

'Basil!' she cried. And then shook her head in bewilderment. 'Basil, what on earth is going on?'

He jumped to his feet at once and came towards her, both hands held out. 'Oh, Mildred, thank God you're here! I thought you'd never arrive – it's been hours since we sent him, absolutely hours.' And he shot Ruby a glance of pure venom. 'I dare say he stopped to gossip with heaven knows who on the way and – '

'Well, there's gratitude!' Ruby cried shrilly. 'Didn't I break my bleedin' neck to get there? An' didn't I 'ave to waste a week'n'an'alf getting this one to come with me? Didn't I 'ave to push and shout at the cabbie, eh? An' you says that! You tell 'im, Miss Amberly, miserable sod what 'e is. You tell 'im! Straight I came to you, didn't I? Straight on account o' that's what I am. Straight by nature an' every inclination. So you mind your manners and be grateful – '

'Be quiet,' Mildred said, suddenly irritable and finding some strength in that. 'Basil, what is this all about? I get some sort of ridiculous message like something out of one of your cloak and dagger stories and – '

'Did you bring the money?' Basil said and moved closer to her and she looked up at his face and frowned. His eyes were dark, for the pupils were dilated with fear, and his upper lip and forehead were wet with sweat, in spite of the coolness of the cellar room. She looked over his shoulder to Claude, the younger of them, and he too was sitting staring at her with a beseeching expression on his face and obviously just as alarmed as his brother.

'What money, Basil? I don't know what you are talking about. Is this some sort of silly practical joke? A game of some kind? You must explain yourself!'

He didn't answer but pulled at the small leather purse she was still holding tightly and tugged it from her fingers and began to fumble with the clasp but at once she seized it back and thrust it into the bodice of her jacket.

'Don't you dare, Basil Amberly! Don't you dare! I've little enough that I may own, but what there is is indeed mine. Now either tell me at once what all this nonsense is, or better still come with me and we'll go home and you can tell me on the way. I have a cab waiting and we shall return to Leinster Terrace at once. Now come along.'

'Not this side o' the new century,' Ruby said at once and moved to lean against the door and she looked over at him and then around at the room, all her original fears leaping up to tighten her throat and dry her mouth. Was she to be abducted, beaten, robbed? But her brothers were there and surely they would protect her? And she looked at Claude sitting on the narrow bench, on which a few towels were lying, with a pile of old and rather malodorous clothes on each side of him, and then at Basil's pale sweating face and knew she would find little defence from them. Yet they had brought her here – and she turned and glared at Ruby and said loudly, 'Well, young man? You have a lively enough tongue in your head. *You* tell me what is happening here and why my brothers are here and why you are preventing their departure, and – '

'Oh, I don't meddle in no family affairs,' Ruby said with a somewhat sanctimonious air. 'It's up to him to tell yer – ' And he looked at Basil with such scorn that she reddened with embarrassment on his behalf.

'If someone doesn't tell me soon I shall just go upstairs on my own and go straight home again and leave you to manage as best you can. Though you'll have to tell me sooner or later if I'm to keep you out of trouble with Papa, which I imagine is part of whatever it is. So the sooner the better. Now stop being so stupid and tell me what it was you brought me here for and why you are being kept here so.'

'I didn't mean to do it, Mildred,' Basil said wretchedly and gazed at her with so lugubrious an expression it seemed he was about to weep. 'It was just for a little fun, you know, a wager or two, no more. I didn't know they were laying such odds and changing them as they did, and when he told me what we owed I was so set about – well, I didn't know how it could be. But he said we can't go home till we've paid and I knew we couldn't sit here all night and that if Papa – if he got home before us he'd tell Freddy to lock up and then what would we do? Oh, please, Mildred, do give them their wretched money and let us get out of here! We won't ever come again and –'

'I didn't want to come in the first place.' Claude's voice came high and thin from the bench. 'I told him I didn't care for boxing, so sweaty and – well, so *horrid*. I much prefer to play whist like any decent chap would, but he insisted and if I hadn't had a bet I'd have looked a sorry baby, wouldn't I? I wasn't to know either how they were changing the odds and –'

'If 'e was to 'ear you suggestin' as 'ow 'e cheated 'e'd have your kishkas out on the line,' Ruby said, almost conversationally, and came away from the door to sit beside Claude, no longer seeming to fear that she or they would run away from him. 'Kishkas is guts, for you ignorant geezers. Listen, you played deep, showing off what toffs you was, and that was the truth of it. We're 'appy enough to bet tanners an' bobs. Even a joey'll do for the likes of us. We're in it for the sport, we are, not for showin' off. But not you, oh no! You 'as to bet with 'alfsovs, don't yer? Well, got yer come-uppance, didn't yer? All yer givah taught yer nothin' about form, did it? So 'ere you are with a big debt to pay, and pay it you shall before 'e lets you out. So the sooner you tells yer sister 'ere what's what, the sooner we can all go and get a noggin, eh?'

'I pay no debts for betting to anyone,' Mildred said strongly. 'My brothers both know that such behaviour is forbidden in our house and would not do it. Of course they have been cheated and so I shall tell whomever this is you're all so frightened of. Debts indeed! More like stealing from innocent boys! They are neither of them yet twenty-one and as such it is not legal, I am sure, for you to take bets from them anyway.

So the loss is yours – if there is any loss, which I take leave to doubt. You people who bet are all – '

'All what?' The voice that came from behind her made her catch her breath and turn at once and she stood there and stared at the man who was standing inside the door which he had so quietly opened.

A short stocky man with eyes as rich and lustrous as Ruby's but with much longer lashes so that he seemed to have a soft gaze – until the glint in the depths of them showed; at which point the sense of softness vanished at once.

A dark and curly man with a shadow across his cheeks where his beard was announcing how long since he had been shaved, and wearing a neat suit and very white linen, with a glint of a gold ring on one short and rather hairy finger.

Looking at him, she felt that the exotic quality she had seen in Ruby was multiplied five times over and she stood very straight as she stared at him, trying hard to keep her face expressionless so that he could not see how alarmed and yet how fascinated she was. He looked as out of place as a tiger would have done stalking down Leinster Terrace and he made her feel as alarmed as though he were indeed a tiger. All the strength and command that she had been using in her dealings with her brothers and Ruby, born of irritation and fed on fear, seemed to slide away and beneath her cream serge skirt she felt her knees become shaky.

But she managed to speak and raised her head and said as steadily as she could, trying not to let her voice shake. 'And who might you be?'

Ruby grinned then and came hopping over from Claude's side to the newcomer, who was still standing quietly by the door. He was barely a couple of inches taller than the boy, for all he was very obviously a grown man, but that did not detract from the menace she felt in him.

'I'll tell you 'oo 'e might be,' Ruby said. 'This 'ere's the fella what is owed all the money. This 'ere's Lizah.'

She stared at the stocky man still standing silently and with his eyes fixed on her, and then looked at Ruby, and she couldn't help it. It was as though someone else was inside her skin and reacting, not sensible Mildred at all. And the someone else began to laugh, softly at first and then more and more loudly until tears were streaming down her face and she was hiccuping helplessly. And all the time the man Lizah stood and watched her, his face quite blank of any expression.

4

'I'm sorry,' she managed at last, and rubbed the back of her hand against her wet cheeks, not caring that it made the kid leather of her gloves darken into ugly patches. 'I didn't mean to be rude, but really – what sort of place is this where the men have women's names? It sounds so ridiculous.'

'Not so ridiculous as *Basil* and *Claude*,' the stocky man said, and he drawled the names in so flat and nasal a tone that Basil reddened and stepped forwards, his hands clenched into fists, and Mildred put up her hand and set it warningly on his sleeve.

'I meant no insult,' she said. 'And I'm sure there is no need for you to give one back. I have apologized for my ill manners. It was just that – I was taken aback.' She let go of Basil's arm and folded her slightly shaking hands in front of her and looked at the man appealingly. 'You have to agree this is a very – ah – unusual situation for me to find myself in and when I am then told that a man such as you is called – ' And to her horror the bubble of laughter rose again in her throat and she had to bite hard on her lower lip to keep it under control. It's just that I'm so frightened, she told herself, biting down even more savagely. It's making me stupid. Stop being stupid –

Amazingly, he produced a thin-lipped smile. 'Well, you got something there, Miss Amberly. I dare say it does sound a bit strange, at that.' His speech was not as racy as Ruby's; indeed it seemed he had made some effort to speak with a better accent, but there was still a nasal resonance about it, and an unmistakable cockney twang. 'I can't say as I'm all that enamoured of it myself. It's a shortening, you see. My name is Lazarus Harris, an' how do you do.' And he held out one hand towards her and inclined his head slightly.

Almost without thinking she stepped forwards and held out her own hand and he took it and shook it punctiliously, if a little more vigorously than she was accustomed to; most of the men to whom she was introduced at Leinster Terrace had fingers that were damp and droopy and certainly never grasped hers so firmly. She could feel the warmth of his skin through her gloves and unaccountably felt her cheeks redden.

'How do you do, Mr Harris,' she murmured and then stepped back again as Basil tugged sharply on her arm.

'You can call me Kid like most people do,' Lizah said, ignoring Basil completely, although he was now standing very close to Mildred and glowering down on him from his considerably greater height. 'Kid Harris, that's me. Known the length and breadth of this city as a winner. Except by some particular fools, that is.' And now he did flick a glance at Basil and she felt him stiffen at her side and she took a sharp little breath in through her nose. The glance had been momentary but so filled with scorn and even menace that a new frisson of fear ran through her.

'Really,' she said and stopped, not knowing what more to say, and Harris looked at her again and she blinked, for now all the menace was gone. His face was rather nice to look at, she found herself thinking; a little dark cheeked perhaps, but friendly. He had rather protuberant eyes, she realized now that he was so much closer to her, and they were a rich brown with a good deal of warmth in them, and his forehead was pleasantly creased with a series of parallel lines, although he appeared much the same age as she was herself. Though that is a considerable age indeed for a woman unattached, a small voice murmured deep inside her and she lifted her head and said quickly, 'I'm sorry. I have not heard of you.'

'You I don't expect to know about me,' he said and there was a note of magnanimity in his voice. 'A woman I don't expect nothing from. Only politeness and respect and this you give.' Again he bent his head and again she wanted to laugh. He really was a very odd little man, she thought, looking at him, aware now that she was a good three inches taller than he was. A solid man, and well built, but considerably below middle height. Just as you are far too much above it, the jeering inner voice said, and again she spoke hurriedly, to drown its nastiness.

'I would hope always to be polite, Mr Harris. Just as I would hope my brothers are. And I must ask why you are keeping them here in this manner, and why I was sent for so strangely? I am sure they have said nothing out of the way to you that would warrant such – such – ah – well, what *is* going on here? I do feel I have a right to know.'

'Indeed you have, Miss Amberly. Of course you have. The thing of it is, they owes me money. More'n it's right for one gentleman to owe another you see, and – '

'Gentleman!' said Basil over her shoulder and snorted. 'A nasty greasy kiky little – '

'That'll do, you!' Ruby had been sitting on the bench beside Claude, watching them and now he was on his feet and running across the room to stand pugnaciously in front of Basil, his back to Kid Harris. 'You been askin' for a pastin' ever since you come in 'ere and I'm in the right mood to give it yer – if the Kid don't lose 'is temper first and flatten yer, which 'e 'as every right to do and every provocation – '

Harris' hand came down firmly on Ruby's shoulder and he pushed him aside, not unkindly but with determination. 'I don't need no mouthpiece, Ruby,' he said. 'I can deal with this one – ' And he looked at Basil, taking his gaze from his feet up his lanky body to his flushed and angry face and then turned to Mildred. 'Not that I intends to waste time on the monkey when I got so sensible an organ grinder here to talk to.' And again he grinned at her, but it was not thin-lipped now. It was a wide smile and his teeth, uneven and with a wide central gap, but very white, glinted at her and made her want to smile back. But she didn't.

'I still don't know what is going on here,' she said stiffly. 'Will you please explain in detail?'

'The detail is a matter of a debt of ten pounds. Ten golden sovereigns, Miss Amberly, that's the thing of it. This piece of cold lockshen here –' He stopped then and smiled even more widely at her. 'I must remember that you're a stranger in these parts, eh, Miss Amberly? This long piece of cold cooked spaghetti – begging your pardon, of course, seeing as he's your brother, but you got to admit he isn't exactly a dazzler of a man – this brother of yours comes in here, on to my patch, swaggering and swanking like some tart out on a – again I must beg your pardon, Miss Amberly. Like some frilly piece o' nonsense on a night out, and throwing himself about more than somewhat on how much he understands about pugilism and how the science of it is at his fingers' ends and considerable nonsense of that nature. And when he hears as how I'm boxing here tonight, and he takes a look at me, he decides with all this great knowledge of which he is so inordinately proud that I'm a loser.'

He laughed then, a sound that was, she felt, meant to be light and amused but which had a savage note in it. He was genuinely angry, even though he was trying to control it.

'Me, Kid Harris, a loser! Now I asks you, Miss Amberly, do I look like a loser? Do I? You don't need to be no expert to answer. Just a sensible person with eyes in her head. Would you call me a loser and lay down a sovereign apiece at odds of five to one the way this pair of ripe idiots you has the misfortune to be related to has done? Just look and tell me that, Miss Amberly.'

She looked at him as he stood there in front of her, his arms hanging lightly at his sides, his feet set neat and foursquare in small and brightly shining patent leather boots and his chest pushed forwards so that his gleaming shirt front, which pouted above his Tattersal check waistcoat, could more easily display the large pearl buttons which fastened it, and shook her head, hardly aware that she was doing so.

'I hardly know, Mr Harris,' she managed to say at last. 'I – I know nothing of such matters. I can only regret that my brothers made any wager with you, on any matter, because they know that their father would object and – '

'I say, Mildred, do stop talking to this wretched creature!' Basil could contain himself no longer, and pushed fowards to stand beside Mildred and glare at Harris. 'M'sister isn't interested in any conversation with *you*. She came here at my request, and not yours. Now leave her be.' He whirled then to lean close to Mildred's ear and hissed at her, 'For heaven's sake, Mildred, give it to him. Ten sovs, and I'll give it back to you tomorrow – or not later than the next day. Claude still has half his allowance at home anyway, so you won't suffer. Just hand it over and let's get out of this damned place – '

'I haven't got ten pounds!' She spoke loudly, not caring whether Harris heard or not, and at once Basil scowled and tried to push her back away towards the rear of the room, but Harris' hand was on his shoulder, pulling him out of the way.

'Not brought it, Miss Amberly? And here's this one swearing on every available object to which he could lay his lying tongue that you would bring it.'

'There is no need to abuse my brother to me, Mr Harris!' she said sharply. 'Any conversation we have is private to us, if you please. I do not interfere with your conversations and I do not expect you to do so with mine. Now, Basil, what are we to do?' She turned again to look at her brother, who was now looking even sicker and yet still furious with anger. 'Why didn't you tell me in that wretched note what you wanted?'

'I said to bring money!'

'Yes, but not how much or what for! I knew I'd need to have money for the cab and that is all I do have – look!' And she thrust her purse at him. 'I had but thirty shillings in my writing desk and that is what I brought. I saw no need to fetch more from my locked box. Why should I? There was no mention of it in that note – you really are a great donkey, you know!' And now she did drop her voice a little and looked back over her shoulder for a moment. 'Why did you not explain properly instead of sending such a mysterious summons? Now what do I do?'

Basil said nothing, just stared at her and then shrugged and turned and went back to the bench where Claude still sat, speechless and with his head drooping, and hurled himself down beside him.

'Do as you please!' he said in a rather high voice that barely concealed his panic. 'I thought you had more wit than – oh, what is the use! Go home, do, and leave us to deal as best we can. I've done all I can – '

And he folded his arms and glowered at her, and her chest tightened with pity, for she knew that mulish look of his so well. He only looked so when he was frightened and trying to be brave. So had he looked when she had had to be the one to go and tell him his Mama had died, when he was just six years old. So had he looked the year or two later when Papa had told him he was to have a new Mama and was to love her and obey her. And so had he looked any time this past dozen years as child after child had come to clutter the Leinster Terrace nursery and push the older Amberlys well into the shallows of family life.

It was not surprising that he had learned to turn more and more to her, his only full sister, as the years had gone by, and now she had let him down; and not only he but Claude too, rather silly Claude who slavishly followed his older brother in all things and never seemed to have a thought to call his own. There they sat, the pair of them, in trouble yet again and needing her, and what could she do? This was not one of their usual pieces of trickery designed to keep Papa in ignorance of their doings, not a situation where she had only to open her eyes wide and lie to Papa, and let him scold her instead of them. This was real trouble and she had proven herself to be helpless to deal with it.

Exasperated at her own uselessness she turned back to Harris, moving sharply so that her serge skirt bellied out a little and made a cold draught of air for which she was grateful, for her cheeks were hot and damp with a combination of the rising temperature of this rather unpleasant cellar room and her own state of mind.

'Mr Harris,' she said with an imperiousness that belied her anxiety. 'We find ourselves unable to discharge this – this so-called debt at present.'

'So-called?' Harris' brows snapped down so low that his rounded eyes seemed to protrude beyond them as he thrust his head forwards, tortoise fashion, to glare at her. 'Are you suggestin', Miss Amberly, that there was some sort o' trickery here? I told these idiots they was wrong, but would they have it? Everyone told 'em not to lay a bet, but would they listen? No, they would not. I took their bet while warning 'em against it. I told 'em to name their odds, and name them they did – at five to one. Such shlemiels! Such idiots – five to one! So they owes me ten pounds, fair and square, and any suggestion that – '

'It's a fair debt, Mildred. For God's sake don't say otherwise,' Basil growled at her from his bench, but she did not turn to look at him. She never took her eyes from Harris' face.

'If any gambling debt can be said to be a fair debt,' she said at length, 'then I dare say this one is. But that does not alter the fact that I do not have that sum to give you. I have just enough to pay the cabman to take us home. If I fail to do that shortly then our family will become aware of our absence and may well alert the police. In which case you would, I think, be more than a little embarrassed.'

38

'Embarrassed?' He seemed to contemplate the word for a long moment and then grinned at her. He really was a most unpredictable man, she decided, moving from what appeared to be cold and malicious anger to joviality in a matter of moments.

'I like the way you speaks, Miss Amberly, I really do. Class, ain't it, Ruby?' And he turned and looked at the boy who was still standing with his fists half at the ready beside him. 'Not like those drawling idiots, but a real classy voice, quiet and nice, you know?' He looked at her again and smiled even more widely. 'Yes, Miss Amberly, I will agree with you that visits from policemen is something I find embarrassing. Not for myself, mind you, but for them. They never finds nothing here, that's the thing of it, and I hates to see them what you might call disappointed.'

Ruby laughed then, a little burst of merriment that made her lips curl in spite of her inner trepidation and Harris seemed to be aware of the change in her and leaned forwards and some more confidentially.

'I'll tell you what, Miss Amberly. Let's you and me go and talk about this here situation somewhere a bit more –' He looked around at the bare room and then grinned again. 'A bit more ladylike. This ain't – isn't the place for a gentleman to entertain a lady so classy as yourself, now is it? I dare say we can reach an agreement about this silly sum of money. It's not the sum that worries me, you understand. It's the principle of the thing –'

'I suspect it always is,' Mildred said sharply and the grin vanished from his face as he looked at her and again fear lifted in her belly and rose to her chest and stole some of the air she had breathed.

But then he laughed again and shook his head, admiringly. 'Like I say, a lady of real class. Well, shall we?' And he crooked his elbow and held it out to her.

'No!' Basil bawled suddenly and leapt to his feet and came across the room as though he had been propelled by a silent explosion. 'Don't you lay a finger on her, Harris! Do what you said you would and beat me, but if you set so much as one of your fat greasy fingers on her, I'll – '

Harris had stiffened and now he said in a low voice that was very clearly heard for all its softness, 'You'll *what*, Mr Basil Amberly? Eh? You'll what? You saw how you lost that bet, didn't you? You saw them carry Levine out on a stretcher, I take it? The blood that was running from his nose, or what was left of it, did not escape your attention? No, I didn't think as how it could have done. I wouldn't waste my time hittin' you, Mr Basil Amberly. I got my standards, you know, and they are high, they are very high. But I am not goin' to let you get away with anything either. You showed one glimmer of good sense tonight in fetching your esteemed sister here to sort matters out. Don't go an' ruin it now with your big mouth.'

'You keep away from my sister – ' Basil said furiously again and moved closer and suddenly Mildred could bear it no longer. Ever since she had set foot in this extraordinary place she had been holding herself in the tightest of control. She had been trying to think of a way, any way, in which she could take her brothers by their elbows and walk them out of this ugly underground room with its heavy smell of male aggressiveness and male intransigence and male braggadocio to safety. Basil and Claude were male too, of course, but not in the way this man was. He stood there in his rather ridiculous over-fashionable clothes with his hair glossy with brilliantine and his finger with its glint of gold ring cocked so that the light caught the deep yellow and made it gleam, but he was far from ridiculous himself. He filled her with a very real fear, but also with a spurt of excitement; and the mixture of the two made her head swim a little and created a rather queasy sensation inside her which, though not entirely disagreeable, certainly interfered with her ability to hold herself in check.

So she stamped her foot and shouted as loudly as she could, 'Be quiet! Both of you be quiet! I don't want another word from you, Basil, do you hear me? Not another *word*. Sit down and be quiet at once. And you – ' And she turned and stared at Harris with as withering a look as she could call up. 'You stop talking in circles and spell it out. What do you want to let us out of here? A promissory note or whatever they are called, for your ten pounds? I'll give you that, and you shall have the wretched money before the end of the week. Tomorrow, probably. Or, you can return to our house and – '

She stopped then as she tried to imagine this man in Papa's hallway in Leinster Terrace – ' – or certainly, you can follow us and wait at the end of the street and your money shall be fetched out to you this very night. But I have had more than enough of all this nonsense and wish to return home at once. I have a cab waiting above stairs with a driver who may well lose patience at any moment and be off, and then what do I do? So, Mr Harris, which shall it be?'

She stood there with her elbows bent and her hands held stiffly closed in front of her, feeling the colour high in her cheeks, and stared challengingly at Harris. But he said nothing, just looking at her.

'She's a goer, ain't she?' The boy Ruby said and laughed again, that same burst of laughter that had amused her so much before; but this time she felt no urge to smile. 'I tell yer, a right goer. Should 'a' seen the way she took on a cabbie up West that wasn't to 'er likin'! A right tongue lashin' she gave 'im. An' now she's done it to you!' And again he laughed. 'Lizah!' he crowed. ' 'Oo's she?'

'Shut your ugly face!' Harris said, almost absently, never taking his eyes from Mildred's face. 'No other choices, then, Miss Amberly?'

'How can there be any other choice?' she snapped. 'I've no money with me. I have money at home. I shall pay your debt as soon as I get there. As I see it, you have no other recourse but to bid us good night and see us on our way.'

'I could keep you here and send your brothers home to fetch the cash,' he said and still there was no expression on his face. Just the same watchful stare.

'Don't be stupid!' she said witheringly. 'The moment they were out of here, they'd fetch policemen to you. Wouldn't you?' she called back over her shoulder and at once Claude said, 'Yes!' and Basil cried loudly, 'No!' to drown him out. 'Of course we wouldn't,' he gabbled. 'Of course we wouldn't. We'd fetch the cash right back!'

'And leave your sister here till then?' Harris said and flicked a look at him and again Mildred saw the scorn in it, and felt, just for a moment, agreement with him. Basil, the weakest and stupidest of her brothers; however easily he could twist her pity inside her, however easily he could manipulate her attachment to him, he was no match for this one.

'Whatever you do I wish you'd do it soon,' she said and turned her back on Harris and went to the bench to sit down beside Claude, who shuffled mournfully along to make room for her. 'I am very tired. So be so good as to let me know what your decision is once you have reached it.' And deliberately she turned her head away from him.

There was a short silence and then Harris went to the door and stood to one side as Ruby, in response to a jerk from his chin, opened it and held it wide.

'Good night, Miss Amberly,' Harris said. 'Take your brothers with you. And see to it they never come back here, for their sakes and for mine. The thing of it is that I have no wish to waste my good energy flattening them on to the canvas. They ain't worth the trouble.'

She lifted her head sharply. 'We can go?'

'That's what I said, wasn't it? Good night I said. I heard it clear. Didn't you, Ruby?'

'Clear as a canary's kiss!' Ruby said. 'Good night. That was what you said.'

She was on her feet and tugging at Claude's arm. 'Thank you,' she said. 'Thank you *very* much. Come on, Basil. It's getting late and we have a long ride back to town. Come along, Claude, for heaven's sake!' for he was sitting staring at Harris with his lower lip lax, and making no effort to move.

'Before he changes what passes for his mind,' Basil hissed savagely and hauled him to his feet roughly and the three of them crossed the room, Mildred bringing up the rear, and Basil pushed Claude through, ignoring Harris completely.

'If you tell me the address of this establishment, Mr Harris,' Mildred said as she reached the doorway, 'I shall see to it the money is sent tomorrow. And after that, there's an end of it. Neither of my brothers will ever return here. Basil! You hear what I said? That neither of you will ever return here – '

But Basil was gone, halfway across the big outer room with Claude, now at last in some control of his scattered wits scuttling along beside him, and neither of them looked back, both making purposefully for the door that led to the staircase.

'You're dam' right they won't,' Ruby said. 'They ever show their faces dahn 'ere and I'll circumcise their bleedin' noses. Not that it wouldn't improve their ugly mooshes more than mildly.' And again he produced his infectious laughter.

'Miss Amberly,' Harris said as she still stood hesitantly looking after her brothers. 'You really are a very polite lady. You're really concerned as they should pay up, aren't you?'

She glanced at him momentarily. 'If they owe it, of course. You say they do. They don't deny it. So, yes.'

'It's written off, Miss Amberly,' Harris said and his voice was suddenly deeper and more resonant and she looked at him again, and now he looked even more like a plump well-satisfied pigeon, for his chin was tucked into his neck and his chest pushed forwards and the laughter that had burst out of her when she had first seen him began to gather again. But all she did was smile and after a moment held out her hand.

'Mr Harris, thank you. You are a very kind – '

'Gentleman?' he said and his full eyes glinted and now she did laugh, but it was not unkind amusement.

'Indeed, yes.'

'Not the nasty kiky little Jew boy that your brother called me?'

Her face crimsoned then as she stared at him. 'He didn't say that!'

'He was about to.' Harris wasn't a pigeon any more. He was standing looking at her with his dark brows raised and she felt the anger that was in him and the affront that filled him and for one brief moment could see her brothers through his eyes; as full of smugness as they were devoid of wit, as arrogant as they were stupid, loud in their criticisms of people they did not know or understand or wish to know. They had clearly behaved like boors, and this man had been deeply offended by them. Yet he had behaved to them as well as he could under the circumstances and now was behaving extremely well, and she took a sharp little breath and said softly, 'I apologize for his – I apologize, Mr Harris. I would not have had him behave so ill for the world. But – I shouldn't make excuses, I know, but since our Mama died and – well, various things, it hasn't been easy for them. Thank you for your forbearance. Good night, Mr Harris.'

'Good night,' he said after a moment and bent his head again in that odd little bow and she walked past him as Ruby, with a great wink, went bouncing off ahead of her to lead the way to the door, the staircase, the cab that waited above and home.

She followed him, not looking back at Harris, but very aware of his eyes watching her, and feeling, suddenly, a little sorry that her adventure was over. It had been an uncomfortable half-hour, but it had been interesting, and she laughed inside her head as the thought came to her; what was the phrase that odd little man had used so often? And then she remembered; that was the thing of it; it had been *interesting*. That was the thing of it.

5

She was in the nursery sorting through the children's clothes, looking for any that required mending but thinking more about last night's extraordinary events than about tattered sleeves and torn seams, when she became aware of Freddy at the door, whispering to Nanny Chewson, and she bit her lip with mortification. The servants would never dare behave so in front of Mama or Papa, yet they did as they pleased with her. To be the ageing unmarried daughter of the house was to be the butt of everyone's scorn, clearly, and the spark of anger that thought created made her speak sharply to him.

'Well, Freddy? Have you nothing better to do than waste Nanny's time in this fashion? I thought the silver at table less than satisfactory last night. A little more attention to your duties than to – '

'I came to tell you as you're wanted at the door, Miss,' Freddy said loftily and looked at Nanny and lifted one brow at her. 'I was telling Mrs Chewson as I wasn't sure it was right to tell you so, Miss, and seeking her advice.'

'I hardly see you need seek advice on announcing my callers, Freddy,' she said, and began to pull off her cambric sleeve covers as she moved towards the nursery door, picking her way over the bricks that Samuel had left scattered on the rug before the fire. 'Put whoever it is in the morning room and I shall be there directly.'

'I can't do that, Miss,' Freddy said, looking scandalized and now carefully not looking at Nanny Chewson, who had gone prudently back to her chair by the fire to continue the work of sorting the children's clothes. 'It would not be – '

'Freddy, do as you are told!' she snapped, well aware of the sneer in every line of the man's body. 'I am not answerable to you or anyone else about my visitors, so be about your business at once!'

Stupid man! she thought furiously as she went along the landing towards her own room, so that she could tidy her morning gown and frizz up her fringe. How dare he be so full of himself! Freddy had once, for a short time, worked as under footman to a baronet and gave himself immense airs as a result. Ever since he had come to Leinster Terrace he had been at pains to point out what was proper behaviour in a gentleman's establishment and since Mr Amberly was well aware of the shakiness of his own gentlemanly status and the problems of being regarded as of high class while engaging in trade, even a most lucrative and respected trade such as his chain of hardware shops, he allowed Freddy a good deal more leeway than he might have allowed other servants, much to Mildred's increasing irritation. Freddy had a way of showing his disgust with all that everyone said or did that was galling to say the least, and this was not the first time he had made it clear that he disapproved of gentlemen calling before the noon hour.

Not that any of the gentlemen who called to see her were ever of the least interest; this one, she told herself as she peered miserably into her mirror and tugged at her disobedient front hair, was probably just another of those awful creatures Papa persisted in sending to make a try with her. To tell the truth she would have been glad to tell Freddy to deny her, but that would have seemed to the wretched man like a victory over her, and she could not bear that, so see the man she would have to, and she turned to go downstairs as sedately as she could, rehearsing in her head the words she would use to get rid of whoever it was as rapidly as possible.

Freddy was standing in the hallway at the table in the centre, ostensibly rearranging the flowers which Mama herself had set to rights that very morning and at the sight of her he jumped to mock obsequious readiness and hurried to hold open the morning-room door, but she sailed past him with her head high, refusing to acknowledge his presence at all. If only Papa could be persuaded to send the man packing, how much more agreeable life would be in this house, she thought. I shall have to find some way to convince him that he would be better served by someone else.

Freddy lingered at the open door after she had walked into the room and went on standing there as she stopped just inside in cold amazement and stared and then felt her belly lurch. For there, sitting in the armchair beside the crackling fire with his feet propped up on the fender and a malodorous butt of cigar burning between his lips, was Ruby.

'What are you doing here?' she cried as Ruby grinned at her over his shoulder and then got to his feet to stand with his back to the leaping flames, and at the same time felt Freddy standing there behind her at the door, taking in the scene with greedy eyes, and her belly lurched again and she felt sick. There was no possibility now that Papa could be kept in ignorance of all that had happened last night, and for a moment she was filled with such a violent hatred of Ruby and Kid Harris, who had undoubtedly sent him here, that she was dizzy with it.

Ruby's bright eyes flickered as he looked over her shoulder and he said loudly, 'Mornin' Miss Amberly. I got a message for you from Father Jay, down at 'Oly Trinity. Your man 'ere told me as to wait 'ere for yer – '

'Father Jay at Holy Trinity?' Mildred repeated, a little dazed, as she stood and stared at him.

'That's right, Miss, him as you told you would make a contribution to 'is special Mission for us poor East End kids,

like. 'E needs all the 'elp 'e can get, does Father Jay, dealing
with the likes of us, and 'e said as 'ow you'd promised 'im
some money an' that, to do 'is good works, givin' of us our
breakfusses what our poor muvvers can't find for us – ' He
stood there, his eyes wide and soulful and as full of wickedness
as an egg of meat, and it was all she could do not to laugh
aloud.

'Of course,' she managed at last. 'Yes, of course. Well, now,
let us see what we can do for you – Freddy!' And she turned
and looked at the servant still standing at the door but with a
much less self-satisfied smirk on his face. Now he looked as
though he had been stuffed and boiled.

'Yes, Miss,' he said after a long moment.

'Freddy, you will go to the kitchen and will bring this young
man some victuals, yes. *Good* victuals. Milk, you know, and
some of that raisin cake Cook made for the nursery yesterday.
And be sure to set it nicely on a tray and bring it at once.'

'In here, Miss?' Freddy tried to gather his forces, but his
defeat had been far too thorough, for she lifted her brows at
him and said icily, 'Of course! Where else? Do you expect me
to deal with my affairs of charity in the kitchen, with all of *you*
listening? That is not the proper Christian way to dispense
alms, as I would have thought you to know. Now be quick
about it, if you please!' And Freddy, now looking as though he
had been carved into slices as well as stuffed and boiled,
withdrew with what grace he could.

'Well, a right nasty piece o' goods that one is an' no error!'
Ruby said and shifted his cigar butt to the other side of his
mouth with a practised twist of his jaw. 'Tryin' to come the old
acid with me as well, 'e was, but I wasn't 'avin' none o' that!
Said as I 'ad no right to come to the front door an' all. Me!
Ruby Marks, no right to come to front doors? Tryin' to send me
down the area to the kitchen door? I should cocoa! Told 'im
straight up I did, if you wasn't fetched on the instant 'e'd be up
to 'is nasty little 'ocks in trouble, so off 'e goes, with his nose

turned up, for all the world like he's got a three-week-old 'erring 'anging round his neck for a cravat – '

But much as she had enjoyed Freddy's discomfiture, she wasn't going to allow this outrageously impudent young person to know it, and she lifted her brows and said sharply, 'Why are you here? I told your – I told Mr Harris last night that if he required the money he was to send me the address to which it was to be dispatched and I would see to it. There was no need to send you dunning me in this fashion.'

' 'Oo's dunning?' He looked pained. 'Did I say anythin' about money? Did I try to suggest I was sent for anythin' but the best o' reasons? Did I say – '

'Then why are you here?' She was beginning to recognize the sort of rhetoric to which Ruby was prone. 'Is it something to do with that – with Father Jay and the tale you told? And – er – ' She felt a moment of compunction; Ruby with his fast intelligence had realized at once how difficult his appearance here could be for her and had lied manfully for her sake. It was churlish in the extreme not to acknowledge his care of her. ' – Er – thank you for being so – um – discreet. To speak of churches and priests was really an excellent idea, under the circumstances – '

Ruby seemed to expand with self esteem. 'Well, I knew I 'ad to do something, didn't I? Got that one sussed out soon's I saw 'im. Toffee-nosed bugger – beggin' yer pardon an' all that, but 'e is, ain't 'e?' And he tilted his head and looked at her as brightly as a sparrow and again she could not help but laugh.

'Yes,' she said. 'He is. A – very toffee-nosed.'

' 'N' anyway, what I said about Father Jay – you could go further an' fare worse than 'elp 'im. 'e's a God palaverer 'n' all that, but 'e don't thump 'is Bible more'n most and 'e's got a decent respect for Yidden – '

She looked puzzled and he threw his eyes to the ceiling in mock exasperation. 'You are an ignorant tart, ain't yer? Yidden, Miss Amberly, is Jews. There's a lot of Jews down the East

End, in case you 'adn't noticed. But there's a lot o' goyim an' all – goyim – that's what you are. Not Jews, see – and some of 'em are right bastards and some of 'em are all right. Father Jay, 'e's all right. Got the best bleedin' boxin' school in the 'ole East End an' that's saying a lot. The Kid, 'e got 'is apprenticeship there – ' He shook his head admiringly. 'And there weren't never a boxer like the Kid. Our Lizah, oh, 'e's the best. 'E'll be a world champion, you see if 'e won't – best bleedin' welterweight there ever was, 'e is.'

Mildred grimaced slightly. 'I do not share my brother's taste for pugilism,' she said a little primly. 'Indeed, I dislike seeing men fight. It seems to me to be barbaric in the extreme. Not at all agreeable – '

'Not agreeable?' Ruby looked shocked. 'Not agreeable? The noble art, not agreeable? 'Ow can you stand there an' – '

'Ruby, I do not wish to discuss the matter. Why are you here? That is what I need to know, not your opinions on the merits or otherwise of fighting.'

'Yeah – well – ' Ruby said, but he still looked ruffled and then the door opened and the housemaid Jenny appeared, her hair still tied up in her morning cap and well enveloped in a calico apron, clearly thoroughly miffed at having been taken away from her duties to bring trays to the morning room for such a guest as the person Miss Mildred was entertaining. Her disgust showed in every line of her face as she set the tray, with its glass of milk and a large half-cut cake and a plate and knife on the centre table and stood stiffly waiting for permission to depart. And because Mildred knew she was as besotted with Freddy and his high flown opinions as her father was, and would tell him all that transpired, she said nothing, but nodded and let her take her bad temper away with her.

Ruby came and peered at the milk and the cake and then cheerfully cut himself a slice and with a great swing of his hips, jumped up to sit on the table with his legs swinging. He ate the cake with gusto, scattering crumbs with great abandon and she watched him, rather aware of the way the warmth from the fire was making his unfortunate clothes give up their smells but not unduly upset by that. It was not exactly pleasant but it was not much worse than the scent of naphtha mothballs of which Papa reeked, or the smell of the heavy beeswax Jenny used for the furniture, or Mama's heavy applications of rose water, meant to disguise the smell of sherry on her breath though not as successfully as she believed.

The more she saw of this impudent boy the more she liked him. He was vivid and alive and intelligent in a way that was foreign to her and also very exciting. Whatever he said and whatever he did he seemed to invest with a drama that was rare in her life and for which she knew she craved. He carried with him, for all his personal squalor, a vision of a world where life was something to be relished and enjoyed and not merely endured. And she ached for that –

'I'll take the rest with me,' Ruby said at length, when a second slice had disappeared after the first and he clearly had no capacity for more. 'Pity to waste it, eh?' and deftly he slid the quarter cake which remained under his shirt and sat there grinning at her. 'Now, to my commission what I was sent to undertake. I got a message for yer.'

'I imagined you had,' she said and he grinned at her, his eyes full of wickedness.

'You ain't expecting this message and so I'll tell yer,' he said, and crowed with delight again. 'It's from Kid Harris and 'e says as 'e'll see yer at Romano's in the Strand tonight at nine o'clock sharp and don't be late.'

She gaped at him, her forehead creased in amazement. 'He said *what*?'

'Romano's, dahn the Strand, 'e says. Bit off my beat, that is, but he's a real West Ender is Lizah when 'e wants to be. For my part I don't think you can do better than eat dahn at Ikey's place in Watney Street, or Curley's caff. Get nosh there and you get the best. But there it is, Kid Harris does everythin' of the

fanciest and that means up West and Romano's, 'e says. So – '
He slid off the table and stood there brushing the crumbs off
his stained old waistcoat. 'Nine o'clock all right?'

'It is certainly not all right!' she said indignantly. 'I never
heard of such a thing! Of course I shall do nothing of the sort.'

'Eh?' Ruby peered at her. 'What'd you say?'

'I said I shall do nothing of the sort,' she said strongly. 'I
never heard of such a thing! What does he take me for? I do
not go to restaurants! I do not accept such invitations from
men I do not know!'

'Don't know!' Ruby stared at her, his eyes a little narrowed
now. ''E's the fella what let your brothers off a sizeable debt.
Remember?'

She reddened a little. 'Of course I do. And I appreciate his –
his forbearance. But that doesn't mean I'm likely to go
traipsing off to a restaurant with him! It wouldn't be proper! I
never go out unaccompanied and – and it's just not possible!'

He stood there, his head again on one side in that birdlike
posture and after a moment shook his head mournfully.

'I thought better o' you, I really did. Told Lizah as you was
a goer, didn't I? I really thought you was. Got a bit o' life about
you, not like most o' these fancy madams what lives up West,
too niminy piminy to take a breath. I thought you was
different. You came down East with me last night, didn't you?
What's so terrible about going up to Romano's then? It's a
decent place, ain't it? Dead posh, as I understand it – don't you
know it?'

'I've heard of it,' she said. How could she not? She knew it
to be a fashionable and expensive restaurant to which her
father occasionally went with his cronies, and to which
her brothers much aspired. 'Of course I have. But that is not
the point. It isn't anything that's wrong with the restaurant – '

'Well, I'm sure it ain't anythin' that's wrong with Lizah,
is it?' He was still standing staring at her, still fixing her with
that birdy sharpness, and she began to feel even more

53

uncomfortable. 'There ain't a woman in the 'ole East End as wouldn't give 'er eye teeth for an invite from Kid 'Arris. I mean, 'e's the *Kid*, you know! Not suggestin' 'e ain't good enough for yer, are yer?'

'But of course he – ' And then she stopped. How could she say what she meant without seeming as Basil had seemed last night; as pompous and as unpleasant? That ladies like Miss Mildred Amberly of Leinster Terrace did not expect to be invited to dine with little Jewish boxers from the East End? That well-bred ladies of a certain class could hardly be expected to meet such persons, let alone dine with them? That she was a person of quality and Mr Harris, whom Ruby clearly admired above all men, was far from being that? The words froze in her throat and she stood and stared at the boy, and behind her eyes her mind raced.

Hadn't last night been the most exciting she could ever remember spending? Hadn't she, after it was all over and the terror had subsided, regretted that she had to return to the humdrummery of mending the children's shirts and being disapproved of by the entire family and the servants for being what she was, so ugly and unmarriageable? Had she not sat in the four-wheeler last night, lurching and rattling back to Leinster Terrace, unable to push the memory of that odd little man out of her mind?

And after all, what was it he was suggesting? Nothing much more terrible than dinner in a restaurant. She had occasionally dined away from home, very occasionally; seaside holidays in boarding houses had meant eating at a public table, and there had been that notable occasion when Papa had taken them all to supper after a pantomime one Boxing Day though the children had cried a good deal and fussed so much that Papa had vowed he would never again repeat the experiment, but she had enjoyed it. The drama of it, the glitter of the lights, the other ladies' toilettes, the sheer uncommonness of it all, had never left her memory.

So why should she not accept this outrageous invitation? It wouldn't be such a sin, after all. Yes, the man was quite out of her class, but he was interesting, and didn't she owe him a debt? He had allowed her brothers to mulct him of his fair winnings, and now he had done her the courtesy of offering her another adventure – and she thought of yesterday and remembered how she had sat watching raindrops run down the window and how Ruby's arrival had made her feel there was something in life worth making the effort to breathe for after all; and she bit her lip and stared at Ruby, trying to find the right words to say all this. And found she was quite unable to.

Ruby for once was silent. He simply stood and watched her think and had she known how she looked to him, she would have understood. For her usual dullness had given way to a liveliness that would have amazed any of her family had they seen it. Her eyes, those dull eyes that were normally downcast anyway, sparkled a little and their yellowness became a rich amber that was far from dull. Her face, long and irregular though it was and oddly shaped though her long nose might be, looked quite different now that she had some animation; it was the heaviness of her expression, almost a sulkiness, that made the men her Papa brought to meet her so unwilling to pursue the acquaintance. Had any of them seen her now, they might have thought it worth the effort –

But she knew none of this as she stood there in her donkey brown frieze morning dress, her hair pulled back unbecomingly from her face in spite of her attempts to create a fashionable fringe, trying to decide what to do. And Ruby, ever shrewd, chose his time carefully and pushed home his advantage.

'O' course I can understand the problems a lady like yourself might 'ave, gettin' the chance to be about 'er own affairs, like, I mean, I dare say you got them all over you, eh? Wantin' to know what you're a'doin' of, and where you're goin' an' 'oo with – but ladies are always doing charity work ain't they? And there is Father Jay – '

'Mmm?' Her eyes, which had been a little glazed as she thought focussed now and she looked at him. 'What did you say?'

'I thought, like, you was worried about goin' out tonight and people fussin'. Like that toffee-nosed bugger – ' And he jerked his head towards the door.

'No,' she said. 'Not really, I mean – ' She stopped. Hateful though it was to have to admit to this street urchin, who obviously lived a life as free as air, just how trammelled she was and how complicated it would be to keep this engagement even if she wanted to, she could not deny that he was right. She would have to lie and scheme and slip out unseen, like a thief from her own house. And that was a most unpleasant notion.

'I thought p'raps you could arrange to come down to see Father Jay at 'is place,' Ruby said almost casually. "E's a good geezer and there's lots o' people o' quality comin' down to go to the Evenin' Services and to see the work what 'e does with us poor pathetic 'eathens – ' His eyes glinted then. 'An' nice pickin's they offer for a good dip, 'n' all – ' And at her puzzled face he added, 'Pickpockets, Miss Amberly. Not me, o' course, but there are one or two o' that kidney around. Still no need for you to fret over *that*. You tell 'em 'ere you're goin' to do some prayin' and a bit of good works for the likes of me dahn East – and go and do yourself some good works up West. That's my advice to you. So, are you goin' to take it? Or do I go back an' tell Kid Harris what was so good to your brothers as 'ow you spit in 'is eye and don't want to know nothin' about 'is nice invite?'

6

As soon as she got there she knew she had chosen the wrong clothes. She had agonized over the matter all afternoon, trying to decide what would look suitable for a place as fashionable as Romano's and yet reasonable for a lady purporting to visit East End priests on an errand of Christian mercy; and had at last settled on her dark blue tailormade with the back skirt pleated and trimmed with black petersham silk and the slightly paler blue gigot sleeves. The little black straw with the grey dove's feathers looked quite tolerable with it and no one seeing her walk sedately down Leinster Terrace towards the cab rank would have given her a second glance.

But now she was here at Romano's, standing just inside the doorway and looking about her, her heart sank. She was so very dull, even dowdy, that surely everyone must stare at her and laugh behind their feathered fans as they smoothed their silk or satin gowns; for every woman who passed her on their way into the restaurant from the lobby where she was standing looked exquisite.

There were short-trained evening gowns in the richest of colours, golds and violets and scarlets, emeralds and crimsons and heliotropes, and the lovely buttery yellow that was all the rage this season, and so much trimming of braid and lace and fringing and fluting that her own subdued costume flattened her spirits even more, if that were possible. And suddenly she was so miserable that she turned to go, wanting to escape before the lofty maître d'hôtel, who had been sent for to deal with her request for Mr Harris' table, had returned. She had been mad to come here at all, mad to consider doing so, even on the terms she had decided and the sooner she fled back to dullness, where she belonged, the better it would be.

'Well, then, here we are! I knew you were the sort of lady to be prompt. A real lady, Miss Amberly is, I said to myself, and I must not keep her waiting. So here I am, arriving at the same time.'

He was effulgent, she decided. That was the only word that would fit, for his evening suit was of the most rich of blacks, and his linen of the most glittering white. The front of his coat, cut away in the normal manner, showed a silk waistband in a deep crimson, fastened with carved jet buttons which was far from usual, and across that was draped a gold Albert. Over his arm he carried a rich crombie overcoat and in his hand was a silk hat so gleaming she could see her own reflection in it.

'Oh dear,' she said and stood staring at him and he smiled widely at her, clearly full of pride at himself, yet very aware of the other people around them; his eyes darted about busily catching others' glances as though seeking reassurance that he looked as he should in this place, and that he had a right to be here. The cocksureness he had displayed last night in the cellar room was not quite so visible now; and she realized that he was as ill at ease as she was, more perhaps. And that made her feel a little more relaxed.

'You must forgive me for not choosing evening dress, as you have,' she said a little stiffly. 'But I thought it important that you should understand that I am not here for pleasure. I mean, I did not come to dine with you.'

He frowned, and stepped aside as a new eddy of people came in from the street and pushed past them to reach the main restaurant. There was chatter and laughter all around them and a rich smell of food and wine and cigars came drifting back from the big room and for a moment, in spite of her determination to do what she had come to do and then to leave, she felt herself regretting her decision. It would be rather nice to stay and eat something delicious, and she thought mournfully of the dreadful dinner Cook had once again sent up, of the thin oxtail soup and the cod that had undoubtedly been a good deal older than it had any right to be and the leathery beef, and then smelled the delicious scents wafting out of the main room, and actually heard her belly rumble. She pressed her hands, both still clutching her reticule, against it as unobtrusively as possible, and said a little more loudly, 'I have brought you the money. Is there anywhere we can go quietly so that I may give it to you to be counted and then go home?'

'I asked you here to have a bit of supper,' he said. 'I didn't ask you here for money. I thought Ruby explained. He usually gets it right.'

'He explained,' she said, and again had to stop as another group of diners came chattering in from the street. They were a particularly glittering group, the women so pink of cheek and lip that she wondered for a moment if they were actresses, for no respectable woman, surely, wore rouge? They went past in a flurry of chypre and eau de cologne with their men, rich and redolent of bay rum, following hard behind, as Kid Harris moved closer to her side to take hold of her elbow, and she stopped wondering about them, concentrating on herself, suddenly alarmed.

'Then what's all this about offering me money?' he said, and his voice was a little rough. 'I don't like insults.'

'I meant no insult!' She was stung and it showed in her increased colour. 'It's no insult to pay a debt.'

'It is when it's been waived, written off, forgotten.' He sounded angry and she felt the familiar twinge of fear from last night back in her belly again. 'I asked you for a bit of supper because I thought you were an interesting lady. I like women with a bit of – of character about them. You've got character.

59

More'n most women have. So I don't expect to be offered money. Don't ever do it again.'

'I won't ever see you again, so it's hardly likely,' she said and tried to pull her arm away from his grip, for he was holding her elbow very firmly and leading her towards the restaurant's main room. 'Please let me go.'

'We've come here for our supper, and our supper we shall have,' he said and then a little more loudly, 'Evening, Joseph. My usual table if you please.'

'Yes sir.' The maître d'hôtel had a bored expression on his face and she knew suddenly that he had no idea who Harris was, but was accustomed to customers assuming a familiarity with the restaurant that they did not have, and she felt, to her own amazement, a surge of protectiveness. This little man had dressed up in his very best clothes and made an arrangement to bring her to a fashionable restaurant where he was in all truth out of place, just to please her, and she was being churlish to object. And, oddly, she wanted to stay with him. He was undoubtedly far from the sort of person she was accustomed to know, and was in some ways rather ridiculous with his pretensions to West End high fashion, and yet there was about him an excitement, a kind of dynamism, which exhilarated and intrigued her. She found herself liking his company and warmed by his presence, and that truly was amazing. *Why* should she feel so? It was absurd.

By the time she had collected her thoughts they were being seated at a table to one side of the restaurant and had menus set in front of them and she looked at hers a little helplessly and then around the room and then at Kid Harris sitting opposite her and the expression on his face made her swallow the words that had risen to her lips. He looked baffled, angry and doubtful all at the same time, and she registered the fact that the table he had been given was a far from favourable one, being set half behind a pillar and in a direct line with the busiest passage-way used by the waiters who were swishing past them at a great rate on their way to and from the servery. Almost as though she could read his thoughts she knew how he was feeling; affronted at being given such scant respect but not certain that making a fuss would gain him anything but opprobrium from the very dignified waiter who was now bearing down on them, and she said quickly, 'I am glad this is your usual table. I much prefer to be a little private. It is much better than being in the centre where all can stare and gossip at you. Especially as I am not dressed as I might be for the occasion.'

His face cleared and he nodded. 'Not my usual table, really, of course, but I dare say it's a busy night tonight and some other devil's taking his time. But if you're happy – '

'As happy as I can be, considering I had not intended to remain.' It was prudent to step back into her more chilly mode, she decided. Give this man an inch and he'd take several miles. And this fascination he had for her must on no account be encouraged. 'I do assure you that I had not meant to – '

'Yes, I know,' he said, and lifted the menu. 'Now, what shall it be? You choose whatever you want. Anything at all. Don't you worry about nothing – you want it, you have it.' And he began to study the large card.

Just reading it made her hungry again and she let her gaze take in the great range of lobster dishes, from patties to grilled in rich sauces to poached in bouillon, and the bewildering list of sole dishes and game dishes and soufflés and pies and puddings galore, and knew that she was defeated. However good her intentions this was a treat not to be missed and she chose a fricassee of lobster and a dish of scalloped potatoes and green peas, and then leaned back in her chair and waited for him to make his own selection.

When the waiter had taken his order, including a demand for champagne ' – the best,' he said loudly. 'Not one of your cheap fizzes, the best – ' at which the waiter looked singularly wooden, he leaned back in his own chair and nodded at her.

'Now, this is a bit of all right, ain't – isn't it? Just what a chap needs, end of a hard day. Did a good bit of business today, I did.'

'Really,' she said and gloom slid into her mind. This was the way her father talked at table, of business and making money, and this was what his guests always talked about, even if they had been invited as potential husbands for her. They certainly never made any effort to speak of matters which might possibly be of interest to a woman rather than to a man of business, and she looked across the table at the corrugated forehead and the protuberant dark eyes and sighed. All men were the same, after all, were they the middling sort like her father and his cronies, or this little East End oddity.

' – but I shan't tell you about it on account of it's boring for ladies. I know that. You must never bore ladies. It's the first thing I tell young 'uns as come to me for education. I tell Ruby all the time. Never bore a lady,' he said blithely and gave her that odd gap-toothed grin of his and inevitably her gloom melted.

'That is very kind of you,' she said. 'Business is indeed a very boring matter. My father talks of it a good deal. I try not to listen.'

'What sort of business is he in?' Harris looked alertly at her, and lifted his brows so that his forehead became even more ridged.

She sighed. 'There you are, breaking your promise already! Hardware. That sort of business. He has a number of shops, and each is as dull as the other. Though why I should discuss my father's affairs with you is really not – '

'Why not? We're going to be good friends, you and me. And we ain't talking about business. Not real business – my sort. We're just finding out about your old man.'

'Old man? He'd be most put about to hear himself so described. He says he is in his prime.'

'You don't like him one bit, do you?' he said after a moment and her face flamed.

'How dare you say such a thing!' she cried. 'He is my Papa and of course I love him!'

'You might love him. Kids can't help loving their parents. It's born in 'em. But liking 'em – that's another matter altogether.'

She stared at him, a little nonplussed, and then said abruptly, 'You said we – that you wish us to be friends. I really must tell you that I am here under – under a form of duress. I mean, I had no intention of eating here with you, and I certainly have no intention of ever doing so again. It is quite improper that you should consider any sort of – er continuing acquaintanceship between us, just as it was quite improper of me to discuss my Papa's business affairs with you – '

'You didn't discuss nothing. I did.' His speech was beginning to sound much more as it had last night, with some care to change the accent, but with only limited success. The more they talked the more relaxed and the less careful he became with his vowels. 'Listen, Miss Amberly – ' He had leaned forwards to speak more confidentially and now he stopped himself and then said, 'What's your first name? I can't go on calling you Miss Amberly all stiff and starchy like that. I'm not the stiff and starchy type.'

'I had noticed,' she said sharply. 'But I am. My Christian name is no concern of yours.'

'Oh, well, I dare say I was rushin' things a bit,' he grinned. 'Wait till the end of the evening. You'll tell me then. Me, you can call me what you like, as long as it ain't Mr Harris, which is for waiters and youngsters and such like. My friends call me Kid. You can call me Kid.'

'I don't want to call you anything!' she cried, almost banging her fist on the table. It was ridiculously difficult making this man understand. 'I keep telling you – I had intended only to pay my brothers' debt when I came here tonight, not to make this into some sort of social encounter.'

'Why?'

'Why what?'

'Why are you so set this shouldn't be a – what was it you said? A social encounter? What's wrong with being sociable?'

'Nothing! I mean, in the right circumstances, with the right people and – '

'Ah!' Now he leaned back in his chair. 'Right, now we got it, eh? I ain't the right person. I'm a nasty greasy little Jew, and you're a Christian lady and too good for the likes of me, is that it?'

She took a deep breath. 'I did not – I do not make any remarks about your religion, nor would I. I know that there are those who do, but I have never been one of them. For my part – ' She went a little pink. 'I'll tell you the truth, for my part, I think religion treats people shamefully. I sit in church and hear the vicar speak of forbearance and love for all mankind and such matters and then watch him after the service wringing his hands in delight as the richer sort talk to him, and quite snubbing the other kind – and I think of the dreadful hypocrisy I see on all sides and I – well, I make no judgements on others' religion when the one to which I have adherence offers what it does. If I were to speak as you say, I would be no better than the vicar, whom I dislike a great deal. So never suggest I did.'

'All right, it ain't religion. Mind you, I think you're wrong. There's good things about it. Keeps people together, doesn't it? At least being Jewish does. It's more to do with people than sermons, being Jewish is. Anyway, if it isn't my religion that makes you not want to know me, is it because you think I'm poor and lives in the East End and you're rich and lives up West?'

'I'm not rich,' she said bitterly. 'I'm fully dependent on my father, and always will be. That is not rich.'

'All right then, upper class,' he said, dismissing the matter of her poverty as though it were quite unimportant, which stung her somewhat; to admit to this total stranger that her father had complete control of the purse strings, even being free to dole out her small legacy from her mother entirely as he saw fit, had been a considerable effort for her. She had become so embarrassed by the turn that the conversation had taken that she had wanted to show Harris that she was not what he thought, a person who valued money above all things, yet now he treated her admission as though it was insignificant. That nettled her and made her speak more waspishly than she intended.

'Very well, if you insist, yes, we are of different classes. Ladies of my sort do not normally behave in the manner you seem to regard as reasonable. They do not accept invitations to dine from strangers, and then go off and sit about in fashionable restaurants with them – '

He produced a smile of total triumph. 'But you're doing it, ain't you? So you ain't so different to me after all.'

'You are impossible!' she flared at him and made to push back her chair to jump to her feet and run as far as she could get from this tiresome man and his ridiculous logic, but even as she tensed her thigh muscles to move the waiter arrived with a bottle in a bucket of ice and a trolley bearing their supper, and began to flourish glasses and napkins, which made not only movement but also conversation impossible.

And when the food was set ready in front of her and the champagne, wonderfully cold and glinting in its dew-hazed glass, invited her to drink it, the moment to protest seemed to have fled. All she could do was sip at the drink in response to his lifted glass – and it really was extraordinarily delicious – and start to eat. And that was even more delectable. She could not remember ever eating anything quite so rich or taste-laden, or at least not since she had first eaten ice cream when she had been a child, and she ate with gusto, savouring every bit of it.

'What's it like, that lobster?' he asked after a moment, sitting with a forkful of sole mornay poised before his lips, and she looked at him and said, 'It tastes very good indeed. Why did you not choose it?'

He seemed to give a small shudder. 'No, not lobster. Couldn't eat lobster. Tref.'

'I beg your pardon?'

'It's tref. Forbidden. Yeah, I know, you don't think there's anythin' much to religion, but to Jews like me, it's everyday things, you see. I don't go to no services much. Got better things to do on a Friday night and on a Saturday morning – but I can't bring myself to eat foods I been brought up against.'

'I know you don't eat pork,' she said, remembering one of her father's guests needing to have some special dish prepared, and he grinned at that.

'Everyone knows that. It's all they do know. That and that we're greasy and make a lot o' money, and so forth. But it's other things as well. It's shellfish. It's meat from an animal that don't chew the cud or have cloven hoofs. It's mixing milk and meat in the same dish. Things like that – '

'It sounds complicated.' She was feeling rather dreamy and comfortable now, for the food had made her a little sleepy, while the wine was sparkling inside her eyes and making everything she looked at shimmer a little. He poured her another glass – the third – and she made no protest. 'And rather a pity too. Lobster is really very good.'

'I'll take your word for it.'

'What would happen if you didn't? I mean, if you decided to eat it anyway?'

He made a small grimace, turning his lips down to make a doubtful crescent. 'I don't know. I just wouldn't – couldn't – do it. It's no trouble breaking the other rules – and God knows there's enough of 'em – but the food ones – ' He shook his head. 'It's what you learn from your Momma. That you can never forget. What your Poppa tells you and your schoolmasters tell you – this you can forget. But what Momma does when you're a kid, this stays for always.'

He was silent for a while and then said abruptly, 'I'm sorry your mother died. That must be very unhappy for you.'

She didn't look at him. 'Yes,' was all she said, and sat and stared down at her glass of wine which stood gently sending its pinhead bubbles to the surface, and whether it was the effect of staring at that or the wine already inside her head she was never to know, but suddenly she remembered her Mama as she had actually looked. It had been almost fourteen years now since she had died of the same diphtheria that had killed Mildred's two sisters, and which she and Basil and Claude had been fortunate enough to survive, and almost that long since she had wept for her, but now, sitting at Romano's restaurant in the Strand, with a total stranger, she saw that much loved face. Lined and tired, and as plain as her own, with the same long features and rather irregular nose that she had bequeathed to her, Maria Amberly looked at her daughter through the bubbles in a glass of champagne and made her feel so lonely and so bereft that tears lifted in her throat, needle sharp, and pushed their way out through her eyes to trickle down her sallow cheeks.

'Hey, hey!' he said softly. 'I didn't think to upset you so.' And he leaned forwards and his hand closed over hers, warm and firm. 'I wanted only to say I was – oh dear, oh dear.' And he reached into his pocket with his other hand and gave her a large white handkerchief. 'I wish you long life, my dear.'

She took the handkerchief and sniffed and rubbed her face and eyes with it, not caring whether it made the tip of her nose red. 'What – I beg your pardon?'

'It's what we say to people as have been bereaved. We wish them long life. It's what upsets the living most, you see. Thinking of when it'll be their turn.'

'It doesn't worry me,' she said and gave him back his handkerchief. It had comforted her to use it, smelling as it did of lavender and tobacco and something else she couldn't quite define but liked. 'I often wish I had died when Mama did. I'd have been no worse off than I am.'

He looked shocked. 'You musn't say that, a young lady like you! You got your whole life ahead of you!'

'And what use is that when it is so deadly dull and miserable and lonely?' she said passionately and stared at him through a mist of tears and the wine's shimmer. Somewhere at the back of her mind a small warning voice tried to make itself heard, to tell her she was behaving quite incredibly stupidly and to stop it at once, but she ignored it without any difficulty at all. 'If you knew, if you only knew, how dismal it is to be there at Leinster Terrace and to know how they all despise me for being so ugly and wish to see me off their hands and wed, and knowing I never shall be – oh, if you only knew you would not speak so about the joys of remaining alive!'

'Ugly?' he said and lifted his brows so that once again his forehead collapsed into a series of tight ridges. 'Ugly? How can anyone say that of you? You aren't a fancy madam, that's true, but you don't need to be. A lady of your character can't ever be called ugly! I never heard such a thing. Not a beauty, no one can't deny, but very pleasant. It's a face I like, anyway.'

She stared at him and now at last the warning voice was able to make itself heard. This was dreadful, quite dreadful. Not only was she sitting with this peculiar man and eating his lobster fricassee and drinking his champagne, while her family, if they thought of her at all, believed she was doing good works at a Mission for poor children, but she was also telling him things she had never told anyone ever before, putting into words feelings she barely dared to admit to herself that she had. And what was perhaps worse, she was hearing him say things to her that she couldn't have imagined any man ever saying, and liking it. To be told that she looked pleasant – it was the kindest remark any person had ever made about her and she put both hands up to her face to cover the heat that she knew filled her cheeks, and did not know where to look.

'Listen,' he said comfortably, and grinned at her. 'Listen, already, don't look like that. A man tells you he likes your face, that ain't no reason to look like you been poleaxed! Have some more to eat. Have some ice cream, some cake, some more wine. Come on, we'll enjoy ourselves. What do you say?'

'No,' she whispered. 'Really, no – I must go home. This is mad. This is quite ridiculous and I must go home and never ever see you again and – '

'So, why?' He lifted his brows at her, his face full of humour. 'Why, tell me? Is home so wonderful? Of course it ain't. You told me that. You don't have no objection to me being a Jew. You told me that. And you ain't the sort of snob some people are, like that vicar. So why not see me again? The thing of it is I like you, and I think you like me. Eh? Am I so bad to like?'

She looked at him, at the face through which beard was once again struggling to escape and creating blue shadows to mark its efforts, at the protruding dark eyes and the corrugated forehead and lustrous curly hair and thought – he's a ridiculous little man. So short, so oddly lumpy, with his thick shoulders and arms so bulging that they strain against the sleeves of his jacket and he can hardly rest them at his sides, so very much everything she found unfamiliar – and yet so –

So what? She tried to clear her muzzy head, but it wasn't easy. All she could see was that face smiling at her and feel the warmth of his hand on hers, for he had reached forwards again to take possession of it, and smell the scent of him, lavender and tobacco and that something else familiar yet indefinable, which she knew she liked. All of it. And as he said, why not?

7

For the rest of her life she was to marvel at herself and the way she behaved during the next few months. Night after night she sat at the dinner table with Mama and, on the rare occasions when he was not dining at his club or with his City friends, with Papa and pick at her food, gleeful in the knowledge that later she would eat much more interesting victuals. She would listen to Papa's interminable droning on about his business dealings, and feel none of the old frustration and misery that had been so integral a part of her life before. Afterwards she would see Mama up to her boudoir and Papa to his study – where the rows of red leather-bound books had no fear of ever being disturbed, for all he ever did was spread a newspaper before his face and sleep off his dinner until it was time to take his whisky nightcap and go heavily up to bed – and then would slip up to her own room and put on her jacket, skewer her hat to her hair, and tucking her Bible under her arm would go sallying down the stairs, head up and face suitably composed, to start living her new life. Her real life, at last.

Freddy would stand at the door, his face carved solid with self control and she would say cheerfully, 'You need not wait up. I shall see myself in and lock the front door. The last service of the evening is not over till past eleven,' and would marvel at how gifted a liar she had become.

Because all the time she was engaged in her Good Works, as the family had come to label her new and abounding interest in Father Jay's East End Mission, she was enjoying activities that she would never have imagined possible.

Sometimes she travelled to her destination alone, but on most evenings he was waiting for her at the end of Leinster Terrace, a cab beside him at the kerb, the horse snuffling peaceably into its nosebag, and would hold the door open in his usual punctilious fashion and help her in. And they would whirl away to the East End to have supper first in one of the steamy marble-tabled noisy little eating houses he frequented along Shoreditch High Street, and eat succulent steaks and crisp fried potatoes, or the freshest and most delightfully steamed halibut and a form of fried fish she had never before eaten but now found delectable, called gefilte fish, and then to do whatever it was he had decided was most interesting for her that evening.

Sometimes he took her to the theatre. She had been once or twice to theatres in the West End, but they had been pallid dull affairs compared to the sort of places to which he now took her. Sometimes it was music halls and penny gaffs where singers and comics jostled with jugglers and animal trainers, peepshows and freaks, but mostly it was real theatres where real plays were performed. Her favourite was the old Britannia in Hoxton Street in the heart of Spitalfields. A great glittering cavern full of red plush and bright lights and the reek of oranges and cakes and the unwashed occupants of the gallery and the pit, it pulsed with life and excitement and that galvanized her. From the moment she first walked in to be ushered to the best seats in the house in the middle of the front row of the grand circle, she felt vivid life, and it was not entirely because of the infectious anticipation of the crowd around her. It was because of Kid Harris, for here, in his own setting he glittered and shone as he certainly had not done at Romano's.

People would come up to speak to him, mostly men in suits as fancifully designed as his own, and even more bedecked with gold rings and charms than he was, to shake him by the hand respectfully and wish him well and ask after his family and when the next fight was to be. Sometimes they would bring saucer-eyed small boys with them to touch the Kid's hand 'for good fortune' or little girls, bashful in their frills, to kiss his blue cheeks, and Kid would bask in the glory of his fame and let his eyes slide sideways to her face to see if she was suitably impressed by the sort of obeisance these, his people, made to him.

At first she would pretend not to notice, sitting with her head bent over the programme he would put into her hands, or staring round at the house, or studiously reading the advertisements for tooth powder and corsets and Macassar oil on the safety curtain, but as time went on, and she became more used to it, she succumbed to his need for her admiration. She would smile at him as he looked at her when yet another supplicant for his gracious greetings came along and nod her head, and he would grin back in such delight at his own splendour that she was filled with warm affection for him. It was very endearing, the way he strutted and sparkled, even when he did so at his most glittering for the ladies who paid him attention. There were some bold women who made no secret of their interest in the Kid, positively ogling him and fanning their sumptuous shoulders in their low-cut gowns as they peeped and fluttered at him, and clearly dismissing her, Mildred, as of no account whatsoever. She learned to pretend she did not notice these other women, but she was well aware of them, and deep inside, so deep she barely acknowledged it was there, she felt triumph. *They* might have bright dark eyes and swelling busts and glossy curls, but *she* was the one who sat beside the man they were staring at and over whom he fussed agreeably. And that was a knowledge that pleased her greatly, or at least it did in those early days.

And the plays; they too pleased her greatly. Great rolling melodramas so full-blooded and riotously emotional that the audience would cheer and groan and weep and laugh in great waves of sound; plays with titles like *The Worst Woman in London* and *A Disgrace to Her Sex* and *The Girl Who Took the Wrong Turning* and *The Girl Who Lost Her Character* and, particularly outrageously, *The Girl Who Wrecked His Home.* Stirring stuff, all of it, and though at first she tried to be serious and sensible and not let herself be swept along on the tide of spurious emotion that battered the audience from the stage, she soon had to give in, and wept and laughed with the best of them, until her sallow cheeks flushed and her eyes shone and he would look at her in the semi-darkness, her face brightly illuminated by the stage in front of them, and beam his pleasure in her pleasure.

Sometimes he took her to the gymnasium again, to see him fight, and sometimes, for more important prize fights, to a hall in Shoreditch High Street, and those evenings made her feel very odd indeed.

It wasn't so much she disapproved of what happened or found it disagreeable as that she found it made her feel so confused. The sight of men stripped to the waist, with legs bare from the knee and their heavily muscled bodies gleaming under the powerful lights that isolated the canvas and rope ring from the spectators, at first made her blush furiously, but she became accustomed to it, for it was so casual and so ordinary to the men themselves that to take exception to such half-nudity was to make herself look – and feel – stupid.

Was it the actual fighting that had the effect on her that so puzzled her? At first she thought it must be; she would flinch as the flailing arms swung and the great leathered fists made contact with flesh in sickening crunches; this sort of boxing was very different from the rather timid, even mincing, version she had seen at the boys' school when Basil had competed, but she soon realized that it was not that. The more she watched the fighting the more she became aware, albeit dimly, of the art of the boxer; of the way the men would weave in and out of each other's reach, each foreseeing their opponent's move and not only blocking it but turning it to his own advantage. There was real skill in it and not just brute beating of one man by another, so it was not that which disturbed her.

Nor, she decided, was it the way the audience behaved, watching with eyes glazed with excitement and lips apart and very moist and shrieking for blood with cries of, 'Kill 'im, the mumser – ' and, 'Kick 'im in the kishkas!' neither of which were phrases she fully understood though she was well able to comprehend the animal aggressiveness that was conveyed by the thick voices.

It was, she realized at last, that it all excited her as well as repelled her so much. The smell of it, the sour heavy sweatiness that she had first met in the basement in Flower and Dean Street, mixed with tobacco from cigars and cheap cigarettes, and heavy ale and sometimes whisky, and methylated spirits and oil from the lamps, and embrocation and witch hazel, all combined to make a powerful mixture that made her heart beat faster, even sometimes tripping in its rhythm so that her chest seemed to resound to an internal thump, and made her feel light-headed. She would watch the fights, unable to take her eyes from Kid Harris' stocky body, with its solid legs with their dusting of dark hair, except down the backs of the calves, where his trousers had rubbed it all away, and the smooth heavy chest and rippling buttocks under the dark shorts, and feel extraordinary.

And ashamed, too, because the excitement she felt did not exist entirely in her head, as all previous experiences had told her excitement did. It affected her whole body, not just beating heart and over-working lungs, but all of it. She experienced sensations deep within her and in her most secret self that she would not, could not, have admitted to anyone. She could barely admit them to herself.

Christmas came and turned sluggishly over to bring 1894, and still she went on serenely, lying through her days at Leinster Terrace and coming alive at night with Kid Harris. No one seemed to notice any difference in her, although she herself was well aware of some. She was plumper, for a start, for she ate with much more gusto now she had escaped from dependence on the awful cooking that was perpetrated in the kitchens deep in the basement of Leinster Terrace, a change which improved her appearance considerably; but more importantly, she was much more relaxed. She often took a nap in the afternoon when Mama was stretched out as usual on her sofa and the children were out with Nanny Chewson, walking in Hyde Park, or, in the case of Thomas and Wilfred, the older ones, at school, for that helped her to cope with the very short nights she spent in her own bed, since it was frequently well past midnight when she came creeping home. There had been times when she had managed to get in a bare few minutes before her father returned to be debouched sluggishly from the cab in which he had slept his brandied way home from his club or the City to drag himself in and lock the front door. Even he had not been able to persuade the lofty Freddy to wait up for him, and Mildred twice had good cause to be grateful for that for on two occasions Papa had been fortunately too befuddled to remember to lock the door and had gone to bed, leaving her to creep in after him, terrified that she might find herself locked out and forced to sleep below the steps in the area and to get into the house as best she might in the morning before the servants saw her.

But so far all had gone well, and inside her new secret regime she blossomed. There was less need now to daydream, though sometimes she would find her mind sliding away on its old paths of ridiculous imaginings, but now it was with pleasure that she let it happen instead of dissatisfied yearnings. Now she had a friend, one of her very own. Not just an acquaintance like the silly Mrs Vance who had been Eugenie Frobisher or the vapid Charlotte Pringle, née Millar, but a real friend who would look at her sideways and laugh when someone said something that struck them both as funny, who would look at a new bonnet when she put it on and nod in approval rather than lift a lip in a sneer and who above all showed in every action that he liked and admired her.

And respected her. She would sit sometimes with her sewing, working busily at it in order to keep up with her domestic tasks so that no one could make any objections to the time she spent on her new-found piety, but thinking her own thoughts as her needle flew, and marvel at that. Respect was something she had never really thought about. To be deferred to as a worthwhile person, to be regarded as sensible, even witty, to be looked up to as an arbiter of opinion, was not an experience she had previously enjoyed. Now Kid Harris gave it to her in full measure – except in one way and she could not help but smile a little as she thought of that.

He had made up his mind to it, quite early in their friendship, that he was to address her by her given name. 'Miss Amberly's all right for other people,' he had said on the second occasion he had taken her to the old Britannia Theatre. 'But we're friends and that means you've got to call me Kid, like I told you, and I got to call you – what am I to call you?'

'I really do not think – ' she had begun primly but he had shaken his head vigorously in the dark corner of the cab so that she could see the passing street lights glint on his white teeth.

'Too much thinkin',' he said roughly. 'The thing of it is, I ain't calling you Miss anything. So what is your name?'

'Mildred,' she said at length, unwillingly, and he had said heartily, 'There! Very nice too. So, Millie it is from now on.'

'No, it is not,' she had said sharply. 'I said Mildred. Surely I am to be permitted to insist that you use it in its full – '

'That don't sound friendly. And it's all about being friendly that I'm interested in. So there it is. Now, tonight, 'ow about trying something different to eat? Like jellied eels?'

'Like *what*?' She had been distracted at once from the discussion of her name and had peered at him in the dimness. 'That sounds very – well, not very agreeable.'

'Jellied eels, I'm told, is a great delicacy. I can't pretend I've had 'em meself on account of they don't have scales the way fish is supposed to, so they're tref and I can't eat 'em, but that don't mean I can't take pleasure in giving my friends a bit o' pleasure, does it? So we shall go to Tubby's place and you shall try the eels and tell me your opinion and I shall have a nice bit of haddock. And then the old Brit and a bit of blood and thunder!'

And so it had been. Despite her objections he called her Millie, always, even though he knew that she disliked it. It was the one area where he showed a stubborn lack of respect for her opinion, but otherwise, she had no complaints at all, and blossomed in the light of his warm approval of her.

One night in January when there was a frosting of snow on the ground and very bright stars seemed to be so low in the sky that they had become tangled in the bare branches of the trees that overhung the Bayswater Road from Hyde Park, he collected her as usual, but sat in a far from usual silence as the cab went its now very familiar way Eastwards. She said nothing for some time but when they reached Holborn could keep silent no longer.

'What is it, Kid? Why are you so gloomy this evening?'

He roused himself and said, 'Gloomy? I ain't gloomy.'

'Quiet, then.'

'Ain't – well, I suppose I am, at that.' He brooded a little longer and then burst out, 'The thing of it is, I got to take you to my Momma's house. She said I got to take you.'

'Oh!' She was silent for a moment and then ventured, 'Do you mean I am invited to meet her?'

'Something like that,' he said.

She laughed. 'How do you mean, something like that? Either she invites me to meet her or – '

'It's more taking you to be looked at,' he said roughly and then muttered something under his breath and she said, 'What did you say?' But he shook his head.

'It doesn't matter. Look, it won't be easy. She's – ' He swallowed. 'This ain't easy.'

'You're making me feel that it is far from that,' she said as lightly as she could. 'Although I really cannot see what is so difficult. It is very kind of your Mama to invite me to her home and I will be very happy to accept.'

'If it was like that, I'd be happy too. The thing of it is, people have been talking. If I get my hands on Ruby I'll have the skin off his lousy back! Jealous, of course, that's the thing. He used to hang around with me a lot, see, and now – ' He waved one hand irritably as though to banish an impertinent fly. 'Anyway, he's told my Momma that I'm going around with a shicksah and she – '

'With a what?'

'You see what I mean?' He shouted it so that his voice thumped onto her head and then went reverberating round the small cab interior. 'You see? Already it's making trouble in what was – what is a nice friendship between me and a lady of class and good taste. Already it's making problems!'

'If you don't explain just what the problems are there isn't much I can do to help you with them,' she said and he reached forwards in the dark cab and touched her hand briefly.

'Yeah, well – ' he began. 'The thing of it is – '

'When you keep on saying that I know you're uncomfortable,' she said. 'Come along now, Kid. Just say it. No need to be uncomfortable with me.'

'Saying what?' he said, diverted for a moment.

'It doesn't matter. Just explain.'

'You remember the day your brothers went on at me because I was a Jew. Despised me for it – '

She was glad of the darkness of the cab as the flush filled her cheeks.

'I'm sorry about that,' she said. 'Truly I am. They mean no harm. At least, I don't think so. It's just that they're – '

'They aren't the point,' he said. 'The thing is – it's just that my family are the same. Every damned one of them.'

'The same?' she said blankly, and then laughed, a rather silly little sound. 'They despise you because – '

'Oh, don't be silly!' he cried. 'It's you! They despise you like they despise everyone who isn't a Jew. They think you're all the dregs, the worst kind of – to go around with a shicksah – a woman who isn't Jewish – it's just about the worst thing a man can do! My Momma wants to see you so that she can give you a bad time! She wants to make sure there ain't no risk she'll have to sit shivah for me on account of you – '

'I don't – shivah?' she said, trying to organize her thoughts. That people like her father, her brothers, everyone who lived in Leinster Terrace, indeed in almost the whole of her London, should despise and sneer at Jews was understandable. It had always been thus; she had heard so many veiled – and not so veiled – sneers about 'the chosen sort' and 'the money-lenders' and 'Hebraic types' that inevitably she regarded that attitude as normal. But that Jews should despise people like herself and her family – that seemed a very odd thing.

She cast her mind back to the one or two Jews her father had brought to visit her. They had not been like Kid Harris, brash and bouncy and exciting, with cockney voices and nasal intonations and glittering gold chains and rings. They had been as citified as Papa, as soberly suited as Papa, as fascinated by his dreary business talk as Papa, and far from despising him and his family and his household had seemed at some pains to cultivate his acquaintance, even though he often behaved with a most unpleasantly patronizing air towards them. Yet now Kid was telling her that his mother – she shook her head in the darkness and contented herself with a repetition of her question while she tried to reorganize her thoughts.

'Shivah? What is that?'

'Mourning,' he said after a moment. 'When a person dies his family sits for a week on low chairs in clothes they've torn to show their grief and their friends and neighbours say the prayers for the dead over them. That's what shivah is. And when a person marries out of the faith, then they do that. And after the week of their mourning they never think or talk about the person again. As if they really was dead.'

She sat in shocked silence. 'Just because a person marries someone of a different religion?'

'Yes.'

'That's disgusting! I mean, I can understand families being upset. I had a cousin who married a Roman Catholic and there was a great deal of fuss. It was years ago and I've never seen her since, I do admit. But no one pretended she had *died*!'

'Well, Jews do. And now someone – and if it was Ruby, I'll destroy him – now someone has told my mother I'm going round with you and – '

She sat bolt upright in the corner of the cab and said loudly, 'I am not going to marry you!'

'I ain't asked you, as I recall.'

'There's no question of it!' She was aghast. 'Friendship is one thing, going out and about is one thing but – this – this idea is ridiculous – I never heard of such a – it really is too much! Take me home at once! Turn the cab about and take me home!' She was becoming more agitated by the minute and leaned forwards and took his sleeve in her hand and shook it, and he put his own hand on top of hers and made an odd little crooning sound in his throat.

'Now, don't get yourself so gefrunzled! No need to get upset! No one's saying any different from what you are. No need to go running away. O' course you're not going back yet. In good time, we go back. Right now, we sort out this business with my mother. The thing of it is, I want we should go and see her. Yes, I do. So you can tell her she's to stop getting in such a fuss herself and it's all right and she can stop making a megillah every time she sees me. And then, when she knows you, and she feels comfortable with you – then, we shall see.'

'See what?' she demanded. 'We shall see nothing because I shan't be there. I am not going to be looked over like some – some prize animal brought from market. To be introduced as your friend would be pleasant. To be regarded as a – some sort of – ' She actually shuddered she was so angry. 'It's the outside of enough! I wish to go home.'

Her agitation seemed to have calmed his for he was now in a much better humour and just patted her hand and laughed.

'What a fuss! Now, do stop! I dare say I explained it all wrong anyway. I dare say I was getting worked up over nothing. She just wants to say hello, give you a bissel cake and coffee, and then we can go to the music hall for the last house, what do you say? No need to get all excited is there? O' course not! The thing of it is, Ruby's been making mischief and I can explain. So – that is what we'll do – see Momma and then go on out – '

He began to whistle tunelessly between his teeth, as happy as he had been gloomy and she could have shaken him in her fury, but he just grinned at her as the cab made one more turn and went rattling over a rather rutted road surface and came to a stop.

'Number seventeen, you said, squire?' The cabbie had leaned over and was shouting in through the window. 'Number seventeen Myrdle Street? Here we are.'

8

Once again, it was smell that affected her most powerfully. She allowed him to shepherd her in through the front door of the small house, unable to do anything else, and stood in the narrow hallway, her head up a little defensively and very aware of all that assaulted her senses.

It smelled warm and rich and in an odd sense affectionate. It wasn't just the heavy odours of food, though there was plenty of that. It was like the fried fish restaurants he took her to sometimes, but there was more than that. There were sweet as well as savoury smells and coffee and tea smells, and beneath them there was the scent of cleanliness, of hard yellow soap and soda and beeswax polish. And when she looked around she could see evidence of the ferocious battle against dirt that was clearly waged in this small house.

The floor was covered with brightly squared linoleum in shrieking yellows and reds which shone with soap, only losing its lustre in places where it had been worn down almost to the canvas. The staircase, which ran steeply upwards on one side of the small hallway, bore a narrow strip of red twill in the centre of each tread, carefully held in place with glintingly polished iron stair rods, and the wood left visible on each side had been rubbed to a deep gloss with beeswax. Ahead of her, just a few feet along, the passageway, which was lit by a single gas mantle in a black leaded holder on which even the chains which controlled the gas supply had been polished to within

an inch of their lives, ended in a door on which the upper
panes had been replaced by glass which was shielded with a
carefully arranged net curtain. She looked at the door and the
light that shone through it from the other side and saw the
shadow of a person standing just behind it, and suddenly her
heart lurched in her chest. She felt real alarm and shrank more
closely to Kid, who was just closing the front door.

'I would really rather not – ' she whispered, not taking her
eyes from the glass-fronted door, perfectly aware that someone
was standing close behind it with an ear pressed against the
net curtain, but Kid took her elbow in his comforting grasp,
and said loudly, 'No need to worry, believe me! Momma! It's
me!'

At once the figure on the other side of the door disappeared
and he grinned down at her, and made a little face, and as
though he had spoken she heard his words. 'What can I do?
That's Momma!' and again she tried to hang back. But he was
much more determined than she, and she felt herself propelled
the few steps along and then Kid's hand came over her
shoulder and opened the door.

'Well, Momma, here I am, and brought a friend you should
say hello to!' he said heartily and she felt the tension in him
for the first time since they had left the cab. He was, she
discovered, as nervous as she was, and that seemed to help.
She stopped hanging back and stood still and straight, her head
up.

The room was a little larger than she would have expected
from the narrowness of the passageway, but so crowded with
furniture that it seemed unlikely that anyone could move about
in it with any ease. A large central table, covered in a red plush
cloth and bearing a big copper samovar on a crocheted mat,
stood in the centre; a broad kitchen range with a grated fire
and ovens on each side, blackened to a luscious ebony that
reflected every spark and lick of flame from the coals glowing
behind the bars; an overmantel draped with the same red plush

as the table but bearing so many vases and ornaments and knick-knacks that it was almost invisible; a glass-fronted wall cupboard in which china and glass and dishes of all kinds were stacked high, with large garishly coloured cups hanging on hooks; a very large and shiny brown horsehair-stuffed sofa, embellished with polished brass-headed nails and several tapestry cushions; a window draped with more red plush, this time trimmed with yellow braid and tassels, and a bewildering number of chairs of varying sizes, all with flat embroidered cushions on them.

And in the largest chair to the right of the hearth a small woman. Even sitting down she looked tiny, with fragile bones and the scrawniest of skins and a face from which every atom of excess flesh had been worn away to show the sharp bones of cheeks and nose and chin, and the darkest and most glittering eyes Mildred could ever remember seeing.

The small mouth opened slowly and the voice that emerged was high and piercing. 'I should say hello? So all right. Hello.'

'This is Miss Amberly, Momma.' He was pushing her forwards gently, a hand on the small of her back. 'Miss Mildred Amberly, my friend.'

'So, your friend.' The woman peered upwards at Mildred and then, suddenly, her mouth opened wider and stretched sideways and she was cackling. 'Pssht, I never saw such a lange locksh!'

'Momma, be quiet!' Mildred felt him go hot behind her as great waves of embarrassment engulfed him. 'You should be – ' He stopped and swallowed. 'Please, Momma. I told you, this is my friend! You should be nice!'

'How do you do, Mrs Harris,' Mildred said, and her own voice was rather higher than usual as a slow anger began to glow in her. 'May I ask what a – what was it? Lange – It's not a word I know.'

'She expects she should know Yiddish, now!' Mrs Harris said, never taking her eyes from her son's face. 'Such an expert! You should tell her what is a lange locksh, Lizah!'

'So, Momma, how about a cup of tea, a bissel strudel maybe? Miss Amberly has come a long way, already – '

'So tell her,' the old woman commanded, still staring at her son, and Mildred thought – she hasn't looked at me at all, apart from that one glance. She's behaving as though I was a piece of furniture or a dog to be talked about and at and around, but never to, and she lifted her head even higher and said loudly, 'I would prefer you explained, Mrs Harris. If you wish me to know what it means.'

There was a little silence as Mrs Harris remained staring at her son, and then she allowed her eyes to shift slowly so that she was looking at Mildred at last.

'A long cold drink of water,' she said at length. 'A lange locksh. A person who is too high for her own good. And thin – ' And her eyes flicked down towards Mildred's feet and again it was as though she could hear unspoken words. The sneer at her flat chest and meagre hips, which remained anything but voluptuous despite so many months of eating the Kid's good food, was loud in the small room.

Kid laughed, a strained sound that was swallowed up by the heavy curtains and the looming furniture. 'Such a jokester, my Momma! Always busy with the jokes.'

'Oh, was that meant to be funny?' Mildred said coolly.

'Sure, it's funny!' Mrs Harris said. 'Ain't you seen what you looks like next to my Lizah? A lange he ain't. He comes up to your pippick! And you want to know what a pippick is? A belly button! That is what a pippick is! Believe you me, you and him, this is a joke!'

She got to her feet, hauling herself out of her chair with some effort, and now Mildred could see that her appearance was deceptive. She was small in height and her upper body was indeed fragile and bony, but from the waist down she was as solid and stocky as her son. She stood now with her fists on those thick hips which were enveloped in a heavy blue stuff gown covered with a very white apron, and grinned. Her teeth were long and rather yellow but suddenly there was a glimpse of the girl she had once been, and of a likeness to her son.

'So, you'll have some tea, Lizah. And some plaver. Strudel I ain't got. Plaver there is.' And she turned and went a little creakingly to the door on the other side of the horsehair sofa and went down a couple of steps into the ill-lit scullery beyond to start banging about with dishes.

Mildred stood still, a little nonplussed. The hostility that had been in the room seemed to have dissolved somewhat and the anger that had begun to rise in her muttered and subsided, although it did not go away entirely.

'Why is she – ' she began to whisper to him but he shook his head and, pulling on her arm, took her to the table and pulled out a chair for her.

'Listen, Millie, understand, please,' he said in a low voice. 'She's a – a forthright lady, my Momma. If it's in the mind it's on the lip, know what I mean? But she means no harm. You always know where you are with her. She says what she says, and then it's over. No hard feelings. Please, don't get gefrunzled – upset.'

'It would help if people didn't keep speaking to me in a foreign language,' Mildred hissed at him, watching the shadows in the scullery as Mrs Harris moved between the gaslight and the door. 'It doesn't exactly make a person feel welcome.'

'You're welcome,' he said, still murmuring. 'Believe me, there'd have been no offer of tea and cake if not – tell her the plaver is wonderful. She's a good cook and – '

Mrs Harris came back into the room carrying a heavy tray and set it down on the table with a clatter and then took the pot across to the grate where a large black kettle was muttering quietly to itself on one side of the fire.

'You've eaten, Lizah?' she demanded. 'I got fried fish, and I got chopped herring and bagels. She wants some?'

'My name is Mildred, Mrs Harris.' Mildred said, fixing her with her gaze as the old woman came back from the fire, her teapot now full.

'So?'

'So call me that!' she snapped and now Mrs Harris looked at her and then at Kid and jerked her head back in Mildred's direction.

'Got a good opinion of herself, eh? Wants to be *everyone's* friend, does she?'

'Momma, stop it!' He sat down with a thump beside Mildred and glowered at his mother. 'Listen, what do you want of my life? You go on and on at me, I'm to bring Miss Amberly to see you. I take no notice, but you go on and on about it, so, punkt, I bring her! And what do I get? Insults to my friend. It's not right and it's not nice and you ought to know better.'

'And you ought to know better than to go shlapping around with shicksahs!' she flared at him. 'You been brought up to be a decent boy, and now you go running around with – '

'I am not a boy, Momma. I'm a man with a life of my own and I choose my own friends, whether you like it or not.' Mildred felt her anger bubble away and took a deep breath in relief. That was what had been the most unpleasant part of the situation: Kid Harris' apparent willingness to let his mother say what she wanted and to behave as she liked no matter how she might make Mildred feel. Now he was resisting she felt much better, and she leaned a little closer to him, staring at his mother with her brows slightly raised.

'So, you're being rude to your mother now? You think you're such a man you can insult your mother and – '

'If you insult my friends, Momma, then I won't put up with it. You said you wanted to meet Miss Amberly. You've met her. Now behave right or we go away. End of argument. Do you hear me? End of argument.' And he sat very still, watching her.

There was a little silence as Mrs Harris stood and stared back at him and then slowly she shifted her gaze to Mildred.

'I insulted you? I meant no insult. I say what I find, and there it is. But if I insulted you then all right, I'm sorry.' She looked now at her son and said, 'So now you're happy? No insults.'

She's frightened, Mildred thought, suddenly seeing the old woman more clearly. She's scared of upsetting him. And she looked at Kid who was now sitting grinning again. Why is she frightened of him? And for a moment she remembered the way he had been the first time she had met him in the cellar room. He had seemed menacing, a heavy man with violence in him, a man who could hurt people and control them with fear of that hurt, and she felt herself shrink away from him, alarm coming to replace the anger.

'That's better!' he said heartily. 'Much better! Now we can be friends, eh? You and me and my friend, Miss Amberly. Now Millie, this you got to try.' He reached for the tray and seizing the knife cut a large slice from the sponge cake that was set on a plate in the middle. 'It's the lightest, the moistest, and the sweetest player in the whole neighbourhood. Momma, a cup of tea for Millie and for me as well, and we'll be comfortable together.'

She hesitated only for a moment and then did as she was told, pouring tea and handing it to them and Mildred took it with a murmured 'thank you' and began to sip automatically. The cups were thick and heavy and she had to concentrate on what she was doing and that helped. She didn't want to think about what had happened in that brief moment, didn't want to look at the fear that had come back. There had been so much pleasure these past months, so much that was rich and exciting that she had managed to forget the origins of their peculiar friendship. Now that memory was pushing against her, trying to warn her, and she put her cup down with a clatter and thought – what am I doing? How did I ever let this happen?

How can I be sitting here in this tiny place with a woman who so obviously hates me? I must be mad. I have to go home. I must go home and stop all this nonsense and – '

Kid Harris had been talking steadily, as the two women sat on each side of him in silence, apparently unaware of the fact that neither of them was actually listening to him and now he repeated a sentence, more loudly, 'Momma, where is it?'

'Eh?'

'The diploma, Momma. The diploma they gave me at the school, when I won my first fight. Where is it?'

'Upstairs. In the back bedroom,' she said and he got to his feet at once. 'Millie, this I must show you. I was seven years old. Would you believe? Seven years old and I got this diploma for boxing. I tell you I was like a – well, I'll fetch it, you'll see.' And he went clattering out of the room and they heard his footsteps go charging up the stairs.

There was a tense silence, crowded with their thoughts, and then Mrs Harris leaned towards her suddenly and grasped her arm in a bony hand. It was a surprisingly hard grip and Mildred thought – did he inherit that from her, too? He holds on to me like this sometimes –

'Listen. You. Miss Amberly – you goin' to marry my Lizah?'

She blinked and pulled ineffectually at her hand. 'What?'

'I said are you planning to marry him? Because if you are – '

She didn't mean to. It just happened. She laughed, tilting her head back and letting the sound of real amusement come out, comfortable and easy. 'Marry him? Of course not! I never heard anything so ridiculous in my life!'

The old woman almost bridled, her face settling into a scowl. 'There's nothing wrong with him! He's a marvellous boy, best of all my children, may God forgive me for making such judgements! You could do worse, God help him if you do – '

'Of course there's nothing wrong with him,' Mildred said and her amusement grew. What did the wretched woman want from her? Assurances of her undying love for her son, or assurances that she hated him? A little of both, probably, she thought shrewdly, and with her other hand, patted the old woman's gnarled knuckles which were still whitening in their grip on Mildred's arm. 'But I have no intention of marrying him or anyone else. We've become friends. It's mad really. We've nothing in common at all, nothing that we could be said to share. It's something that just happened. But all it is is a *friendship*. He knows my brothers, and that's how I know him. It means nothing. I have a dull life and he entertains me. That is all.'

They could hear his footsteps moving about upstairs and then coming back towards the staircase and the old woman said quickly, 'Listen, you swear? On your mother's life?'

'She's dead.'

'I'm sorry, you should forgive me. I wish you long life. On your father's life, then. You swear you won't marry my Lizah?'

He was clattering down now and Mrs Harris almost shook her arm in her impatience, never taking her eyes from Mildred's face. 'Swear already, on your father's life – swear it.'

'Oh, for heaven's sake,' Mildred began but again the old woman shook her arm and said, 'Swear it.'

'Oh, all right.' At last she managed to pull herself away from that tight grip. 'Anything you like. I swear. Will that satisfy you?'

'Say it. Say "I swear I won't marry Lizah Harris, on my father's life." '

Mildred grimaced and rubbed her arm as she heard his footsteps reach the bottom of the stairs. 'Oh, all right!' she said hurriedly as Mrs Harris leaned closer, looking threatening, and repeated the words while feeling more than a little absurd, for it was so melodramatic; more like the things that happened on the stage at the old Britannia than real life, and as Kid came back into the room, slamming the glass-fronted door behind him, the old woman nodded, apparently satisfied, and leaned back so that her face was in the shadows and no longer illuminated by the central gaslight that hung over the table.

'So here it is!' he said jovially, and sat down between them again. 'My first winnings! Now I get fat purses and make a good thing out of side bets, but when I got this, believe me, I felt richer'n I have any time since! See, Millie?'

She looked at the oblong of paper covered in elaborate copperplate script, with his name, Lazarus Harris, carefully embossed in the centre and nodded.

'It's beautiful,' she murmured. 'Beautiful.' And then lifted her head and said very deliberately to the face in the shadows. 'Like your cake, Mrs Harris. That is beautiful too. I enjoyed it. May I have another slice?'

'You like it?' She leaned forwards and stretched for the cake plate and knife. 'You've got good taste, I'll give you that. So tell me, you bake cakes yourself? Or are you too rich to have to do such things?'

'I don't bake cakes,' Mildred said and took the plate that Mrs Harris thrust at her. 'But I'm not rich either. I live with my father.'

'You should see, Momma. Real class, that house. In Leinster Terrace, right by Hyde Park, lovely. One of these days, I promise you, I'll get a house like that for you – '

'And Queen Victoria will come and eat my plaver,' Mrs Harris said and got up and took the tea pot back to the range to refill it from the hissing kettle. 'And the moon'll come down and turn into cheese and we'll all eat smoked salmon every day.'

'Just you wait and see.' He leaned back in his chair and stretched. 'Just you wait. One of these days, when I'm a world champion and got it all, my own gymnasiums, my own stable of fighters, you'll see. You'll have the moon, sure, and plenty more besides. Eh, Millie?'

'No doubt,' she said and stood up. 'Mrs Harris, I really think I must leave now. It has been – I am happy to have met you.'

And she held out her hand and after a moment the other woman took it and shook it perfunctorily.

'We may meet again some day,' Mildred said formally and withdrew her hand and put on her gloves, and Kid Harris got to his feet and leaned over and hugged the diminutive old woman who stood quietly beside her tea tray, and said jovially, 'So, Momma, I'll be home late, all right? No need to worry none. I'm all right. And now you've met my friend, you're all right there too, eh?'

'Yes,' Mrs Harris said, though her voice was colourless. 'Yes. All right. Good night, Miss Amberly.'

'Goodbye, Mrs Harris,' Mildred said firmly and turned and went.

9

It was never quite the same after that meeting. So much so that she did make herself think very hard about giving up her friendship with Harris altogether. His mother's hostility had been more than unpleasant, she felt; it had been illuminating too, making her see the situation much more clearly. What had been just a ridiculous adventure now took on darker undertones. She wasn't just flouting convention in sneaking out of her father's house to go to East End music halls and theatres and cheap restaurants; she was actually taking risks not only with her own well-being but also that of others.

Often, as she was falling asleep at night, she would see again Mrs Harris' face, shadowed and watchful under her gaslight as she stood and watched her son go out of her home at Mildred's side, and what she saw there wasn't hostility and anger so much as fear and hurt. And that distressed her.

But giving up the liaison was not as easy a matter as it might have been. First there were her own inclinations. The thought of returning to the humdrummery of life as it had been before that evening last September was a painful one, so painful she could not countenance it, for it was her evenings with Kid Harris which made her days tolerable. Without that respite she could not imagine living at all.

And there was also the matter of Kid Harris himself. He was as determined she should continue with the friendship as she was unwilling to relinquish it. When she told him she thought she should stop going out to meet him, he threatened to come to the house to speak to her father and insist on her right to do as she chose. When she tried to tell him she was bored and no longer interested in spending time with him, he shrugged the words away as patent nonsense. It was not possible, to Kid Harris, that any person on whom he had set the seal of his approval could ever find him anything but enthralling. There were many childlike qualities in this little man with the blue cheeks, but this was the most childlike of them all. The people he liked must, of course, like him, and there was an end of it. And that innocent certainty of his in fact made him even more likeable.

And so they went on, she still managing to escape detection at home and becoming ever more adept a liar about time ostensibly spent at Father Jay's club (to which she had persuaded Kid Harris to take her on a visit so that she could trim her lies with details which would add a gloss of believability to her tales) and he seeming quite unperturbed about anything. Whatever her mood, he was sunny and pleased with himself, pushing aside any efforts she might make to talk of serious matters and wanting only to show her how generous and carefree he was. He seemed to be never happier than when sitting with her amid a crowd of his friends, ordering large quantitites of food and drink for them and generally being the centre of attraction. And she would sit quietly beside him and try to imagine a life in which she did not share such jaunts, and would see it as very bleak indeed. And yet, it seemed to threaten to become just as bleak if matters went on as they were – and she would close her eyes against her confusion and try not to think of anything at all except the here and now, which was, after all, agreeable enough.

At least he did not embarrass her with any unwanted physical advances. Their friendship remained just that, and quite unadulterated by any lover-like behaviour on his part. He would hold her arm to guide her, would put his hand on hers to make a point, and was much given to taking her by the elbow, but there was never anything lingering in any of these touches, nothing that could alarm her in the least. Her virtue, she knew, was totally safe with him. And whether this was because he felt no attraction towards her in that sense, or because he was holding himself rigidly controlled, she did not know and did not care to think about. It was bad enough that she experienced those strange and exciting sensations when she watched him boxing; to regard him as anything more than a friend was literally unthinkable.

So might they have gone on for many more months had Kid Harris not chosen on a very rainy night in February to take her to see the last night of the pantomime that the famous Mrs Lane was putting on at the Britannia. The ever popular Marie Lloyd was in it and there were to be guest appearances by Ada Reeve and Marie Kendall and the Lupinos, a very special night indeed. Kid Harris had only the week before won a fight in Shoreditch which had carried a huge purse of a hundred pounds and was feeling extremely pleased with himself, in spite of the fact that he still had a fading bruise on his right cheekbone and a healing cut across his right eyebrow, and in consequence was in an even more lordly mood than usual.

'None o' your rubbish, Millie!' he said expansively. 'Tonight we sits in a box. I've ordered some fizz for you, and there we shall sit and how they'll all stare! It'll be a good show and we'll be as good a show as any of 'em!'

She did not argue. She had tried to persuade him several times to understand her problems regarding dress. To leave her home in an evening gown was impossible, for no one would ever go to a Mission to help a priest in such a rig, so she nearly always wore her quiet tailormades, alternating the blue with the dark brown, and had stopped paying any attention to the differences between herself and the other women who attended the Britannia and Kid's other places of entertainment.

Let them strut in their vivid colours and low-cut bodices and frills and trimmings. She would sit demurely in her tailormades and not care a whit.

So, on this occasion again she said nothing about the grandeur of sitting in a box, quietly settling into the little gilt chair at the front of the box, and not thinking at all about how visible she might be to the rest of the house. In this she was quite unlike Kid, who always knew exactly who was looking at him and who was speaking of him and who was approving of him, and basked in such attentions. Now he sat beside her, sumptuous in a new set of evening clothes which were even more handsome than the last, delighted to be seen so clearly.

'I don't know why I never took a box before,' he confided to her as at last the orchestra struck up and the house lights slowly dimmed. 'You get a lovely view of the stage 'n' all from here – '

And they, she thought good-humouredly, get a lovely view of you, as slowly the great tableau curtain rose and the huge wash of light came pouring out to illuminate the front rows of seats and even more their own eyrie, part way up the right side of the wall beside the stage.

The pantomime was indeed delightful, and within a matter of minutes she was immersed in it, following the adventures of the character played by Marie Lloyd, one Princess Kristina, who had sundry adventures while carrying a lamp about with her at all times. The lamp, Mildred soon realized, represented her virtue and in one scene, when she lost the lamp, Miss Lloyd immediately became a very different character; no longer retiring and girlish, but forward and brazen, and the audience howled their delight as Marie Lloyd with a set of sidelong glances that were as wicked and knowing as those any woman ever delivered, took them all in her hand and squeezed their hearts until they shrieked for more. And Mildred was as entranced as anyone in the house, leaning forwards on the parapet of the box and laughing immoderately and clapping delightedly as the plot unfolded itself in one obvious but vastly enjoyable scene after another.

By the time the curtain came down to mark the first interval and the fruit sellers and the cake peddlars were out in force in the aisles below them and the people in the gallery were scenting the air with their pigs' trotters and fried fish and oranges – for the gallery always resembled a vast continuous picnic – she was very relaxed and happy. It was like one of those earlier evenings when she had first embarked on this silly mad caper, when she had first come to the Britannia and discovered what a place of joy it was. Whatever happens in the future, she thought confusedly as she accepted a glass of the champagne he gave her from the bottle in a bucket of ice which had been set ready for them at the back of their box, whatever happens, I am enjoying this. Live for the moment – just for now, and *enjoy* it –

And then the door snapped open and Kid Harris turned his head lazily, expecting to see those of his friends he had spotted in the audience below coming to pay court, and she did not look at all, for the same reason. But then she heard the voice and her chin snapped round and she stared, her mouth half open and her belly somersaulting with shock.

'Mildred!' Basil stood in the little doorway with his back to the light that was coming in from the passageway outside so that his face was shadowed, but it was unmistakeably him and she stood up quickly, spilling some of her champagne as she did so. 'What the deuce are you doing here?'

She had seen little of him for some time; ever since the night when she had rescued them from their pickle, both he and Claude had kept themselves very much to themselves at home, hurrying out in the morning to their respectable employment and spending more evenings at their club than at home. And that had suited her well enough, for she knew that they would have been far less easy to gull than her father, who was, she knew, always glad to see as little as possible of the children of his first marriage, finding them an embarrassment now that he had another nursery full and a whining ailing wife to boot. So, seeing Basil now was an added shock, for he seemed to have grown more than she had noticed on the few occasions when she had passed him on the stairs at home, or had seen him hurrying down the front steps to the street on his way out. He looked formidable as he stood there filling the doorway with his height, if not his bulk, and she pressed her hands together to still their shaking as she looked at him.

'Basil!' she said. 'I – how very – I mean – '

'And with this horrible creature!' Basil stepped forwards and stared at Kid Harris who now came slowly to his feet and stood with his legs slightly apart and his arms hanging loose and yet clearly tensed at his sides.

'Good evenin', Amberly,' he said quietly. 'It's been some time since I saw you. Not layin' any more bets, then? Given up your interest in matters pugilistic, have you?'

'I'll deal with you in a minute,' Basil said and straightened his shoulders and she thought fleetingly of the timid way he had sat slouched on the bench at the back of the cellar when these two had last been in the same place, and could not help but feel a little lift of approval. He had indeed come on in more ways than one during the past six months. 'Mildred, put on your hat and we'll be going.'

'Going where, Basil?' She sat down again, feeling the need to do so, for her legs had begun to tremble in reaction to the alarm the sight of him had created in her. 'I am quite well able to get myself home, thank you.' She stopped and then added daringly, 'I usually do, you know.'

'What do you mean, you usually do?' He stepped forwards now so that his face was in the light coming up from the noisy orchestra stalls below them. 'Have you been here like this before?'

She laughed a little shakily. 'Basil, you are a donkey! Why should I not have been? I am as free as you. Freer perhaps, since I am older. I am well past the age of my majority, after all.'

'Don't talk such rubbish,' he said shortly. 'And put on your hat and come away at once. A girl like you, in a place like this! It is ridiculous.'

'Why?' She looked over her shoulder at the crowds below and then tilted her chin to take in the grand circle and the balconies and galleries above it. 'I see many women and girls here who seem to be safe enough.'

'Safe!' he snorted, sounding more like his father than he knew. 'These ghastly females, greasy Jew girls and tarts and – '

'That is enough, Amberly.' Kid Harris did not move, still standing with his hands loose at his sides, but the sound of his voice made Basil rock back a little on his heels. 'You owe me an apology for that. And your sister. Make it and get out of here.'

'I apologize to no one,' Basil cried passionately. 'I don't know what is happening here and it's better perhaps that I shouldn't be told, for if I hear what I suspect I may, then you will not live to tell the tale and – '

Harris said nothing. He did not even seem to move at all quickly, but she heard the sound as his hand met Basil's cheek and the even more sickening sound as Basil's head cracked back on his neck and she jumped to her feet and threw herself at Harris and cried, 'No!'

But it was too late to stop either of them. They were staring at each other with so much venom that it was almost palpable in the air, making her catch her breath in her throat and then Harris said in a voice she hardly recognized, 'Get out of the way, Millie – '

It was that which seemed to galvanize Basil, for he howled at the top of his voice, 'Millie! You bastard, who are you to call my sister "Millie"?' And with a great deal more courage than sense hurled himself at Harris, who, moving with a fluid ease, set his hands up at chest level, the fists lightly formed, and began to punch at Basil rhythmically and methodically, each blow hitting home with the same revolting sound and she cried, 'Stop it! Kid, Basil, stop – For pity's sake, *stop* it – '

But it was like shrieking in a dream for no one could hear her. The two men were thumping at each other furiously; Basil, for all his lack of Kid's skill and experience, making good use of his much greater height and dodging and feinting blows while occasionally managing to land one of his own on Harris' face, which made an easy target for him; whereas Kid Harris had to reach upwards to hit him and so leave his body vulnerable.

The rest of the house had by now become aware of what was happening in the stage box, and people in the gallery were leaning over the rail, at grave risk to themselves, to see all that could be seen and to shout encouragement. In the balconies and the Grand Circle the interest was no less intense, and in the orchestra stalls below people were all looking upwards so that their faces made a white sea in the prevailing colours of red from the plush-covered seats and black from the men's clothes.

There were people thundering along the passageway outside too, and the door, which Basil had kicked closed behind him now was flung open and three men came pouring in, clearly intending to separate the two fighters and so put an end to the fracas.

But they were too late, for Harris, using every atom of skill he had, had forced Basil to turn round and had pushed him back against the low parapet of the box, and then, punching hard and fast, made him lean back and over as Mildred, now almost frantic with fear and her own rage and excitement, tried to pull Basil back, convinced he was going to fall head first out on to the people below him.

And so he did, for no matter how many people tried to seize on Kid Harris' pumping elbows as he rained punch after punch on Basil's rapidly swelling face and bleeding nose, the punishment went on and on and slowly, agonizingly so to Milly as she tried to hold on to him, Basil toppled over the edge of the box and went down, his arms and legs flailing as Kid Harris continued with his relentless steam engine action, his elbows going like pistons and his fists threshing the air.

How she ever got down there she was never to remember. All she knew was that she turned and ran blindly, pushing her way past the men who were still trying to control Kid Harris' rage and round and down the small flight of stairs that led below, bursting at last through the curtained doorway to where Basil lay, spread out on the floor between the rows of seats, and looking dreadful. On each side of him people milled and chattered, one of them making a loud fuss about how his own neck had been nearly broken when Basil had landed on him from above.

'I wouldn't worry, ducks,' someone said as she flopped down beside Basil and with her hands shaking tried to feel his face to see if he was still breathing. ' 'E didn't come down fast, and 'e's that tall 'e was nearly down 'ere before 'is feet left the box, like. And 'e landed on that fat fella there and that made it easier for 'im.'

He was breathing, and she touched his face and he groaned and opened his eyes.

'Basil?' she said. 'Are you all right?' and he closed his eyes with a grimace of pain and she knew her question had been fatuous in the extreme. 'Oh, you idiot,' she cried and fumbled in her bodice for the handkerchief she usually kept there, so that she could mop his face. 'Why did you do anything so stupid? You must have known he would do this to you!'

'If he's done anything to you I'll kill him,' Basil managed to say hoarsely and then closed his eyes again as tears of pain squeezed out beneath his lids.

'I – don't be so stupid – ' she began but then someone was leaning over them and pulling her away.

'Come on now, Miss. Let the dog see the bleedin' rabbit. We've got a show to get on 'ere and it's time we was on the way again. Let's 'ave this fella out somewhere where 'e can get 'isself together and we can all get to rights again – '

There were several of the theatre's uniformed attendants with the man, who was wearing an evening suit so old that it looked green and so crumpled it looked like an elephant's skin, and at a sign from him they swooped on Basil and lifted him up, paying no attention to his groans, and carried him out with Mildred hurrying along behind them to the doors at the side, and then along the passageway to the foyer of the theatre. Behind her she heard the orchestra strike up its sprightly music again and then it was muffled as the auditorium doors were closed, and the audience settled down to enjoy the rest of the show for which they had paid, having much enjoyed the impromptu free one they had witnessed during the interval.

Kid Harris was already sitting in the foyer, his legs sprawling as he lay back in a chair that had been fetched from an office, as a woman in a red dress bathed his face with a towel which she dipped from time to time in a bowl of water beside her. As the blood was mopped from his face and transferred to the water it reddened so that it began to match the woman's gown and, feeling suddenly sick, Mildred turned away and looked to where Basil had been laid down on a bench.

'You want to clean 'im up, then, ducks?' someone said and brought a bowl of water to her and after a moment she took the towel she was also given and imitating the actions of the woman attending to Kid, began to clean up Basil's face as he lay and groaned under her attentions. Slowly the other people began to melt away, going back to more interesting activities, until just the manager and the two men and their attendants were left.

'I'll call a coupl'a cabs for you, then?' The manager was clearly anxious to get rid of them all. 'You be on you way and no questions asked. I know the Kid, and I don't want to make nothing nasty out of this. But you'd better be on your way, or we'll 'ave the bloody rozzers round 'ere making pests o' themselves when no one wants 'em. Sooner you lot's gone the better. You'll take 'im then, Mrs Mendel? An' then you can take the other one off – '

'I want a doctor for my brother,' Mildred said shortly over her shoulder. Under her careful fingers his face was beginning to show more clearly the injuries he had suffered and they were not as bad as she had feared. A rapidly darkening eye, an area of puffiness on the left of his face and a badly swollen lip which had split where it had been pressed against his front teeth seemed to be the worst, though there were other bruises and lacerations of less severity. But she was worried at his dreadful pallor and the way he lay with his eyes half open and showing no real awareness of his surroundings.

'Take him to the London,' the woman in the red dress said. Her voice was rather deep and had a familiar ring to it, and Mildred looked at her over her shoulder and the woman looked back at her and raised her brows slightly in a not unfriendly grimace. 'They're used to these things there. And they'll see you get back up West all right. I dare say the boy'll be all right once he's had a bit of sleep and a chance to get the stiffness out of his bones. But make sure to keep an eye on how he sleeps. If he sleeps too deep, wake him up. If you have trouble waking him, get the doctor to see him again fast. All right?'

Mildred nodded. 'Thank you – what about him? Is he all right?' And she craned her neck to look at Kid Harris, who was still sitting silently, his head a little slumped, paying no attention to anyone.

'Oh, he's all right,' the woman in red said cheerfully. 'More annoyed with himself than anything else, if I know him. Silly devil – ' And she pushed his shoulder in an oddly playful gesture that made Mildred's brows snap down.

'Perhaps he's hurt too. Perhaps he should be at the hospital,' she said stiffly. 'I'll take him. He's a friend of mine and although I'm very angry with him – ' she swallowed and closed her eyes for a moment. 'Although I'm angry with both of them, I wouldn't for the world have anything happen to him. As soon as a cab comes I'll take them both – '

'Oh, I can manage this one,' the woman in red said and stood up more straightly and dusted her hands together. 'I've done it often enough before. Great shlemiel that he is. Been doing it for years for him, come to that.'

She lifted her head and looked at Mildred and smiled widely at the sight of her frown. 'Don't look like that,' she said. 'I'm his sister Jessie. And you must be his shicksah, I suppose?'

10

They sat side by side in the echoing space of the marble-floored waiting-hall, silent and glum, the thick reek of carbolic and harsh yellow soap sharp in their noses as they listened to the occasional cry of a child or the shout of a distressed patient, and found nothing to say to each other.

Or at least Mildred did not. Jessie Mendel had tried several times to start a conversation, but Mildred had sat mulishly with her mouth clamped shut, refusing to look at her, let alone speak to her. The nurses, blue and white and rustling and deeply disapproving, had taken both Basil and Kid away to cubicles where they had rattled curtains closed upon them, and made it very clear that neither of the women was at all welcome. They had to sit and wait, and although Mildred had tried to use the sort of imperious West End voice she had heard her father employ to considerable effect in such situations, it had done no good. The senior nurse, a girl probably younger than Mildred, had looked at her down her snub nose and said icily, 'Only patients are permitted to enter cubicles. You are not a patient. Be so good as to wait on the bench there. If you are troublesome I shall be obliged to fetch the porter to remove you.' And Mildred had looked over her shoulder at the large and forbidding man in serge and brass buttons who was standing magisterially still and watchful by the main doors and, furious but impotent to do otherwise, had sat down beside Jessie Mendel.

The great clock ticked on the far wall, ominous and heavy against the white tiles, and still Mildred sat there, staring down at her hands clasped in her lap, and glowered. Her head was bubbling with a tangle of thoughts and feelings and she didn't know which was distressing her most; her sense of her own stupidity, for it had been stupid in the extreme even to start on this mad trapsing around the East End which had landed her in this dreadful situation; anxiety about Basil's welfare, for he had looked so very white and sick when he had been half led, half carried to the cubicle by the small and masterful nurse who had taken charge of him; concern about Kid Harris, who had been bleeding steadily if sluggishly from the cut above his eyebrow which had opened up again in the fight; fury with both of them for being so lunatic as to start fighting in such circumstances, and over such a cause – was she not a free person, entitled to make her own decisions about what she did and where she went? How dare they fight over her as though she were a prize in a boxing match? – and, simmering beneath all of it, cold anger at the woman in the red dress, now with a rabbit fur cape slung over it in a casual and rather beguiling manner, who sat beside her.

How dare she, she thought furiously now, how *dare* she try to be friendly and to start conversations with me after calling me names as she had? Mildred had heard the word shicksah before. Mrs Harris had used it, and she had been very aware of the scorn with which the word had been filled, and knew it to be an insult. And now Kid's sister had used the same insult; and Mildred sat and glowered and tried to think of what she could do to repay her in kind.

'Listen, why are you so broigus with me? What have I done?' Jessie said then and she shoved with her shoulder at Mildred so unexpectedly that she almost lost her balance and was at risk of toppling sideways off the bench. 'Eh? Why don't you talk?'

'It would help if people spoke to me in simple English,' Mildred said frostily, unable to maintain her sulky silence any longer. 'If you wish me to understand, you must use words I recognize.'

'Hoity toity,' Jessie said equably. 'What did I say that you couldn't understand? Broigus, was it? Bad-tempered, that is. Annoyed. *Broigus*. You can hear what it means – the word sounds like what it is, don't it?'

'Not to me,' Mildred snapped.

'All right, I'm sorry, already. So I'm not one of you hoicke fenster people – ' She stopped then and laughed, a pleasant sound deep in her throat. 'You see my problem? Here we all talk this way. You say I'm not talking English to you but to me you don't talk English when you don't understand what I say. It may have some Yiddish in it, but believe you me, it's English. East End English. All right, so I don't talk like you, who lives where all the houses have high windows, is what I mean to say, but that don't mean I ain't got nothing to say you won't want to hear. Does it?'

For the first time since they arrived at the hospital Mildred turned and looked at her companion. She was sitting very straight, her arms crossed on her bosom and her head tilted a little and as Mildred's eyes met hers she grinned, showing very white teeth, as uneven as her brother's, but on her they looked particularly attractive. They gave her a crooked smile that was full of warmth and amusement. 'Does it?' she repeated, and smiled even more widely.

'I don't know what you mean,' Mildred said and turned away. 'And frankly, I am not particularly interested. I want just to get my brother out of here and take him home. Nothing more.'

'And what about my brother?'

'You can take him anywhere you like,' Mildred said shortly. 'He's nothing to do with me.'

'Hey, I thought you were his friend?' Jessie said. 'What sort of a way is that to be with a friend?'

'He's no friend of mine,' Mildred said and let the bitterness display itself in her voice. 'To beat up my brother like that, and – '

'I saw it, you know. Saw what happened. I was on the second row, underneath your fancy box in the stalls. I could see. And from where I was sitting it was your brother who went looking for mine. And who, I think, hit out first.'

'I'm well aware of that. But Kid Harris – he's the older of the two, and the one with all the – the benefit on his side. He's a trained boxer. To fight like that with a boy as young as Basil, and to throw him out of the box like that – he could have killed him.' Mildred's voice began to rise as her anger rekindled. 'It was the most stupid and dangerous thing anyone could possibly have done, but he didn't stop to think. He just threw him out of the box and – '

'Ah, poppycock!' Jessie Mendel said and laughed aloud. 'I tell you, I saw what happened. That box wasn't more'n ten feet above the ground, and your brother's a good six-footer ain't he? Lizah hung him by his ankles so he had only a couple of feet to go, and he made sure he landed on a nice fat 'un. Believe me, your brother was hurt more in his dignity than what he was in his head.'

'And then, how dare you,' Mildred said, refusing even to contemplate the possibility that she might be right about what Kid Harris had done. 'How dare you call me names?'

Jessie's eyes widened in genuine amazement. 'Names? What names did I call you?'

Mildred took a deep breath. 'That word that – schick – something.'

'Shicksah? It means a girl who isn't Jewish! By some people, I can tell you, that ain't no insult. It's a compliment. No one'd choose to be a Jew, not if they could be born to be West End madams like you. You want that I should shout Jew girl after

108

you in the street the way I've had it shouted after me, sometimes? I don't like it when they do it, but I don't see it as an insult, on account of it's what I am. And shicksah is what you are. A girl who isn't Jewish.'

Mildred sat and stared at her, taken aback. The other woman smiled at her, friendly still, and shook her head. 'You're tired, that's what it is. Tired and upset. It made you br – it made you take offence. Being worried does it to some people, don't it? Me, when I get worried, I eat.' She shook her head in mock self reproof. 'My Momma and Poppa have another of their fights, and my Poppa comes round and wants to stay at my house, so what do I do? I don't shout at him and tell the silly old fool to go home the way I should. I make up a bed for him and then I go eat a plate of bagels and herring. My husband died, God rest his wicked soul, and I tell you, I got half as big again.' She looked down at herself, and unfolded her arms and smoothed her hands proudly over the front of her dress. 'Now I got me a new fella paying me some attention and I ain't eating no more. And Gotse Dank, it shows. Not bad, eh? Turn of the year, I weighed thirteen stone. Now I'm down to eleven and a half. Six weeks of loving – it does a lot for a woman.'

Suddenly Mildred felt her face go hot. She had been so pleased with herself and her appearance because she had plumped up during this past four or five months, since she had been seeing Kid Harris, but now she was embarrassed, as though Jessie had made her think disgusting thoughts.

'Well, anyway – ' she began and then shrugged her shoulders. 'I wish they'd hurry up! I want to take Basil home as soon as possible. If it gets much later, Papa may be home and then – ' She stopped and bit her lip. Getting home again was indeed going to be a very real problem, for now it was well past eleven o'clock, and there was no sign that Basil was to be released to her care yet. But that was a bridge, she told herself sententiously, to be dealt with when it came into view.

'Listen, why don't you stay down here, with me? Let your brother go home his way – put him in a cab – and no one won't say nothing. Fellas, they can stay out as late as they like, come home looking like something the cat would be ashamed to know, let alone to bring in, and no one says nothing. But for a woman – ' She shook her head. 'For a woman, and a single one at that, it ain't so easy. So stay here, tell your brother to cook up some tale or other and slip home tomorrow when it's quiet and no one won't notice.'

'Don't be silly,' Mildred said shortly. 'If I'm not at breakfast they will look in my room and then everyone will know at once that I've been away all night.'

'At breakfast? You all sit down to breakfast like it was a supper?'

'Of course.'

Jessie shook her head wonderingly. 'I always say, you might as well be abroad, we're all so different. In all my life, I ain't never sat down to a breakfast. A piece o' bread, a bissel butter on it or cream cheese, and you eat it on your way to school or to work – ' She sighed. 'But to sit *down* to breakfast? That must be nice.'

'No it isn't,' Mildred said. 'Not in our house. My father sits there behind the paper and Mama looks green and the boys squabble at each other and – '

It was absurd. Not ten minutes earlier she had been hating this woman with her glinting dark eyes and cheerful smile, had thought her vulgar and horrid, but here she sat in the waiting room of the London Hospital's casualty department, pouring out all sorts of silly details about life in Leinster Terrace. She talked of the way the little boys ran riot, no matter how much Nanny Chewson tried to bring them up properly, because of their mother's silly partiality for them and refusal ever to admit they did anything they should not, and of the way Mama spent such long hours on her sofa asleep, and of the way her own life dragged on drearily in ever deepening ruts and indeed of the general awfulness of everything, and all the time Jessie sat and listened and nodded and watched her with those dark and lively eyes and said nothing. Until at last Mildred stopped talking and sat looking down at her hands on her lap again.

'Well,' Jessie said at length. 'I can see why you like to come down here. That all sounds real miserable. Why don't you just get out altogether?'

'What?' Mildred lifted her head and stared at her. 'How do you mean?'

Jessie shrugged. 'You're a grown woman. You don't have to stay there with 'em if you don't want to. Come down here, down East. You can have a room in my house. I got a proper house all to myself, you know. Not one of these two-room affairs, my place. I got two bedrooms upstairs as well as the two rooms downstairs. *And* gas and water laid on. None of your taps in the yard, by me. It's water right in to the scullery! As good a place as my mother's and father's. You saw that, didn't you? Nothing wrong with that, is there? No – nothing. Lizah fixed it for them when he started to make good money, with his first few fights, and for him it had to be the best. So it is. But there's three of them living there and only me in my place. So come and move in. I could do with the rent and the company. You need a place to live, and what could suit better. You could go further and do a lot worse.'

'I've no money of my own,' Mildred said dully. For one glorious moment it had seemed that the thick dark curtain that hung over her life, making it so gloomy and dull, had twitched and shown her a glimpse of a whole new life beyond where she could do as she wanted when she wanted, and would never again have to sew nightshirts for her brothers or sit dumbly being looked over by a man her father was trying to persuade to marry her. But at the mention of the word 'rent' the curtain twitched back into place, as dark and impenetrable as ever. 'My mother left me a small amount, but my father has the full control of it until I marry. So I might as well have nothing.'

Jessie lifted her brows, amused. 'Have I got money? You think because I'm a widow I got money? Believe me, my old man, rest his wicked soul, left me gornisht mit gornisht – nothing with nothing. A spieler like him – he was a gambler, see – lost all he had and a bit more besides before he goes and falls under a brewer's dray one night two years ago, and us only married a year. I tell you, he left me more debts than anything else. But I work, see? I work for Joe Vinosky, as married my sister Rae, and I pay my way. I got my house. I got my furniture and bits of pieces when I got married, and that's all. So, you can do the same. You can sew, can't you?'

'Sew? Of course,' Mildred said. 'It's all I ever seem to do, sometimes.'

'Then sew for a living. Come and live at my place – I won't charge you no big rent – get a job on the finisher's bench at Joe's, and punkt! You're an independent woman. And maybe then my brother – ' She stopped and looked at Mildred sideways, and for the first time there was more to her expression than simple warmth and openness. She had a calculating look about her.

'The thing is,' she leaned forwards confidentially, 'thing is, Lizah needs to be taken in hand. My Momma'd go mad, she heard me talkin' this way, but what she don't know won't hurt her. Lizah's had any number of the Yiddisher girls round here. Any number. They all fancy him, good-looking boy like him. Struts a bit, got a name for himself, so naturally they give him the eye. But there ain't none of them he's ever been interested in the way he's interested in you. And for my part, shicksah or not, I think you'd be good for him. I've seen him lookin' at you – '

'What? But I've never seen you before tonight!' Mildred's head was spinning, she was so startled at what Jessie was saying, and she seized on the only thing she could hold on to. 'You're talking nonsense about – about me and Mr Harris – '

'Listen, dolly, I been around! I seen you at the theatre with him. I seen you at Curly's place and one or two others. Always kept well out of sight, of course – Lizah gets upset if he thinks the family's too busy with his affairs – and I tell you, I *watch*. And you could make that boy be sensible for once in his life. Give up this boxing game. It'll kill him if he goes on like this – ' And she looked over Mildred's shoulder towards the still curtained cubicles and her face was bleak for a moment. 'A boy can box, can get his head broken and his nose battered and come to no harm, please God. But a grown man? Lizah's twenty-five already. How much longer can he go on like this? Three years? Five years? And then he'll be just another meshiggeneh – a mad thing, sits around the cafés talking of the old days, no memory, no common sense left in his poor fuddled head, a schnorrer for the rest of his days. I don't want this for him. With you, I think I got a friend who also won't want this for him. So come and live with me down here, and we'll fix it. Momma'll come round to the idea. Poppa, he'll do what Momma says – so what do you say?'

'You're mad,' Mildred said. 'Quite mad – ' and suddenly remembered Mrs Harris' hand, biting into her arm in the kitchen in Myrdle Street as she made her swear on her father's life that she would not marry her son. But she pushed that memory away as ridiculous, and clumsily got to her feet and moved away, towards the curtained cubicle where Basil was incarcerated, not looking back. This was dreadful, quite dreadful, she told herself as she tried to keep herself from shaking. She had never heard anything so stupid in all her life –

As though in response to a signal the curtain rings rattled and the fabric was pushed aside with a flourish and the nurse came out, shepherding Basil, who still looked white but much more in command of himself.

'This one can leave,' the nurse said. 'The doctor says he is fit and there is no need for any concern. The bruises can be treated with arnica from time to time if it is felt to be necessary.

The other one will be ready to leave shortly, I believe – ' And she looked over her shoulder to the other cubicle. 'Though I gather he has needed some stitches to a cut – '

'Stitches? Good. I said I'd show him – ' Basil muttered thickly as Mildred, moving quickly, came to his side and took his arm ready to lead him towards the main doors. 'And I did. That man – '

'Be quiet,' Mildred said quickly. 'And come along. We have to get a cab and get home as fast as possible.' And without so much as a glance in Jessie Mendel's direction she began to lead Basil away, and he came willingly enough, wincing a little as he put one foot in front of the other, clearly feeling a pain inside his head at every jarring movement he made.

Again there was a rattle of curtain rings as the other cubicle was opened, and she heard Kid's voice as he came out, protesting at something the nurse was saying about returning to have his stitches removed.

'I can't,' he was saying. 'I got a big match to fight the day after that, so I'm coming back to have these stitches out in three days. I don't need no five days – I heal quick, I do. Got good healing flesh, I have – Millie!'

Clearly he had seen her going towards the door and was coming after her and she pushed on Basil's arm, urging him forwards, wanting only to get out and away, not wanting to speak to Kid at all. But Basil could not, or would not, be hurried. And there Kid was, his hand grasping her upper arm in that familiar grip.

'Millie – where are you going? I have to talk to you. Don't go rushing off like this – I have to talk to you. We have to sort this out and – '

'There is nothing to sort out,' she said, keeping her voice as flat and calm as she could. 'I have to get Basil home. Excuse me – ' They had reached the door and the man in serge and brass buttons was holding it down. 'I need a four-wheeler,' she said to him as she reached his side. 'Is there one available?'

'Outside the main gates, t'other side of the yard.' The man pointed. 'There's always one or two there. Take it easy now –' And she went through the door out into the bitter dark cold of the February night, Basil's arm held firmly under her hand as Kid Harris came lumbering after them.

'Listen, will you stop a minute? I can't talk to a person's back! Millie!' he cried, but she did not halt, did not change the rate of her marching, pushing Basil ahead of her as fast as she could. He at least seemed not to care that his opponent was so close; he seemed to want to concentrate solely on keeping himself upright, and she was grateful for that. If they started arguing again it would be more than she could cope with, she told herself, more than she could tolerate. She would lose her temper, weep perhaps – it would be dreadful. Thank God for Basil's pain and the silence it ensured in him.

They had reached the gateway and were through it and out on the other side and into the Whitechapel Road where, to her intense relief, she could see two four-wheelers waiting, their drivers standing to one side round a burning brazier full of charcoal where a nightwatchman sat pondering over a hole in the pavement. 'Cab!' she called imperiously and felt Basil wince at the sound of her voice. 'At once –' And one of the drivers hurried over and began to help her get Basil into his vehicle.

'Millie, this is dam' well ridiculous!' Kid Harris blazed and she felt his hand pull on her arm, whirling her round so that she had to look at him. 'Stop trying to pretend I ain't here, for God's sake! I have to talk to you!'

'Oh no, you don't,' she said very loudly, needing to hear her own voice, needing to be sure she said what had to be said. 'I never want to speak to you again, do you hear me? Not now or ever. Keep away from me – I was crazy ever to agree to see you at all, but I'm not crazy now. You understand me? I never want to see you again ever. Go *away* – and to the devil with you!'

11

March blew itself in with gales and rain that drummed the entire household into a state of cold misery. The children couldn't go out to walk in the Park and became more fractious than ever. Nanny Chewson's elderly mother died in far away Norfolk and she went home 'to put matters to rights', as she explained darkly, leaving only the housemaid to cope with the little boys, and Maud caught a severe quinsy and had to keep to her bed for weeks on end. Edward in consequence developed a furious rage with every aspect of the way his house was being run, and took to his club, staying there for as many nights as he slept at home, which was a mixed blessing for on the nights he did choose to return to his hearth and household, his temper was even more unreliable than it usually was.

All of which helped to distract attention from Mildred and her state of mind. To say she was unhappy was to understate the situation gravely. She went through her days in a frozen haze, her face drawn and looking more sallow than ever, and her eyes blank and dead. Now she was no longer eating good suppers, and had lost what little appetite she had ever had for the appalling cooking that was the staple fare at Leinster Terrace, she lost all her agreeable plumpness and became positively gaunt, and violet shadows appeared beneath her eyes and in her temples.

And nobody at all noticed.

She had managed to get Basil back into the house on that dreadful night and up to his room without anyone being disturbed, and next day he had managed to get out to his office without his father noticing what he looked like, for he had clearly had a disagreement with his own digestion the night before and was far from well; and from then onwards life had slipped back into its old painful rut as though nothing had ever happened to disturb it. No one seemed at all aware of the fact that her interest in Mission work seemed to have completely evaporated; no one paid any attention to her at all, any more than they ever had. It was as though whatever she did was invisible to her family.

There were times, indeed, when she sat in the window seat in the drawing room staring out at the relentless rain, and wondered whether any of it had actually happened. Surely she had imagined it all? Had it not been just another of those stupid fantasies she had been used to weave all her life to hide herself from the dreariness of reality?

But even she could not convince herself of that. There *had* been a Kid Harris. There *had* been those long months of evenings spent where lights were bright and voices were loud and laughter was raucous, where people ate and drank and shouted at each other with a gusto that had expanded her soul and made her realize that after all life was worth the trouble of living it.

But now as her horizons shrank and her very body shrivelled and lost its resilience she knew that those joyous months had been a cruel trick that Providence had played upon her. Bad as life had been before, it had been tolerable. After all, she had never known anything else, so she had rubbed along well enough. Not happy, of course, but not actively miserable.

But now she was precisely that; a walking breathing mass of unhappiness that sometimes threatened to burst its confines. There were times, sitting as usual beside Mama at the mahogany dining-room table, hearing her bleating on and on about the children and the latest piece of impertinence from Cook or Jenny or Mary, when she wanted to shriek her hatred of all that made up her existence, when she actually had to bite her tongue and hold hard on to the sides of her chair, out of sight beneath the spread of the tablecloth, to prevent herself from doing so.

The nights were the worst. When she went up to her room and crept between the cold sheets to lie beneath the weight of her blankets, staring up at the ceiling where the street lights from beyond her window created strange shifting patterns, she would pray with all the passion of her unbelieving soul for death to come in the night. Just to slide into sleep and never, never, *never* have to wake up and face living inside her own skin for another moment – that would have been the best she could have hoped for herself. But even that was denied her, for as one who had long ago lost her piety and turned her back on the beliefs which everyone else seemed to hold, she had not even the right to seek any help from Providence.

And she would close her eyes and ache to weep, longing to cry and relieve her pain that way, but no tears ever came. Only, at last, an uneasy sleep which was so bedevilled with dreams, some of which were so horrendously full of Kid Harris that she could hardly bear to think of what she and he did together in them when she emerged from the darkness of the night into yet another day, that she never felt at all refreshed by her slumbers.

Both Basil and Claude avoided her. They slid into a new pattern of life, telling their stepmama that they wished to spend longer at their places of work, and therefore would not take breakfast at home, preferring to wait till they got to their offices, and would probably dine at their clubs as often as not, and she had shrugged and made it very clear that she was uninterested in their living arrangements. They had their own incomes, drawn from their inheritances from their mother (being males they were allowed to have what was their own, and did not have to bow to their father's control of their use of their money) and from their employment. So they were able to use their father's house largely as an hotel, and this they did.

In the past when they had been more visible about the house, Mildred had felt closer to them. They had always been that little more important to her than anyone else, since they were her full kin, and she had thought they felt the same concern for her. Now she was not so sure. It was true that Basil had allowed himself to become embroiled in a fight with a man he considered unsuitable for his sister to know, but had that been, she asked herself bleakly, because of her, or because of his own amour propre? Did he feel it was below his dignity to have his sister regarding an East End boxer as her friend or below hers? She strongly suspected it was the former.

As, slowly, the weather improved and she could escape occasionally during the day to walk in Hyde Park, she began to feel a little less ill. She was still eating poorly and sleeping uneasily, but when at last she could exercise again, stretching her long legs under her heavy serge skirts as she walked briskly along the asphalt paths between the dripping bushes and the wide expanses of sodden grass, she began to feel a little better. And that meant she could think more clearly.

She was determined not to think about Kid Harris. That was a chapter in the past; but she did think about his sister. She had put ideas into Mildred's head that wriggled around like worms, and however hard she tried to push them away, back they came.

To leave her father's home and rent a room somewhere, and pay her own way by working for money? It seemed a mad idea, an impossible notion, fit only for her fantasies. But slowly, it took hold. To be able to get away from her father's home and her father's influence, to be an independent woman; and away flew her imagination, settling her in a charming little flat with a pretty sitting room and bedroom which she would leave every day to go to her employment. It took her a while to decide on an employment that would fit into her fantasy, but then she remembered a girl she had once seen long ago when she was very young, in a flower shop in Oxford Street, looking charming as she tied her flowers into elegant bouquets, and she imagined herself doing that with great skill and success, and earning large sums from it.

Her daydream grew, spread its wings and soared; now she had not only the employment in the pretty flower shop and the lovely little flat to go home to each night to dream of, but also friends. Faceless but delightful, they fluttered around her head, laughing and chattering and making much of her as they visited her in her flat, or went with her to tea shops and theatres and –

And then her fantasy shivered and died in a shower of falling sparks, for the only person she could manage to see beside her in a theatre was Kid Harris. It was as though her fantasies were no longer her own; it seemed he had calmly walked into her head and taken over, and whenever she tried, as she went striding through the park, to see herself in her shop with her flowers, there he was, watching her. When she tried to see herself in her little flat, once again he sat himself down on the facing chair and stared at her. However much she struggled to rid herself of him, it was impossible. It was as though he had engraved himself on her mind and was never going to leave her. Ever.

There were times when she was afraid her control would burst; that she would start to shout and scream at her images, and then another set of fantasies would fill her head. She was going mad, quite mad, and she watched in horror as stiff starched nurses came and held her down as she shrieked and wept and roared her rage at Kid Harris for invading her imagination so cruelly, and saw herself carried off to some mysterious shadowy place labelled 'asylum' – and then she would find herself standing stock still in the middle of the path that led through to the Long Water, her eyes wide and tears streaking her cold cheeks. It was indeed a dreadful time.

The weather changed again, became softer and gentler, and the green spikes that had peered uneasily above the black soil of the park flower beds took courage and shot up, dragging their flower buds with them, and she stood sometimes and stared at the crocuses and snowdrops that carpeted patches of grass beneath the trees and watched the still unopened daffodil buds nodding at her and thought that possibly, just possibly, one day soon, she might feel better, that perhaps things would go back to being what they had been, before the events of the winter. A dull life, but at least not a miserable one, was all she wanted; and the crocuses and snowdrops seemed to mock her a little, telling her she still had to wait – and inside her head, deep inside, the wriggling ideas curled and beckoned. To have a place of her own, and a job that would pay for it –

It was in the first week of March that the first message came. Freddy came to the drawing-room where she was sitting after luncheon to tell her that 'the messenger from Father Jay's is below and wishes to speak to you.'

She stared at him blankly.

'Who?'

'The messenger from Father Jay's,' Freddy repeated woodenly, staring at a point somewhere three inches above her head.

'Father – oh! Yes,' and she bit her lip. She had almost forgotten that convenient lie that she had used to get herself out of the house during her wild days; Father Jay, the man who ran the boxing club at his Mission in Spitalfields. Suddenly she could see the boy Ruby sitting at Mama's sitting-room table and gobbling cake and milk and looking at her with those impudent eyes of his and she took a sharp little breath in through her nose and said, 'Tell him I have nothing for him today. I am sorry. See if there are some food scraps in the kitchen, and send him away.'

Freddy departed and came back a few minutes later, more wooden than ever in expression.

'He says he has an important message to give to you directly, Miss.'

'Does he, indeed?' She tightened her lips. Ruby indeed it had to be, for only he could be so cheekily persistent, and she would not see him. She knew precisely what his message was and wanted no part of it. 'Then tell him he must take his message away undelivered. I am too busy. The – ah – Mission demanded too much of me. I still feel the need of rest. I – er – I may be beguiled into doing more work again if I speak with this messenger, so it is better I do not. Tell him that.'

Somewhat to her surprise, Freddy had not returned, obviously having successfully sent Ruby about his business, and she had for a little while felt some pleasure at contemplating how downcast Ruby would be. He prided himself not a little on always completing his tasks, and this time he had failed.

But he wasn't so easily defeated, for he returned the next day and the next and the one after that until Freddy began to look as though he would explode with passivity whenever he came to tell her, yet again, that Father Jay's messenger was waiting below to speak to her. She managed to go on refusing for some time, but at last Freddy stood there and stared directly at her and said that he 'couldn't take it upon himself to deal with the matter any further and perhaps it would be better to arrange for the boy to return at some time when the Master could speak to him,' and she capitulated. She had to.

'I shall see him in the morning-room,' she said stiffly. 'Put him there. And tell him I shall be down directly.'

She left him kicking his heels for fully ten minutes before, at last, going unwillingly downstairs to speak to him. She had dressed herself that morning in her dark blue merino and had not bothered unduly about dressing her hair well, settling for pulling it back off her face into a tight bun, and abandoning any effort to create a fashionable fringe. She looked tired and drab and was well aware of it, and cared not a whit.

'Well?' she said harshly, standing just inside the door of the morning room. 'I have told my servant to tell you that I have no wish to hear your message.'

Ruby had been sitting on the fender, swinging his feet and warming his hands at the coal fire that burned brightly there and he looked perkily over his shoulder at her, grinning, to answer her. And then stopped and frowned and got to his feet and came across the room to stand in front of her and stare up at her, his face crumpled with concern.

'Cor, stone the bleedin' crows, but you look godawful!' he said, his dark eyes wide. 'I mean, what have you done to yourself? You wasn't no oil painting before, but you looked perky enough. Now you looks like you died last week an' forgot to tell anyone! 'Ad the fever, 'ave yer? Is that why you wouldn't come down and have a chinwag an' that?'

'I have no wish to talk to you or to hear of anything from whoever sent you,' she said flatly. 'I have sent enough messages back to you to make that clear. So go back to whence you came and tell – say that. I have no wish to hear anything at *all* from anyone – '

'Oh, Father Jay'll be that upset!' Ruby said and went skipping back to the fire to stand in front of it and warm his tight little buttocks in a wicked imitation of an alderman. ''E'll be upset enough to see you lookin' so poorly, but 'e won't be all that surprised. 'E ain't bin feelin' all that up to the blunt 'imself. P'raps 'im an' you oughta – '

'Will you be quiet!' she snapped. 'I am not interested, do you understand? And do stop this stupid lying. I have no wish to hear any messages from anyone and that is an end to it. You do not need to take a parson's name in vain just to tell me that – '

'You didn't mind takin' it in vain when it suited you,' Ruby said and grinned again. 'Oh, come on, ducks! No need to go daft over this, is there? The Kid, 'e says as – '

She opened the door with a sharp twist of her wrist and then went across the room and took hold of Ruby's collar.

'Out,' she said. 'At once. I will not tell you again. I have no wish to discuss this with you or anyone else. If you come here again I shall be constrained to fetch a policeman to deal with you. Go away at once.'

'You'll be sorry,' he said, but he went, allowing her to lead him to the front door and to open it and push him out on to the top step. She was well aware that behind the green baize door at the back of the hall Freddy was listening, agog, and she didn't care.

'I doubt it,' she said and closed the door firmly in Ruby's face and turned and went upstairs to the drawing-room with all the dignity she could muster, shaking inside in case Ruby went on with his nagging and rang the doorbell again.

But he did not, and when she reached the drawing-room and went to the window to look out, unable to prevent herself from doing so, the street was empty. He had gone, wasting no time about it, and for one incredible moment she felt a sense of desolation creep over her. The sight of that self satisfied young face, the sound of that perky impudent voice, had brought back with great poignancy all the memories she had of the pleasure there had been in life during those magic months, and she stood at the window, holding the curtains in a white knuckled grip, holding on to her self control.

And she succeeded. That day at any rate. But it could not last.

During the last week of March the weather once more decided to become capricious and an unseasonable warmth crept into the air. The trees blushed green with anticipation and the daffodils bawled their delight with wide brazen mouths at the warm air that stroked them and she stopped being miserable and became instead angry.

She woke up one morning to see the sunlight gilding the rooftops of the houses across the Terrace and felt herself tight with it. How *dare* the likes of Kid Harris cause her so much unhappiness? How could such a one as he persist in invading her dreams and her daylight thoughts as he had done? It was now fully a month since that awful night at the old Britannia and still she felt the fury of it all, and she went through the day, doing the normal domestic tasks, instructing Jane and Jenny and Mary on the way the spring cleaning, due to be started after the first day of April, next week, was to be done, with her anger just under control but simmering steadily. He had to be told to leave her be. He had to be told that she was no longer interested in him or his doings. He had to be forced to leave her mind and let her be at peace again –

Once again circumstances conspired, or seemed to, to make her behave as she should not have done. Her father returned home early to change for yet another dinner in the City, but this time he was far from being in a bad mood or anxious about his evening. Mama's quinsy had been better this past week, and she in turn had been less given to whining complaint, and this may have put him in a better humour; but whatever it was he spoke jovially to Mildred as he left the house shortly after six to go to Guildhall; and that made her feel in turn a little more relaxed. And then Mama said in a dying fall that she was going to bed early and disappeared, leaving Mildred once again completely alone in the drawing-room with the long hours stretching blank and empty in front of her.

It was almost inevitable that she should reach the decision she did. The warmth in the air was so reminiscent of how it had been last September and the silence in the house was so thick and familiar that she found herself feeling as though all the intervening weeks had been little more than a bad dream.

And shortly before ten o'clock, she found herself in her bedroom, putting on her serge jacket and pinning her black straw hat to her head.

It was not exactly a planned thing, but neither was it totally spontaneous. It was almost as though she were on the outside of herself watching it happen, as though none of her actions were under her full control. It seemed that she was doing what had to be done, without thinking. And what had to be done was that Kid Harris had to be told to leave her in peace. He had interfered enough in her life already, and he had to be made to leave it. That he had for the past four weeks inhabited her mind rather than her life in any real physical sense was almost beside the point. She only knew that until she told him of her anger at how he had behaved, and how unhappy he had made her, she would have no peace at all.

So, with all her old stealth she went down the stairs, past the gaslight on the landing, turned down as usual in the evening to an economical half light, across the tiled hall, walking on her toes to prevent any clattering of her heels, to the front door. She opened it gently, slowly, so that there should be no risk of rattling the chain that dangled on its inner side and then, still moving with practised slow ease, she was out on the front step, and pulling the door gently to behind her so that it closed with only the lightest of snaps.

She stood there poised on the top step, listening hard, to make sure no one inside the house had heard her go, clutching her reticule with its precious front-door key safely tucked into it, and then, when she was sure that all was as silent as it needed to be, turned to come down the steps.

And as she reached the bottom his hand came out of the shadows and seized her by the elbow.

12

'I knew you'd come out eventually,' he said. 'You could have done it sooner, though. It's been damned uncomfortable out here some nights. Cold – '

'I – go away,' was all she could say. 'Leave me alone. I don't want to talk to you – ' and then stopped short, for wasn't it precisely in order to talk to him that she had come out at all? She had expected to have to go and find a cab and go out to the East End in the way she had been used to, to hunt through the more familiar cafés and theatres, not to find him here at her very doorstep. That would have given her time to think about what she would say to him when she found him. But now he was here, and all she could do was stand dumbly looking at him.

Ruby had been right. He didn't look as though he was feeling well at all. His face had a pinched look it had never had before, and his corrugated forehead shone a little damply in the soft gaslight from the street lamp behind him and his eyes, those wide and rather full eyes, had an expression of anxiety in them.

'Millie,' he said and let go of her elbow at last. 'Millie, are you all right? You look – are you all right?'

'Don't call me Millie,' was all she could say. 'My name is Mildred.'

'Have you been eating right? You've gone thin again. You need one of Barney's good salt beef sandwiches.'

'I need nothing of the sort,' she said. 'I just need to be left in peace. I came out to tell you to leave me alone, that – '

'You knew I was here?' He seemed to pounce on that.

'No, of course not – '

'Then you were coming to the East End to look for me?' He still sounded eager.

'No! I mean, I just came out for a walk – '

'You never ever told me no lies, Millie, did you? You used to tell 'em here, I know, on account of here they don't care about you, but I care about you and you never told me no lies. Are you tellin' me one now?'

She looked up at his face again and then away. The expression on it was so anxious it made her want to cry. 'Yes,' she said after a moment. 'Yes, I suppose I am.'

'Then you did come out to talk to me? To find me and talk to me?'

'Yes.' It was almost a whisper.

'Oh, glory alleluia!' he cried at the top of his voice and at once she reached for his arm and shook it, terrified that someone would hear and come investigating. But he just laughed and took her hand in his and held on to it tightly, staring at her in the dim light and grinning hugely.

'I've been feeling awful,' he said simply. 'Awful. Night after night I've been coming here, waiting outside, hoping you'd come out. I felt so bad, and I missed you something dreadful, Millie. I even lost a fight two weeks after you went. Me, lose a fight!' He shook his head in disbelief. 'Would you Adam 'n' Eve it! Me! I know what it was, o' course. The thing of it is I wasn't concentrating. A boxer has to concentrate, but I was thinking of you, in the third round, and whoops, there I was, gone.'

'Were you hurt?' She looked closely at him. 'Did it do any damage?'

'No,' he said. 'No, I'm all right,' and his hand closed warmly on hers. 'Does it matter to you if I'm hurt or not?'

She pulled her hand away from him, nervous suddenly. 'It matters if anyone is hurt. I hate to see people suffer – You – you made my brother hurt – '

'Yeah, I know. I'm sorry about that – ' He stopped then and said awkwardly, 'Listen, Millie, I told you. I missed you this past month something awful. I ain't been eating or sleeping right – it's been dreadful. And the last thing I want to do is upset you again, not now we're talking. But though I'm sorry for his hurting I can't say I'm sorry about hittin' your brother on account he behaved like a – well, he carried on in a way that'd make any man hit out. He talked about the people in the theatre that night – my people, the ones I live with and – *my* people – he called the women in the theatre Jew girls and tarts, as though bein' one meant a woman was always the other as well, and I couldn't be doing with that now, could I? And he wouldn't apologize, so I hit him. And I have to tell you, if he walked down here right now and said it again, I'd hit him again. I'd have to.'

'There are other ways of dealing with – with things you don't like, aren't there? Do you always have to hit people?'

'Mostly,' he said. 'I'm not as good with words as you are. Maybe you can talk your way out of trouble – well, I know you can. You talked your brothers out of big trouble with me, didn't you? That was the only time I ever let anyone welch on a bet, you know that? The only time. And all because of the way you talked. Like I said, a class lady, you. But me, I'm just a boxer. An East End boxer, and I don't know no better way to sort out a foul-mouthed devil than hittin' him. But I want you to know that whatever your brother said and whatever I did, it shouldn't make no difference to us. To me and you – '

'Stop it!' she said and knew her voice was shaking. 'There is no me and you – I mean, it's mad. We were both crazy to think we could be friends and – '

'Could be? But we were,' he said. 'Weren't we? Good friends. You can't say we weren't. And I don't see why we can't still be.

I've missed you so bad, Millie – ' And again he put his hand over hers, and again she felt the warmth of him move into her skin, into her muscles, into the very centre of her.

There was a rattle of wheels and a cab turned the corner of the Terrace from the Bayswater Road end and she jumped back from him as though she had been bitten. 'Go away!' she said. 'For heaven's sake, go away! If that is someone who knows me and tells Papa – oh, please go away!'

'No! I've too much to say to you – '

'Please, there'll be such trouble! Suppose it is Basil or Claude – oh, I couldn't bear it again! Please – '

The cab was slowing down as the driver pulled on his reins and swore at the horse and almost in an agony of fear she pushed on Kid's chest, making him move away so that he was out of the immediate pool of light thrown by the street lamp.

'I'm not going,' he said. 'Let's see who it is first. I'm not going – '

The cab driver hauled on his reins more cruelly than ever and the horse stopped, rolling its great eyes as the bit caught its soft mouth, and the cab driver jumped down, leaving the reins on the horse's back, and opened the door of the cab as she stood there not knowing what to do. To be out on the street at this time – it was dreadful for a respectable young woman. And here was – who? Basil or Claude she could deal with. A visitor she could not. But who would visit at this hour of the evening? And she caught her breath as the cabbie hauled a bundled shape out of the cab's interior.

' 'Ere you are, guv'nor – safe and sound. Blimey, you is in a mess, ain't yer? It'll take me now till midnight to clean up after you, an' no error. Cost yer, this will – ' Scolding steadily, the cab driver led the bent and shaking figure towards the steps and then caught sight of her standing there and called out, 'Gawd, miss, 'ere's a mess, if you like! This geezer's bin took good an' ill and they put him in my cab, would yer believe? My bleedin' luck! You work at this 'ouse, then? Can yer find your mistress 'n' get 'er out 'ere and see to it someone pays me for bringing this back and for cleanin' me cab?'

'I'll pay you,' she said, and stepped forwards, fumbling in her reticule. 'Here, I'll take over. Papa? What happened?'

He groaned, trying to stand up in the circle of the cabbie's arm and failing. 'Took ill,' he gasped. 'Bad oysters, I swear it. Bad oysters – ' And he retched and the cabbie made a face and pushed him up the steps towards the front door.

'Better get 'im in before he starts casting up his accounts all over again,' he said and reached for the doorbell. 'Nasty, that'd be – '

'No, I'll open the door,' she said swiftly, suddenly seeing how Freddy's face would look if he came and found her out here. 'No need to bother anyone till we get in – ' And she ran up the steps and with shaking fingers pushed her key into the lock.

'Millie!' Kid came running up the steps behind her. 'Let me help. You can't manage him alone – '

'No!' she cried, scandalized. 'You can't come in! Can you imagine what would happen? Here, cabbie, get him in and sit him down there – I'll get Freddy – here, Kid – ' And with fingers that shook with urgency she unbuttoned her jacket and pulled it off, and dragged her hat from her head. 'Here, take these. Don't let Freddy see them – he'll know I was out and he'll tell tales. I'll get them afterwards. Leave them in the area, on the steps – I'll find them – '

'No,' Kid said and took the jacket and hat. 'I'll wait for you and give them back m'self. Come out as soon as you get him sorted out – '

'I can't – '

'You'll have to. I'll wait for you – ' He looked over his shoulder at the street and at the cabbie, now staring at him with great interest. 'You, take him in and be sharp about it – ' And he pushed the cabbie, still half carrying the groaning Mr Amberly, in through the door. 'Millie, I'll wait for you – '

'Not in the street, for heaven's sake! Someone will see you!' she hissed.

'In the park then,' he said after a moment, watching over her shoulder as the cabbie at last relinquished his burden to a chair that stood against the wall. 'Promise, or I won't go! I'll stay here and – '

The green baize door at the far end of the hall began to open and in a fever of anxiety she cried, 'All right! All right – the park. As soon as I can. Now, please go *away!*' And he melted back into the shadows of the steps and she felt more than heard him disappear from sight behind her, just as Freddy put his head round the baize door, his mouth half open in amazement.

'Freddy!' She moved forwards with all the aplomb she could muster and stood beside her father. 'The master is ill. This man – he is concerned about his cab. It seems it has been – ah – spoiled – ' She looked down at her father who was sitting leaning back, his face as grey as asphalt and sweating heavily, the front of his costly evening clothes bearing very disagreeable evidence of just how ill he was feeling. 'See to it he has what he needs to deal with it and then come and help me fetch the master upstairs. Hurry now. And you – ' She turned to the cabbie as Freddy nodded, for once shaken out of his professional stolidity, and went back to the kitchen. 'What is the fare that is owed to you?'

'Arf-a-sov'll cover it nice, lidy, takin' into account the state o' my cab,' the man said, cocking a knowing glance at the hallway, and its costly furniture and decorations. 'Not much to a flash cove like this one, is it, arf-a-sov?'

'Nonsense,' she said crisply. 'Half-a-crown is more than enough. But because of the trouble you have been put to, I will give you twice that, and I am being more than generous.' And she held out five shillings which she took from the pocket in her skirt.

The man sniffed. 'I'd 'a' done better if the other geezer 'ad paid me,' he said disparagingly. ''E looked like a sensible bloke, 'e did.' He peered round. 'Where's 'e gone, then? It'll take more'n one to get this 'un up these stairs an' no error.'

Her face reddened and she bent over her father to hide it, pretending to be anxious about him, though there was clearly no need. His colour was slowly improving and his breathing was loud and clear. 'He was – he was just a passer-by,' she said. 'And has gone – '

A slow grin spread over the cabbie's face. 'Passer-by, was 'e? Seemed a mite familiar for just a passer-by, way 'e followed you up them steps.'

'Listen,' she said desperately, feeling the man's knowing eyes on her, though she could not bring herself to look at him. 'If you want your half sovereign you will have to earn it. When Freddy returns from the kitchen, help him take my father upstairs and you shall have the money – '

'Fair enough,' the man said heartily. 'I knows when I'm on to a good thing, don't I? I'll 'elp you and you'll 'elp me, an' very nice too. All right, squire!' And he turned his head as Freddy reappeared, a bucket of water and a bundle of rags in his hands. 'You just shove that stuff outside an' come back an' I'll 'elp you get this lump o' misery up to his bed. It's where 'e longs to be and where 'e ought to be, and where 'e's goin' to be.' And with a vast wink at Mildred, he bent to take Mr Amberly by the shoulders.

The next half hour was busy and unpleasant, as they settled her father in his room and undressed him and put him into his bed, at which stage she was allowed by the men to come in and wash his hands and face and chest and make him clean and comfortable. He lay there on his high pillows, still groaning, as she dealt with him and when she had finished, he opened his eyes and looked at her lugubriously from their bloodshot depths.

'You're not a bad girl, Mildred,' he muttered, his voice still slurred, for clearly his indisposition owed as much to over-indulgence in brandy as to any oysters. 'You got your uses. Not a bad girl, for all you look the way you do – got your uses –' And he fell asleep as suddenly as a child and lay there snoring thickly, and she looked down at him and felt her gorge rise with revulsion.

It was not just the look of him, with his mouth hanging open to show unappetising vistas of furred tongue and yellow teeth set in the middle of his sagging jowly face, nor was it the way the room smelled of brandy and scented soap and sickness. It was the anger that was in her that choked her. She had cleaned him up, made him comfortable, dealt with as unpleasant a piece of self-induced nastiness as any woman should ever have to deal with for a man, and all he could say was that 'she had her uses'. No thanks for her efforts, no apologies, no regrets for making so disagreeable a vision of himself. Just another insult about the way she looked, that was all.

With savage self control she collected the dirty towels and bowl and took them to his dressing room to deal with them, and then, turning the gaslight down to the quarter, went and peered through the adjoining door into her stepmother's room. She was lying on her back too, snoring softly, and Mildred went over to stand beside the crumpled bed and look down at her.

She had been a pretty woman once, Mildred thought, remembering the way she had appeared when her father had brought her to meet his motherless children: a slight and simpering thing with fair fluffy hair and round pale blue eyes and a china doll complexion, she had sat with a fixed smile and looked at the gawky fifteen-year-old Mildred, and as though she had said it aloud, Mildred heard the pity in her thoughts. A poor plain creature, Mildred Amberly, Maud had thought, pleased with her own undoubted charms; poor plain Mildred.

And now she lay in a half-drunken sleep, reeking as ever of sweet sherry and with her pink and white cheeks collapsed and soft and a little veined over the cheekbones, and her body that had been so sweetly plump sagging with the efforts of her four childbirths and no longer so sweet. Did that hateful man in the next room tell her she 'had her uses'? Did he ever thank *her* for what she did for him? I've never heard him do it, Mildred thought and stepped back as Maud stirred in her sleep and snorted softly.

She stood outside on the landing, staring down the stairs at the hallway below. It was quiet and still again, for Freddy had sent the cabbie on his way – and heaven knows what tales the man had told to those avid ears! – and retired to his own part of the house. She was again free to do as she wanted. To stay here and go to bed or go down the stairs, and open the front door and slip out and run to the park to –

To what? She stood very still and closed her eyes against the richness of the scene before them and tried to be honest with herself. To fetch my jacket and hat and then say goodbye for always, as I promised myself I would, and then just come back to this house where I will never be thanked for anything I do, nor loved nor admired. Out there in the darkness of Hyde Park there is waiting for me a man who does admire me. Who, perhaps, loves me. I don't know, but perhaps – he missed me, he said. Missed me something awful, and her lips curved as behind her closed lids she saw the woebegone face as it had been when he had said the words. He's ridiculous in so many ways. He is three or more inches shorter than I am so that he has to tilt his head to look into my face. His speech is exotic and often lazy and larded with words I don't understand. He is an alien to me, a man from a world I know so little about. How can I find him, as I do, so exciting? How can I behave, because of him, like a kitchen maid told she can't have followers, sneaking out of my own home in the dark nights, going to places which are seedy to say the least, dangerous at the worst? How can I do it?

She opened her eyes and stared again at the polished mahogany furniture and the red turkey carpet and gleaming satin polished brass amongst which she had lived all her life and saw it for the sterile prison it was. 'I can do it,' she whispered aloud, 'because everything else I do is so dreadful. That is why.'

And it was a bad reason for feeling as she did about the man waiting in the park. She had to admit it now; she could no longer deny the fact that had been battering at her mind all through this past month of misery. She was obsessed by him. The thought of his face made her belly lurch. The touch of his hand made her chest tighten so that she could hardly breathe. Her dreams were laced with sensual experiences with him that amazed her when she recalled them in her waking hours. Altogether he had moved into the fabric of her in a way that had changed her completely. She would never be the same again, whatever she did now. And feeling like that is no basis for any reasonable discussion.

But all the same what I am going to do now, she told herself, is go to the park and talk to him. That is all. I shall go to the park and talk to him – what harm can there be in that?

And she went softly down the stairs, leaving her parents snoring in their lonely rooms behind her, to slip out of the house into the darkness.

13

It was not, after all, as warm as she had thought. Without her jacket she shivered a little and that made her walk faster, clattering along Leinster Terrace from street lamp to street lamp and not caring if anyone heard her. It was now late, anyway; she had heard the clock chiming half past eleven as she had slipped out of the house, and that meant that most law abiding citizens would be in bed – and who could be more law abiding than their neighbours in this respectable stuccoed street?

She hovered on the kerb of the Bayswater Road, looking first westwards towards Notting Hill and then eastwards to Marble Arch and Oxford Street and all was still. Not even a late cab was trotting up the wide expanse and she took a deep breath and plunged across the road to the other side where the trees from the Park hung over the railings to make a shadowed damp place well away from the light.

After a moment she turned eastwards to make for the Lancaster Gate. He hadn't said where in the Park he would wait for her but that surely would be the nearest, and it should be open still.

It was, and she stepped inside feeling the roughness of the gravel beneath her light shoes as she left the paving stones behind, and stood for a moment in the darkness.

It was very still. Behind her an occasional horse clopped by, making its way homewards to a warm stable, and there were one or two hurrying foot passengers, but their scarceness only served to underline just how quiet and empty it was here in the black-leaved fastness of the Park and she stood there poised, almost ready to turn and run away, back to the warmth and security of Leinster Terrace.

And to its misery, she thought and stepped forwards with a confidence she didn't really feel, peering into the darkness. 'Kid?' she called softly, and then again, more loudly, 'Kid?'

There was no answer and she stood still a while longer, her head up, trying to listen. Her eyes were getting more accustomed to the darkness now and she could see ahead of her the blackness thinning where the path from Marlborough Gate crossed the Lancaster Gate path on its way to the Broad Walk, and beyond that the massing of the trees on the far side of the open spaces that flanked the paths. She could smell more clearly too, now, the delicate scent of daffodils and new leaves and crushed grass and that heartened her, and she stepped even further into the Park and called more loudly, 'Kid? Where are you?'

Still there was no reply and she felt a stirring of alarm that had deepened the pool of fear and doubt that had been lying low inside her ever since she had first stepped out of the house this evening, expecting to take herself to the East End, and she was suddenly ashamed of herself. At her age, to be afraid! Of what? There was nothing to fear but her own fear, she told herself stoutly and started to walk along the Marlborough Gate path towards the Broad Walk. He must have come into the Park further up, she told herself, at Porchester Terrace Gate. She would have to meet him, somehow. And she walked sharply, feeling the chill of the night air creeping into her through the fabric of her gown.

Now and again she stopped and listened for footsteps and called again, but still there was no reply and she thought – I'll go as far as Porchester Terrace and then give up. He must have changed his mind – and desolation filled her and she began to hurry, trying to escape her own doubts.

It happened so suddenly that it seemed the world had turned itself upside down and then lurched back, leaving her breathless and yet wanting to scream. At one moment she was half running and the next she was held hard by strong arms that would not let her move, so that her feet scrabbled helplessly in the gravel, and as she opened her mouth wider in an attempt to force out a sound, any sort of sound, she remembered for the first time the tales the kitchen maids sometimes told of footpads and thieves in the Park. And her head began to spin so that she felt sick.

'Millie, where was you, for Gawd's sake?' His voice was loud in her ear and she thought at first she had imagined it, so terrified was she but his breath was warm on her face and she could smell him too, that mixture of bay rum and tobacco and whatever else it was that was so uniquely him and she felt her fear begin to subside. But what took its place was almost worse, for she felt tears rise in her and burst from her throat so that she was weeping bitterly, feeling her cheeks wet and her nose blocked and her eyes hot, and then he had both arms about her, and was pushing her face down against the rough shoulder of his jacket.

'Millie, boobalah, what is it? Millie, don't take on so, oh, my dear, *dear* Millie, don't – please, don't cry so – I can't bear it – '

He moved then, taking one arm from behind her so that he could touch her face and he fumbled for her chin and with hard fingers pulled on it and she opened her eyes and looked at him, so close to her and tried to speak and could only gulp.

'Ah, boobalah!' he said with great tenderness. 'Such a frightened little girl!' and lifted his chin and kissed her. His mouth felt hot and dry against hers and she tried to speak, to tell him he mustn't, so that her lips opened. And that seemed to galvanize him, for he was no longer tender, but was suddenly very urgent indeed, thrusting his tongue against her own in a way that was so desperate she was amazed.

139

'I can't – ' She managed to pull away from him and turned her head away. 'I can't breathe – ' she said and he laughed and reached into his pocket and she felt soft linen against her nose.

'Blow!' he commanded, and after one startled glance at his face just visible in the darkness, she did so, needing to rid herself of the tears that had so nearly choked her.

'Did I frighten you?' he almost crooned it. 'I didn't mean to, boobalah, believe me I didn't, I wouldn't frighten you for the world – ' And again his arms were round her and he was kissing her, but this time she could breathe through her cleared nose and had no excuse for pulling away.

And did not want one. The effect that the touch of his face on her skin had was extraordinary. It was such as she had dreamed it would be on those long, miserable nights in her hated lonely bed, exactly like that. Her skin crawled across her belly and back as their cheeks met, and she found herself opening her mouth greedily to him, wanting to kiss him as much as he did her.

When they had moved she did not know, but she suddenly realized that they were no longer on the gravel path, but on something soft and yielding and he was pulling her down, inexorably, so that her knees buckled under her and she was on the grass and he was beside her. Wet grass, black grass, scented grass, with flowers all round her. She could smell the daffodils even more strongly now, and the scent of them, mixed with the scent of him, made her dizzy with excitement and she reached both arms out to hold on to him, stretching herself along the grass to relieve the cramped position she was in.

And there they were, side by side, facing each other and she could feel a daffodil leaf brushing the back of her neck as he lifted his head and looked down at her, and she said with a soft giggle, 'Something's tickling me – ' and he laughed too and kissed her again.

'Millie, please, let me. I have to – please, Millie?'

'What?' She looked at him again in the darkness, seeing his eyes glinting at her. 'What did you say?'

'Please,' he said, and now his voice was thick. 'I must – you want me, and I must and – ' And now it all changed. Not his cheek touching hers but his hands, pulling at the bodice of her gown and then tugging at her skirts and reaching, stroking, holding. She felt the buttons on the front of her gown part and gasped as suddenly his hand was there, inside her clothes and touching her skin, and her nipples hurt sharply as his hand found one and again she gasped and tilted her head upwards.

'Ah, Millie, my own Millie, you're the same as me, you are, you are. You want me as much as I want you – ' And he bent his head and she felt his lips against her breasts and could not breathe at all. This was unbelievable, and somewhere deep in her mind she cried – it wasn't like this when I dreamed – it wasn't like this when I dreamed – it's better, better, better –

When it happened all she felt at first was amazement. He lay on her, pulling at his own clothes and at hers at the same time, wriggling, grunting a little as he concentrated, all his actions rough and urgent, and she lay there beneath him looking up over his curly head at the stars that she could see caught in the tree branches above her head and thought – so, this is what it's like? This is what it is meant to be? Just this? And he pushed himself at her, forcing her legs to part and then tearing at her drawers. She felt a surge of cool air as he heaved himself upwards for a moment to be sure he was arranged as he wanted to be, a coolness that made her embarrassingly aware that she had become richly moist with excitement and which gave her a sudden urge of sensation quite unlike any she had ever had before.

But then the coolness went as he pushed himself into her, hard and determined, and she cried aloud as she felt him cleave his way through her and tried to clamp her legs together more tightly, to stop the hurt.

But it didn't stop, and again he pushed his body against her so that she had to let her knees fall apart and now he was pushing himself in and out of her, hard and rhythmic, his head thrust back so that it blocked out the starlight above her, making its own patterns against the sky.

Still it hurt, but it was different now. Excitement rose in her as the sharp sensations burnt against her awareness and she tried to hold on to each one as it came to her, but every time the feeling changed and swept her away onto a different one, and she tried to concentrate, to understand all that was happening, and could not.

The sensations rose and grew and she found herself clutching his shoulders, holding on hard and bending her own head back so that her skull pressed against the ground and she closed her eyes, wanting the sensations to go on and on. It was good. It was dreadful, it was wonderful, it hurt and she didn't want it to stop.

But it did stop, suddenly. He thrust himself down on her yet again, but this time didn't rise, but remained close to her, jerking his pelvis, as he seemed to try to push right through her, and she heard him cry out, a thick guttural sound. And then he collapsed against her, and lay panting a little, his mouth pressed into her neck and making her skin feel wet and cold.

'Oh, Mildred!' he said. 'Oh, Mildred!' and lay still.

She lay still too for a while and then moved experimentally. 'Kid?' she whispered and then, as he showed no response, said it more loudly. 'Kid!'

At once he woke and turned his head towards her. 'Mmm?' he said sleepily.

'Kid – I – ' And then to her amazement she was weeping again, with huge sobs coming from her and he lifted himself up on her and peered down and said, 'Millie – oh, Millie – don't – ' and rolled off to lean over and touch her cheek.

But still she wept on, rocking her body against the grass and suddenly he made a soft little sound in his throat and then repeated it and she knew he was laughing.

'You didn't, did you? You didn't and you want to – oh, Millie, you are such a girl, boobalah – such a girl!' and his hands began to move again, stroking her, across her bare thighs where he had pulled her stockings away, up and on into the centre of her, moving his fingers as rhythmically as he had moved his body. She tried to resist at first, but then knew what he was trying to do and moved her own body in rhythm to match his and then at last there they were again, the sensations, the feelings that had made her dreams so terrifying and exhausting and so distressing.

But now there was no distress in it. Only need and urgency and more need and she went on moving and so did he and then it happened; as inevitable and as familiar as though it had happened a thousand times before, although it had never happened before, except in restless dreams, and this was so much better –

They lay side by side on the grass for a long time, she staring up at the sky and he dozing a little, his mouth once more against the side of her neck and she lay very still, not wanting to disturb him, feeling a need to be kind to him. She was half dreaming, half thinking and neither seemed to make any sense, and it didn't matter anyway –

The sound of the clock came from a long way away but sleepily she listened. First the four notes of the first quarter – ding, dong, ding, dong – and then the second quarter. Half past something, she thought – then the third quarter came softly singing through the trees, and a tiny worm of anxiety stirred in her. The final quarter rang and now she opened her eyes wide, fully awake. It must be midnight and here she was, still out of the house and in such a state of disarray – and she reached for her skirt, wanting to pull it down to tidy herself as the first single note of the hour came singing at her. And stopped. Just one note and she caught her breath and sat up so sharply that he rolled away and sat up too, staring round in startled bemusement.

'It's one o'clock!' she cried. 'Oh, my God, it's one o'clock! Freddy must have locked the house by now! He knows Papa is in and – oh, God, what am I to do?' And amazingly it mattered more to her than what had gone before. It was as though worrying about the time and how she was to get back home without being discovered made the reason for her lateness unimportant.

'Don't worry.' He was pulling at his own clothes, setting himself tidy. 'I'll look after you, Millie. Don't you fret – I'll take care of you. Oh, Millie!' And he came across the small area of grass that separated them, shuffling on his knees, crushing once again the daffodils which had been flattened beneath them and which had been trying to recover. 'I – That was incredible, wonderful – I've been wanting you so bad I didn't know what to do with myself. It's crazy, ain't it? I never felt like this before about any girl ever. Not ever. Was it good for you?'

She was on her feet now, and smoothing her gown over her hips, very aware of her torn drawers beneath it, and of the gaping spaces in front of her bodice where the buttons had been lost. 'Good? – ' She swallowed. 'As good as what? It's never – I mean – I don't know.'

He scrambled to his feet and came to stand close beside her, peering up at her in the darkness. 'You was a virgin, Millie?' There was an odd note in his voice, a kind of awe, and he said it again, a statement this time. 'A virgin.'

She felt her face flame in the darkness. 'What do you think?' she said savagely. 'I'm not one of your – in my world unmarried ladies always are.'

'Oh, Millie, did I hurt you?' He sounded concerned but there was more than that in his tone, a sort of triumphant hopefulness, as though he wanted to be told that he *had* hurt her, not badly, but enough, and she frowned, bending her head to fiddle uselessly with a rip in her gown. 'No – well, yes. Oh, not – it didn't matter – '

'But you liked it? I made you feel good? Tell me I made you feel good. I want you to feel good so much – '

'I – ' She swallowed and looked at him and he smiled and set his head to one side. 'Tell me it felt good,' he said again and she could not lie to him, and nodded and her face stretched itself without any conscious control from her and she found herself smiling a wide and tremulous grin.

'That's all right then,' he said with great satisfaction and turned and reached for a bundle that was on the ground beside him. 'Look, here they are. Your jacket and your hat. The jacket'll cover what's happened to your dress. You'll be able to fix it won't you? I'm sorry I tore it, Millie. I didn't mean to. But I wanted you so bad it was like – ' He put his arms round her and kissed her. 'But you know what it was like, don't you?'

'I don't know anything,' she said and pulled away from him. 'I don't know what – I can't think how it all happened, I'm not – '

'I know,' he laughed. 'You ain't that sort of girl. They all say that. I ain't that sort of girl – but you don't have to say it. I know you're not. You're a lady. Real class you are.'

She had stiffened, stopping the buttoning of her jacket and staring at him in the dimness.

'What did you say?'

'That you're a real lady – '

'No – before that. That's what they all say? Are you saying that – ' But she could not go on, and bent her head and swallowed, not wanting to look at him any more.

'Am I saying what?'

'It doesn't matter,' she said dully and bent down to retrieve her hat, and stood turning it between her fingers, trying to smooth the small brim which had bent beneath the pressure of their bodies.

'It does. If it matters to you it matters to me. Tell me what it was you was going to say.'

'They all say that,' she repeated after a moment. 'I'm just one of lots, aren't I? A plain and stupid old maid you've had a game with and – ' Again tears filled her eyes; not painful urgent ones this time, but tears of loss and desolation. For a little while it had been all so rich, so real, so important, and now she saw it for what it was: a cheap and nasty adventure. This was the inevitable result of the whole sordid business on which she had embarked last autumn, travelling secretly to slums to spend time with slum people, learning slum ways. And now she stood in the middle of Hyde Park in the small hours of the morning in torn and stained drawers feeling soiled and degraded and sick. And she closed her eyes and took a deep breath and then turned and without another look backwards, ran as fast as she could towards the Lancaster Gate and home. Horrible, hateful, but *safe* home.

14

He caught up with her as she reached the Lancaster Gate, and it was just as well, because the gate had been fast closed. She stood there pulling uselessly on the great padlock that held them together, crying furiously and noisily, so noisily that she did not hear him come up behind her.

He took hold of both her elbows from behind and held on, even though she tried to shake him away, and just stood there as her tears blew themselves out in a storm of weeping. And then, as they lessened and became first occasional sobs and then just a few hiccups, said reasonably, 'You can't get home without me to help you, so you might as well let me talk first. I won't let you go till we do, so be sensible like you usually are.'

'I don't feel sensible,' she flared at him. 'I feel dreadful – '

'Don't say that.' He spoke softly and pulled her round so that she had to look at him. 'Please don't, because it ain't true. It was good loving for you as well as for me. I made sure it was. Didn't I? I know I did – '

'With all your experience I dare say you do know. I dare say all the others say it, too, just as they always say they're not that sort of girl. So if they say that you're so good at – at what you call loving, then it must be so. How can I know, ignorant as I am?'

'Listen, I didn't mean to upset you, saying what I did! But be reasonable, Millie – a bloke like me, what do you expect?

I'm not one of your West End types, all eyeglasses and namby-pamby mincing around! Maybe they don't need no – maybe it ain't important to them to have women in their lives, but for me and people like me, ordinary people, believe you me, it is. The thing of it is, I'm a man and I ain't cut out to be a monk. So – '

'So I'm just another one of the things you need,' she said bitterly. 'Like fights and gold chains and salt beef sandwiches. Just something you need, that's all. An ugly old maid who ought to be grateful, I suppose, and – '

His grip on her tightened. 'Don't ever say that again to me, you hear me? You are not ugly. You are not an old maid. How can you be? You and me is goin' to be married – '

There was a small silence and then she said carefully, 'How can you be so sure?'

'Because I wants to marry you, and you wants to marry me – '

She took a sharp little breath. 'How can you say that? You don't know. How can you be so sure that I do?'

He peered at her in the darkness. 'Of course you do!' He sounded uncertain for the first time. 'I mean, back there in the daffodils – it was obvious you love me! You know you do – you wanted to be with me, didn't you? You wasn't acting, was you?'

'Acting?' she repeated. 'No, I wasn't acting.'

'Then we'll get married. It'll be problems, I dare say, but we'll sort it out. They'll come round – '

'Who'll come round?'

'Families – ' he said vaguely. 'You'll see. They'll get used to the idea.'

'Even if I'd agreed that I was going to marry you, I don't see how you can say that,' she said, trying not to let herself imagine the reality that might lie behind the words he was using. Married? To Kid? And living with him? Where? And on what? Houses cost money, and for all his lavish spending when they had been going out and about together, she knew that all that Kid had he earned from fights. To set up a home took more than the occasional windfall which was, after all, all that his income was. And what chance was there her father would release to her her small legacy, which would be useful, if not the whole answer to her needs, once he met this man? 'My father is not – not an easy man.'

'Your father? I wasn't thinking about him.'

'Oh!' She was startled. 'Then who were you thinking about? My Mama is just my stepmother, you know. I doubt she'll care much what I do. Except perhaps for regretting having the use of me about the house.'

'I was thinking about my family,' he said. 'Remember what I told you? About how they go into mourning when a person marries out of the faith? Remember how my mother was with you?'

She reddened in the darkness. 'I'm sorry. I was being – I suppose I'd forgotten – ' And how could I forget? she thought then, when his mother had spoken so to me, when she made me promise I would never marry her son? A far-seeing woman, Mrs Harris. She had known this was going to happen; and for a moment she hated her for being so perceptive.

'You thought it more likely there would be objections on your side, and that they'd be more important,' he said shrewdly. 'After all, your people are much better quality than my lot, aren't they?'

Again there was a silence as she digested that and then she said abruptly, 'This is all nonsense, isn't it? It's been mad from the beginning. For me to have agreed to know you at all was mad. To be here with you tonight is even more – and to talk about marrying – ' Her voice trailed away and she stood and stared into the darkness over his head and felt the chill of the night air in her bones and ached to go away and crawl into her bed and sink into total oblivion. It was all too much for her to cope with any more. She was tired and dispirited and felt oddly detached now. It was as though all this was happening to someone else, a someone else she did not particularly care for, and she closed her eyes and took a deep breath.

'I shall have to climb over, I think,' she said as calmly as she could. 'Will you help me?'

'Of course. Here, it isn't as difficult as it looks. I'll get up first, get you up and then go down the other side to catch you – '

At once he was all action, shinning up the ornamental ironwork of the tall gate, leaning down to reach out a hand to help her do the same once he was safely astride, using his jacket to protect himself from the blunt spikes that adorned the top, and half in a dream she obeyed his instructions. Had she been less tired, less bewildered by all that had happened tonight she might have been too frightened to try, for the gate was well over eight feet high and created a formidable barrier to her in her muffling long skirts, but within minutes she was down on the other side, caught by his strong arms, and standing in the Bayswater Road.

'Listen,' he said. 'We'll talk about this later. Let me get you home, and tomorrow – tonight, eh? – we'll meet, go to supper, we'll make plans. I'm goin' to marry you, Millie, that's the thing of it. So you might as well agree now. Haven't you noticed I always get what I want? Soon's I saw you in the gym that night I thought – this is a class lady and she's goin' to be my lady. An' that's how it's worked out, hasn't it? You might as well give in – '

'I have a mind of my own, for heaven's sake!' she flared. 'You make me feel as though I were an object you saw in a warehouse and coveted.'

'I did covet you. Good word, that. I coveted my neighbour's sister – ' He laughed. 'Yeah, imagine that! I'll have those brothers o' yours for misbocher – '

'What?'

He sighed. 'The sooner you learn a bissel Yiddish the better for both of us. Misbocher, family. They'll be my relations – '

'You see how ridiculous it all is?' she said despairingly. 'Can you imagine the sort of fuss there'll be if I even suggest it? And anyway, I haven't said yet that I want to – '

'Oh, Millie, come on! You aren't one of these simpering madams that play games with men, are you? You don't say no when you mean yes. You're a woman, you do what you want, when you want. Like you wanted there in the Park – ' And he looked back over his shoulder through the gate to the grass and grinned softly. 'And you wanted it, didn't you? So don't go playing no games with me. Say you want to marry me, and be done.'

She opened her mouth to tell him again that it was impossible. They were too different, too hopelessly divided by their past lives, their families, every aspect of themselves. She had even made a promise on her father's life that she would not. And she listened with amazement as the words came out.

'Yes, I want to. I want to marry you. I don't know why, and I know it's impossible but I want it. And not just because you decided, either. It's my own decision, not yours.'

'Well, there you are then. Home, now. You look worn out – '

'Thank you,' she said a little tartly.

'Listen, Millie – ' They began to walk along the Bayswater Road, he with his arm tucked tightly into hers. 'There's something we got to get clear. You got to stop all this business o' thinking people are getting at you about how you look. I said you looked tired. This wasn't no insult. It was just the way it is. You look tired out, and entitled to. No need to get sharp about it, is there?'

'I don't mean to be sharp. It's just that – well, I ought to be used to it, I suppose. Being plain. It's not as though I was ever any different, even when I was a child. People used to ask my mother if I was accomplished and you could see them thinking – she'd better be – she's got nothing else to commend her, poor thing. But I'm not accomplished at all. I can't sing and I have no conversation and I'm dull as well as plain and – '

'No,' he said strongly. 'No, no, *no*. I won't have it. Plain you ain't. Interestin', yes. Different, yes. But plain an' dull, no conversation? That's nonsense, an' I won't listen to it. First time I heard you talk I thought – there is a lady. And you've got a lovely voice, an' all. Low, like. Most women you hear talkin' it's like a henhouse, cluck cluck cluck – ' And he lifted his own voice an octave and clucked to such good effect that she chuckled, for all her weariness.

'That's better. Bit of humour, that's what we need. I don't want to hear you ever talking that way again. Understood?'

'Yes,' she said and stopped walking. They were at the end of the Terrace and she peered along its length and bit her lip anxiously. But there was no one about at all, not so much as a late roisterer, and she untangled her arm from his and said, 'Listen, Kid, I – '

'Call me Lizah,' he said. 'Everyone calls me Kid. For you I want to be special, you know? Real close, like the family. Lizah.'

'All right,' she said. 'Lizah – listen, I want – ' And then she stopped and looked at him and said, 'I've just remembered. You – there in the Park, after you – when you – Well, anyway. You called me Mildred. I used to beg you to call me that, and you wouldn't, said I had to be Millie. But then you said Mildred to me – '

He was silent for a long time, so long she thought he hadn't heard her and she bent her head to look in his face, for his own head was bent too, but then he glanced up at her and said awkwardly, 'I know. Did you mind?'

'Mind? No. I was – it felt different, that was all. Why did you?'

'Because it was different. Mildred,' he said and grinned at her and then leaned forwards and tilted his chin up so that he could kiss her and she returned it. No passion now, just closeness and kindness and a feeling of rightness and she smiled too.

'I must go in,' she murmured. 'If I can get in – '

'I'll come with you – '

'No. Let me see first if I can manage. If I need you I'll wave. Stay here – and wait – '

'We'll meet tomorrow? Tonight? Nine o'clock, like we used to?'

'Nine o'clock,' she said. 'Like we used to.' And turned and went, slipping along the railings towards the house, worried about being seen even though the street was deserted.

She tried the front door first, fitting the key she took from her pocket hopefully into the lock, but of course it was bolted and she stood for a moment, trying to think. The kitchen door? Perhaps that would be unlocked. And she turned and went down the steps and down to the area below, leaving the gate open at street level. The kitchen door was locked, but to the far side of it, almost in the corner, there was a small window half open, and she went across the paved yard and stood on tiptoes and reached up, pulling herself up by muscular effort, to look in. It was, as she had remembered, the pantry window and she could see just below it to the broad marble shelf where Cook left food to cool, and tried to visualize other things that could be there that might create a hazard. And felt reasonably secure in her certainty there was not.

She went back up the area steps to the street and waved and there was a glimpse of white as his hand was raised and he waved back, and with one last gesture of her arm she returned down the steps, this time locking the gate behind her. Thank God, she was thinking, that Cook was so lazy and slapdash in so many ways. To leave the pantry window open was stupid in the extreme, but she had done it, and Mildred was deeply grateful.

Getting up to the sill was much harder than she would have expected, even though she hoisted her skirts and tied them round her middle to free her legs, and her muscles were shrieking in agony by the time she managed to hook one knee on to the narrow sill. But from then on it was fairly easy, and for the first time she could remember she was grateful for her thinness, for she was able to wriggle through the small window, tight fit though it was, and emerge on the inner side.

She sent a meat pie flying as she landed on the marble slab, and began to fumble in the dark to pick it up but then decided to leave it where it was. Let them think a marauding cat had done the damage. Any attempt to tidy it would be easily detected and would immediately prove that a human agency had been at work.

The pantry door opened on to a stone-flagged passageway that led to the kitchen and she stood there smelling the mixture of old cabbage and paraffin from the lamps and tallow and soda and yellow soap and tried to catch her breath. Her fatigue was growing by the moment, seeming to double itself every time she made a move and as she untied her skirts her legs felt so heavy she wasn't sure she'd be able to drag herself up the stairs to bed. But it wasn't far now and she went across the dim kitchen, which was glowing softly in the light from the banked up fire, towards the far door that led to the second passageway which ended in the green baize door.

It happened just as she opened the kitchen door, so pat that it seemed that it was her own action that brought the flood of light into her eyes and made her stand there blinking and holding her hand up to shield them. There on the other side of the door someone was standing, holding a lamp in such a way that nothing could be seen behind it, and she blinked and turned her head away and said, 'Who is that?'

'Well, well!' The voice was soft and amused. 'I been waiting for you. Time you got here. Been doing your Mission work have you, then? Been out preaching the gospel to the poor, is that it?'

'Freddy!' she said and then tightened her lips. 'For heaven's sake, put that lamp down! You're blinding me!'

'And very suitable too, I'd say. It was what they used to do to sinners in the Bible, wasn't it? Put their wicked eyes out?'

'I don't know what you are talking about,' she said, pretending an insouciance she was far from feeling, and tried to push past him to go towards the front of the house and her own room. Her heart was beating thickly in her chest, for now she was filled with fear, far more than she had ever known before. She had thought she was alarmed earlier, when she had been talking to Kid – Lizah – in the street, and the cab bearing her father had arrived, but this fear was twice that. It filled her mouth with a metallic taste and made her head spin.

He didn't move, and she had to stop and said loudly, knowing her voice shook and knowing equally that she was not able to do anything about it, 'Will you let me pass?'

'Not till I know what's in it for me if I do,' he said, and the insolence in his voice was so clear it seemed to ring in her head. 'Why should I do something for nothing? If you want to go trolling round the town like some dollymop, there's got to be something in it for me not to tell your Pa and Ma, hasn't there?'

'You're drunk,' she said, aware for the first time of the smell of him. Beer, mostly, and a lot of it laced his breath and now, as he laughed, she had to pull her head back, it was so disagreeable.

'And why shouldn't I be? It's good enough for that old sod upstairs so it's good enough for me. A chap's got to do something to drown his sorrows when he finds himself caught up with the sort of rubbish you lot are – ' And he turned his head and spat and she heard the spittle ring as it landed on the stone floor.

'Go to your room at once,' she said, with all the dignity she could gather around her. 'I will see to it that you are dealt with in the morning. Good night – ' And again she tried to push her way past him.

But he held his ground. 'Oh, yes? And what'll be the result, do you suppose, when I tells the old sod that you've been larking about with some Jew boy out of the gutter? Eh? He won't be as interested in what you've got to say about me then, will he? Oh, I'm not daft, you know. I heard what that cabbie said and I saw that character hanging around! I know the sort he is – and that boy that kept coming here with his messages and his cheek – Father Jay my arse! And don't you look so old-fashioned at me! Ladies I watch my tongue for, but you ain't no lady. So I can say what I like to *you*.'

She stood very still, trying to think what to do and what to say. Freddy stood swaying a little in front of her, the lamp in his hand tilted so that the flame smeared the glass chimney with a black streak, and stared at her, his eyes, red and bleary, mocking her with his insolence.

'I don't care what you say or what you do,' she said at length. 'I am tired and I am going to bed. Now let me pass – ' And this time she set her hand in the middle of his chest and pushed hard so that he had to give way. Or so she thought because although he seemed to yield as she pushed past him, he did not, and she felt his arm come round her waist and hold on as she tried to get away.

'Come on,' he said, in a thick voice. 'Give us a kiss an' a bit o' what you been giving your fancy boy out there, whatever that was. If a stinkin' slummer like that's good enough for you, then why shouldn't I have a bit o' fun 'n' all? You might have a face like the back of a bus, but a woman's a woman when all's said and done. All cats are grey in the dark – ' And his breath, hot and beer-reeking was on her face and she could bear it no longer. She whirled and, with all the strength she had, hit out. But she kept her eyes tightly closed as she did so, not able to look this hateful man in the face.

She felt her fist hit something soft, felt his head snap back and heard his yell, but still she didn't look. She just turned and ran blindly for the green baize door and the stairs, and bed. It was the only place she could think of going to that would be safe.

15

Like it or not, she had to come down to breakfast. She had woken from the deepest of sleep with a great start when Jenny came in as usual to clean and light her fire and then had lain there, her eyes closed, trying to find the courage to open them in the new day. But that didn't help, for in the dull orange glow behind her closed lids she saw herself in the Park with Lizah and then saw herself in the dark kitchen passageway with Freddy and the juxtaposition of the two images was so disagreeable that she snapped her eyes open to stare up at her ceiling, trying to think what to do.

Could she perhaps pretend to be ill, and keep to her room? No one would care much, and it would give her time to gather her thoughts and make sensible decisions about what was to happen now. For in the clear light of this March morning it was very obvious to her that last night she had run mad, stark staring mad. To marry Lizah Harris – it was out of the question, no matter what had happened between them. He had to be told and she had to return to normal living as soon as possible; but she needed time, and the only way to get that was to feign illness –

And that would make Freddy believe she was afraid of him, and he would go to her father and – she sat bolt upright and swung her legs out of the bed. She had to be there at breakfast whatever happened, had to be at table to see what the situation was. Hiding here would make matters worse, not better.

Claude, who had taken lately to breakfasting at home, was already deeply involved with his bowl of porridge when she reached the dining room, his head down over his busily working spoon and he greeted her with no more than a grunt and seemed ill disposed towards any further conversation, which comforted her. At the foot of the table the tea equipage waited for Mama and behind it stood Jane, also waiting woodenly for instructions. Mr Amberly came into the morning room just behind Mildred and went straight to his place at the head of the table, saying nothing at all to anyone, but waving one hand imperiously at Jane.

In the subsequent bustle of supplying the master with his wants, his bowl of porridge and his plate of kidneys and eggs and his tea in its double-sized cup as well as his newspaper no one paid any attention to Mildred at all, not even Maud when she came drifting in, pale and a little damp about the forehead and interested only in taking a little black tea, and no food at all. And Mildred's spirits began slowly to stir and lift their heads above the parapet of her fear. Perhaps, after all, there was no outcome of last night's events? Perhaps Freddy too had woken to realize how stupidly he had behaved and had decided to say nothing to anyone?

But then, the door opened as Jane left the room behind her, and she knew he was there; she felt him come in. She did not have to turn her head to know it was he and she sat rigidly, her cup at her lips, trying to pretend she was drinking tea in the normal manner and very unsure of her success.

'Extra postage is due on one of the letters just arrived, sir,' Freddy murmured into Mr Amberly's ear. 'Shall I pay it, sir?'

'Eh?'

'Extra postage due, sir. Tuppence, sir,' he murmured a little more loudly.

'Who's it from?'

'Can't say, sir,' Freddy said. 'It's addressed to madam, sir.'

'Hmph,' Mr Amberly said and turned his head and squinted at the letter on the salver that Freddy was holding towards him. 'Send it back to whoever sent it. I'm not paying tuppences for any fool that can't be bothered to stamp a letter properly.'

'What is it, Edward?' Maud looked vaguely down the table at her husband, suddenly aware that her name had been mentioned. 'A letter for me?'

Her husband ignored her. 'Take it away. Give it to the postman,' he grunted and returned to his paper as Maud lifted one hand towards Freddy to take the letter from him. But he stared insolently at her and walked past her and out of the room, taking it with him.

For a long moment Maud gazed down the table at the back of her husband's newspaper, patches of red appearing in her pallid cheeks, but the spark of her anger seemed to die as fast as it had been kindled and she let her shoulders sag and went on sipping her tea, her eyes down as she stared at the table-cloth.

Quite why Mildred interfered she did not know. It was, perhaps a combination of things; her own tension, for she was so taut inside she felt that if she moved she would give out plangent little sounds, and her anger at Freddy, exacerbated by the way he had walked past his mistress with that look on his face which so clearly displayed his scorn, or perhaps it was her new mood of foolhardiness, for after what she had done last night, anything seemed possible.

'I will fetch your letter back, Mama,' she said loudly and got to her feet. 'You need not fret about the twopence. I think I can manage to find that for you.' And she went to the door.

The newspaper at the head of the table rustled and was lowered. 'What was that?'

'I said I will fetch Mama's letter,' she said even more loudly and looked at him with her chin up. 'It is Mama's letter and you have no right to send it away.'

He stared at her, his reddened eyes squinting in the thin morning light. His face looked yellow this morning and seemed to sag more than usual. 'I said it was to be sent away. I pay no tuppences for the sort of fools that write rubbishing letters to Mrs Amberly. I've told her so before, have I not, Maud?'

'Yes, Edward,' she said after a moment, still keeping her gaze fixed on the tablecloth.

'So sit down and mind your business,' he growled and again glared at Mildred.

'It is as well I did not mind it last night, Papa,' she said, her courage sharpened by her anger. 'Had I done so you'd be sitting there in the hall yet, in as disagreeable a state as any man – '

'Hold your tongue!' he shouted. 'How dare you speak so to me? A man eats a bad oyster and – '

'More costly liquor than bad oysters,' she said and held her ground by the door, and Claude looked up and threw a scared glance from his father to his sister and then got to his feet and positively scuttled from the room with a muttered ''Bye – ' Basil was coming in as he reached the door and Claude pushed on him, hurrying him out again, and Mildred saw his startled face and his anger as Claude firmly closed the morning-room door behind them, and could have laughed. But she did not, remaining staring at her father, and not knowing for the life of her why she had started this stupid argument. What did she care for Mama and her letters? Was it not true that all she ever got were silly gushing fusses from those of her old school friends who still remembered her and wished to maintain the acquaintance? Why should she, with so many of her own affairs to concern her, become embroiled in this manner?

Because he is a bully and I hate him, she found herself thinking as she looked at her father. And sooner or later I am going to have to deal with him for myself. So I shall deal with him first for Mama –

'Go to your room!' He was on his feet, his face empurpled now with fury. 'How dare you speak so to me, you great stupid creature! I keep you here, eating your ugly head off at my expense, and will have the keeping of you till the day you die, no doubt, for no other one will take you off my hands, and you dare to speak so to me? Where is your gratitude, girl? At your age you should have your own establishment! Since you do not and are dependent upon my purse, then by God, you will mind your manners and behave yourself!'

'I am well aware of my lack of an establishment, sir,' she said, and reached behind her to hold on to the doorknob. Her legs were trembling so that she needed something to give her a sense of security. 'I would perhaps be less of a trouble to you if I were to be allowed my own money. My Mama left me a small competence to which I am, I believe, fully entitled. Give it to me and I will gladly leave this house and live on my own.'

'Mildred!' Mama spoke for the first time, turning her white face towards her. 'Be quiet, you stupid girl! I never heard such insolence in my life! How dare you! Tell your Papa you are sorry for your ill manners at once!'

'I have no cause to apologize. I wished only to fetch your letter for you and – '

'The letter does not matter,' Maud said and looked appealingly at her husband. 'Did I complain, Edward? Indeed I did not, and I would not wish you to think I had. I care nothing for the letter. I had nothing to do with any of this, I do assure you – '

He paid her no attention at all, still standing there at the table, his newspaper crumpled in his hand as he stared at his daughter.

'What did you say?' he said thickly.

'I asked for my own money, Papa,' she said. 'I have a wish to live on my own. It is I believe worth about one hundred and fifty pounds a year. I could find a small set of rooms for that and – '

'She's gone mad,' Edward Amberly said flatly, shifting his gaze for the first time to his wife. 'D'you hear me, Maud? The girl has gone mad. It is a case of her excess blood running to her brain, and curdling there. I have heard it happens to spinster women, and now I can see it. Send for the physician and see to it she is dosed.' And he threw down his paper and came stamping down the room towards the door. 'Get out of the way, girl. I have to go to my office at once. I have no further time to waste on an old maid's megrims.' And he set one hand on her shoulder and pushed her aside so roughly that she almost stumbled and had to let go of the doorknob to steady herself against the far wall.

'I wish to have my own money! – ' She said it again, even more loudly, knowing there was a note of pleading in her voice and hating herself for it, but he had opened the door and was gone out into the hall and she could see Freddy standing there, his master's glossy top hat and heavy overcoat in one hand and his silver topped walking stick in the other, staring lumpishly at the wall in a manner that made it abundantly clear that he had listened to every word said in the morning room.

'Send for the doctor, d'you hear me, Maud?' Edward Amberly shouted as he shrugged on his coat and seized his hat and stick. 'The girl's run mad – ' And he went stumping out of the hall, leaving Freddy to close the door behind him.

'At what time, madam, would it be convenient for Cook and me to come for our orders this morning?' Freddy said smoothly as he came back into the morning room to stand deferentially behind Maud's chair. 'Shall it be as usual?'

'What? Oh, yes, I suppose so. Oh, I have to see Nanny Chewson – let Miss Mildred deal with that – will you, Mildred? I am sure all will be well when your Papa returns – I do wish you wouldn't provoke him so – it makes it all so difficult – ' And her voice trailed away as she pushed her chair back from the table and got to her feet. She looked even more pale now, and her forehead was gleaming with sweat. 'I really must lie down for a while – I do have the most tiresome of sick headaches – ' And she went out of the room and towards the stairs, leaving Mildred standing against the wall in the morning-room and Freddy just outside the door.

'Mama, I do not wish to see any doctor!' She went after her, not caring any longer that Freddy was standing there. 'I will refuse! It is not an illness to wish to have one's own money – '

Maud stood half way up the stairs, clutching the banister in one hand and she swivelled her eyes and looked down at Mildred and shook her head. 'Oh, please, Mildred, don't tease me so. I do feel very sick – I really cannot – ' And suddenly, she made a retching sound and turned and, stumbling a little, ran up the stairs, one hand over her mouth.

'Three bottles she got through yesterday,' Freddy said in a conversational tone and Mildred turned and saw him standing beside her, gazing up the stairs at Maud's disappearing figure. 'Three bottles o' the master's best sherry. Used to be one a day, and care took to hide the fact, but now it's three and she much cares who knows!'

He shifted his gaze to Mildred's face now, and grinned. 'Mind you, so far, I'm the only one as does. And she pays me handsome to keep it that way. I don't mind tellin' *you* whatever it is she gives me to hold my tongue, on account of you're the same as she is, really, ain't you? Not booze, o' course. Still enough of a lady not to be at the booze, though the way you're going I don't give it more'n a few months. You'll be knocking 'em back with the best of 'em down the East End, you will. But there, it don't really make no never mind what a person's poison is does it? Slummers or sherry, it's all the same.' And again he laughed. 'Money in my pocket.'

She said nothing, standing there staring at him, her hands folded in front of her. She had to think, and she needed peace and quiet and time for that. She was losing control of her situation, that was the thing and she heard her mind whisper, 'that's the thing of it – ' and at once an image of Lizah lifted in her mind's eye, his corrugated forehead and bulging dark eyes and grin as vivid as if he were there in front of her. And almost without knowing she was doing so, she allowed her face to relax into a wide smile, a happy and contented smile, and for the first time Freddy looked disconcerted.

'I ain't playin' games, you know,' he said sharply. 'A bloke's got to look after hisself and I'm good at doing it. So don't you go thinking as I'm wind and water like the miller's cat, because I ain't. I mean what I say.'

'I'm not sure what it is you are saying,' she said coolly, for the first time feeling she had some control after all. He had been rattled by her response and that made her feel better.

'I'm saying that unless you comes across with a sov or so each week, your dad's going to know what happened last night. He's going to know about you sneakin' out of here to hang around with low company and creeping back in through the pantry window like a thief. And then he'll know what's what, and he won't start saying as your brains are curdling for want of a bit of how's your father, neither. He'll know what you was doin', you Berkeley Hunt, you –'

She tightened her lips, not knowing what the epithet meant, but hearing the sneer in it and guessing it to be as nasty a term as any to which he could lay his tongue. But she was not going to let him know that he was having any effect on her.

'It really doesn't matter to me in the least what you say,' she said and again managed to smile, filling it with as much of her own sneer as she could. 'It's quite irrelevant. I shall be in the morning room to give Cook her orders at ten o'clock, tell her.' And she turned and went upstairs, walking with as composed an air as she could muster, leaving him staring up after her, completely silent for once.

In her room she closed the door and bolted it and stood staring round. Jenny had made the bed while she had been at breakfast and emptied the slops and cleaned her wash stand and the room stood as it usually did, quiet and neat and empty of any real personality. She had never tried to make it any way a sanctum of her own, with her own decorations and pictures, knowing full well that to persuade her father to expend any money on her would be a waste of effort, and anyway not feeling any real need to do so. There had been a time, in her long ago girlhood, when she had kept scrapbooks and mementos and pressed flowers like other girls, but it had been many years since she had felt any desire to do anything like that.

And now she was glad. If this room had been in any sort a haven, marked with her own emotions and life, it would have been hard to leave it. As it was, she felt no sense of affection for it at all, any more than she did for any other aspect of her life here at Leinster Terrace, and went across the room to her wardrobe and opened it and stood looking at the contents.

There was not a great deal. She had always had a small dress allowance; even Edward Amberly expected to provide that for the females in his household, but she had never cared that it was a singularly niggardly one. She had not needed much in the way of clothes, for dressed up or not, she still looked what she was, plain and gawky, and anyway, where did she go? Her need for good clothes was very small, and so the same evening gowns had sufficed for many years. She reached forwards now and touched the green ribbed silk that hung on the end of the rail and then the blue spotted voile she wore in the summer. She could not recall how old they were, and the same applied to the sensible morning dresses and skirts and blouses that were arranged on the other hangers. None of it startling, all of it serviceable, and in good repair. What more could she ask?

She reached behind the green ribbed silk and brought out her small japanned box with the red flowers on it. The key she drew from the small chain she always wore around her neck, her only adornment, and slid it into the lock.

Her savings from her dress allowance and the few money presents she had received from her brothers for her birthday, when they had forgotten to buy her a gift as a memento, lay there in a small chamois leather bag and she took it out, and untied it, undoing the strings carefully and smoothing them as she went. It was important not to rush this moment, she felt obscurely. It was a significant one and as such to be savoured to its full.

Equally slowly she counted her money. There were eighteen sovereigns and three Bank of England notes, two for ten pounds and one for five pounds. A goodly sum to have saved from such small beginnings but not a great deal altogether, for what she had in mind. In addition she had twenty-seven shillings in her writing desk and a further two shillings and eleven pence in her reticule. She piled it all together on her lap, sitting on her bed with her box beside her and counted it.

Forty-four pounds, nine shillings and eleven pence. Not much on which to build a whole new life. But enough, she told herself sturdily, and swept it all into the little chamois bag and drew the strings tight before tucking it firmly into the pocket at the back of her skirt, where it hid itself beneath the folds and thumped against her legs as she moved. That was a comforting feeling, as though she was carrying all her future behind her, and her lips curved at that thought.

It was remarkable how calm and relaxed she felt. She should have been now as she had been when she had first gone down to the morning room for breakfast, taut and anxious and unsure of herself. Yesterday had been so incredible a day, so extraordinary a day, that her ability to walk so calmly through this one amazed her. But there it was; she felt much better than she would have thought possible.

And she knew why she did. It was not because of any affection she might have for Lizah, nor because of his wild talk of marriage the night before. That was now all as dreamlike as the incredible experience that had gone before it. She refused now even to think about what Lizah had said, or what promises he might make. All she knew was that the plan that had jumped fully fledged into her mind when she had opened her mouth in the morning room and demanded of her father her own small inheritance was all that now mattered to her.

She had decided then and there that whether he gave her the money or not, she was going to leave this house. Whether Freddy told tales about her or not, she was not going to remain here. No matter what happened, she was going to take hold of her own life and live it, for good or ill, on her own and not be beholden to, or concerned about, anyone else. She had had enough of being second to everybody, and often third or fourth. She would be first, central, the *only* one from now on.

She was going to accept Jessie Mendel's offer of a rented room in her house. She would go there and live with her and then, in due course, find herself paid employment. And there she would set about making her ridiculous fantasy of her own flat and her flower shop occupation come true.

Mildred Amberly, she told herself, Mildred Amberly, you are going to escape. *Really* escape.

16

'Well, I don't like it,' Lizah said again. 'That's the thing of it. I just don't like it.'

'I was not concerned with whether you would or would not when I decided to do it,' Mildred said equably. 'It was my own decision, after all.'

'But why? I told you we was to get married, that they'd come round to the idea and we'd get married, eventual. Why go off half cocked like this and run out? It's all so – '

'I told you why. Freddy – '

He seemed to swell in front of her eyes. 'That lump o' villainy! I'll have his blood for that. I'll go round there and I'll sort him out so he can't ever think of – '

'I've already told you, Lizah, that if you do anything of the sort I shall never speak to you again. And I mean it. The man is dreadful but that does not give you any right to attack him. It is much better simply to walk away from him. And anyway, it was not just because of him. There are other things – living there – it is all so – ' And she shrugged her shoulders, unable to put into words how she had felt that morning and how inevitable her action had been.

Remembering now she marvelled at how calm and collected she had been all day. She had gone downstairs and interviewed Cook to give her her daily orders – and even took the trouble to suggest that she cooked the meat a little longer tonight in order to avoid sending it to table as tough as last night's beef had been, although Cook's scowl showed what a waste of trouble that was – and then had gone about her normal day's activities as though nothing at all out of the ordinary was going on.

She did the flowers and helped Nanny Chewson prepare the little boys for their morning walk and then sat with Mama and stroked her aching brow until at last she had said she felt a little better, and then spent the afternoon sewing in the morning room as usual. But shortly before the tea tray was brought into the drawing room at half past four o'clock she slipped away to her room and, moving carefully and quietly, had packed her few clothes in a large Gladstone bag and then, at the time when she knew all the servants were safely ensconced in the kitchen taking their own tea, had fetched it downstairs and taken it out of the house and down into the area, to hide it behind the coal cellar door.

And there it had remained while she took tea with Mama and then helped put the little boys to bed and finally ate dinner with Mama and Claude and Basil at seven o'clock. Even if Papa had been there, she had thought as she sat and pretended to eat the execrable soup Cook had sent up, she would have been as comfortable, but she could not deny she was glad he was not. He had sent a message to say he was dining at his club tonight and the rest of the family clearly felt much happier in consequence. Certainly Claude and Basil were cheerful enough and talked to her and Mama a good deal instead of eating in surly silence as they usually did; and she had for a little while watched them and thought – perhaps after tonight I shall never see them again. Perhaps they will refuse ever to speak to me? But though that was a melancholy thought it did not at all distress her. She was going, at whatever cost. That was all that mattered.

And then the boys had made their excuses and left and Mama had drifted away to her bed and she had gone up to her room and sat there, waiting till the clocks struck the quarter before nine. And then had put on her pelisse, as offhandedly as if she were doing no more than going to the corner to post a letter, and gone downstairs and out of the house. She did not look back at any point except when she had closed the front door behind her; and then she took her door key and slipped it through the letter box. No turning back, now.

Her Gladstone bag was where she had left it, quite undisturbed, and she had picked it up and looked over her shoulder through the brightly lit window into the kitchen. Cook was sitting by the fire, her skirts pulled back to her knees and her boots up on the fender, her head thrown back on her rocking chair and fast asleep, and beside her Jane and Jenny and Mary sat and whispered to each other while at the table she could see Freddy with a black beer bottle beside him and a racing paper spread out in front of him, and for one mad moment considered rapping on the glass and waving a farewell. But then she smiled at herself, and went quickly up the area steps and along Leinster Terrace to their usual meeting place, to stand and wait for him, her bag at her feet and her hands tucked into the sleeves of her pelisse for warmth.

Now they sat facing each other at a small marble-topped table at a restaurant in Oxford Street, the Gladstone bag beneath the table between them as he tried to decide what to do next. He had brought her here to talk because she had ruined the evening, he had told her with an air of grievance. He had planned to take her to the Britannia tonight for the show and then to have a supper at the Warsaw restaurant in Brick Lane.

'Not fancy, but a real good place for a nosh up, and you don't 'arf look in need of it! But how can I take you there, when I don't know where you're goin' after that? I took it for granted you'd be staying with your folks until such time as we could get our plans made, but now you've gone and ruined it all – '

'I've ruined nothing,' she said, sitting with her head bent and watching herself stir her tea. 'I knew nothing of any plans you had made, did I? I knew only of what I had decided to do. And do it I shall. I shall find a room in a respectable hotel, since you say it is not possible to go to your sister tonight and – '

'I didn't say it wasn't possible to go to Jessie's tonight!' he said irritably. 'I never said any such thing. What I said was that it wasn't right to go there at all – '

'Why not? She invited me. I think she meant it. I didn't consider her the sort of person who says things on impulse and later regrets them.'

'She isn't. She – if she said it, she meant it. But it won't do, Millie, it really won't do!'

'Why not? You have not said why not. Only that you would prefer I did not. That is not enough of a reason.' He called me Millie, she thought then, and felt a little trickle of cold across her shoulders. He called me Millie.

'Because – oh, damn it, why do you have to be so pig-headed?' he snapped and threw himself back in his chair. 'It's one thing for me to tell them I'm to marry a shicksah from the West End, ain't it? It's another to say, "oh, yes, she's left her family, lives down here with Jessie" – can't you just see it? She'll go meshuggah, my mother, meshuggah!'

She looked at him now enquiringly, and he shook his head irritably. 'She won't put up with it,' he said flatly. 'She'll go mad, she will. I can talk her round in time, I swear to you. If you go on living at that house, if she knows you're rich and respectable. But let her get the notion that you're – '

'I am not rich nor ever have been,' she said and again bent her head to look at her tea cup. 'I told her that, as I recall, when we met.'

He waved that away. 'Not rich? Listen, she knows what rich is! It ain't so much havin' cash of your own to spend, like you think it is. It's living in a decent house, having servants, all that. And you're chucking all that away when it's the best card I got in my hand. Can't you see that?'

'Is it so essential to you that your mother agrees to our getting married?' She still did not lift her head.

'Important? Well, of course it is! How can't it be important? She's my mother, for Gawd's sake!'

'I do not care what my father says. I have not spoken to him on the matter, nor do I intend to. But if I did and he objected, it would make no difference. Not if I had decided for myself that it was what I wanted to do.' Now she did lift her eyes and looked at him very directly, her thick dark brows raised to sharp circumflexes and he looked at her uneasily and then dropped his own gaze.

'You don't understand,' he mumbled. 'How can you understand? Do your lot go and carry on like you was dead if you marries out o' your faith? Eh?'

'No,' she said. 'But the way they would behave would add up to the same thing. I have left my father's house and that means my reputation is destroyed and I shall never be able to return there, even if I want to. Which is very unlikely.' She allowed herself a thin smile. 'From now on, I might as well be dead to Papa for all the care he will have of me.'

'It's not the same thing,' he said again, and now he sounded sulky. 'All of 'em, my mother, my father, my sisters – they'd turn their backs on me. You got to see what that'd mean – '

'Your sister Jessie wouldn't,' she said softly.

'Jessie?' He looked up then. 'I'll bet she would. It's one thing to tell you to come and stop by her, though why the silly bitch said it I'll never understand, but it's another altogether to think o' me marryin' you. She wouldn't go for that. No Jewish family ever does – '

'But she did,' Mildred said. 'She sat there with me in the London Hospital and told me I would be good for you. She said she wanted me to marry you – '

He gaped at her, and then his own brows snapped down, hard. 'I don't believe you.'

'I have never lied to you yet,' she said as calmly as she could. The cold trickle between her shoulder blades had thickened and spread.

'Why should she say that? She knows how Ma is – and Poppa – he'd be as bad – and – '

'She said what your mother wanted, your father did. Or something of that sort.'

He made a face. 'She's right there. But I just don't – ' He shook his head. 'Well, all right. If she's on my side, that helps.' He began to brighten. 'Listen, Millie – ' and he reached for her hand but she took it from the table and set it on her lap beneath the marble top. 'Listen, doll, maybe it's not so bad as that. Maybe we can fix things. As long as my mother don't know you're with Jessie – '

Her temper, which had been simmering just below the surface, finally erupted. 'Is it not enough that you have already accused me of lying to you without now suggesting I should tell lies? I am to move in with your sister as long as I keep the fact a secret? Why should I? So I choose to leave my father's house for reasons of my own, and that makes me an – an unacceptable person in your family's eyes? I must put on a show of riches before they can be convinced that I am a suitable person to marry you? If that is how they think, then I must tell you I despise them. If their faith in God means so much that they grieve over a child who leaves it to marry, as you say they do, how can their grief be assuaged by the appearance of riches? Every word you say makes me – '

'Hey, hey!' He was staring at her, amazed. 'What are you goin' on about? Don't you understand nothing? It ain't to do with the faith as such. I mean, it ain't to do with religion! At least, not properly – oh, how do I explain to someone who ain't a luntsman what it's all about – '

'It would help if you did not use words I do not comprehend,' she said icily.

'That's all part of it!' he said. 'Can't you see that? Listen, a luntsman – it means someone from the same land as you, someone of your own kind. You don't have no understanding of what it is to be one of us, do you? You and your sort, you've lived in this country for ever – but my lot – we've been on the run for ever. We've been spat on for being Jews, we've been murdered and robbed and raped and always we've run to somewhere new, somewhere we can try again. And every time it gets bad again – the people get jealous if we do well, they hate us if we don't, we can't do nothing right. Strangers never can. So we run. My parents ran here when times started to be bad in Poland and Russia for Jews. It's worse now, and people are coming in their thousands, thousands and thousands – but my parents, they saw the trouble brewing and they got out among the first. So, they come here, they don't speak a word of English, but they learn. They learn fast. They got nothing, but they got each other and the people who came from the same village they did. Their luntsmen. And they leaned on each other, right? They needed each other to lean on, strangers in a strange land and all that! My father – he don't care about God, for Gawd's sake! I've heard him *curse* God – and anyway, I don't think he believes he exists. But he goes to the synagogue all the same and he sticks with his own kind and he says his prayers. But it's not because of what he believes! It's because of what we was. *Strangers*. And if we stop caring about each other, and sticking close together, we're in dead trouble. That's the thing of it. That's why it matters people stay inside the faith. It ain't the faith itself, you understand. It's the staying inside that's important.'

She sat and watched him as much as she listened to him. His whole body was animated and excited, not just his face, as he lifted his hands and used them to punctuate his speech, and his face was alight with the drama of what he was telling her and for the first time since she had been with him this evening she felt again the wave of warmth and affection he could create in her, and of which she had been so very aware last night.

He stopped at last and looked at her appealingly and she nodded. 'I see,' she said. 'Yes, I see. I'm sorry if I – I did not wilfully misunderstand.'

'I know you didn't,' and again he reached for her hand, and this time she let him take it. 'It isn't that I don't love you, Mildred. I do love you, very very much. You know that, don't you? It's just that it's all so complicated – ' And now his voice drifted away and he looked at her and his eyes glistened with emotion and she felt an odd sensation and then realized it was embarrassment. 'Mildred, do you love me?'

She blinked at the directness of the question. 'I – that's an odd thing to ask, considering – I mean, last night – '

He waved a dismissive hand. 'Never mind last night. I mean, it was great and all that, but it was only sex, wasn't it? It's love I'm talking about. I've told you I love you but you've never said it to me, have you?'

She sat and thought, looking at him, scanning his face as though she were taking an inventory. Love him? She wasn't sure what he meant. She had been obsessed with him, that was for certain. For weeks she had thought of no one else. But was that love? And she had been excited by him. Last night's experience had been extraordinary, not so much because of how he had behaved as because of how she had been. She had caught fire and been as eager as he was. Was that love? And now she had finally left her home to come to him. Was *that* love?

'It's not that – ' she heard herself say and saw his face harden and added hastily, 'I was trying to think – Was it because I loved you that I left my home? But it wasn't that. I had to do it. Even if you hadn't been there I would have had to go, maybe not so soon, but it would have happened. So it isn't that – '

'You haven't said yet whether you do love me or not.'

'I don't know!' she said. 'What do I know about love? I said I'd marry you, didn't I? Isn't that enough?'

'No,' he said. 'It isn't. Because getting married won't be so easy. I've tried to make you see that. It's going to be even harder, now you've walked out. I suppose you couldn't just sort of sneak back so that no one knew you'd gone?'

'I've left my key behind,' she said flatly. 'And I do not wish to return. Whether I marry you or not, I've left.'

'I shouldn't have said that,' he said after a moment. 'Sorry.'

'No, you shouldn't.' She looked down at the table again, at the half-cold cup of tea and pushed her chair back. 'I must leave now if I'm to find a respectable hotel tonight. If I leave it too late I shall be turned away as being of dubious character.' She stopped then. 'That is something I shall have to get used to, no doubt, but I need not make it more difficult for myself than I must. So I must leave now – '

'Oh, don't be so daft!' he said and leaned over and held on to her arm so that she could not stand up. 'I'll pay this bill and we'll be on our way East. I'll take you to Jessie's if you insist. We'll sort out when we get there what you're goin' to do, and how I shall look after you and – '

'I do not need you to look after me. I shall take care of myself.'

'Oh, be your age, Millie! You'll be living in the East End now! You don't think you can walk around the streets there as comfortable as you was here, up West, do you? It's rough and tough in our parts. You've never had no trouble there on account of I've always been with you, but believe me, if you went out on your own you'd soon see what it was all about. So we have to work out when I can see you and take you around. Otherwise you'll have to stay indoors with Jessie – and – '

'She said I could work with her. As a – a finisher, I think she said.'

He stared at her and then burst into laughter so loud that people at adjoining tables turned to look at him. 'A finisher? You? In Joe Vinosky's sweatshop? I should cocoa! Jessie's got to be crazy even to think it. Ten, eleven hours a day over the bench, five of 'em working in a space no bigger'n a couple of graves, and no air and no chance to catch your breath – or she's crazy! She's forgotten how it used to be when she started. It's all right for her, she's hardened to it, but you wouldn't last five minutes. And anyway, I won't have you working for Joe Vinosky, and as for my sister Rae – she'd murder you and have you on toast for breakfast without no butter, believe me. She's a real slave-driver, that one. Jessie can handle her, but you – you'd be mincemeat to her.'

'Then I'll find other employment,' she said as sturdily as she could, but it was not easy to be as brave as she sounded. To work ten or eleven hours a day in a sweatshop did sound more than she could deal with and a long way from her flower shop idea. 'Perhaps I can come back here during the day to work, in a shop perhaps or – '

'No!' he said. 'No girl o' mine has to work. I'll see to it you're all right. You stay at Jessie's all day, and in the evenings, when I can get away, I'll take you out. It'll be boring, I dare say, but you'll be all right that way. As long as you've got me to look after you, you'll come to no harm.'

'No,' she said. 'I don't want it that way. I want to find employment.'

'Millie, don't be so stubborn – '

'If you are to be as tiresome as this about it, then I shall not go to your sister. I shall do as I said and seek a hotel and then a set of rooms somewhere and find myself work to pay my way. I – ' She swallowed hard. 'I dare say you mean kindly, wishing to take care of me as you say, and I know it is how it should be for women. But I have been looked after all my life and it has been dreadful – quite dreadful. I have no wish ever to be looked after by a man again. Oh, don't look like that! I want us to be – I mean, I do want to marry you. I don't know what love is, or whatever it is that is in me that makes me want to marry you, but I will not be looked after by you. I must take care of myself.'

He shook his head. 'But you can't say that. Not and be *married*, Millie!'

'Why not?'

'Being married to someone means you take care of 'em – '

'Then why cannot I take care of you?'

'Ah, but you will! You'll keep house and cook and clean up and all that, the way women do, and when we have kids, you'll have them to run after an' all. But you got to have me to earn the money for it all, haven't you?'

'I don't see why,' she said, feeling her obstinacy rising in her. 'I believe I can earn my own living. I intend to try. And anyway, you know yourself that we cannot be married so quickly. You have to persuade your mother and the rest of the family. Or are you willing to marry me without their consent, after all?'

He was silent and she lifted her brows at him. 'You see?' she said and she made it as gentle as she could. 'I will have to take care of myself, won't I? And the sooner I begin, the better.'

17

Jessie's house, Mildred decided, was delightful. It was small, very small, with the narrowest of passageways that led into a tiny kitchen and an even tinier scullery, and at one side of it a little parlour, and two bedrooms above. There was a tap in the scullery that brought water right into the house – no outside pump for Jessie – and there were gaslights in every room, even in the bedrooms, as Jessie pointed out with some pride.

'Lots o' the other houses down here, they got gas in the kitchen and the parlour, but that's it. Upstairs it's oil lamps and candles, and that means a lot o' work. But I made this place real comfortable, didn't I? You like it?'

'I like it very much,' Mildred said fervently and stood in the doorway of the room into which Jessie had shown her. It was the small back bedroom of the house and it contained a neat bed, with a red blanket as a counterpane and a very plump pillow at the head, a wash stand and a wardrobe, as well as a small table and a wicker armchair beside the small fireplace. The floor was covered in cheerful red linoleum and there was a strip of bright blue and green carpet on the hearth and at the side of the bed. The cotton curtains at the little window were red too, and the whole room glowed with jollity.

Mildred conjured up a memory of her room at Leinster Terrace, in all its pallor; the floor had been carpeted all over, it was true, but in a dismal shade of light brown, and the bed had been higher and clearly better sprung than this one, but shrouded in a dull cream damask, and the window had been curtained more lavishly, but in the most ugly of yellowish Nottingham lace. It had been much more costly and a great deal larger than this little box of a room, but here she saw peace and contentment and, above all, cheerfulness.

'It'll be a pleasure to see it used, to tell you the truth,' Jessie said. 'I fixed it up like a bedroom see, when we moved in, not wanting it to be empty like, but I had it in my mind that one day we'd use it for a kid. But there, it never happened – ' And she looked bleak for a moment and Mildred glanced at her and impulsively put out one hand and set it on the other woman's arm.

'Well, I dare say you'll marry again,' she said. 'I mean – ' She reddened then, embarrassed at her own temerity. 'You said to me that night at the hospital that you – ah – had – that someone was paying you some attention – '

'Oh, him!' Jessie said cheerfully. 'Gave him the push weeks ago. Got too big for his boots, he did. Thought he was entitled to a bit more than what he was getting. It's one thing to share a woman's bed from time to time, quite another to think that gives him any rights in her purse. So he got his marching orders fast.'

She leaned down and took the Gladstone bag from Mildred's hand and walked past her into the bedroom to drop the bag on the bed. 'I'll light a fire for you in a minute,' she said. 'The coal's down the back – you can fill a scuttle any time you like.' She looked at her then and her face was smooth and expressionless. 'About fellas – my brother – I thought you'd given him his marching orders. That night at the hospital you didn't seem best disposed towards him. And now he's brought you here.'

Mildred followed her into the room. 'I did try to stop seeing him,' she said, and she sat down on the bed and Jessie sat down beside her. 'I tried very hard. But it was impossible – ' She contemplated her hands on her lap. 'It might have been easier if I'd had other things to do. But as it was – ' She looked up at Jessie. 'As it was I could think of no one else. So – ' She shrugged. 'It's a long tale with which I won't worry you, but here I am – '

She wanted, very much, to tell her everything. Of the way it had been in the Park and how she had felt about what Lizah had done with and to her. She felt the need to pour it all out in words and also felt sure it would be safe to do so. This woman in the red dress – a different style gown to the one she had been wearing when they first met, but still in the same jolly colour – was so warm and friendly and inviting that telling her everything would be very easy and comforting. And she looked at her again, opening her mouth to speak, and then closed her lips. Friendly and amusing though she looked she was, after all, Lizah's sister. It would not be right to gossip to her of his doings.

'Well,' Jessie said after a moment, clearly aware that she had meant to say more but had had second thoughts, but choosing to be diplomatic about it. 'Well, then, here you are! And welcome too. Now, come on down, and I'll make you a bite of something and then we can talk – '

'You must be tired,' Mildred objected. 'I mean, you have to go to work in the morning – '

'I do and all!' Jessie said and moved to the fireplace. 'But I can work on as little sleep as you'd never believe. Famous for it, I am. And I want to sort all this out before I go to my bed. Now, I'll set a match to the fire to warm the room for you – '

'It's all right,' Mildred said. 'I don't want to put you to any trouble making fires – '

'I shan't after tonight!' Jessie said as the paper caught at the touch of the vesta she had set to it, and then the sticks began to crackle gaily. 'I won't run after you like you've been used to, and never think it. No servants here, is there? So you clean your own room and set your own fire and clear the grate and that. Do you know how?'

'I've seen it done often enough,' Mildred said.

''T'isn't the same as doing it,' Jessie said sapiently. 'But you'll find out. Trial and error, it's the only way. Come on then. Leave this to burn up nice and we'll go and see Lizah off the premises.'

Mildred followed her down the narrow stairway, hearing her heels clatter on the bright linoleum that covered the centre of the treads, and found herself yawning. It must be late, she thought a little fuzzily. I didn't meet Lizah till nine o'clock. Must be nearly midnight –

But neither Lizah nor Jessie seemed at all sleepy. Lizah was sitting at the table in the middle of the small kitchen when they reached it, and he looked up anxiously as they came in. 'All right, is it?' he said to Mildred. 'You and her going to get on all right?'

'Of course!' she said and smiled at Jessie. 'I told you, it was Jessie's idea I come here. That was why – '

'And we ain't like you lot,' Jessie said. 'Men, always fighting and arguing among themselves. Women've got more sense. We'll shake along nice, we will. Eh, Millie?' And she grinned at Mildred over her shoulder as she busied herself with the kettle on the range.

There was no point in trying to stop people using the diminutive of her name, Mildred decided, and looked around the room instead of protesting. It was as red as her bedroom, with curtains and cushions and tablecloth all in what was clearly Jessie's favourite tint and it made the whole room feel warm and a little stuffy and infinitely safe and comfortable. She sat down on the chair that was on the other side of the table to Lizah and managed to stifle another yawn. 'Yes, I'm sure we shall,' she said.

'Only one thing to settle,' Jessie said and came and plonked a large brown tea pot in the middle of the table. 'Money. I got to have my rent, see. Make it all shipshape and right, eh?'

'Of course – ' Mildred began but Lizah overrode her. 'How much d'you want for the room, Jessie?'

'Five shillings,' Jessie said, and slid her eyes sideways at Lizah, and then grinned as she saw the expression on his face. 'Oh, all right. I thought it was worth a try, eh? Three bob I had in mind. Sound fair enough to you, Mildred?'

'It sounds – ' Mildred began but again Lizah broke in.

'One and six,' he said.

'Two and nine, and I'm doing myself down,' Jessie said promptly.

'One and nine and that's robbery.'

'What do you take me for? A charity queen? I'll settle at two and six and that's my last shout.'

'Make it two bob and you've got yourself a deal.'

'You're on,' she said cheerfully and stood up and went to the scullery to fetch a plate. 'There you are, Mildred. As nice a room as you'll find anywhere in these parts, for a very fair rent, coals thrown in, except if it gets real cold and you burns a lot. Then it'll be a penny a scuttle, for every one you have over six in a week. Fair enough?'

'Er, yes – ' Mildred was dazed and it showed. 'I have no idea what sort of costs there are and – '

'How much you got, Mildred?' Jessie sat down with a little thump and looked at her, her face glowing pink in the light from the gas mantle which hissed and plopped cosily over-head. 'I ain't being nosy, mind, but you've got to think ahead. I always say that. That's why I've got this place, even though my old man, rest his wicked old soul, left me with so many debts. I count every penny and make 'em all work. And unless you got a lot of pennies, you're going to have to get some work to do.'

'She's not working for Rae and Joe Vinosky,' Lizah said. 'I'll tell you that flat for a start. Can you see her in those bleedin' workshops? I ask you, can you?'

Jessie looked at her judiciously. 'Mmm – well, no,' she said at length. 'No, I can't say as I can.'

'Then we'll have to think of something else – '

'I could fetch her home some work to do here. Joe uses outside finishers a lot. If I tell him I want more work at home he'll let me have it. And I'll get the best rates from him. Let him know someone else is going to do it and he'll screw the rate down to nothing. But – yeah, that'll do nicely. She could sit here, cosy as you like, and do felling and a few buttonholes – can you buttonhole, Millie? No? It don't matter. As long as you don't have thumbs where you ought to have fingers, I'll teach you. You look nimble enough – what do you say, Lizah? Let her work here and then there's no trouble with Joe and Rae and no one to tell Momma nothing until we choose to talk to her and – '

'Will you both stop talking about me as though I weren't here!' Mildred managed to shout her down at last. 'I would like to make some decisions on the matter for myself, you know! I left my father's house because I had no chance to think or do for myself and now I have you two doing the same thing to me! Now, I will decide for myself the rent I should pay – ' And she looked very firmly at Jessie. 'And the sum you first mentioned sounds fair to me, more than fair. I will gladly pay you five shillings for that room and for the heating and – '

Jessie stared at her and then slowly grinned. 'Bless you, girl, you're a right plucked 'un! Don't be daft! Two bob's a very fair rent for a room like that. There're people letting 'em out down this street for half that, so I've no complaints at two bob. But you never say right out what you want, do you? You've got to bait a bit – bargain, see?' Mildred looked puzzled. 'There's right and wrong ways of doing things and baiting is the right way to settle prices. Believe me, you're paying a fair amount – '

'Anyway, you won't be paying it,' Lizah said loudly, 'I shall.'

Mildred's face flamed as red as the tablecloth. 'You are doing nothing of the sort!' she snapped. 'I have sufficient funds of my own to pay my way until I find an occupation that will earn me sufficient for my later needs. There is no need for you – '

'Need don't come into it,' Lizah said. 'It's what I want to do.'

'It is not.' Mildred's voice was low now. 'It is what *I* want to do that matters.'

'But I say as I *want* to pay!' He sounded bewildered now. 'Why are you so difficult, Millie? All I want to do is what's right and – '

She closed her eyes. 'Do not call me Millie,' she said very quietly. 'And I shall pay my own way. I wish to hear no more about it.'

'Shut up, Lizah.' Jessie's voice made Mildred snap her eyes open. 'Leave her be. She wants to pay her own way? Good luck to her. You spend your whack taking her out and about a bit. It's going to be damn dull sitting here on her own, day after day, working. Let her earn for herself if she wants, and keep herself. If that plan suits you, Millie – Mildred?'

Mildred looked across the table at her and the smile on Jessie's face widened and she closed one dancing dark eye in a cheerful wink, and Mildred's spirits, which had begun to spiral downwards, took an upwards turn.

'It's hard to say,' she said as honestly as she could, feeling she could be as honest as she liked with this woman. For the first time since this whole confusing business with Lizah had started she began to feel less frightened, less aware of struggling on her own in a hostile and complicated world. This woman could be the real friend she had always so much wanted. 'I've never worked for money, you see. I'm approaching thirty and never had to think about such matters. I still hope to persuade my father – or his lawyers if need be – that I have a right to the money my mother left me, but otherwise I have never had any dealings with money. If you say I will be able to earn enough at such work to keep myself, why, I will happily do it. I can sew, heaven knows. All the sewing at

Leinster Terrace had been done by me for many years – ' Her face split in a sudden happy smile. 'I cannot imagine how they will go on now I am no longer there. Nanny Chewson will have to do it all, sheets and table linen and all as well as the children's clothes, for it is certain Mama will not!'

Jessie nodded. 'Then you can do the work. I'll help you, so don't you fret. And when we've sent Lizah on his way, we can settle down to a real cosy prose and see what's what. On your way, Lizah. Your room'll be more welcome than your company – you can come back to see her tomorrow – '

She got to her feet. 'I'll go upstairs and make sure it's all to rights for you, Mildred,' she said diplomatically. 'Then Lizah can say his good nights and be on his way – ' And she went out of the room and they heard her go clumping up the stairs and could hear her whistling loudly as she moved about in the little room overhead.

There was a silence between them and then Lizah said stiffly, 'You didn't have to take me up so sharp about the rent. I only wanted to help.'

'I'm sure you did. But you have to understand that help is only acceptable if – if it is necessary. I am not so useless that I have to be petted like a child. I am able to pay my own way, and I insist that I shall do so. You have no responsibility for me – '

'I reckon I have,' he said softly. 'After last night.'

She was silent for a long time, and all that could be heard in the small room was the plopping of the gas and, above stairs, Jessie's whistling. 'I – what happened last night was something quite – it has nothing to do with anything that is happening now,' she said carefully. 'Do you understand me? I do not wish you to think that because you did what you did that you have any need to feel responsible for me.' She went a little pink. 'I believe there are names for women who regard a man as indebted to them if they share such activities.'

He laughed then, a soft amused little sound that made her feel better, for it sounded much more like the old Lizah, the one with whom she had spent so many amusing, outrageous evenings. 'You, a brass? Don't make me laugh! As if anyone would ever think such a thing!'

'Yet you offered to pay my rent,' she flared at him and then looked away.

'That was out of friendship,' he said stiffly and got to his feet. 'Nothing more. And if you suggests otherwise then you do me a downright insult.'

She looked up at him and tried to see the expression on his face, but it was not easy for, now he was out of the pool of light thrown by the gas mantle, he was in the shadows. 'As long as it was not meant that way –' she said, knowing there was doubt in her voice.

'It wasn't.'

'Then I accept that. I just wanted it understood that I am independent,' she said and also stood up.

'Bloody independent,' she heard him mutter in a half whisper and then he said more loudly, 'Yes. Independent. I get the message. Listen, I got to go now. You'll be all right?'

'I think I shall be very much all right,' she said and lifted her head as Jessie's moving footsteps came out on to the upstairs landing and down the staircase. 'Your sister will be an excellent companion, I am sure.'

'She's all right,' he said and turned for the door as Jessie came in. 'I'm going, Jess. You know where I am if you want me. Ruby'll always find me for you.'

'Why should I want you?' she cried jovially and winked again at Mildred. 'Me and Mildred here, we'll get on fine without you. On your way, then,' and she leaned across and gave him a hearty hug and beat him across the back and urged him towards the front door.

He looked back at Mildred as he reached the kitchen door. 'I'll see you then,' he said and she nodded, but said nothing and then he was gone, Jessie shooing him along for all the world as though he were a recalcitrant child.

'Well!' she said when at length she came back into the room and sat herself down firmly at the table. 'Now we can drink our tea. It's a bit stewed, I dare say, but none the worse for that. Sit you down, then, Mildred, and we'll talk easy about things. We'll do nicely, you and me. And sooner or later, you'll sort out how you want it to be with Lizah.'

She cocked a sharp little glance at Mildred as she passed her a large cup of very dark tea. 'I know how it is – you don't know what you want with him, do you? Now you want him, now you don't – '

Mildred positively gaped at her. 'How do you know that? I mean, I didn't say anything about – '

'Oh, men!' said Jessie and set her elbows firmly on the table, holding her cup between her capable hands in front of her mouth and watching Mildred, bright-eyed, over the rim. 'They has that effect on all of us. One minute we wants them and only them, can't so much as breathe without 'em, the next it's to buggery with the lot, and leave me alone, who needs 'em? We've all been through it.'

'Oh!' Mildred said blankly, not knowing what else to say. She had indeed been feeling precisely that, even if she would not herself have couched it in quite such terms, and as she thought now about Jessie's words she felt a warm glow begin to develop inside her, and welcomed it. It was a good feeling to have a friend like Jessie Mendel. A real friend, at last.

'Listen, now. You tell me how much money you got and then we'll plan accordingly, all right? I'll work out how much work you need to do to keep yourself and we'll sort that all out tomorrow. But right now, a nice cuppa and away to bed. Here you are, then, Mildred. Welcome to Jubilee Street! It's a pleasure to see you here!' And she raised her cup at Mildred who lifted her own in response.

A toast drunk in tea at a kitchen table, she found herself thinking absurdly. How much more suitable could it be? And she nodded and repeated, 'Jubilee Street – Welcome to Jubilee Street,' as she took her new home into her life.

18

It was amazing how rapidly she settled to that new life. Within a week she felt as though she had been living there for years, and Leinster Terrace and all its doings seemed remote and unreal.

But not so unreal that she did not think about how to deal with what she had left behind there. She wrote a letter on her first day in Jessie's house, addressing it, after much thought, to her stepmother. It would be easier to express her contrition for any distress she might be causing; to offer anything which smacked in the least of an apology to her father was out of the question.

So she told her stepmother that she had felt she could no longer continue to live in a house where her presence was, she knew, unwanted. 'My father,' she wrote, 'has made it abundantly clear that I am a burden upon him, and I feel this to be an insupportable position in which to find myself. I shall, therefore, earn my own living in the future. I do, of course, wish to you and my stepbrothers every future happiness, and trust that you will continue in good health. I would be grateful if you could convey to my brothers my regret that I was unable to bid them farewell. I suspected that any attempt to leave in a more ceremonious manner would have caused considerable recriminations, which I was anxious to avoid. I would also be grateful if you would inform my father that it is my intention to seek through the law the full use of my mother's legacy to me.

I do not append my address, preferring to avoid any confrontations in future. Letters sent to the General Post Office in Old Street will reach me. Yrs in affection, Mildred Coulter Amberly.' And she signed it so even though she knew that including her dead mother's surname in her own was in effect an insult, a reminder to her stepmother that she was but a second wife.

After careful thought, she then wrote another letter, this time to her father's solicitor in Finsbury Pavement. She had never used the services of a man of law in her own right, and knew no other way to seek access to her legacy. Hitherto she had not worried unduly about it. It was just something that existed somewhere in a shadowy background and would no doubt come to her when the time was ripe. She had never before had any real need of money and so had never concerned herself about it.

But now all was different. She needed the money very much indeed. She and Jessie had worked out that if she did not earn, her forty-four pounds would last her for at least a year, for her needs were small.

'And I'm a fair manager,' Jessie had said cheerfully. 'You can eat with me, on account of feedin' two works out as cheap as feedin' one sometimes. It's amazing what I can do with a piece of soup meat and a pennorth of pot herbs. A dinner fit for a king, that is. You can live on ten bob a week here, easy. And when you do start working, you can earn as much as that in a week easy, if you put your mind and needle to it. There are people living on that and feedin' a couple of kids 'n' all in these parts. So you're rich.'

But not so rich that she felt she could ignore her legacy. She wanted to earn money for herself – that was becoming an ever more important factor in planning for her future – but she also wanted to feel safe. And that meant saving as much of her money as she could, to keep in store for the time when she could no longer work. She was not sure when or how that might be; she had just a hazy vision of herself in a state of elderly uselessness and wanted to prepare against that day.

This was what she told the lawyer, expressing herself in direct and simple terms.

'I need the money my mother left for me,' she wrote. 'And I need it now. I am now in my thirtieth year, having recently celebrated a birthday, and I believe myself fit to take control of my own property without my father's consent or control and without the supervision of a husband. I therefore ask you to investigate the provisions of my mother's will and tell me whether I may have this money, and when. Letters sent to me care of Old Street Post Office will find me – '

And then she set about thinking of work. Despite Lizah's objections, Jessie took her on the third day after she came to live in her house to see the workshop where she spent her days, leaving her little house at seven in the morning and returning any time after six at night, clearly tired but still with some of her native energy in her.

'It's not so bad,' she told Mildred cheerfully as they walked through the long street past the flat-fronted little houses northwards towards Clark Street. 'The others talk and laugh a bit and it's friendly enough. And at least he keeps the place dry and clean. There are shops I know where the girls have rats runnin' over their feet while they work, and they have to hang their dinner bags on the wall to stop the buggers getting at their food before they do. Old Joe knows better'n that, at least – '

But not much better, Mildred thought in dismay as she stood in the doorway of the workshop and looked around. It was on the third floor of a house that abutted a school on the corner of Clark Street, and they could hear the children shrieking outside in the playground as they climbed the rickety wooden stairs. It was still only a little after seven, but the children, some of them very small, were already there, for their parents, as Jessie had explained to her, left them there on their way to their work.

'Nowhere else for them to go,' she gasped as they reached the end of the last flight of stairs. 'They're safe there. Noisy little devils, ain't they?'

But it wasn't the noise of the children, shrill though they were, that Mildred found disturbing. It was the smells which assaulted her from all sides. The stairs reeked of cats and dirt, and as they passed the second floor, of a particular cloying sweetness and Jessie had laughed when she had seen her wrinkle her nose.

'Old man there, Jack Cohen, makes coconut ice, sells it down the Lane,' she said. 'Tastes better'n it smells, thank God – Come on, here we are – '

The workshop was the most tightly packed room Mildred had ever seen. Overhead were skylights so grimy that little light filtered through, and gaslights were hissing with great naked flames to illuminate the work benches, of which there were three. On the far side was a bank of whirring sewing machines over which grey-faced men were bending, pushing heavy pieces of cloth through as the bobbins in front of them bounced and jumped with the speed of the treadles which each worker was frantically pedalling. On each side of the three benches women sat, barely able to see each other over the masses of garments that were piled in front of them, and all had their shoulders hunched and their heads down as they watched their fingers fly through the fabric, as behind them a great pressing machine hissed and fussed out great gouts of steam as the man who operated it disappeared and reappeared in the mist like some horrid ghost in a pantomime. But there was nothing pantomimic about all this; it was very serious and very real indeed, Mildred thought as she smelled the acrid reek of damp cloth and tailor's soap and chalk and, above all, human sweat. And felt sick.

Not that the workers seemed to object. They were chattering at the tops of their voices, laughing a good deal too, and as Jessie came in there were cries of welcome and banter that she replied to with great aplomb, and Mildred lingered at the door watching her and thought – I wish I was like that. Able to look at people and laugh and just be happy – but I'll always be what I am. Quiet and dull and plain –

'So Joe and Rae ain't here today!' One of the women on the nearest bench called. 'So you think you can play games, sleep late, come sauntering in here like a bleedin' duchess, already! Listen, Jessie, misbocher to the guv'nor you may be, but you're also a worker here, and I'm in charge right now. So what's in it for me I shouldn't tell Joe the time you comes to work, eh?'

'A frosk in pisk,' Jessie said at once and everyone laughed.

'Listen Jessela, the day you hit *me* in the face'll be the day you turn up your toes for good,' the woman said, but without rancour. 'So, who's the mouse at the door, already? You getting so fancy schmancy you got yourself a maid?'

'This is my friend. Just come to live down here. From over the other side o' London – ' Jessie said, and waved her hand vaguely at Mildred, who stepped forward nervously. 'Just visiting, see, a friend. No more'n that – '

Mildred felt eyes on her and knew she was being looked over as critically as she ever had been in her father's drawing room and she felt her face fall into the same sullen lines it had been used to under those circumstances, and someone called, 'So smile already! We don't bite!' and almost against her will, she felt her lips lift. These people are really rather agreeable, she thought, surprised. They're not staring to be critical or to judge me. It's just that they're interested –

'Good morning,' she said, and bobbed her head and one or two called back, 'Good morning!' and then returned to their work. Clearly there was little time to waste in this place and soon she felt that they had lost interest in her, and she could just watch and listen as they went on with their own chatter, paying her no attention at all.

The garments they were making were men's overcoats, thick in cloth and richly lined in satin and she watched as the women, with expert flicks of wrists that must have been as strong as iron, turned the sewn coats briskly from side to side as they stitched in the satin linings, whipping their needles along at an incredible pace. Some of them were sewing buttonholes, setting stitches so close together it seemed to Mildred that it must take hours to make just one hole, yet they grew beneath those nimble fingers at an incredible rate and she thought – I can't do this sort of work! I can smock a child's nightgown, sew a few seams, but this? For hour after hour? I would never survive it –

But Jessie came towards her with a parcel, dragging it in front of her with both hands. 'Here you are,' she said quietly. 'Can you get back with this? Don't try to work on it till I get home. I'll show you how – they're tricks to the work, it ain't as tough as it looks, believe you me.' And Mildred took the parcel, and almost reeled, it was so heavy, and with one last grin from Jessie to sustain her, and a nod from the women on the nearest bench, escaped into the odorous hallway to start her journey back to Jubilee Street.

'I'll see you about seven,' Jessie called after her. 'Don't worry about supper. I'll bring a couple o' pieces fish 'n' 'taters from Corb's over in Whitechapel. Just make sure the kettle's on the hob – ' And Mildred nodded and dragged her parcel down the stairs and out into the street, grateful for the fresh air.

It took her a good deal of time to get back to the house. The parcel was so heavy that the rough string that tied it cut into her hands and she had to stop and rest it every little while. But that didn't matter, for it gave her the chance to look about her.

At first she had been alarmed by the streets of the East End. Her own part of London, quiet, restrained, respectable, with passers-by neat and busy and politely behaved, could have been on another planet, let alone in another country. Here the streets buzzed with life and busyness. There were stalls on every corner, some selling fruits and vegetables, great piles of earthy potatoes and golden onions and glowing carrots jostling the bright oranges and, occasionally, greenish bananas, and others piled high with old clothes and boots. There were men selling papers and women selling sweets from grubby trays and men with cats' meat slices threaded on long spears and okey-pokey sellers with their pink and white confections and pitch and toss players, all huggermugger in the greasy streets, filling them with noise and life and excitement. There seemed to be a pub on every corner and as she reached each one, she drew back into herself a little, alarmed by the smell of gin and beer, even at this hour of the morning, and very aware of the reeling noisy people who clustered round the doors like bees at a hive. But they paid her no attention and she was able to slip by safely enough. Indeed, no one paid her any attention at any time. It was as though she had been part of this street furniture herself for all her life, so easily did she fit into it, and she was grateful for that.

It was not so easy to slip into the work that Jessie had provided for her. After that first evening when Jessie sat with her and showed her how to fit the linings into the coats and how to make the special long felling stitches that held them there she spent her days at it, but it was agony for the first few. Her wrists ached abominably and her fingers stung with the many injuries she did them with the sharp needles, and became rough and sore, so rough that even touching her own skin made her jump with pain. Jessie showed her how to rub her fingertips with soap before starting to sew, so that she had some protection, and also how the soap film made the work slide more easily through her hands, and at night she rubbed them with lanolin, and at last, it got easier.

By the end of her first month she was putting the linings in ten coats a day, which was half the output of the experienced people working at Clark Street, but she was content enough. Joe Vinosky, who had been told by an expressionless Jessie that she was doing the extra work herself, in the evenings, to get herself a bit of extra cash, paid the fully experienced rate of tuppence a coat. 'If he knows it's you, ducks, and you a starter, he'd only give you a penny a coat, the tight-fisted old devil. So keep quiet about it and you'll do fine.'

And to Mildred's delight she did do fine. Each week Jessie brought home her wages of eight shillings and fourpence, and Mildred would at once give her tenpence, which was her payment to Jessie for the effort she made fetching and carrying for her.

'It isn't right you should do all that dragging, to help me, and not get paid for it. I have to give you something for it,' she had insisted, and they had settled on the rate of a penny per parcel and both had been content with that. Then Mildred handed over her rent of two shillings and added another two shillings for her food, for it was agreed they would share their cooking costs as a matter of commonsense and economy. That left her three shillings and sixpence each week, and on that she felt rich. She could save it and add to her other little store of money and when she worked out that she could grow that to a magnificent fifty-three pounds by the end of her first year of independent living, she was elated, as excited as if she had been given a small fortune.

When she told Jessie proudly of how well she had organized her finances Jessie made a face.

'You don't want to get too worried over it, ducks,' she said. 'You got to do some livin' too. I mean, I'm all for saving for a rainy day, but what about spendin' for the sunny ones? Clothes, now – ' And she smoothed down her newest gown, which this time was in a rich raspberry velvet lavishly draped over the hips and so tight at the waist that it showed off her undoubtedly magnificent bust to great effect. 'You want to get yourself a couple o' nice things to go out with Lizah in. It was different when you was stuck up West, but now you're one of us, he'll expect you to look good – '

'I'm not spending money on clothes,' Mildred said shortly. 'I have enough that is serviceable and I can easily make another gown cheaply if I need one. I have no wish to waste my money so.'

'Well, that's up to you, o' course,' Jessie said taking obvious delight in her own appearance as she primped in the mirror over her fireplace, for they were sitting in the kitchen as usual. 'But you still don't want to get too excited about savings. Things can go wrong. There can be slack times when the work just ain't there to let you earn the money. Or you can get ill – '

'I'm never ill,' Mildred said stoutly. 'I have an excellent constitution. So you will see, by the end of my first year I shall have saved enough to bring my total to fifty-three pounds and maybe more. I shall always make sure I have enough. I will not waste a penny, not even if I am able to get my legacy from my mother. I still have great hopes of that – and when I have it, oh, Jessie, you will see what I shall do! I have such plans!'

'Plans with Lizah?' Jessie said, cocking a sharp little glance at her through the mirror.

'I don't know,' Mildred had said and reddened. 'It's not – I mean, I'm independent now. I only make plans for myself – '

And Jessie had grinned at her knowingly and made another of her interminable pots of tea and said no more. But Mildred knew she was still thinking of Lizah and making plans for her with her brother, but she refused even to think about that.

Not that she never thought about Lizah. He came often and sat in the kitchen to talk to her, trying to persuade her to go out as they had been used to do, but she was less willing to do that nowadays. The little kitchen and her bedroom upstairs had become very dear and comfortable to her, hot and stuffy though it became as April and May gave way to blazing June, and she felt so tired after a day's sewing that she wanted nothing more than to stay put, her feet up on the fender and a cup of tea at her side as she drowsed through the evening. She was content and settled in a way she would not have thought possible only a few weeks ago.

At first Lizah complained about her unadventurous ways and tried to persuade her to change her mind, but as she showed herself more and more unwilling to go out he became less and less eager for her company, so that by the middle of June he came to visit no more than once or twice a week, which made Jessie frown a little, but pleased Mildred well enough. She felt more and more tired, less and less interested in dealing with him and Jessie took to watching her with sharp eyes and wondering.

In late June, Mildred found herself forced to look clearly at her situation in a way she had been trying not to do for some weeks. She had at first wondered what was happening to her, but then put the changes which she noticed in her constitution down to the change in her circumstances. The lassitude, the feelings of sickness, the differences in her body's rhythm, all of these she well knew could occur to any woman who had altered her way of living as drastically as she had done. There was no need to be concerned any further than that, she told herself, and would sit and sew industriously, letting her mind wander as it usually did over her familiar fantasy of small flat and friends and flower shop, refusing to think of anything else.

It was eventually Jessie who made her pull herself out of fantasy into reality. She was in the scullery one morning, washing out the bowl and jug from her room, her head bent over the sink, when Jessie came in and stood leaning against the door jamb watching her. Mildred, who had woken feeling particularly weary and ill at ease this morning kept her head down over her work, and would not look at her.

After a long pause Jessie said abruptly, 'Millie, how much longer are you goin' to go on like this and not talk about it?'

'Talk about what?' Mildred still kept her head down, scrubbing at her already clean wash bowl with all the energy she could muster.

'Oh, come on, ducks. This is me, Jessie Mendel, remember? Not the cat from next door what ain't got more sense than whiskers. When is it due?'

'When is what due?' Still she kept her head down.

'The bleedin' baby you got inside you, that's what,' Jessie said loudly. 'An' I've got a right to ask, seeing as I imagine it's going to be misbocher of mine. I mean, it's Lizah's, ain't it? So what are you goin' to do about it?'

19

'Oh, my Gawd,' Lizah said. 'I never even bloody well thought about it. Would you believe it? After all these years I been puttin' myself about and I never even thought about it.'

'A right pair you two are!' Jessie said tartly. 'You never thought and she never knew.'

'How could I?' Mildred lifted her head wearily. Even talking seemed an effort. 'I have no experience of such matters. I should have considered the possibility, I know, but I did not. So there's an end to it. No point in talking more, is there? Here I am, and in this state, and I see no sense in discussing what might not have happened. Because it did.'

Lizah shook his head and moved a little as though to come and sit down beside Mildred at the table. He had been standing just inside the kitchen door ever since he had come in, his hands thrust into his trouser pockets and his chin tucked down hard into his collar, clearly in a state of some confusion which sat uneasily on his usual jauntiness. Lizah Harris not quite sure what to do or say was not a scene familiar to any of the people who knew him. But even as he moved forwards he stopped and looked at the rigidity of her back as she sat there, and stood still.

'Listen, Millie, I'm sorry. I really am. I wouldn't have done this to you for the world, if I'd ha' thought. I know how to take care of a girl, and I should have done, but dammit, it was all so – ' He looked sharply at Jessie who was sitting in her usual chair by the grate and his voice dropped, became more confidential. 'Well, you know how it was. I mean, we didn't exactly plan nothing and – you know how it was!'

Now he did move closer and stood on the other side of the table and, resting his fists on it, leaned closer to her.

'Look Millie, I'll get it all fixed. I'm really sorry, but I can put it right. I'll arrange it all with old Mother Charnik, over at Christian Street. She'll sort it out. I'll pay, dolly. It won't be no problem – '

She looked up at him, puzzled, and he stared back at her, his eyes glistening with emotion and his forehead even more tightly corrugated than usual.

'What?' she said dully. It really was very strange; she had been feeling uncomfortable and uncertain for some weeks, refusing to consider what might be the cause, but now she had been forced to face up to it and knew for certain that she was pregnant, she felt so much worse. It was as though the knowledge of her state gave her permission to yield to it, and now she felt sick most of the time and often was sick, retching her heart out in the scullery as Jessie, tutting a little, wisely kept out of her way and left her to get on with it till she felt well enough to come trailing back into the kitchen. Now, trying to understand what Lizah was saying, she felt her gorge begin to rise again, and she thought – hold on. Control it. Hold on –

'I said I'll get it all fixed. You won't have to worry. I'll even get the old girl to come here to you. You won't have to go over there, so no one will know from nothing. I'll bring her here, late, and that'll be that. I wouldn't have knocked you up for a fortune, Millie, I really wouldn't. I'm sorry – '

'Maybe she don't want Mother Charnik,' Jessie said sharply. 'Yet.'

Mildred closed her eyes and took a deep breath and then opened them again and looked at Jessie. 'Who is Mother Charnik?' Her voice sounded thick in her own ears; heaven knows what I must sound like to them, she thought muzzily.

'She's the midwife in these parts. And everything else, too,' Jessie said and her voice was still harsh. 'She'll bring a baby alive as often as not, but if you don't want to wait that long and don't care much for it then she'll bring it sooner. Do you understand me? Don't you have the likes of her up West?'

Mildred stared at her, and with one hand wiped her upper lip, which was beaded with sweat. 'There was a midwife when my stepmother had the children,' she said. 'Came in the last week and stayed till the monthly nurse took over. And then Nanny Chewson, of course, once she came – ' Her voice drifted away and again she closed her eyes. It would be rather nice to be able to go upstairs and lie down and sleep, she thought. It was getting very warm in here.

Unbidden, a memory lifted into her mind; waking late one night at Leinster Terrace, hearing the doorbell and sitting up in bed – how long ago? Perhaps three or four years, now. And hearing whispering voices in the hall, and slipping out of bed to investigate and peering out of her bedroom door to see the figure of a tall man going into Mama's room and hearing Papa's voice. 'I'll wait downstairs, Horner. Only be in the way here. And for the love of heaven keep quiet. Don't want the whole damned household afoot – ' And he had looked up as though he had known she was there watching and she had shrunk back unseen into the shadows, but hadn't gone away.

Not until the man had come out of Mama's room half an hour later and gone downstairs and she had heard Mama weeping had she gone down a flight, not caring now whether Papa were to come and find her or not, for Mama sounded so piteous, and she had crept into Mama's bedroom and there she had lain in her bed, her face twisted into jowly shapes by her tears and at the sight of Mildred she had cried even more loudly.

'I should not have let them do it. I should not have let them do it – ' she kept saying and Mildred had sat on her bed beside her and stroked her forehead until she had calmed down and said softly, 'Not let them do what, Mama?' And Maud, eaten with her pain and her distress and her loss had let it drip out, in disjointed phrases and tangled words, telling her stepdaughter how it had been; Papa certain he wanted no more brats, four in the nursery was quite enough and he had three more already eating their heads off under his roof, and that was an end of it, and how he had arranged it all, bringing the man to her, making her have it done – and now she lay in her bed and wept and bled and wept again and Mildred had wanted to weep with her. She had not understood completely what it was that had made her stepmother cry so much, but that she was in sad pain, that much she knew. And it was due to her father. She knew that too.

Now her eyes snapped open and she stared at Lizah.

'Are you telling me you wish me to kill this child?'

Lizah stood up and put his hands back in his pockets. 'Child – ' he said. 'What child? Ten, twelve weeks ago there weren't no child. There's no child now. How can there be a child in just ten, twelve weeks? In another six months, half a year, then tucka, maybe a child. But now? All you have now is an embarrassment, a problem you got to deal with. A problem I got to deal with. It was my fault and I got to put it right.'

'That wouldn't be putting it right,' she said and frowned, trying to think clearly. 'When I knew, when I had to know, I thought – please let it be all those weeks ago, so that it never happened. Take me back to the Park so that I can say no, and run home and not let it happen. But I couldn't change it. It *happened* and I can't – ' She gave a little choking sound, half a laugh, half an exclamation. 'I can't *un*happen it, can I? What's happened is there. It's for always – and now you're saying you want to – that you can – it's mad.'

'Not mad,' he said flatly. 'Sense.'

'What can be sensible about trying to kill a child?'

He closed his eyes in exasperation. 'Millie, for Gawd's sake, be your age! This is the real world, not your fancy schmancy one where people sit around having tender feelings and enjoying 'em all the time. Down here we got to be practical. *I'm* being practical. I want we should get married one of these days. I don't know when, but one of these days. And do you think my mother'll ever – if you have a baby now, before we get married do you think she'll – ' He threw his hands in the air. 'You tell her, Jessie. You explain to her about Momma. About how she'll be over this.'

'As God is my witness,' Jessie said. 'I love my Momma. But it's none of her business.'

'What? Are you out of your mind? You always was a stubborn devil, but this is – tell her, Jessie! Tell her she's got to get rid of this mumser! I can't bring Momma round to me gettin' married if she's in this state, can I? And I want her to come round, believe me I do.'

'Trying to get rid of my child is no way to make me feel you want to marry me, Lizah,' Mildred said and managed to stand up. She felt the need to be in command of the situation and she couldn't do that when she had to look up to him. 'If you love a person you want their child. I think maybe – ' She stared at him and then shook her head slowly. 'To tell the truth, I don't really know. But I think perhaps that is one of the reasons I want this baby.' And she set one hand on her belly, as though to protect it.

'Of course I want us to have kids, Millie,' he said and now he sounded petulant. 'Of course I do. But the thing of it is, not *now*. Now is not the time. It's not just Momma, either – ' He stopped and looked sideways at Jessie. 'I didn't want to say it, but I've got to, I suppose. It's a bad time for me, financially, you understand? I got into a bit of a game at the spieler in Osborne Street and they've set Jack Long's lot on me – '

Jessie caught her breath sharply. 'What? How do you mean?'

'I can't pay, and they say I got to. You know how it is – ' He grinned a little crookedly then, with all his old charm, and turned to look at Mildred. 'Remember how we met, Mildred? Your brothers, they had a bad debt and I was mad. I was real mad. Bad debts upset a person. No one's got the right to bet when they don't have the necessary to cover if they lose. I was so mad at your brothers that – that only you could have talked me out of it – doing 'em a mischief, you know? Well, now it's my turn. I was as cocky as your bloody Basil, and that's the truth of it. I thought I could beat the bank and I didn't manage it – '

'Faro,' Jessie said disgustedly. 'Bloody faro. When will you learn? A bit of poker or solo or klobiosh ain't good enough for you. You've got to go fancy with Ruby Michaels and that lot down at Osborne Street – '

'So what's to do with you? You win a few and you got to lose a few. Now I'm on a losing streak, so there it is. I can settle with Mother Charnik for whatever she needs. But for more than that, I'm out. I'm plain boracic, and there it is. So, you see, Mildred?' He turned to her appealingly. 'It's just not the time for no kids.'

'Not your time, perhaps,' she said. 'But it is mine.'

'What?'

'I'm the one who is pregnant. Now. So I can't choose any time, can I? It's been chosen for me.' She turned her head and looked at Jessie. 'She says it will be at the turn of the year. She worked it out for me.'

She smiled then and Jessie smiled back and for a moment a bubble of intimacy hung between the two women, excluding Lizah. He stood outside the charmed circle of their femininity, their understanding of themselves and each other through their bodies, and as though he knew he was excluded, he shuffled his feet and said loudly, 'I told you. Jack Long's lot are after me and they can get nasty. I'm getting out of the way for a while. So if we're going to get Mother Charnik we've got to get a move on.'

'We're not getting her,' Jessie said flatly and got to her feet. 'Not till the turn of the year. Then is soon enough. Go away, get your money together for your debts and don't worry about a thing. I'll look after her.'

'That's easy said. Of course I worry. I'm going to marry her, ain't I?'

The nausea that had been threatening to overtake Mildred began to subside and she sat down again. 'Lizah, perhaps we ought to talk about that,' she said carefully.

'Listen, I understand.' He was standing legs apart, with his fists hanging loosely at his side in his old pugnacious style. 'You want to have this brat and you want to give it a name. So I'll just have to sort things out. We got a few weeks, one way and another. I'll talk to Momma. You too, Jessie, eh? For all you got some crazy ideas, Momma listens to you. And maybe I'll talk to Poppa – ' He looked troubled and some of his pugnacity seemed to ooze away from him.

Mildred shook her head. 'You misunderstand, Lizah. I'm not telling you I want to be married. Quite the reverse.'

'Eh?' He stared.

'I'm not sure that would be the right thing to do.' She said it patiently, needing to explain carefully and needing to make him understand the first time she told him. Long arguments of the sort at which Lizah was adept could not, she felt now, be tolerated. 'I don't want you marrying me just because I'm pregnant – '

'I asked you before I knew,' he said sharply and lifted his chin angrily. 'Don't make me out some sort of bastard who – '

'I'm not, I do assure you, trying to say anything bad about you at all,' she said. 'Listen, please, and hear me out. I am not sure *I* want to get married just because I'm pregnant. I know it's the usual thing in cases like this.' She managed a little grin. 'Even in the smart parts of town, you know, these things happen. I know of other women of whom it has been whispered that the christening came a deal nearer the wedding than was seemly. But I don't want it to be like those. I don't wish to marry just for the sake of a child. I believe I can care for my own child, on my own.' She lifted her head with an oddly proud little gesture. 'I would never have thought I could keep myself at all. Had I known what I know now six, or even ten years ago, I would've left my father's house long since. I can earn and live as long as I am sensible. Well, being pregnant need not change that. I work here, at home – ' And again she flashed a conspiratorial look at Jessie. 'And there are two of us to help each other. If Jessie is willing to keep me here while I have my child and will go on fetching me my parcels, then I think I can manage well enough. Then afterwards, if you still want to, why, then we can talk about marriage. I will be better able to think properly about it. Even though – ' She hesitated.

'Well?' He was standing and staring at her, his face a picture of confused feelings. That there was relief there was very evident. He wanted to behave as he believed a man should. He wanted to take care of his woman and to take care of his child, but at the same time, he wanted to do it in his own way and in his own time. And here she was giving him just that opportunity. Yet, being given an opportunity by a woman undercut his own sense of masculine pride. Mildred could see the thoughts chasing themselves over his expressive face and felt an odd emotion in connection with him. She felt sorry for him, and that was something very new. She had been frightened by him, obsessed with him, amused and repelled and delighted by him; to feel pity, however, was strange. It made him seem even shorter in height than he was which was rather odd, she thought.

' – I made a promise to your mother,' she finished.

His brows came down again. 'To my mother? What do you mean?'

'When you took me to see her. That night – she made me promise I wouldn't ever marry you. On my father's life, she said I had to promise.' She stopped then. 'I must say I didn't take it very seriously at the time. It was all so silly, you know? Like a bad melodrama. Not real at all. But now – ' She shook her head. 'Now I think about it a lot.'

She bent her head and looked down at her fingers, laced on the table in front of her. 'It troubles me a lot because I hate my father so, you see. I – ' She swallowed. 'I have found myself wishing him dead. He has refused to allow the lawyers to give me my money and it seems he has the right to exercise such control. My mother's will was so made that only if he says it is the right time for me to have the money may I have it. If he never says it, then I will be denied my legacy from her for always.'

She lifted her head and looked at him with her eyes wide and candid. 'You see, Lizah? I hate him so much that I wish him dead. And your mother made me promise on his life that I would not marry you. And though I am not superstitious – and it is surely mere superstition to take such promises seriously – I cannot help but feel wrong about it. Perhaps it is because of my condition. I have heard that women do not think as clearly as they usually do when they are as I am, and I know my stepmother has always been – captious – when she has been increasing. So I feel I should wait – '

He still stood there looking at her and now his face was sullen, and no longer showed his thoughts so clearly.

'That's all stuff,' he said at length. 'I think that's all a lot of stuff. I think it's much easier than that. You just don't want me no more. I don't do so well in the fights lately and you've heard. And I've lost a lot of money betting trying to make up for what I ain't winning so you don't want me no more. You think I'm a layabout, a no-goodnik, and you ain't interested in me, even though you ought to have a man with you at such a time. But now I'm in trouble – '

'That is wicked!' she flared at him and her face was white with anger. 'How dare you say such a thing! This is the first I have heard of you having such trouble. Do you think I ever cared about how much money you had? For all I knew when I first met you, you had nothing! There was no evidence to suggest – and you saw how I lived! For all you knew, I was the one with money! Of course I did not choose to go about with you for such a reason! You insult me to suggest it – and you insult me now to say I am speaking to you as I am because you are no longer plump in the pocket!'

He looked at Jessie and she made a face at him. 'Don't look at me! I'd heard a few words around that you weren't doing too well – Momma said she was worried – but I didn't say a word here. Did I, Millie?'

'Why didn't you?' Mildred said, looking at her.

'Because I knew before you did what the situation was with you, madam! And I saw no need to upset you for no reason, just yet. It was only rumours.'

'Well, it's true,' he said sulkily. 'And I'm sorry, Millie. Didn't mean to insult you.'

'All right,' she said after a moment. 'We shall forget it.' And there was a long silence then and at length he took a deep breath and turned to the door.

'I've got to go. I don't like to stay anywhere too long these days. The word goes about and I don't want to meet Long with a broken bottle in his hand waiting when I come out. Listen, I'm going to Southend. Just for a few days. Maybe pick up some fights at the booths there. It's summer – you never know. I'll see you when I get back – later in the year. September time, thereabouts.'

He lingered at the door as the two women remained in their place, silently watching him. 'You're sure you don't want Mother Charnik?' he said then, in one last despairing throw.

'No,' Mildred said. 'No thank you. This is my baby and I am going to have it. Goodbye, Lizah. Take care of yourself.'

'Yes,' he said and went. And they sat and listened as the front door banged closed behind him.

20

It was, by and large, a tranquil pregnancy. Once the initial nausea had settled down, which it did before the third month was over, she felt remarkably well, and could spend long hours sitting in the small kitchen with her head bent over her work and her needle flying without feeling at all bad. Her skills increased fast, and by the end of the fifth month, even though the August weather became thick and sticky as the heat pushed down relentlessly into the narrow East End streets, she was felling the linings into fifteen coats a day. Her earnings increased in proportion and she was able to tuck away more savings into her japanned tin box, which she kept in her wardrobe in her small back bedroom. And that made her very happy, even though the lawyer to whom she had applied for her legacy still reported to her that they could do nothing; her father still refused to agree to sign the necessary documents. But if she could earn enough to save as well as live, she would tell herself optimistically, returning the key of the box to the chain round her neck and tucking it into her bodice, that mattered less and less.

Jessie worried a good deal about her at first, fearing she was overworking and concerned because she ate only sparingly. 'You need to eat for two!' she would cry, piling Mildred's plate high with pieces of pale boiled chicken on Friday nights, and adding masses of potatoes over which she poured melted spoonfuls of pale amber chicken fat. 'Come on, now, think of your baby! Oy, I'd give a fortune to be in your shoes! Me, I have to watch every mouthful or I get like a horse, and you can eat all you like and stay like a stick, and still you won't eat! There ain't no justice!' But she would laugh and pat Mildred's back and then try to urge her to eat great slabs of lockshen pudding, which she made with vermicelli and apples and butter and lemons, until Mildred, struggling to push the food down, thought she would burst with it.

But she didn't. She did, however, start to look a great deal rounder. The flat breasts over which she had mourned so often began to swell and lift and sometimes, after she had taken her bath in the battered tin tub Jessie would set before the kitchen range, she would stand and peer at herself in the dark and rather spotted old mirror over the mantelshelf and marvel at what she saw.

The nipples, so much larger and darker, and those rich curving lines would excite her, and she would run her hands over herself and then on to her rounded belly and her smooth thighs, which though still thin, shared some of this unusual new bloom, and think of that night with Lizah amongst the daffodils. And she would close her eyes with shame at how specific were the feelings such thoughts created. There were times when she wanted him very badly, wanted again to feel that urgent use of her that he had made, wanted once more to feel his fingers touching and encouraging her the way they had on that dark March evening; and she would then open her eyes and, moving briskly, wrap herself in her nightgown and drag the bath to the door and call for Jessie to help her empty it. Such thoughts were not to be tolerated; they were sick and stupid, she would tell herself angrily, and might harm the baby, for did they not cause a tightening of her belly and those deep inside feelings? That cannot be good for a growing infant, she would scold herself, and must stop.

And stop they did. She always had an ability to control her thinking. It had been a very necessary survival skill during the bleak years of her growing up and living in that cold and stiff Bayswater house that had been her home. To be able to remove her mind from present misery and transfer it to a fantasy world where she could control what happened and make sure that all events were to her pleasure and benefit had been essential to her sanity. And now that ability came into good use.

She would sit and sew and think of her baby, and visualize exactly how he would be, and what sort of person he would grow into. She saw him small and helpless and in such deep need of her that only she could please him, and that was a thought that made her feel so good that she would smile as she worked, watching her baby cry and others – Jessie, usually – trying to placate him as he cried more and more; and then watching herself pick him up and seeing him at once cease his weeping and start to smile. It was a most agreeable vision; and then she let her images grow and stretch themselves, so that she saw her baby become a sturdy little boy with a beautiful body and strong arms and legs and a brain so sharp and alert that every lesson he was given he immediately learnt. He still loved and needed his mother more than anyone else in the world, of course, but everyone else admired and petted him – it was a lovely dream with which to fill her head as she felled the heavy overcoats with hot sweating hands and an aching back.

She did, once or twice, try to imagine her baby as a girl, but this was much more difficult. Whenever she conjured up a girl baby in her mind's eye she saw ugliness and scrawniness, not beautiful sturdiness. She saw dullness and slowness, not sharpness and alert thinking, and she came to the conclusion that this was because she was in fact carrying a boy. Jessie would add to her conviction by sometimes coming and looking at her and trying to decide what sort of baby was hiding within the shroud of her belly. She would stare at Mildred judiciously as she stood at the scullery sink washing their evening supper dishes and say, 'You're carrying that baby very high – it's a boy, you know.' Or, 'There's a lot of you there in the front – that means it's a boy – ' and even once offered to use the wedding-ring test.

'You tie a thread to your wedding ring and hang it over your belly and if it's a boy it goes back and forth and if it's a girl it swings in circles,' she said. And then laughed. 'But seeing you haven't got no wedding ring, better you don't try it. No use using mine – it's not my baby – ' And she would make a little face and Mildred would hug her affectionately, knowing how deeply Jessie envied her.

'Once this baby's here and I can get out and about more,' she promised, 'we'll do something about getting you married again. It isn't right someone so young and charming should be alone. You'll see – this time next year you'll be married and have a baby of your own on the way – '

'Listen to her! A shadchan yet! A matchmaking shicksah! I like it – but no one else'll play the game with you, dolly, so forget it. If the good Lord means for me to have babies, he'll send me a fella. If it ain't meant – ' And she shrugged. 'It wasn't when I did have a man, after all. We tried hard enough, God knows – ' And she grinned reminiscently. 'Never stopped, he didn't, and that's the truth of it. But there it is – if it ain't meant, it ain't.' And she would laugh again, but her eyes weren't amused at all.

As August limped wearily into an equally hot September, Mildred became less and less willing to go out into the streets in daylight. She had been used to go out late in the afternoons, when she had done her day's share of sewing, to buy their food, having learned many of the skills from Jessie. She knew that going to the stalls just before they closed up for the night paid well, for the stallkeepers were eager to get rid of as much

215

stock as they could. Vegetables that were still saleable late in the afternoon were no longer fit to eat after spending the night languishing in a stuffy outhouse somewhere. Only the poorest could be persuaded to take cabbages that were slimy with dying leaves or carrots furred with mould. So she would go from stall to stall with Jessie's plaited straw bag in her hand and dicker over what was available to get the lowest prices and then go to the fish man and try to find a piece of haddock or cod that was not too tired to be edible.

She did not buy the Friday night chicken; that was a task that Jessie insisted on keeping to herself, though she would take Mildred with her, and she learned to enjoy their late shopping on Thursdays. Jessie would make a progress down the market, shouting greetings to old cronies and teasing the men and generally making what almost amounted to a royal progress. And at the chicken stall she would prod the birds that hung, glassy eyed and limp, from the cross rail, trying to assess how much flesh there was beneath the feathers and then would stand and watch as the old chicken woman, her knees spread wide to accommodate the sag of her sacking apron, would set to work to pluck the bird of her choice for her, her fingers moving with as much speed as Mildred's did when she sewed, so that feathers flew and they all coughed and sneezed.

And then they would take the naked pimply thing home and Jessie would show Mildred how to draw the bird – and great were the celebrations when they found she had chosen well and there were lots of golden globules of unlaid eggs inside – and then how to kosher it, salting and soaking and singeing it to make it fit for a good Jewish household to eat. Then she would simmer it for hours with carrots and onions and parsley root to make the soup into which she would put the cooked vermicelli she called lockshen; delectable food, and Mildred would eat it and remember the nastiness of the dinners at

Leinster Terrace and marvel at how much better the living was in the poverty of the East End.

But now her pregnancy was so advanced that it was obvious, the joys of shopping for chickens and all their other necessaries had to go, she felt. No longer could she walk among the crowds in her state and with her hand naked of any wedding ring. That there were others in a like situation who cared not a whit for anyone's opinion and went wherever they chose mattered not at all to her. However much Jessie tried to persuade her, she refused to venture out until it was dark.

October and November slid away, and now she became more active with preparations for the baby. She had been curiously unwilling to organize herself in any way, feeling a sort of superstitious dread of doing so. Perhaps if she was too confident in her expectations her baby would die? But Jessie would have nothing to do with such notions.

She came in late one Monday evening, dragging a big wooden box with her, and dumped it on the kitchen table before slumping in front of the big fire that Mildred had kept tended all day. Her day's sewing, completed and neatly piled, stood on a chair in the corner waiting for Jessie to take it back to the factory next day, and she was resting with her head back against the crimson cushions of the big chair, half asleep, when Jessie came in.

'There!' Jessie said, with great satisfaction. 'What do you think?'

'Think about what?' Mildred was bewildered, still half asleep.

'A crib,' Jessie said. 'It came in today to the factory – Joe's bought some fancy new machine and it came all packed up in this and as soon as I saw it, I thought – a crib. What do you say?'

'A crib?' Mildred stared at the wooden box. 'You want me to put my baby in that?'

'Of course – but not till it's fixed up. A bit of padding on the inside, all sewn in, and a touch of rubbing down and polish on the outside – it'll look lovely. You'll see! As soon as I've had some supper, I'll fix it – '

And she did as Mildred sat sleepily in her chair and watched her. Jessie sewed cheap pink rep into the inner part of the box, over layers of tow she had brought in the market as she had come through on her way home and though Mildred had protested a little at the colour she had been too sleepy that evening to care enough to make a major fuss. She knew of Jessie's predilection for all tints of the colour red, and it really didn't matter, after all –

But next morning she did care and she had looked at the finished work, which really had made a very workmanlike crib, and felt a stirring inside her that was the baby and thought, almost in panic – I've done nothing for this child. Nothing at all. I've just dreamed the time away – and she took the crib and set it in her room on the floor beside her bed, and then went to look at her underwear. She did not have a great deal but there was enough and she selected two chemises and a nightgown she could manage without and hurried downstairs with them. And for once setting her money-making work to one side, she spent the rest of the day cutting out baby gowns from the fabric of her underwear and sewing and smocking them into shape.

And it really was, she told herself happily, rather nice to be handling delicate fabric again. The heavy woollen coats that made her back and wrists ache so much seemed a million miles away as the white cambric slipped through her fingers and she found herself humming softly beneath her breath as she worked.

After that there was no stopping her – nor Jessie. Both of them sewed busily now, using fabric that Jessie once again brought from the market, with strips of lace that she managed to get hold of too, and by the beginning of December the top shelf of the wardrobe in Mildred's room bore several diminutive nightgowns and pilches, vests and binders and long baby dresses, as well as a good number of muslin as well as towelling napkins. There were even two bonnets, which Jessie had rather inexpertly knitted, but which were pretty enough, and mittens and bootees that Mildred had sewn out of soft woollen material. And finally, a large and very ornate pink shawl, with bright embroidery on it, which Jessie had found and brought home with such pride that Mildred had not felt able to protest, even though she hated its decorations of great tumbling red poppies in bud and in flower, in profile and in full front-facing exuberance. Jessie had held it out to her, her face alight with pride and pleasure in her own skill at finding so splendid a thing in her favourite colour, and Jessie now was too important a person to Mildred to be hurt in any way. In time, she promised herself, Jessie would forget she had ever given it, and Mildred would be able to leave it at the back of the wardrobe and never use it.

And then it all went sour. The long months of dreaming and waiting that had made her so happy seemed now to be interminable. Her body was no longer pleasingly round, she told herself, but hideously distorted. She hated the great smooth dome of her belly, with the navel now turned quite inside out, perched on the top like an obscene pink cherry. She hated the heavy veined look of her breasts, so high and round that they felt like someone else's stuck on her chest wall, not hers. She hated the way her back ached and her legs dragged and the frequency with which she had to hurry out to the cold dark privy in the back yard because of the way the baby kicked against her bladder, and mostly she hated the queasy sensations she felt as it moved within her. It was an active baby and often woke her from her sleep, and she almost began to hate it too.

But then, one afternoon when it was dark outside with clouds lowering, heavy with unshed snow, the sense of deep boredom and dreariness and irritation lifted suddenly. She had woken feeling rather less weary than she had been lately, and had indeed found herself bustling round the kitchen tidying it, and then the scullery, scrubbing it clean with a surprising energy, and had then settled to her work as usual and felt quite capable of dealing with as many as twelve coats today. But as she sat at the table there was another of the hard tightening spasms across her belly that she had become accustomed to, and she had leaned back a little to let it pass, as it usually did, before getting on with her work. And felt a sudden hot gush come away from her and soak her legs.

She stood up and lifted her skirts and stared in disbelief at the state she was in. Had she wet herself? She had not been aware of any need to run to the privy again, and anyway, even when she did go, she did not produce this volume of water – and then she caught her breath in excitement as another spasm of tightness crossed her belly and pushed out yet more liquid. It had started; she was about to give birth and it was as though the darkness outside had quite disappeared, leaving every-where bright with excitement.

She did her best to mop up the floor and then, moving carefully, undressed and mopped up herself and then put on her nightdress. She knew little enough about what was to happen to her in the coming hours except that it would be hours; she remembered that from what had happened when her stepmother had given birth. So she was not too anxious; Jessie would be home in plenty of time.

But by the time Jessie did come home at nine o'clock, for the factory was going through one of its busy periods, she was having strong pains every ten minutes and was beginning to be fearful that she would have to deliver her baby all on her own, and fear trickled into her and made the contractions seem harder to bear than they had been. A great deal harder to bear – she was in fact in tears when Jessie came into the kitchen and took one horrified look at her before turning and rushing out again.

'I'll be right back with her!' she called as she ran. 'Just hold on, Millie – I'll be back with her as soon as I can – '

By the time she did come back, the pains were coming at three-minute intervals and were tight and hard and sore and Millie was half lying, half sitting in the big chair, her head thrown back and sweating heavily. She was alone, all alone in an agony of pain and no one cared whether she lived or died and she was going to die, for what else could happen to her but that? She and her baby, alone and frightened as they were, were meant to die –

And then Jessie was there beside her again, this time with someone else who was dragging at her nightgown, pulling it unceremoniously upwards to reveal her huge belly and she scrabbled helplessly, trying to pull it down again and be decently modest, but those strong hands were no match for her.

'So hold her hands already, Jessie!' It was a harsh voice, high and cracked and ugly and Millie shrank away from it as she had shrunk from the hands on her nightgown. 'I got enough trouble seein' what's goin' on here without her gettin' in my way!'

'Go away – ' Mildred tried to say. 'Go away and leave me – I don't know who you are – go away – ' But no words came out. Instead she found herself holding her breath and pushing downwards, as though she had a compulsion to turn her whole body inside out. It was dreadful, as though she were no longer in charge of herself. She had become a gasping panting object that did nothing but tighten its throat and push obscenely downwards and outwards –

221

It seemed to go on for hours, with respites so short that they were a cruel mockery. The desire to push would lessen and go and she would open her mouth to speak, as soon as she had caught her breath, wanting to tell the old woman she could now see as the owner of the hands and the voice to go away and leave her unmolested, but then it would be there again, and she would feel her face get hot and engorged as she pushed and grunted and pushed again.

And then it all blurred again and ceased being pain and hard work, but became a great crest of excitement, as the pushing went on and at last she felt it happen, felt the great mass of the thing that was making such urgent demands on her ease itself and come through her. She felt the wet heat on her thighs and then heard a loud cry from Jessie, a wordless cry that was so full of emotion that it seemed she was about to weep, and even louder words that she could not understand from the old woman, and then another push and it all slithered away from her, and the old woman was holding it up, a grey and pinkly streaked object with a curly rope dangling from it. And then it opened a great cavern of a mouth and let out a mewling sound that made Jessie clap her hands and the old woman cackle with laughter.

And then, at last, Mildred found herself back in her own mind again, and no longer crowded out by her own body. For so long, it seemed, she had been unable to think or do for herself at all. She had been driven entirely by physical forces she had never known existed in her and now she stared up at the ceiling, amazed to find herself lying flat on the hearth rug. She had no memory of getting down there, and now she blinked and shook her head as Jessie bent to tuck one of the cushions behind her head.

'Let her lie there a while,' the old woman commanded. 'I got to get the afterbirth. It'll be a few minutes yet – we got time. Here, the cord's cut, you can have her – '

'Her?' Mildred said, amazed. Her voice sounded cracked in her own ears. 'Did you say her?'

'A dolly of a little boobalah,' the old woman said and came back once again to drag her nightgown up – Jessie had carefully pulled it down – and start to meddle with her. But Mildred hardly noticed that. She was trying to absorb what the old woman had said.

'A girl,' she said wonderingly.

'Yup. We got all women in here – an' very nice too,' the old woman said and cackled loudly. 'Here, already, give a push – like before. The afterbirth is almost ready – come on – a push – that's it – here we are – ' And again a rush of warmth and wetness, but a sense of relief as well.

'A girl – ' Mildred repeated and closed her eyes, not wanting to look at the fact.

'She's lovely,' Jessie crooned. 'Little boobalah, what a beautiful baby! Look at your baby, Millie! Here she is – all beautiful for you – ' And she thrust the child, wrapped in a towel, into her arms and now Mildred had to look.

The baby was smaller than she had expected, and far from beautiful. She had a face so crumpled and so red with fury that she looked rather like a crimson walnut, Mildred thought, and her head was covered with tufts of matted blood-streaked dark hair that made her look very old. But then she opened her eyes and stared upwards and opened her mouth and bawled loudly and Jessie laughed delightedly.

'Hark at her!' she cried. 'Such a pair of lungs on her – she's wonderful! And the colour of her! She's as red as one of the poppies on the shawl I got her – Ain't she, Mother Charnik? Ain't she just like a poppy? A lovely baby, Millie. She's lovely! Mazeltov. May God bless you both – ' And she bent and kissed Mildred and looked at her and then at her red-faced baby and began to cry.

And the baby lay on her mother's belly and stared upwards with her red crumpled face and her dark eyes wide and considering, as though she could actually see the world into which she had been born.

BOOK TWO

21

'Joobee – joobee, joobee, joobee,' Poppy said obediently and Jessie crowed and clapped her hands and crowed again.

'She said it, she said it, Mildred – listen – say it again, Poppy, boobalah, say jubilee – '

This time Poppy said nothing, chewing the head of the Dutch doll that was at present her most favourite object and letting the spit dribble down her chin. Poppy liked the feeling and made it happen more, blowing round the doll's wooden head to make more bubbles which plopped softly on her skin. Jessie dug into her pocket for a handkerchief and dried her face as Poppy screwed up her eyes and mouth and tried to escape the huge and determined hand that was so much bigger than her face.

'Leave her alone, Jessie, please!' Mildred said and leaned forwards and took Poppy from her arms, though Jessie tried to hold on, unwilling to relinquish her grip. 'It's bad enough we're out here at all without getting her all worked up by fussing her – '

'Who's fussing?' Jessie demanded and pushed her face close to Poppy again. 'Mmm, boobalah? 'Oo's fussin', den? Auntie Jessie isn't fussing, is she, den? No, not a bit. Just wants her little Poppy to see the fun and remember it all – jubilee – say jubilee, baby – '

'Oh, Jessie, do stop,' Mildred snapped irritably and hoisted the baby on to her other hip. She was getting heavier by the day now, a bonny sturdy child with well-muscled legs and bottom and, as she leaned sideways and tried to see her aunt's face round her mother's body, Mildred again felt the stab of anger that so often sharpened her tongue these days, and tugged the baby round so that she couldn't see Jessie. And Poppy's face puckered and she began to wail, at which Jessie began to cluck even more loudly and ran round Mildred to her other side, pushing without a qualm past the other people standing at the pavement's edge, so that she could coo the baby back into a good temper again.

'Poor little object, out here in crowds like this – ' one of the old women standing beside Mildred muttered, loud enough for Mildred to hear. 'Bleedin' ridicluss, bringin' a kid aht 'ere the way things is – '

'She has as much right to be here as anyone else,' Mildred said at once, enunciating every word with freezing good breeding; speaking well had become something of an obsession with her now that the baby was beginning to imitate all she heard. The sloppiness of the local speech hadn't worried her at all in her early days here, but now – 'Historic events affect people of all ages,' she added and turned her back on the old woman who made a heavy grimace and said, 'Hoity toity, Madam Muck 'n' I don't think – ' and jostled her so that she could get in front and stand there triumphantly blocking the view.

'Oh, come on, Mildred. We'll do better further on,' Jessie said loudly. 'By the corner o' Watney Street. The stalls are all out still and we might pick up a coupla bits an' pieces while we're down there.' Jessie was never averse to a little shopping. 'Got all the rag, tag an' bobtail here – ' And she began to push her way through the crowd and Mildred perforce had to follow her.

Poppy, sitting on her mother's hip, watched over Mildred's shoulder as faces and shapes bobbed past her, her dark eyes wide and watchful and glinting with intelligence and some of the people who caught that wide stare smiled back in spite of themselves, for her face was so round and rosy and her dark hair so curly and bouncy that it was difficult not to find the child agreeable to look at; and at once Poppy smiled back, opening wide her little cavern of a mouth with its few rice grains of teeth and gurgling with pleasure, for she was a friendly child, not yet showing any signs of shyness or fear of strangers.

Around her the sunlight reflected on the shop windows, shimmering and bouncing in bright sparkles and the bunting, great red, white and blue swathes of it, fluttered and swung in the light June breeze as the crowds shouted and sang and shimmered too, as brightly dressed as the flags over their heads, with many people wearing cheeky patriotic cockades in their hats, so that even more brave red, white and blue gilded the bright day. In years to come the memory of all she saw that day would sometimes come to Poppy in vivid little flashes; the sight of coloured flags or little whirling paper windmills on sticks or the sound of brass bands pounding could bring before her older eyes sudden visions of the Commercial Road on the day when Queen Victoria celebrated her Diamond Jubilee. Her mother and her aunt would laugh and deny that she could possibly remember, for she was still some months short of her third birthday when the old lady had travelled through London in her great open coach, hunched and globular, with her head covered in a white cap so that she looked for all the world like an ebony egg with its top removed, so how could she remember? But that day when Poppy sat on her mother's hip and was bounced along the road amid the shouting cheerful crowds and past the great brewery horses jingling and glittering with brass and the stallholders adorned with their pearl-buttoned best suits she watched and listened and soaked

227

it all up to store it deep in her infant memory. Young as she was, those dark eyes and sharp ears missed little of what went on around her. And what she absorbed she retained. For always.

But she fell asleep after a while, soon after Mildred had at last relinquished her hold and given her to Jessie to hold. Jessie had the strength to carry the child for long hours, showing no weariness at all; Mildred, thin as she was, simply did not have the reserves of energy that the rounder Jessie enjoyed; so it was on Jessie's ample front that Poppy fell asleep in the middle of the afternoon, and went on sleeping until the two women had escaped the crowds and come wearily home again to Jubilee Street.

'Funny to think of it, really,' Jessie said as she waited for Mildred to unlock the front door. 'This street was named after the last King's jubilee, you know – ages ago it was. Well, it must have been, seein' the old Queen's older'n God. Can't imagine ever having a king, can you? Have to soon, mind you, I dare say. She can't go on for ever, can she? Lawks, but my feet hurt!'

'If you wore better boots they wouldn't,' Mildred said tartly, and turned to take Poppy, now starting to wake up, from Jessie's arms. 'I'll put her down. Give her to me – '

But Poppy was fully awake now and was not interested in being tucked into her crib in the quiet room upstairs. She wanted company and shouted loudly enough about that desire to make sure she got it, and Mildred gave in wearily, as she usually did, and took her through to the stuffy kitchen and tied her into her high chair before pulling off her hat and starting to make some tea.

'That's why I've got to do it, you know, Jessie. She's getting too clever by half,' she said abruptly as Poppy sat and banged the flap in front of her with the wooden spoon that was tied to it by a ribbon. 'It's not good for her.'

'How can it not be good for her to have two of us to take good care of her?' Jessie said, and her voice was high and passionate, and somewhere deep inside Poppy fear stirred and she banged the wooden flap of her high chair even harder, kicking her legs too, to make it all feel better inside. 'You can't do it all on your own – '

'Why not? She's my baby, isn't she?' Mildred had been bending over the range, riddling the clinker to bring the flames leaping again to make the kettle sing, and now she straightened and turned a flushed face to look at Jessie. 'Are you trying to say I'm not fit to take care of my own child?'

'Of course I'm not,' Jessie said, uneasily, and now her voice was low and placatory. ''Course not. How can I say that? I've never had no kids o' my own. So what do I know? Only ever looked after my brothers and sister when they was little. Much like you, o' course. I mean, we're neither of us great experts, are we? So why not help each other? I can help you, take some of the load off you – '

'She's no load,' Mildred said shortly. 'I can manage her perfectly well. And I'm sick of sewing. I never want to see another coat and lining as long as I live.'

'But you know you can earn a living with 'em,' Jessie said swiftly. 'Eh? You knows where you are with the rag trade. Been in it all my life, I have, and can tell you, it won't ever let you down. This idea you've got – it's mad. How can you expect people to come and buy that sort of stuff from you when times are hard, eh? When there isn't much gelt around, you spend it on what you got to have, not on what you'd like to have – '

'Rubbish,' Mildred said and plonked down on the table the freshly filled brown tea pot and went to the kitchen to fetch cups and saucers. 'When times are hard people spend *more* on what they want, not less. Look at you. As soon as the slack time comes you go and buy another red dress – '

'But I'm not everyone, I'm different. I'm me,' Jessie said. 'Just because I'm a meshuggeneh it doesn't mean other people are too – '

'They're the same as you are,' Mildred said and sat down and began to pour the thick dark tea in the cups, and some milk and hot water and sugar in a separate cup for Poppy. 'They'll buy my cakes. You say yourself you like them – that they're good – '

'Of course they're good. You've learned a lot about cooking this last year or so. I'd never have thought you could learn out of books, but there it is. But can you cook,' Jessie said, 'good enough to keep yourself and this little dolly here? That's what I'm not sure of – here, boobalah, let Auntie Jessie give you your milk and – '

'No!' Mildred said sharply and took the cup from her hand. 'I'll give it to her when I'm ready. Leave her alone, Jessie, for heaven's sake – '

'What did I do?' Jessie cried and threw herself furiously back in her chair. 'All I want to do is help, all I want is to be nice and all I get from you is bad mouthing and a load of complaints. What did I *do*, already?'

There was a silence and Poppy reached her hands out towards her cup and Mildred busied herself with it, holding it as Poppy tried to feed herself, and the milk ran down her chin and she laughed, and held her hands out to her aunt and laughed again, her head tilted to one side like a bird. And Mildred, seeing that, reddened.

'I'm trying to bring her up my way,' she burst out. '*My* way, not yours. I don't want her to be like these – these people round here. She's my daughter, not – not anyone else's and I want to bring her up the right way. Already she's got the name you gave her – I tried, remember how I tried to use the name I wanted her to have? But no, you wanted her to be called Poppy and the way things were when she was born, what chance had I to stand up for myself? So Poppy it is, and I hate

it. You know that? It's a name I hate! And now other things –
you trying to teach her to talk and – '

Jessie sat with her head bent, staring down at her hands on
her lap, not looking at Mildred and most of all not looking at
the baby.

'I see,' she said at length. 'I see. I'm not good enough, is that
it? I'm common and ordinary and cheap and you – '

'Oh!' Mildred cried and got to her feet to run round the table
and lean over her. 'Oh, Jessie, I'm sorry! I didn't mean to make
it sound so – really I didn't. It – it's just that – I don't explain
it well, but I know what I want so much. I want the best for
her – the very best. And I thought you did too, and I don't
think the best is here in Jubilee Street – '

'You're damned right it isn't,' Jessie said. 'It's a lousy place
to live. But I've done the best I can with this house to make it
cosy and nice and warm and clean, and I keep away from some
of the neighbours who aren't any better than they have to be,
as well I know, and I do try – I care as much about Poppy as
you do. And I'm sorry if – about her name – but she looked so
much like – and she suited it so well that I – well, I'm sorry.
And she doesn't look like an Emily, does she? Look at her –
those cheeks, that hair, how could you call such a dolly Emily?
Bright as a poppy she is by looks, by nature, so by name. Oh,
Mildred, don't take her away from me! Don't go away and
leave me! I've been so happy this past three years having you
here – it's not my fault Lizah behaved so bad and never come
back like he promised – '

'I don't want to talk about him,' Mildred said abruptly and
went back to her chair on the other side of the table. 'You
agreed. Not another word about him, not ever.'

'I know I did. But time changes things. And it's been a long
time since I promised. And he's entitled to see his own child,
Mildred, even if he didn't do the decent thing by you – '

'He's known where we are this past two years,' Mildred said and leaned back in her chair. 'I'm not going looking for him if he can't be bothered to come looking for me.'

'He's ashamed, Mildred. Ain't you got no feelin's for what a man goes through? You knew him when he was doing good things, up in the butter he was. But this past coupla years – ' She shook her head. 'I've heard. I don't miss much, I don't. He's been on a right losing streak, he has, poor lobbus! No wonder he keeps away. My mother he sees sometimes, this I do know, though she don't tell me. As long as you live here with me she won't tell me a thing about Lizah, or about anything else come to that.' She looked bleak for a moment and then shrugged. 'Well, that's the way of it. Can't do nothing about that. One of these days things'll change, and Lizah'll get back in the pink again and come and see her and then you'll get married and Momma'll come round to the idea and everything'll be lovely – only stay here till then, do me a favour, Mildred – '

Mildred shook her head. 'It's no use sitting waiting for things to happen, Jessie. Life doesn't work that way. You ought to know that. You have to go out, and make it do what you want – ' And she leaned forwards suddenly and touched Poppy's hand. She had stopped banging her wooden spoon and instead was pulling to pieces a scrap of paper she had found on the table. 'That's one of the things I have to teach her, don't you see? That she has to go out and make things happen for herself. And I can't teach her that if I don't do it myself, can I? So, I'm going to make things happen for me – and for her – even if I do have to leave you. But I'm not going far, Jessie. It's a bus ride, really, that's all. You'll be able to visit. And I want you to visit, as often as you can. It's just living together that–' Her voice trailed away. 'It just won't work any more. If I don't go soon, we'll start having disagreements and may even quarrel, and I couldn't bear that. Let's part friends – and stay friends – '

Jessie ignored that. She was sitting extremely upright and staring at Mildred, her cheeks very red, almost the same colour as her shirtwaist, which was a particularly clamorous scarlet. 'A bus ride? Not far? You mean you've already found somewhere?'

'Yes,' Mildred said, but didn't look at her. 'Yes, I have. It's the other side of the City – in Holborn. I thought – I wanted to get away from the East End, you see. It's not that – I mean, there's nothing wrong with it round here – well, not a lot. Not here, in Jubilee Street with you, anyway. But I wanted to get away – '

'Holborn,' Jessie said in a flat expressionless voice. 'Holborn?'

'Yes,' Mildred sounded eager now. 'In Leather Lane, just before you get to Gray's Inn. There are so many sets of lawyer chambers there, do you see, and many well run bachelor chambers too, and I know I can build up a good custom. I dare say I can go further West in time, as far as Bloomsbury, perhaps, for customers. I found a house with a splendid kitchen, quite splendid. A big range, with two excellent ovens as well as one for raising bread, in which I can make meringues, I am quite sure, and there will be space in the scullery for one of these new Rippingille's oil stoves. I've seen a very sensible one that will take several cakes at a time, and which has top burners, too, for bains-marie, you know, where I can do custards, and though it will cost forty-two shillings and sixpence, it will soon pay for itself. There are two bedrooms, just as there are here, so that Poppy may have her own room to herself, which she will need soon, you know. She cannot share with me for always. A growing child needs her own air, of course. And when she starts school – '

'School? *School*? What's the matter with you, Mildred, wishing the child's life away? She's a baby, just a baby! She won't go to school for ever – why already make such a fuss about – '

Mildred shook her head. 'Time cheats, Jessie. It's cheating already and you should know it. She isn't a baby. She's a big girl already – look.' And she got to her feet and came and lifted the flap in front of Poppy's high chair and unfastened the strap and set the child down on the floor on her feet. She stood there for a moment, her fists clenched in front of her in a pose uncannily like a boxer's and then, legs well apart, began to walk, lurching forwards purposefully towards the shiny horsehair sofa on the far side of the room. And Jessie sat and watched her with none of her usual crowing delight in the child's prowess, her face closed and blank.

'You see what I mean?' Mildred said softly as Poppy, with one last shaky step, finally lost her battle with gravity and tumbled forwards to land on the edge of the sofa, there to try to climb up its slippery side. 'You see? Only a few days ago it seems I was feeding her at my breast. Now look at her – she eats solid food on her own, drinks from cups, walks about, talks quite a lot. Another few weeks and it will be school and growing up and learning and – and I want her to learn to be a lady. I mean no insult, Jessie, you know that. But she is entitled, surely, to have as fair an education as her mother had? And I was reared – '

Her voice faded and she sat and looked at Jessie as Poppy at last succeeded in her struggle to achieve the high alps of the sofa and bounced noisily on it, laughing, and then Jessie said flatly. 'Yes. You was reared a lady. So she's got to be. Which means I can't have the caring of her – not ever – '

'Of course you must go on caring,' Mildred said. 'Please, Jessie, don't be angry. I mean no harm to you, you must know that. But she – '

'Yes. She comes first.' Jessie got to her feet heavily and began to clear the cups and saucers from the table. 'When are you going?'

'I'm – I'm not sure,' Mildred lied. 'I have to sort things out. There are items I must buy, handbills to be printed, advertising my service, do you see, and then as soon as I know – '

'When are you going, Mildred?'

Mildred bit her lip and looked up at Jessie, standing tall and heavy against the light from the window, her round face reflecting the rosiness of her shirtwaist, but looking drawn and almost haggard for all its roundness. She has plumped up a good deal this past two years, Mildred thought, irrelevantly. She needs another gentleman to pay her attention or she will become very large indeed –

'I thought, another week, Jessie,' she said at length and Jessie nodded and moved heavily out to the kitchen with the cups and saucers and tea pot.

'You'll let me bath her tonight? Seein' as I won't be able to after this week?'

'Every night till we go,' Mildred said fervently. 'You can give her her meals, everything. And – ' She jumped to her feet and ran out to the scullery to take Jessie's hand in her own. 'I shall always call her Poppy, I promise. You are quite right. She isn't at all an Emily.'

Jessie grinned crookedly. 'Well, I suppose that's something. And you'll let me visit a few times? I won't come too often – '

'Oh, please, Jessie, as often as you like! I don't wish to cut us away from you!'

'No,' Jessie said. 'I'm sure you don't.' But she knew they were both lying. And so did Mildred.

As for Poppy, sitting bouncing on the horsehair sofa, she also knew something was not right, as small children always do know, but she had not yet the words to put to her feelings, however powerful those feelings might be. And she buried them deep inside herself together with her memories of the Jubilee celebrations outside, the sounds of which were still drifting in past the closed windows, to keep for always. Right from her earliest days Poppy Amberly had a very long memory indeed.

22

Poppy lay on her back in bed, her knees pulled up and her hands linked behind her head, trying to decide on a story to tell herself tonight. She had several books of her own – seven to be precise – but she knew them almost by heart now and anyway Mama never let her have a light in her bedroom at night. She said people had to learn to be brave and they never learned if they had nightlights, so that was that. And even if Mama let me have a nightlight, she told herself now, it wouldn't be bright enough to read by. So it doesn't matter that it's dark in my room. It doesn't matter at all. But she didn't feel as brave as she tried to pretend she was.

But at least it wasn't as dark as it might be. As soon as Mama had heard her prayers and said good night and closed the door firmly behind her, Poppy had been out of bed and twitched aside the curtain Mama had so carefully closed and was back in bed again even before Mama reached the bottom step. So the light from the gas lamp outside could seep in and make the blackness not quite so thick.

She was careful not to look around the room. The big cupboard in the corner where the door did not close as tightly as it should was not at all a worry to her. The chest of drawers on the other side was not pretending to be a crouching lion, waiting to spring, any more than the chairs were really great big insects standing up on their long legs waiting for her to go to sleep so that they could hop across the room and bite her –

She took a deep breath and held her knees together even more tightly and stared up at the ceiling, straining her eyes to see the patterns the cracks made. They were nice patterns, a bit like rivers on a map, the sort of maps she had in her book called *The Wonders of God's Beautiful World* which was all about places so far away and so peculiar that no one she knew had ever seen them. The ceiling patterns weren't a bit frightening; in fact sometimes they gave her ideas for stories to tell herself. But tonight it was unusually difficult to find such a story; generally she managed very well indeed, having to choose between being the Princess in the tall tower, or the Good Fairy who came to help her, or the little girl who lived in a house in the middle of the forest with the animals and cooked and looked after herself, all on her own, all day and all night. But not tonight, and she wriggled against her pillows and tried to concentrate.

But still the stories wouldn't come. She was too aware of what was going on in the house below her, and after a while she gave up trying, and let herself listen, and smell, and think about what was happening in the kitchen.

First the smells. Coconut cakes, she decided, and seed cakes, and perhaps a lemon one too. The house always smelled of cooking, and usually it was agreeable cooking, like tonight, cakes and biscuits and sweet sugary fruit-filled breads, and she was glad of that for there were times when it was a horrid smell, like old dirty clothes being boiled. That was when Mama put her big meat puddings, wrapped in their greyish greasy cloths, in the copper boiler in the kitchen, and stoked up the little fire beneath it as high as she could so that the water bubbled and plopped and gurgled round the string-tied parcels. Poppy hated the days Mama did that, and not only because of the smell. It was also because of the meat, for when Mama made the puddings she stood there at the scrubbed wooden table in the middle of the stone-flagged kitchen and cut the meat with a huge glittering knife, chopping it smaller and smaller and smaller – but however small she chopped it, Poppy could always remember how the meat had looked before she started. Which was like a piece of the bleeding weeping animal it had come from, a cow or a sheep or a baby lamb – and Poppy would close her eyes and try not to remember the pictures of those animals in her book *Father Giles' Farmyard* for fear of crying.

No, no nasty puddings tonight, nor frying smells either. They weren't as bad as the meat ones, but still they weren't as pleasant as cakes and now, lying in bed, she lifted her head and drew a long and lingering breath in through her nose, letting the sweetness of the scent fill her. It was almost as good as the left-over cake mixture that Mama sometimes baked for her in small tins that she could tuck into the ovens at the sides of the big ones, and made her feel almost as full.

Sounds came to her too; the faint clang that was the door of the oven on the big range being slammed shut and the tinny rattling sound that was Mama refilling the oil tanks on her Rippingille's stove. If she was using that one tonight, Poppy thought, she was working extra hard, and making a big order; which meant she would be up a long time and be very tired in the morning and consequently cross, and Poppy stopped enjoying the smell of the coconut and seed and lemon cakes and thought about what she would do if Mama was cross in the morning.

Perhaps she could put her coat on when Mama wasn't baking and go and play in the playground of the school in Baldwin's Gardens until the big children heard the bell and had to go in to the big red brick building in long lines, marching as they went. Then she would have to come home again but perhaps by then Mama would not be cross any more – and, oh, please let me soon be a rising five and make it the time for me to be one of the children at the Baldwin's Gardens School allowed to march in at the end of the line with all the others instead of being a baby they all jeered at and wouldn't play with –

There was a new sound from below and she lifted her head from her pillow and began to listen in good earnest. A thumping on the front door and then Mama's steps going along the lino covered passage to open it, and voices – Mama's, low and sharp at the same time and somehow strange, and then a very unusual sound inside this house. A man's voice.

Poppy sat fully upright and listened harder than ever. It was a deep rumbling sound, like the one made by the men who looked after the stalls in the street outside or the ones Mama paid to deliver her cakes and puddings to her customers. Those men were never allowed to come into the house but had to stand on the step outside – that bright clean step which Mama scrubbed and buffed with a special white stone every morning – while the heavy cake trays were brought out to them, for Mama said she had to be careful, a woman alone with her child as she was, to do all that was proper. And that meant no men must come into the house. Perhaps, Poppy thought hazily, men were dirty and spoiled the cakes and made them fall flat inside the oven as they sometimes did, which made Mama very cross indeed; but it couldn't be that, for now this man was right inside the house. Poppy could tell that by the way his voice was so much louder and the way it came booming up the stairs so clearly that she could hear the words he was saying.

'It wasn't all that difficult to find you. I had only to ask the lawyers. I knew you had been in correspondence with them this past five years and more – and they told me – '

'They had no right – ' Mama's voice, sharp and strange still, and something else – frightened? Poppy knew a lot about what it felt like to be frightened. 'No right at all – '

'Still, here I am. Will you talk to me, Mildred?'

'I – there is little to talk about, I imagine.' Still Mama sounded strange, but sharper now and a little more like herself.

'You have felt no need to seek me out this past five years or more. Why now?'

'These are difficult times, Mildred. Very difficult – the war – '

'The war!' Mama sounded sharper than ever now. 'What has that to do with you coming to see me? I find that – '

'You will understand when I explain, perhaps,' the man said, more loudly now and Poppy could almost see her Mama shake her head and made a face.

'Hush – ' she said. 'You'll wake her – '

'Wake who?'

'I – quiet. Come in here. And please be *quiet* – ' And Poppy heard the footsteps go further along the passage and heard the kitchen door close with a little snap. And after that she couldn't hear anything at all.

She lay there on her back for a long time staring up at the patterned ceiling and trying to think about who the man might be and why Mama had allowed him to come into the kitchen. And who were The Lawyers who had sent him? Friends of Auntie Jessie, she decided after a while. Auntie Jessie has lots of friends for she always talks of them when she comes. Perhaps she has friends called The Lawyers and they sent this man. And maybe he is a prince in disguise who will bring gold treasure in a great chest and go on one knee and open it in front of Mama and it will be full of wondrous coins and necklaces and rings like Auntie Jessie's only bigger and lemon cakes and coconut cakes, all little and sweet and bouncing about in the chest – and she fell asleep without having to find a story to tell herself after all.

'You look – um – well – Mildred. Very well,' he said and then, as she stared challengingly at him let his gaze slip away.

'If you have nothing more honest than that to say, I wonder that you bothered to come,' she said tartly. 'I look ten years older than I should, and small wonder, working as I do. And I am hardly dressed or primped to receive company at present.'

'Company? I'm hardly that! As your brother – '

'A brother I have neither seen nor heard from for so long no longer seems to be an important part of my life,' she said. 'I doubt you feel differently.'

'Even if I did, you give me no encouragement to express warmer feelings.' He frowned and then looked appealingly at her. 'Come, Mildred, ask me to sit down at least, and let us talk. I dare say I did behave badly to you when we last met – but I was much younger then. Just a boy, after all. Times have changed and I with it. And you know it was not easy for me, or for Claude. You had brought great disgrace on us all and – '

'Disgrace? What disgrace? Who was to know of my doings? I had but gone away, that was all. I see no disgrace in that.'

'Oh, come Mildred, don't try to be – I mean, you did after all go off to the East End – and now live here – ' He waved his hand vaguely in the direction of the front door. 'It's hardly Leinster Terrace out there, now is it?'

'And so much the better for me that it isn't,' she said. 'The people here may lack gentility, but they more than make up for such a lack in good heartedness. Well, sit down. You take up too much space standing there like a great booby. You appear to have continued to grow.'

He smiled at that, and obeyed her instructions, taking a chair beside the big kitchen range. 'I am now an inch over six foot,' he said proudly. 'And better muscled too. I joined a good gymnasium, don't you know, and took pains to develop myself better. It seemed to me – ' He swallowed and stopped, embarrassed. 'Claude looks well too. He is not so well grown as myself, but well enough, well enough.'

'And the rest of them?' She could not bring herself to speak any names, nor could she look at him, preferring to fuss over the cakes that stood cooling in rows on her big kitchen table.

'Well, the rest of them? Let me see – Wilfred is working in the Acton shop and will be moving to the new one at Shepherd's Bush soon – or so it is planned – '

'Wilfred? But surely he is at school still? He was always a good scholar as I recall – '

'He is seventeen, Mildred. Well able to be of use in the business, and Papa saw no sense in leaving him in school longer – '

'Papa,' she said and took a sharp little breath in through pinched nostrils. 'And Thomas and Samuel and Harold? Are they working in the shops as well?'

'Now, don't be sharp Mildred. Of course not. Thomas and Samuel are both doing well enough at the City of London School, and Harold, it is hoped, will be able to join them in a year or two. They are well and fit – '

There was a silence as she sat down and stared at her hands on her lap and Basil watched her covertly, unsure of how to continue what he had to say. He had not entirely lied about her appearance, he decided, as he looked at her. Mildred would never be anything but excessively plain, of course, but she had improved somewhat since her girlish days. She wore her hair pulled back severely from her forehead beneath a neat white cap and this, far from exaggerating the length and unevenness of her nose and her rather long chin gave her face a strength it had certainly not displayed when she had tried to hide so much of her brow beneath a frizzed fringe. Her eyes seemed to be larger too, somehow, for her face certainly had a pleasantness about it that had been lacking when last he had seen her and her figure, though still thin, had lost some of its gawky awkwardness. When she moved about her small kitchen she did so with economy and dispatch and even a certain grace and now, as she got to her feet to bend to her oven and remove from it a large round and very golden cake he said impulsively, 'Indeed, it *is* good to see you looking so well, Mildred. I had feared what I might see when I came, but as it is – '

'And what did you expect?' She set the cake on the table and with one expert twist of her wrist ran a knife between the tin and its sides and set it tipped at an angle to cool before decanting it onto the rack that stood ready. 'A bedraggled crone, no doubt, living in filth and squalor? One who has been abandoned and left to rot as she deserved, wicked fallen creature that she was?'

'Of course not,' he said uncomfortably. 'But when I heard that you had had a child – '

'From the lawyers, no doubt.' Her voice was scathing. 'I should have known that any attorney *he* employed would be less than reliable in his dealings. My correspondence with the man was not intended to be broadcast wholesale, and I have no doubt he was well aware of that. But I was hoping too much to think such a one might behave in a professionally sound manner – '

'Oh, come, my dear, you do him an injustice. I heard many of his conversations with Papa. He did well by you, indeed he did. Time and again he begged Papa to allow you to have your legacy, saying he had your assurances that you would not remarry ever and that you had a child to care for – but even in your widowhood Papa was adamant – '

'Widowhood? Did Mr Poynter tell Papa I was a widow?' She had been putting another cake into the oven and now she straightened up and stood staring down at him, her hands set against the frosty whiteness of her apron, which looked even whiter against the dark stuff of her gown. 'Perhaps you are right and I did do the man an injustice. And what did he say to that?'

'He said he had to see your marriage lines before he would agree to sign the necessary documents.' Basil looked away and mumbled it. 'And Mr Poynter said no more – '

'And rightly so,' she said equably and returned to her table to continue beating at a bowl of cake mixture. 'For I am indeed no widow. I am as I was when I left Leinster Terrace, plain Miss Mildred Amberly.'

'Let me get my hands on that blackguard and I'll teach him to abuse my sister so,' Basil began wrathfully but she shook her head at him and even smiled a little.

'You did that once before, as I recall, and it did you little good,' she said. 'There is no need. I choose to live as I do.'

'Are you happy, Mildred?' He stared at her and after a while she stopped the rhythmic beating of her cake and set the bowl down on the table and lifted her chin and looked at him.

'Happy? What is happy, Basil? Are you happy? You look happy enough sitting there – you are wearing good clothes on that improved frame of yours and I see that the last of your young skin disorders has left you. You seem a prosperous happy enough man of – what is it now? Twenty-three or thereabouts? Yes, it must be, for I am thirty-three. As I say, you look happy enough. But are you? Do you enjoy your work? Have you a young lady in whom you have an interest? At your age it seems a reasonable supposition, but I cannot tell from looking at you. So tell me – are *you* happy?'

He reddened. 'As for that, I can – I asked you first.'

'Very well, I shall tell you. I do not know if I am happy. I am, however, content enough. I earn my own living, mine and my child's. And I do more than that. I am, I am pleased to tell you, amassing some savings of my own. They are not large sums, but they are mine and they grow steadily if slowly. I am beholden to no one, no one at all.' She lifted her chin with a touching air of triumph. 'I may not be as rich as you and the rest of the family. I may not be permitted to have the money my dead Mama wished me to have and which – he – her husband refuses to permit me to have, but I am content and successful in my own way. So, does that satisfy you?'

'I wish you did not hate him so, Mildred. Not to be able to give him his name – ' He shook his head. 'You must hate him a great deal.'

'My father?' she said after a moment and with great deliberation. 'Mr Edward Amberly, my father? My dear Papa? I

can name him without any difficulty at all. As for hating him
– pooh! I have neither time nor energy for that. I lose no love
for him, of that you can be sure, but – '

'Please, Mildred – ' He swallowed. 'I wish you would not
speak of him like that.'

'And what has he ever done for you that you should defend
him?' Mildred flared at him, and returned to her cake mixture
and began to beat it so ferociously she bade fair to break the
bowl to pieces in her hands. 'I was so miserable in that house
I gave little thought to others' unhappiness, but I now know
that you probably had no better a time in your own way, than
I did. The man is monstrous in his selfishness and his greed
and his – '

'No, Mildred, I cannot let you speak so.' Basil was on his
feet now, and in the small low ceilinged kitchen which was lit
only by the faint light of a single gas jet plopping over the
mantelshelf and the firelight and so seemed even smaller
because of the many shadows, he seemed gargantuan. 'Not
until you hear my message. If you say too much now you will
not be able to give my request a fair hearing.'

'If you seek to persuade me to come cap in hand to beg his
forgiveness or any such nonsense you may forget it,' she said
roundly, and began to put her cake mixture into the prepared
tin which stood ready, smoothing it with the back of a wooden
spoon with gestures of such controlled ferocity that it was
amazing that the mixture did not splash about the room.

'No, I do not suggest that. But I have to tell you that they
are in a state of great distress, and I thought perhaps if you
came to visit and made your peace – ' His voice trailed away as
she snapped her head up and looked at him with her eyes so
dark and sharp that they seemed actually to glitter at him, like
a steel knife.

'*I* make my peace! I would have thought it was his duty to
beg *my* forgiveness for the way he had behaved towards me

that made it necessary for me to leave his house – ' She stopped then. '*They* are in great distress?'

He nodded. 'Mama,' he said simply. 'Poor creature, you must pity her. I never saw such a wreck of a woman at the best of times, for I will not hide from you, Mildred, that since you left she has taken to liking sherry a great deal more than is good for her – '

'She did that long before I left,' she said shortly. 'Is she ill?'

'She is prostrate with terror. Not because of us, of course, although she is kind enough to say she is, but because of Wilfred, you see. He is only seventeen, I know, but he's a well-made lad and could pass for older, and swears that no matter what she or Papa do or say, do it he will. And – ' He grinned suddenly and for a moment the small boy who had been her petted brother peered out of the man's face at Mildred. 'I tell you, Mildred, do it he will. He's turned out to be a well-plucked 'un, has young Wilfred. Remembering what a monster he was as a child, it amazes me that he's grown up to be so good a fellow. So you see, Mama is so set about that she does not know what to do, and Papa does not understand her misery and so that makes her worse – ' He sat and gazed at her mournfully for a long moment and then burst out, 'Oh, Mildred, it is so hateful there! I know it has never been the happiest of homes, but it is the only home I have, and I would wish to see things better than they are. I will feel better in what I do if I know I have done all I can to make matters better for Mama. She is but a stepmama, I know, but she has been kind enough in her own way. And I thought if you would come and see her – you could perhaps help her see that – '

'You must explain yourself better than that.' Mildred put the last cake in the oven and, straightening, began to rub her weary back with both hands. 'What about Wilfred? Why should my visiting her make any difference to what Wilfred does?'

'You might be able to persuade him not to. You always could when he was small, as I recall. You were the only person he listened to. He drove Nanny Chewson quite demented then, you'll remember, and all she can do now is sit and weep, so she's no help. Mama does need you, Mildred. And if you choose a good time, when Papa is away from home, perhaps – '

She was staring at him with her brows snapped together. 'You've changed less than I thought,' she said. 'You still don't explain fully what's in your mind. You give half the story and that in so garbled a fashion it's incomprehensible. So, explain properly what it is you are concerned about, if you want me to take you seriously.'

He shook his head and again managed to smile at her. 'I'm sorry, Mildred. I dare say I'm not at my best with words, at that. A man of action, you see.' He lifted his chin proudly. 'That's it, you see. I'm to join the City of London Rifles and go to South Africa to fight, and of course, Claude comes with me. And now Wilfred swears he will go too, so everyone is at such sixes and sevens that I'm demented with it all. Please come and sort it all out, Mildred, just as you used to do when I was a boy? Please?'

23

The second week in September, 1899, was the most exciting week Poppy Amberly had spent in all her life. First of all, on Monday, Mama took her shopping for special clothes. For Mama to leave the kitchen on a Monday was a very unusual thing. Generally it was a day when she was very busy sending out the cakes and pies and pasties she had baked on Saturday and Sunday, but this Monday Nellie Milner, the girl from the house on the corner of Leather Lane and Holborn, who some-times came to help at busy times, had been fetched early and instructed on all she had to do, and given lists of what was to be given to which of the delivery men, and Mama had told Poppy to put on her red coat and straw hat with the cherries on it and had polished her boots till they shone like liquorice straps, and taken her shopping.

And that was the next wonderful thing. Not only did Mama buy Poppy new chemises and drawers and black stockings and extra sturdy boots and two green serge dresses and three new white pinafores to wear when she went to school; she also bought her a pencil box with a lid that swivelled in which there were not only three pencils and a pen holder and two shiny golden pen nibs, but also a long thin slate pencil and five sticks of chalk, one pink, one blue, one yellow, one green and one white. Poppy clutched the box and looked at Mama and said, 'Oh,' and then 'Oh – h – h,' again, because she was too excited to say anything else. And although she did not realize just how much the delight she felt made her face shine and her eyes widen, Mama certainly did and perhaps that was why the next exciting thing happened.

They were on their way out of the shop, Gamage's at Holborn Circus, when they passed a counter on which there were displayed small hats made of fluffy white fur, and Poppy stopped to look at them, while Mama rearranged her parcels to make them easier to carry. The man behind the counter leaned over and smiled at her and said, 'Aren't they pretty, Miss? And look at this – ' and showed her a muff made to match, with twisted white cotton ropes with which to hang it round your neck and she took it, and tugged off her straw hat with the cherries so that she could put the muff's rope over her head, and tucked her hands in it and whirled, crying, 'Mama!'

And Mama looked and smiled and came and picked up a hat, too, and tried it on Poppy's head, and let her look in the mirror the shop assistant held out and now Poppy could see what she looked like. And it was wonderful. Her hair seemed to be as curly as the fur on the hat, though a different colour of course, being as dark as the hat was light, and her eyes seemed even to Poppy to look very bright and shiny and her cheeks very round and rosy.

'How much are they?' Mama said to the shop assistant and he beamed and said very quickly, 'Three shillings and elevenpence the pair, madam,' and for a moment Poppy thought she would burst with hope and misery all mixed up together, for Mama looked serious and anxious and began to shake her head; but then she saw Poppy looking at her and she smiled again and said, 'Why not? After all, why not? It's ridiculous nonsense. But why not?'

Poppy stood there, not knowing what to do with the happiness inside her as the man took Mama's money and wrote out the bill and reached over his head for the little wooden holder to put it in. He twisted it down and put the money and the bill in it and then reached up again and turned

it back and Poppy, who stood staring upwards, waited for him
to pull the handle that would send the wooden holder full of
money swinging its way across the ceiling of the shop to the
high glass enclosure in the middle where a woman in thick
glasses sat and kept untwisting the holders and refilling them
and then sent them swinging back. And the shop assistant saw
her watching him and laughed and said, 'Would you like to do
it, little Miss?' and came round and picked her up and held her
high so that she could pull the handle. And that was the next
wonderful thing that happened that week.

But there was still more to come. After they had got home
and found that Nellie had done everything perfectly and had
even been sensible enough to use the extra time she had to
scrub and polish all the cake tins, Mama was in so happy a
mood that she had time to sit by the fire with Poppy on her lap
and tell her stories. Poppy could hardly remember the last time
this happened and she sat there with her head on Mama's
shoulder, watching the flames behind the bars of the kitchen
range and listened dreamily as Mama told her not only
Cinderella but *Snow White* and *Red Riding Hood* as well.

And then it was tea time and they made toast at the fire, so
that it came to the table covered in alternating black and brown
bars the way Poppy liked it best of all, and on the toast they
had Mama's special jam which she had made only a few weeks
ago when the stalls in the market had been covered in the great
heaps of red and golden plums which had been so cheap that
year because there was a glut, and then some raisin and treacle
tart which Mama had found time to make just for them and not
for the delivery men. Oh, a wonderful tea time, as they sat
there opposite each other and ate and ate until Poppy thought
she would not be able to swallow another little bit, and then
found she could, and Mama sipped her tea and watched her
and was quiet, but not at all cross. Just having Mama not cross
and tired was treat enough. To have all this as well was – well,
wonderful.

They had just finished half of the raisin and treacle tart when there was a knock at the door and Mama let Poppy answer it, and now she was getting used to lovely things happening and didn't even feel particularly surprised to see Auntie Jessie there. She stood on the doorstep, smiling that great big smile of hers, wearing a lovely shiny black hat with purple feathers on it and a purple cloak over a bright crimson skirt with stripes of darker red on it, and looking bigger than ever. Every time Poppy saw Aunt Jessie she looked even bigger, which was how Poppy knew that grown-ups went on growing just like children did, only they grew sideways, instead of upwards. Now Poppy cried out delightedly, 'Auntie Jessie, Auntie Jessie, I've got a lovely new pencil box and a hat and muff – come and see – oh, do come and see!' and grabbed her hand and pulled her into the kitchen.

And then it all became even nicer, for Mama gave Auntie Jessie tea and seemed happy to see her, which was nice, for sometimes Mama was a bit cross when Auntie Jessie came. But not on this wonderful day. Nothing could go wrong on this wonderful day, Poppy decided as she paraded her new clothes and especially her hat and muff for Auntie Jessie to see and then showed her the pencil box. Even when they stopped talking to her and started to talk to each other, the way grown-ups always did in the end, it went on being nice, for she had her new pencil box to play with. Mama said she was not to use any of the things in it till she started school, because it was a school pencil box, but she could swivel the lid and take everything out, and then put it all in again and that was quite enough to enjoy for the present.

'Thank you for coming, Jessie,' Mama said, and Jessie laughed.

'Don't thank me, doll. You know my problem's keeping away from here and you and the little one. I don't need no inviting. So it was a real pleasure to get your letter. Especially as I don't get much in the way of letters at the best of times.

Postman thought I was coming into money.' And she laughed, a round comfortable laugh, almost as round and comfortable as she was herself. She was eating a piece of the raisin and treacle tart and she didn't at all mind opening her mouth when it was full, though Mama made sure Poppy never did that. It didn't seem to matter with Auntie Jessie, though; whatever she did was always all right.

'It's just that – well, I have a decision to make,' Mama said. 'And it will help to talk of it with someone.'

'And what other someone do you have but me?' Jessie said, but there was no rancour in her voice. 'So, tell me, what's the problem?'

'I had a visitor last night,' Mama said, and Poppy pretended to go on counting her pencils but naturally began to listen.

'Oh?' Auntie Jessie sounded very interested too.

'It – it was my – it was Basil. You remember Basil?' Poppy felt Mama look at her. She didn't have to see her do it. She knew she was watching her and wondering whether to send her away, and she began to count the pencils very obviously, being very busy with them so that Mama would know she wasn't listening at all.

'Basil? Your brother Basil? Well, I'll go to the foot of our stairs!' Auntie Jessie said loudly and Poppy worked harder than ever at not looking as though she was listening. But it was no use.

'Poppy, my dear, take your new clothes upstairs and put them on your bed. And then you may lie on your bed and read your books. I shall come and tell you when it is time to get ready for sleep,' Mama said and Poppy just for a moment considered making a fuss and asking to stay downstairs here by the fire. After all, with Auntie Jessie sitting there – but she looked at her Mama's face and knew that would be a silly thing to do, and went upstairs, taking her new clothes with her, and sat on the bed and heard the rumble of their voices from below and longed to know what they were talking about. Mama, with a brother? Nellie from the corner had brothers including one who was very old – nearly twelve – who wore short trousers tied with string and a very torn jacket and an old cap over his eyes, and sometimes shouted after Poppy in the street. Did Mama have someone like that? And where was he? Nellie's brother lived in her house with her, but Mama had no brother here. It was all very odd. So odd that there was no sense in thinking about it so she put her new clothes on the chair by the bed and then took her *Grimm's Fairy Tales* book from the shelf and began to look at the pictures from the stories Mama had told her before tea. It was still being a wonderful day, even if she hadn't been allowed to stay and listen to the talk downstairs.

'Listen, what harm can the kid do, even if she hears?' Auntie Jessie said as Poppy went disconsolately up the stairs, her new clothes and pencil box carried carefully before her. 'Why keep secrets? Kids don't understand half what you say in front of them anyway.'

'Poppy understands a great deal more than you might think,' Mildred said. 'She's exceedingly quick.'

'I know,' Jessie said fondly. 'Sharp as a tack, that one. But all the same, what harm if she knows? Secrets ain't good in families.' Her face darkened a little. 'Believe me they ain't. And I got something to tell you, on account I don't reckon secrets – I don't care what he says – '

'You see, Jessie – ' Mildred hadn't been listening to her. 'You see, I do have to make up my mind what to do, and quickly, and for once I'm – ' She shook her head. 'I just can't think clearly. I need to be told what to do – '

Jessie laughed. 'You? No one tells *you* what to do, or what not to do. I thought you were potty, you know that, when you started this cake lark? What did you know from cooking, after all, only what I'd taught you while you lived with me? And I'm not a great cook – but you were right and I got it wrong. You're making a marvellous living here, marvellous – '

Mildred went a little pink. 'I have no complaints. Business is steady and quite good.'

'Quite good? Don't tell me! Someone as careful as you are to go and buy a piece of frippery like that fur hat and muff for Poppy? This is me, Jessie Mendel, Millie! Not the cat to be turned off with boobahmeisers – none of your tales for me! You must be coining it.'

'I'm doing quite well,' Mildred said, looking down at her hands. 'I'm thinking of taking over the house next door, as a matter of fact, and putting in extra ovens and taking on some girls to help full time. I can sell all I bake, so why not bake more? But that isn't the problem – what do I do about Basil?'

'What does he want you to do?'

'He wants me to go to Leinster Terrace,' Mildred said baldly and sat and stared lugubriously at Jessie. 'It's been five years and I've heard nothing from them, and now suddenly he just comes here and tells me to come to the house and see Mama and the boys – '

'Why? I mean what's happened all of a sudden? Is there someone ill? Your father maybe? I wish no man ill, naturally, but if he should die, please God, that would be useful, hey? Then you could get your inheritance and no problems!'

'Don't be wicked, Jessie,' Mildred said, but the rebuke was perfunctory. 'It's not that. It's this war. Basil and Claude and even Wilfred – they're all joining the army and going to South Africa and Mama, it seems, is in a terrible taking over it and he wants me to come and sort it out – ' She grinned crookedly. 'Although what I can be expected to do is quite beyond me. Basil thinks I can make Mama feel better about it, but how can I? If she does not want them to go – well, it will be Wilfred she is concerned about, of course. She won't mind if Basil and Claude go – '

'Go and see her,' Jessie said decidedly.

Mildred stared at her. 'But didn't you hear me, Jessie? What can I do? If I thought I could really be of some value, it would be different, but I remember Wilfred well enough. A most stubborn boy, who did what he wanted, neither more nor less. If he says he is going, go he will. So what use is there in getting myself all – I have not been there for five years. It's a long time. A great deal has happened – ' Her voice trailed away. 'A great deal – '

'Poppy has happened, and they have a right to see her.' Jessie was sitting very straight in her chair and her round cheeks had become rather pink. She had even stopped eating her raisin and treacle tart. 'And what's more she has a right to see them.'

'What?' Mildred looked startled.

'Never mind what your Mama wants or your brother wants, Millie. You don't owe them nothing – not a thing, the way they was with you, not caring nothing for you, not ever, but Poppy – now, that's different. She's a person, ain't she? A person with *relations*. But as far as that poor little mite knows she's only got you and me – and not much of me. No, I'm not complaining. I dare say I would encroach more than I should if I did come round more often. I have to be kept at a distance or I eat everything up. I know me as well as you do, Mildred Amberly, so don't go thinking I'm daft. But that ain't the point. What matters is Poppy and a kid's got the right to know her own blood. She ought to know her grandparents and her uncles and that.' She stopped very deliberately. 'And she ought to know her Poppa and her other grandparents an' all.'

Mildred became very still. 'I told you. I don't want to talk about that,' she said in a flat voice.

'Well, maybe you don't. But I do. An' you're goin' to listen, like it or not. Hear what I got to say and then you can decide what to do about your brother and going round to their place. But first I got to tell you that Lizah's back.'

There was a sharp little silence and then Mildred said carefully, 'Oh. Is he?'

'You've every right to be angry, every right to feel like what you do. But that don't alter the fact that he's that little mite's Poppa and she got a right to know him. He's changed, Millie – ' Her voice softened, became less strident. 'It'd really upset you to see him, and that's the truth of it. He turned up at my door three weeks ago, looking like – well, I don't know. Been in America, would you believe? Boxing and that, and not doing too good. And now he's back, skint again, and looking real sorry for himself. Or did. He's feeling a bit better now he's had some o' my good food in him, and looking better too.'

'Three weeks?' Mildred said. 'And this is the first I've heard of it? Am I supposed to be pleased to know now, grateful to be told at last? And ready to welcome him like a conquering hero or some such?'

'I knew you'd be angry. So did he. But that wasn't why he said not to tell you. He's ashamed, that's what it is. Dead ashamed. He's even too ashamed to live at Momma's house – not till he gets on his feet proper, he says. Till then, he's livin' with me – and he used to be so cocky.' She shook her head and her eyes shone with the easy tears of nostalgia. 'Such a strutter, that one, so full of himself. But now – he looks like someone pulled the plug out of him and half his innards drained away. He asked about you and the baby, first thing he did, that was, but said not to tell you. Not till he can get himself on his feet again, he says, and come round like a mensch – like a real man, you know? With presents for you and Poppy and a bit of gelt in his pocket, like he used to be – '

'As if I cared tuppence for that!' Mildred blazed, anger boiling over at last. 'How dare he treat me as though I were – like some sort of – I was never one of those people he set such store by who count a man's worth only in the contents of his pockets! He insults me by thinking it – '

'No, he doesn't. But he would insult himself if he did not come to you as a man of some property. Until you understand that about him, you understand nothing. But like I said to him, and I'm saying it to you now, what you two wants is beside the point. It's Poppy.'

'Poppy is perfectly happy as she is.'

'That's as may be. I'm glad to hear it. But she ain't going to be a little one for ever. I used to think that, but I know better now. She's going to get older, ask questions, want to know this and that. Like who her Poppa is. And she's got a right to know. Well, why not get it all over and done with? Go and see your people at Leinster Terrace, and come and see Lizah at my house. And then you ought to take Poppy to see my Momma. She's not been the same since my Poppa died, believe me. She's an old lady after all – she won't behave bad to you – and she's entitled to see her grandchild, ain't she? Entitled.'

'She could have seen her any time she wanted to, if she'd asked. Any time, this past five years. But she never called, never said a word – why should I – '

'Oh, Millie, Millie, don't be that way! Sure people ought to do things different. Sure they ought to be good and kind and nice. And no one ought to be poor and no one ought to have to work all the hours God sends baking cakes to keep herself and her baby, and no one ought to have to work in a stinkin' sweat shop and no one ought to be a widow that no one wants and who gets fatter every time she turns round. But the world ain't like that. It's full of things and people that aren't what you'd like 'em to be. So do you have to be the same? Can't you go there? Make an effort? Take your Poppy to see her rich relations and bring her to see the poor ones and tell her they're both as good as each other. Different, but just as good. Teach your Poppy to be a mensch – a good person – and you can't do that if you ain't one – '

She was still sitting there very straight, with her round face stained with red patches on the cheeks and Mildred looked at her and blinked and then suddenly got to her feet and went over and bent down and hugged her.

'Jessie, you really are – I'm sorry. I should let you come more often, and I don't really know why I don't – '

'Because a little of me goes a long way. I'm like salt herrings – one you can enjoy, two keeps you awake with a raging thirst all night – ' But she looked pleased and lifted her great arms and put them round Mildred's narrow shoulders and hugged her.

By the time Mildred had gone upstairs to tell Poppy she could come down again she had fallen asleep, lying curled up in her bed hugging her book and with her new pencil box clutched in one hand. So, together her mother and her aunt undressed her and tucked her into bed and went downstairs to spend the rest of the evening planning what Mildred was to do next. And if by the time Jessie left, wrapping her purple cloak around her to keep off the chill September mist in the dark streets outside, Mildred was relieved to see her go, she would not have dreamed of saying so. A little of Jessie did indeed go a long way, but the exhaustion she left behind her was well worth it, Mildred thought as she stood on her doorstep and watched the large shape dwindle away into the darkness. She does make me remember the things I could so easily forget.

24

The exciting week went on next day, right from the morning. Poppy woke as usual to the smell of baking but today didn't wait till Mama came to fetch her for breakfast as she usually did. She got up and put on the wrapper Mama had made for her out of her own old blue one, and which had frills round the edges which Poppy liked very much, and went downstairs, her bare toes curling a little on the cold lino, and pushed open the kitchen door and stood looking in.

It is strange, Poppy thought, looking at the small room, bright and warm and smelling so sweet. I think this room is inside my head as well as outside, in front of me, and she closed her eyes and she was right. She could still see the room in every tiny detail: the shiny black range with the glowing fire and mantelshelf over it with its pink china clock and matching candlesticks and the pretty purple and blue vases with spills of curly paper which Mama used to carry a flame from the grate to the gaslight over the table; the shelves on each side of the range, tucked away alongside the chimney breast, where the blue and white dishes were displayed and the cups hung on hooks; the big scrubbed wooden table in the middle where the cakes stood, too many of them to count, waiting on their racks to be cool enough to set on the trays ready for the delivery men, and beyond, in the scullery, Mama apron-wrapped at the copper, tugging out the freshly boiled plum duffs and meat puddings with her great wooden tongs, her hair tied back and her face shining with the water from the steam that curled round her like a cloud. And somewhere inside her head Poppy knew that always and always the kitchen would be there; wherever she went and however old she grew, she would always be able to close her eyes and walk into Mama's kitchen and smell the good smells of fresh cakes and pies and puddings.

She opened her eyes and found it was a little different, after all; Mama had come out of the scullery, drying her hands on her white apron and was standing looking at her, her head tilted a little, and seeming – not exactly cross but not very pleased, either, and Poppy smiled and said, 'Hello, Mama.'

'Slippers. Where are your slippers, naughty girl?' Mama said, but she wasn't really cross after all. Poppy could tell from the sort of not-quite-there sound in her voice and she ran across the room to stand on the rag rug in front of the fire.

'I forgot,' she said. 'Mama, can I wear my hat and muff today? Can we go somewhere so that I can wear my hat and muff?'

'Come along, I'd better carry you – next time remember your slippers,' Mama said and held out her arms and Poppy jumped into them and let Mama carry her out to the lavvy in the back yard.

'If I promise to be very good and not get them at all dirty, can we go somewhere, Mama, please? It's the only thing I ever want to do, ever, ever – ' All the time she chattered, until Mama brought her back inside to sit by the fire while she got ready the bowl for Poppy to wash her face and hands and brush her teeth, but not once did Mama say anything. Yet somehow Poppy knew it was all right to go on chattering. There were times to be quiet, and there were times to talk. And this was a talking time.

When she had finished her breakfast bowl of bread and hot milk with a little butter and a spoonful of honey in it, and had had her hair brushed and tied back into its ribbons, Mama took the last cakes out of the oven and set them on the table and then, at last, sat down to drink a cup of tea from her own special big cup. Mama had once told Poppy how hot the baking made her and how thirsty she became and explained that was why she needed such a big cup, and Poppy sat on the small stool that was her special one, set at the end of the fender, and watched Mama drink her tea and knew the time had come not to talk. And sat quietly.

'Poppy,' Mama said at last, and so suddenly that Poppy almost jumped. 'Poppy, we shall go out today.'

'Oh, Mama, thank you, thank you so much – ' Poppy jumped up and was about to hurl herself across the room at her mother, but she held up her cup warningly.

'It will be a – oh, heavens, how do I explain? We are to visit some people.'

'In my hat and muff?'

'In your hat and muff, if you wish. Why not? Let them see how charming a child you are – ' And Mama leaned forwards and touched her hair, tucking back one of the curls which had escaped from its ribbon.

'I'll go and get ready!' Poppy cried and ran to the door, but Mama called her back.

'Don't you want to know who they are? The people we are to visit?'

'Er – oh, yes,' Poppy said, thinking only of the hat and muff calling her so loudly from her cupboard in her bedroom upstairs. 'Yes, please, Mama.'

'Your grandmother,' Mama said it slowly and rather loudly. 'And your uncles. And perhaps – possibly your grandfather.'

Poppy stood at the door and stared and then shut her eyes to make sure the kitchen was still inside her head and was safe and comfortable still and then opened her eyes again. The outside kitchen looked safe and comfortable too, but it didn't feel it. Not with Mama looking at her so seriously.

'Oh,' Poppy said, not knowing what else to say. It was very odd to be talking about grandmothers and uncles when she had never heard of them before, but everything was like that really, changing all the time and being strange. New people came, like Nellie Milner, and old people went, like the delivery men, and it was all very peculiar, but it didn't matter so long as when she shut her eyes she could see the kitchen safe and familiar inside her head –

'You must be very polite and quiet when we are there,' Mama said. 'They are very – it is a different sort of house, you see, from this one. Rather big.'

'As big as Gamage's where we got my hat and muff?'

'Not quite – oh, how do I make you understand? Well, you'll just have to wait and see. We'll go on the omnibus – '

And there it was, another wonderful day beginning. Her new clothes and an omnibus as well. And the first day at school to look forward to tomorrow as well – it was almost more than any person could think about, Poppy told herself, and ran to get ready.

It wasn't hard to be quiet when they got to the place they were going to. All the way in the omnibus, sitting at the front downstairs where Poppy could look out and see the backs of the horses, she had chattered happily, pointing out to Mama all she saw, from shops to beggars, boot boys to elegantly dressed ladies, but when they reached the end of the journey and Mama shepherded her out onto the street and the bus conductor lifted her down before the driver whipped up the horses again to make them go clattering off down the road, she fell silent. The street they were in was so very wide and the traffic so very heavy and the houses that towered over her so very large that she began to feel rather alarmed. And when she turned her head and saw that on the other side of the road there were no houses at all but very high railings – much higher than those outside Baldwin's Gardens School – and very tall trees and a great deal of grass she found herself even more alarmed and shrank closer to Mama's side and took one hand out of her muff and took Mama's gloved hand and held on tightly.

Mama stood there very still, making no attempt to move onwards and Poppy looked up at her and saw her staring over the railings into the Park, and she looked herself to see what Mama was staring at; but there was only grass and little knots of trees under which the grass looked dark and shadowy and Poppy pulled on Mama's hand and said in a small voice, 'Shall we go home again now, Mama?'

Mama seemed to start and then glanced down at her, and Poppy looked up at her and decided that she looked particularly well today, in her dark stuff dress with the neat jacket over it to match and her new hat with the little veil in front. Poppy smiled at her and said, 'I do like your hat, Mama! Not as much as I like mine but you look very well in yours!'

And Mama laughed and bent down and hugged her and then began to walk along the road, beside the houses instead of by the big frightening Park. And Poppy was glad of that.

'When shall we go home, Mama?' she asked again, and Mama shook her head.

'Not yet, Poppy. We have come to visit people and we must go and see them. Now we are here. We didn't come out just to ride in the omnibus and walk. I have too much baking to do to spare time for that. I only wish I could – I will be losing a good deal of money today and annoying some of my regular customers as it is. I worked half of last night and shall again tonight, I dare say – so please, Poppy, don't fuss about going home just yet –'

'I'm sorry, Mama,' Poppy said, but Mama just held her hand tightly and said no more.

They turned away from the big road after a while and into a smaller one, though the houses were still as large and then, as Poppy became even more worried, because Mama was holding her hand so tightly and that meant that she was worried, they stopped in front of one of them. And Mama walked up the steps and rang the bell.

It was strange inside the house. It was dark and large and it smelled, but not of lemon or coconut cakes or plum duffs. It was a thicker harder smell which Poppy did not like at all, and she moved closer to her Mama as the man who had opened the front door walked ahead of them into the dimness towards a door on the other side of the big hall which looked to Poppy to be at least as big as the front of Gamage's where they had bought her hat and muff.

'Is that my uncle, Mama?' she whispered, tugging on Mama's skirt, but she just turned and frowned and set a finger to her lips, looking very annoyed, so that was that. No more talking at all after that, Poppy well knew and she bit her lip and put her hands back in her muff and followed Mama into the dangerous darkness.

It was not so dangerous after all. Another big room but not so big that it was frightening, and full of furniture – tables and chairs, sofas and bureaux – and, it seemed to Poppy, people. A lady was sitting on a velvet sofa and some men were standing about or sitting on chairs and Poppy stood beside Mama when she herself stopped walking, right beside the sofa where the lady sat, and tried to pretend she wasn't there.

'Well, Mildred,' the lady on the sofa said and her voice was high and thin and made Poppy think of the sort of sound the kettle made sometimes when it whined to itself that it hadn't quite boiled yet. 'Well, this is indeed a surprise. Basil said you would come but I did not think you would. So I was glad of your note. It gave me time to consider and to arrange – it is better that he be from home, after all – ' The lady stopped talking as though it was just too much effort to go on, and Poppy stared at her, fascinated, for she seemed a very odd-looking lady to her. Her hair was a pale yellow and was piled high on her head in many curls, but they looked so very odd, as though they were made of cotton from Mama's sewing box, that Poppy wanted to laugh. The lady's face was strange too, being full of lines and rather soft and it reminded Poppy of the doll she had once had that she had left, forgotten, on the doorstep when it was very hot, and when she came back to find it, its face had melted.

'Good afternoon, Mama,' Mildred said and Poppy felt her head lift as though someone had pulled her hair from behind, and she stared at Mama and tried to understand. Mama calling someone Mama? It was so silly that suddenly she laughed aloud.

'And this is –?' the thin kettle voice said and the lady looked at Poppy and Poppy looked back, still fascinated. Someone had painted round pink patches on her cheeks, just as had been painted on the face of the doll that had melted.

'This is my daughter, Mama,' Mama said – and Poppy could still not understand that. 'This is Poppy.'

'Poppy? How quaint,' the lady said and lifted her hand towards Poppy as though she were going to touch her. But she did not, and stopped looking at her and said to one of the men, 'Basil, my dear, fetch a book or a toy from the nursery for – er – to entertain our – er – ' and again her voice died away as the kettle's did when the fire fell low in the grate.

'Poppy, this is your Uncle Basil,' Mama said and put her hand onto Poppy's back so that she had to walk towards the men. 'And this is your Uncle Claude. How are you, my dear?' And Mama leaned forwards and kissed the cheek of one of the men and Poppy watched and marvelled. Would this remarkable week never cease to amaze her?

'And this – it cannot be Wilfred, can it?' The other man, Poppy decided, was the nicest of them all, for he was smiling and jolly and had rumpled hair rather than the smooth sort the others had, and he looked at Poppy and said cheerfully, 'Hello!' which no one else had done.

'Hello,' she said. 'Are you an uncle too?'

He laughed loudly and threw back his head in a way Poppy thought very beguiling. 'An uncle! Oh, blow my buttons, that's a ripe 'un! I suppose I am, if you're Mildred's – I say, Mildred, it is good to see you! Oh, I used to lead you such a dance, didn't I? I remember it well! I missed you when you went, and that wretched man Freddy started to get so tiresome – you were always so good at dealing with those sticky situations! It is good to see you – and I do like your little sprig here! Very charming and all that.'

'Thank you, Wilfred,' Mama said and put her hand onto Poppy's back again and directed her to a chair beside the large fireplace, and obediently Poppy went and sat in it, though she would much rather have sat beside the man with the rumpled hair and talked to him. He seemed to be a nice person, much nicer than any of the others who were all behaving as though she weren't there. It was strange to have people do that and Poppy fiddled her fingers inside her muff to remind herself that she was very much there, sitting in a hard chair beside a hot fire in a big rich room with more furniture in it than she had ever seen anywhere, and listening to rather dull grown-up talk. Sometimes such talk was interesting; it always was when Auntie Jessie was about. But these grown-ups weren't nearly as nice as she was, and Poppy yawned.

'Well, Mama, have you been keeping well? I hope so,' Mama said, and Poppy decided to stop listening altogether. She would think about one of her stories, instead, she decided and she bent her head and looked down at her muff and started to think about being a princess. It was easy to think of that when she was looking at such lovely white fur and sitting in such a big rich room.

'I've been very poorly,' the lady on the sofa said. 'Not that anyone in this house cares. No one cares. I thought you did, until you went and left me – though I know you had your reasons, of course, but all the same, to leave me alone with no female to support me – it was very selfish of you, Mildred!'

'Was it, Mama?' Mildred said and looked at Wilfred who winked at her. Both Basil and Claude had repaired to the back of the room and were standing by the window staring out woodenly, patently not joining in the conversation.

'Everyone is so selfish nowadays,' Mama complained loudly and wriggled on her sofa. 'When I was a girl I would never have dared to treat my parents so, to be so cruel and unfeeling – ' And she began to weep. Mildred looked at her, feeling the old sense of helpless irritation rise in her and glanced swiftly at Poppy, but she was sitting there in her chair, her booted ankles crossed beneath her serge coat and dress and leaning back with her eyes closed. Thank heavens, the child's fallen asleep in this warm room, she thought.

'I am sure no one is meaning to be cruel, Mama,' Mildred said. 'It is not always possible for people to do as their parents would wish, of course – ' She stopped as Wilfred suddenly guffawed.

'Indeed it is not,' he said loudly. 'I keep telling Mama that. What sort of milk-and-water son does she want, I ask her? Does she want a great ninny to sit and whine at her feet and never set foot in the world? She would have something to cry about then, I tell her, but as it is, all I can say is that at this time, when my country needs me, I must do what all good mothers must want their sons to do, and that is to be a soldier for my country – '

'Rubbish!' Basil said loudly from the window embrasure. 'You want just to get away from any restraint and kick up your heels in foreign parts. You have as much patriotic spirit as – as a flea and will jump as hard and as fast if any danger ever comes near you – '

'You, of course, are going to South Africa out of a great spirit of duty and self sacrifice,' Wilfred said and his voice drawled now. 'Such a hero you are, that you give no thought at all to the fun of it and the adventure – For my part, I am more honest. I am indeed seeking adventure and if at the same time

I can be of use to Queen and Country, why, so much the better. And you, Mama, should be glad I am made of such stuff – '

'Well, I am not,' the wail came from the depths of the sofa cushions into which Maud had now buried herself. 'I want my boys safe and sound at home at my side. I cannot prevent Basil and Claude, of course, for I am just their stepmother, but you are my own dear boy and so young – ' and the wail grew louder.

'It's all my eye and Betty Martin, you know, Mildred,' Wilfred said cheerfully above the din. 'She knows I shall go no matter what she says or does. Papa says it is a good idea – well, he would, for it will save him money to have me in the army, I dare say – so there is nothing Mama can do. Basil said you could make me change my mind and quieten her that way, but I'll lay old Kruger's boots to a penny candle you won't.'

'I have no intention of trying,' Mildred said calmly, at which another wail went up from the sofa. 'It is no business of mine, so how could I? I cannot pretend I fully understand what all the fuss is about anyway. Why must we fight in South Africa at all? What harm do the Boers ever do us? But if you want to go, then there's an end of it. You'll come back a sorrier man than you went, I've no doubt.'

'If he comes back at all!' Maud raised her flushed face from her sofa cushions. 'Oh, Mildred, tell him how wicked and selfish he is! He might be injured or even killed and what should I do then?'

'The question is, Mama, what should *I* do then?' Wilfred said. 'Tend hell fires or work as an imp, do you suppose? Or do all soldiers killed in battle go straight to heaven to play their harps? I doubt I should enjoy that. All the most interesting people I know are very devilish, especially the ladies.' And again he winked at Mildred.

'Oh, Mildred, what shall I do?' Maud cried again and Mildred got to her feet.

'Mama, I came here not to argue with you or Wilfred, but to introduce my daughter. Whatever happened – whatever I chose to do, she is after all, your step-granddaughter. And you – ' She looked at the three men. 'You are her uncles. I thought it only right that she should know you. But you have showed no interest in her at all. Except perhaps you, Wilfred – ' and she smiled briefly at her half-brother. 'For which I thank you. Happily she is too young to know she has been snubbed, but I know it. And I tell you honestly, I think it unkind, indeed, wicked of you to treat her so. Whatever sin I may have committed, she is a child, and deserves better at your hands – '

She stood there in the middle of the room, her chin up, and in the chair by the fire, Poppy, who was now only half asleep, stirred.

'Dammit, I'm sorry,' Basil burst out and he came across the room towards her. 'I meant no harm, but what do I know of small girls? If you wish me to play with her, say so, but I cannot say that I really know what else I can do. I never had much to do with these – ' and he jerked his head towards Wilfred, ' – when they were little, so why do you expect me to know how to deal with infants now? They are a mystery to me. I am glad you came. I wanted you to come, to help Mama to understand that – to persuade Wilfred – oh, what's the use!' And he flung himself out of the room, leaving the door swinging behind him.

But almost at once he returned, moving absurdly, ludicrously, backwards, and Mildred felt rather than heard what happened there behind her and she stood with her shoulders rigid and her back to the door as once again it swung open.

'What the devil d'you mean by rushing out like that?' the voice growled and at the sound of it Poppy woke up and sat up in her big chair, staring in terror at the source. 'Can't a man come into his own house and find peace and decent quiet in it? What goes on here? What the devil – '

269

Mildred turned and stood with her chin up. 'Good afternoon, Papa,' she said and Poppy, at the sound of her voice, scrambled down and came across the thick carpet to stand at Mildred's side, and clutched for her hand, and found only skirt to which she could cling.

'God be damned, what goes on here?' The man who stood there staring at them was, Poppy decided, the biggest and ugliest she had ever seen, for he had a vast belly and above it a face so red and so whiskered that his eyes seemed not to be there, though there were slits for them. He smelled ugly too, pungent and harsh, like the pubs past which Mama always made her hurry when they went out.

'I have come to visit, Papa,' Mama said and she put her hand on Poppy's shoulder. Her voice was very flat and odd but quite loud. 'And I brought my daughter to meet her relations. This is Poppy, Papa.' And she set her hand behind Poppy's shoulders yet again and urged her gently forwards so that she was standing almost in the shade of the big man's belly.

'This is *what*? Do you dare to bring this gutter creature, this by-blow, here? I found out those lies, and never think I was ever beguiled by them – widowed, indeed! You are a slut and this object here is a slut's brat. And what the devil is it bedecked in? Take it away and yourself with it. There is no place for you or the creature here, so don't come whining your troubles to me. You made your bed, so you get out and go and lie on it!' And he turned and went stamping out of the room, shouting for the man to open the front door and see these people off the premises at once, leaving them all in silence behind him.

25

All the way home Mama sat in the omnibus in silence, staring ahead of her but, Poppy knew, looking at nothing at all. Her eyes looked too dull for her to be actually seeing, and that made Poppy shiver and sit as close to Mama as she could. But she didn't feel really frightened any more, the way she had when she had been at the rich house. Some of the things they had all talked about had been difficult to understand, even when it was about herself, and that had made her feel cold and shaky inside – or had until Mama had spoken so loudly and said such surprising things. Poppy stared at the shops and houses outside the omnibus as it went swaying down Oxford Street towards home and the safe warm kitchen and remembered Mama's voice, high and strong, telling them all how stupid and wrong they all were to behave so to her daughter; and that is me, Poppy thought, and deep inside her warmth rose and swelled and made her feel good.

'Mama,' she said and tugged on her sleeve. 'Mama, I'm ever so glad we're going home. May we have a boiled egg at tea time? I like boiled eggs. Just you and me and boiled eggs by the fire?'

Mama looked down at her and then suddenly set her arm about Poppy's shoulders and hugged her. 'An egg by the fire, just you and me –' she repeated. 'Oh, yes, Poppy, we shall have just that. And hot toast and some seed cake and we shall sit there and be cosy and just be us. No one else at all. Just us. We don't need anyone else, do we?'

'No, Mama,' Poppy said fervently. 'No horrid uncles or – '

'No,' Mama said and then hugged Poppy again. 'Though I would not wish you to think they are all bad. They aren't, you know. Basil and Claude – they are very foolish, I dare say, but they are so frightened of him, that's the trouble. They're all so frightened of him. I used to be, too, so I can't cast stones – ' She was talking to herself now, and not to Poppy at all. 'As for poor Mama – she has been destroyed by it. To see the way she ran after him and grovelled – faugh! It made me sick!'

'It made me sick too,' Poppy said at once, wanting to please Mama, glad to see her so awake again and with her eyes looking bright instead of dull.

'Now, Poppy, you must not speak of matters you do not understand.' Mama seemed to shake herself a little. 'And I dare say I was wrong to let you hear such – I should have realized it would happen so – oh, well, anyway, no more talk of this. We shall just go home and have boiled eggs for our tea and forget all about this afternoon. Now hush – ' And she tweaked Poppy's hat into position, for it had been set awry by her hugging, and made room for some people who had just got on the omnibus to interrupt them, for they had been the only passengers until now.

'That man didn't like my hat,' Poppy said after a while, in a whisper. Even though Mama had said to be quiet, she had to talk about that. 'He said I was bedecked. That's a nasty thing to say isn't it? I'm not bedecked. I'm wearing my hat and my muff and they're beautiful.'

'They're very beautiful,' Mama said. 'But now, Poppy, just sit quietly and – '

But Poppy was not ready to sit quietly yet. 'Nellie from the corner, she's got a grandfather and he doesn't say she's bedecked even when she's wearing her torn ordinary things to come to work for you, Mama, so why did that man say it to me? Is he really my grandfather?'

'I'm afraid he is – but you need never see him again.' Mama was whispering too. 'But we shall not speak of it now. You must not disturb the other passengers. No more chatter, now, do you hear me? Wait till we reach home – '

And Poppy subsided, knowing she must, but determined to talk again about the horrible man when they did reach home. Because anyone who said nasty things about her hat and muff had to be a very bad man indeed, and she wanted to say so.

But when they reached home Auntie Jessie was there, sitting in the kitchen waiting for them.

'I couldn't wait,' she said without ceremony as they came in. 'I told Joe at the factory, Joe I said, I got important business so I ain't working this afternoon, and you can put that in your pipe and lump it, and I came straight over an' got the key from Nellie. Brought a bit of schmalz herring for our tea, a little treat, an' you can tell me all about it. I knew you wouldn't stay there for your teas. They don't do that up West, do they? Ask visitors to stay an' eat. Got to have proper invites there. I know all about it. Better here, eh, Poppela? Our sort of people, when someone comes, they have to eat, be family – better that way, hmm?' And she opened her arms and Poppy ran to her and was hugged till she could hardly breathe.

'He said I was bedecked, Auntie Jessie! The horrible man said I was bedecked! I'm not, am I? It's a lovely hat and muff – '

'They're beautiful and you're beautiful in them,' Auntie Jessie said. 'The most beautiful Poppy in the world.' And Poppy laughed and whirled to speak to Mama. But she looked cross now, and was standing there unpinning her hat and smoothing the veil and frowning.

'I don't want her to grow up vain and foolish, Jessie, please. She looks well enough; but there is no need to make such a matter of it! I wish I'd never bought the things, now, for she

273

has thought of nothing else since. Poppy, take them off immediately and put them away. I do not want to hear another word about them or – '

'But he was horrible, Mama! I never want to have any grandfathers ever if they are as horrible as that. Do I have to have them?'

Jessie crowed with laughter. 'Will you listen to the boobalah! The head she's got on her, it's a miracle! But Millie, tell me, was it so bad? What happened?'

'Poppy, go upstairs – '

'You're wrong, Millie! Believe me, you're wrong – ' Jessie leaned forwards. 'Listen, last time we talked you promised me, you remember? You said no more secrets.'

'I made no promises.' Mildred's face was stony. 'You said it. I didn't, so – '

'Well, I'm saying it again. Secrets make troubles. Let the child listen and learn – she'll come to no harm. Tell me what happened.'

'He was horrible!' Poppy burst out. 'A great big horrible man. The other men were silly, except for the curly one, he was all right and the lady cried a lot, she was silly too, and there were ever so many chairs and tables and it's dark and scary when you go in and there are stairs up to the front door outside as well as inside and no one said have a cup of tea like you always do and Mama does and there were no nice smells like here and the man who was horrible, the grandfather, he smelled worst of all – '

'Poppy, for heaven's sake, child!' Mildred said and Poppy looked at her, a little scared and then, emboldened by what she saw, said, 'Well, it's true, Mama. You know it is. All of it. Do I have to go back there ever?'

'Perhaps,' Auntie Jessie said and Mama frowned and said sharply, 'Why?'

Auntie Jessie shrugged. 'Who knows how things turn out? People change, they get ill, die even. There comes a time when you have to think again, make new decisions. One day she may have to go back, even if you decide you don't want to right now.' She grinned. 'I get the idea you agree with our little one here. You won't be going again.'

'No,' Mama said shortly and looked at Poppy and she clapped her hands delightedly and took her hat and muff and ran to take them up to her room.

As soon as she had gone Mildred said swiftly, 'I'd really rather you didn't talk about it in front of her, Jessie. I know I said – but all the same, it isn't good for her, all this upset.'

'She seems to me to be dealing with it nicely. I never saw a child look less upset, believe me.'

'Perhaps not, but she's an odd child. She thinks more than most, I suspect, and hides a lot. And there's another thing – I don't want her to feel – ' She shrugged, and her face seemed to go blank. 'I want her to feel always loved and wanted, whatever she looks like. To make a fuss over prettiness is a way of making a sin out of ugliness. I don't know how she will look when she is older – now she is pretty enough, as all children are, but later perhaps – '

Jessie looked scandalized. 'That one, later? A beauty. A complete beauty! What else? With those curls and that skin and that little face? And she's got your eyes, amber eyes they are, like the best dark amber, lovely – '

'I told you, Jessie, no fuss about looks, or I will have to make rules about you coming here again and – '

'Yeah, yeah, I know. But about the visit, tell me, what *happened*?'

Mildred managed to smile, a little crookedly. 'Poppy said it all. The house was as I remembered it, too lavish by half, and altogether stifling, and my stepmama did indeed cry the whole time, and the boys – my brothers – were tiresome. And then he came in. I had chosen the time carefully to be sure he would not be there, but I was wrong. Or perhaps someone told him I was coming, for I had sent Mama a note. I did not wish to

275

alarm her – anyway, there he was, and very unpleasant he made himself. I was not surprised.'

'What did he say about our boobalah?'

'He said nothing of her. Referred to her as "it" and my "by-blow" and said I was to take the brat away. Sent for the footman and had us escorted from the house.' Her face darkened even further. 'And only Wilfred protested. My own blood brothers stood there like stuffed monkeys and let him rant and said nothing. He roared at Wilfred too, of course, but at least he stood up for us.' She shrugged. 'There is no need to speak of it again, Jessie. We shall never go back there while that man is there, whatever you say. I have promised Poppy so, and there's an end of it. There will be just she and I. She said that – ' She stopped beside the table, holding her apron in her hands, ready to put it on. 'She sat there in the omnibus and said she wanted boiled eggs for tea and just she and I by the fire. And she will have what she wants. Just she and I – '

There was a little silence and then Jessie said in a carefully neutral voice, 'Without me, then.'

Mildred flushed. 'Of course not. We shall go on as we always have. You visiting us and we visiting you – ' She grinned then, a little awkward suddenly. 'Not as often as you would like, perhaps, but if you had your way you'd live with us. We've been through all that before – '

'Well, that's something,' Jessie said and heaved herself from her chair to go over to the range to make the tea, for the kettle had started to sing more purposefully. 'The child won't lose by having an aunt as well as her mother by the fire sometimes, I promise you.' She made the tea, pouring the kettle slowly and deliberately, not looking at Mildred. 'And what about Lizah?'

'What about him?'

'You said you'd bring Poppy to see him. You agreed with me he had a right – and that she did too, to know her other relations. Not just her West End ones.'

Mildred closed her eyes for a moment. 'Oh, Jessie, give me a chance, will you? Haven't I had enough to put up with today? Don't start harrying me to go and see Lizah – '

' – and my mother – '

'Yes, yes, I know, I remember. Your mother. But give me time. I promise I'll arrange it. Poppy shall meet them – and then we'll see. But not just yet. I can't cope yet. And anyway, I must consider Poppy. I cannot think it's good for her, all at once like this. Be reasonable, Jessie. I try very hard to listen to you, even when it goes against the grain with me. At least give me credit for that and don't rush me.'

'I won't rush you,' Jessie said. 'And I won't rush Poppy. But don't leave it too long, Mildred. It gets to be a habit, you know, not doing things. You stand and look at fences and they grow like they was bushes, higher and higher, and then you think you can't ever get over 'em, so you don't even try. Lizah's a good boy at heart – it won't hurt you to try again – '

'He's a man, not a boy.' Mildred was sharp, almost as sharp as the knife with which she was now slicing bread to be toasted.

'By me, he'll always be a boy,' Jessie said. 'How many eggs should I put on? She can eat two, the little one?'

'Of course not! That would be far too much. Don't make her greedy too, Jessie, for heaven's sake!'

'Ah, pfft – ' Jessie made a soft sound with her lips. 'Such a terrible influence I am on this child! It's amazing she loves me. But you do, don't you, dolly?' And she held her arms wide again as Poppy came back into the kitchen, her pinafore ready to be buttoned on the way Mama liked best, and hugged her so that she almost disappeared into her capacious bosom. And Poppy hugged her back, for she was Auntie Jessie and though she was almost as large as the nasty grandfather had been, she was a much, much nicer person. In fact, Poppy thought, Auntie Jessie was really very beautiful.

And the next day Poppy started school and that completed the most exciting week in her whole life. Mama walked with her to Baldwin's Gardens, making sure she looked neat and tidy with her hair tied in neat bunches at the back and her new pencil box and her slate and her indoor shoes carefully stowed in a bag which had her name embroidered on it, and when the bell rang she joined the lines of children walking into the great sooty red-brick building, turning to wave at Mama who was standing outside the gates with all the other mothers. She wasn't a little girl any more, she was a big girl, Poppy Amberly, a big girl, not a baby, but a grown-up sensible girl who had to do work, learning to read and write and count and thread beads and sew. No more would she sit in her room and struggle alone with the hard words in *The Wonders of God's Beautiful World*. She would have teachers to help her and tell her what to do, and not just Mama when she had time. No more would there just be Poppy and Mama. Now there would be Poppy and Mama and her teacher. And Poppy looked at her mother and waved and felt sad for her that she couldn't come into school as well and have a lovely time with teachers and beads and books. How sad, thought Poppy as she plunged fearfully yet cheerfully into the maelstrom of her school life, immersing herself in the smell of chalk and ink and disinfectant and unwashed children, how sad to be Mama and not have anything so lovely to look forward to each day!

She was right to feel sorry for Mildred, for Mildred was indeed unhappy. It was not just parting with her daily companion that distressed her. She had been fully prepared in her mind for it, had been braced for the time that would come when she would have to let other people take care of her precious child, when she would have to relinquish her control of Poppy's mind and her behaviour, allowing others to guide her. She had managed to hold Jessie at bay – well, at least partly so – but she had known that school days would mean an irrevocable change. Poppy would cease to be hers as she had been all these past five years, and would belong to others, and eventually to herself. But sad though that thought had made her, it did not distress her nearly as much as what had happened at her father's house, and nor did it worry her so much as the fact that Lizah had returned to the edges of her life.

Jessie's words turned and writhed in her head as she walked back from Baldwin's Gardens to her ovens and the day's work, and went on doing so as she beat eggs and kneaded yeast dough and washed currants and chopped almonds. Every time she opened the oven she thought of Jessie cooking for Lizah; every time she withdrew another golden cake or pie she thought of cutting a slice of it for Lizah; every time she sent out another consignment of her finished cakes and counted the money she had earned she thought of having Lizah to help her with her business. Even when Poppy came home for her midday meal, brimming over with excitement and chatter about all she had seen and done with the other children and Miss Rushmore, her teacher, Mildred thought of Lizah. And was furiously angry with Jessie in consequence.

But, she told herself, as Poppy, still chattering but now full of the good dinner Mildred had made her eat – despite her protestations that she wasn't at all hungry and anyway she hated semolina pudding – went back to school for the afternoon, it wasn't really Jessie's fault. Sooner or later this day had to come. I did not produce Poppy all alone. She does have a father, however unsatisfactory he may be in some respects, and that means I may not stand between them.

Or does it? Surely, as the person who has cared for her day in and day out since her birth, I am the best person to know what the child needs? If I decide that she is better off not knowing that ne'er do well, that foolish man who thinks that what matters is the appearance of wealth rather than real worth, that coward who runs away from his responsibilities rather than facing up to them, and whose first response to the news of his child was to suggest destroying her, who can say I am wrong? There would not be another anywhere who would not agree with me.

But that did not comfort her, for others' opinions mattered nothing to her. For Mildred it was essential only that she had a good opinion of herself; if she felt she had behaved well, then others' censure ran off her like water from her newly greased cake tins. The trouble was that when she thought of Lizah, her own body let her down and confused her thinking. She felt again that crawling of need across her back, that sweet deep ache that only he could relieve. The worst part of the visit to Leinster Terrace for Mildred had not been Edward Amberly's display of spleen and ugliness; it had been the sight of the Park and the little cluster of trees with the long grass beneath them where the daffodils grew in March – and she shook herself and went grimly back to rubbing down loaf sugar to make the icing for a special cake she had been asked to bake for the wedding of the daughter of the licensee of the Golden Fleece at the other end of Leather Lane. There were some things it was not right to think about at all.

But one thing she should think about and that was what she was to do about Poppy and Lizah. He *did* have a right and so did she; so what right had Mildred to prevent them from knowing each other, just to protect herself? It was that which she thought about constantly, that day and for many days afterwards, indeed for some weeks. And found no answer at all.

26

And yet there was an answer there, and she found it inadvertently. By taking so long to decide what to do about taking Poppy to meet her father, she found the decision taken from her hands.

Late one Friday evening in October, when the lamplighter had come round not long after tea, for now the days were drawing in the evenings were becoming wintry, Mildred was sitting by the kitchen fire picking over raisins and listening to Poppy read to her. She glowed as she listened, for the child had come on by leaps and bounds in this first month of her school life. She had herself taught Poppy to read when she had been an eager four-year-old with what seemed like an inborn passion for books, and had been amazed then at the speed with which she had picked up her alphabet and come to recognize the shapes and meanings of words on the page, but now she was remarkably fluent. Mildred listened with a half smile on her lips and her fingers flying over her task as Poppy read eagerly from her newest book, Mrs Nesbit's *The Treasure Seekers*, which had been loaned to her by Miss Rushmore at school. There were a few words over which her tongue tripped – though only the very longest ones – but she was clearly enjoying the story hugely. And Mildred listened and watched and enjoyed her enjoyment.

The rapping at the front door was an intrusion they both resented, Poppy frowning and reading more loudly in an effort to overwhelm the noise, but she had to stop when Mildred set aside her bowl of raisins and went out to the passageway to unbolt the front door and peer out into the dark street.

'Millie? Let me come in – oh, am I glad you're here! I was afraid you might be out – '

'Where do I ever go in the evenings?' Mildred said, mildly enough considering how little she relished the interruption. 'I'm always here. What's the matter?'

'I'll tell you, give me a minute to catch my breath, and I'll tell you – ' And Jessie pulled off her hat and pelisse and flopped, panting, onto Mildred's chair by the fire, almost sending flying the bowl of raisins which had been left perched on the fender. Very unusually, she made no effort to hug Poppy, but sat there fanning her sweating face with her hat and Mildred, closing the door against the chill of the passageway, frowned. She must have run from the omnibus to have got herself into such a lather, and that she also failed to make her usual fuss of Poppy, now sitting staring open-mouthed at her aunt from her small stool, betokened great agitation.

'Let me make you some tea, Jessie,' she said, her mind going at once to the practical remedy for all problems in Jessie's world. 'And I've got a ginger cake that broke when I turned it out, so we're having it – then you can tell us what it is that's – '

But amazingly Jessie waved the suggestion away. 'No – no, listen to me. We've got to stop him, Millie. My Momma will go mad, it'll kill her, we've got to stop him. You've got to help me – '

'Jessie, for heaven's sake, what are you talking about? I've never seen you in such a taking – ' And nor had she. Jessie had always been the practical one, the sensible one, the person who strode through everything in the same cheerful insouciant way, be it joy or tragedy, but now she sat there panting and sweating and staring at Mildred with an expression of such anxiety on her face that she looked like an imitation of herself rather than the real person Mildred had known for so long; and anxiety sharpened in her. 'Now, calm down, take your time, and tell me slowly what it is that has distressed you so.'

Obediently, Jessie took a deep breath and leaned back in the chair, clearly trying to compose herself, but the look of anxiety in her eyes did not lessen.

'I was out, you see. Tonight – I was out with Nate Braham – he's started bein' serious about me, and I need a bit of attention, even from the likes of Nate Braham – and we went out to supper at his sister's place, being it was Friday night. And we were talking about this and that and Nate started arguing about when it was that Marie Lloyd did that last show of hers at the old Britannia, and got it all wrong and wouldn't be told. He's a stubborn devil, that one. So I said I had the programme from the show at home, I'd go and fetch it and show him he was wrong. Thank God there was the argument, or I wouldn't have got home till late and who knows, Nate might have come with me and I'd not have gone into the kitchen at all and – anyway, I got home, to get this programme, must have been about nine, half past – house empty of course. I didn't expect him to be there – '

'Expect who?' Mildred was trying very hard to be patient.

'Lizah!' Jessie said irritably. 'Who else? Usually of a Friday night he comes with me to Momma's but tonight Momma told us she was going to bed early, on account of her cold, wouldn't be making no Friday night supper, which was why I said I'd go to Nate's sister in the first place – and I thought, Lizah'll go out with his friends somewhere, Friday night or no Friday night. So, I wasn't surprised the house was empty. But after I got the programme from upstairs, I thought – did he bank up the fire before he went out? It'd be just like him to let it go out – so I went in the kitchen to see, and there it was, on the table – '

'What was?'

'So let me tell you! There's this note. He says he's going to South Africa, he's going tomorrow from Southampton, and not to try to stop him and give his love to Momma. I ask you! Just like that! We've got to stop him, Millie. He can't do it, we've got to go to Southampton and get him back – '

Mildred had pulled a chair forward from beside the table and was now sitting staring at Jessie. 'Get him – but why? He is his own man, Jessie, free to do as he chooses, surely. He always has so far – ' And she looked a little grim as she said it. 'Why expect him to change now? You didn't stop him when he went to America.'

Jessie shook her head in a fever of impatience and almost howled the words. 'That was different, for God's sake! For a start we didn't know he was going till he came back and told us he'd been there, and for the next thing he didn't go to America to be a soldier. And that's what this is about. The great shlemiel's going to fight in this ferstinkeneh war o' theirs and get himself killed. It's dangerous bein' a soldier! And what's it got to do with him anyway? Eh? This war – all about taking gold and diamonds from a lot of poor bloody farmers that never did no one any harm as far as I can see – '

'Jessie!' Mildred said, scandalized, and glanced at Poppy who was sitting with her eyes wide open, fascinated by every word. 'Your language!'

'Oh, oh, I'm sorry – Poppy, boobalah, you never heard nothing, not a word, did you? No you didn't – but Millie, can't you see how dreadful it all is? He's not a soldier, for God's sake! Our Lizah, fighting a war?'

'He's fought in the boxing ring often enough,' Mildred said dryly.

'That is totally different, and you know it,' Jessie snapped. 'There he was making a living. A lousy living, but a living. He fought for money, for a purse, for a bit of attention. But this? This is just asking for trouble, to go fighting in wars. That's real fighting, the sort that kills fellas. And if anything happens to Lizah it'll kill my Momma. All she's got is us two – sure there's my sister Rae, but she thinks of nothing but Joe Vinosky and that business of theirs, and there's Wolfie but he went off to

America Gawd knows how long ago, and who knows where he is now or what he's doing? So there's only me and Lizah. And for Momma the one that matters is Lizah. If anything happens to him – ' She literally shuddered. 'Believe me, Mildred, it don't bear thinking about.'

Mildred sat there silently staring at her and Jessie stared back, her eyes huge in her face as she put every atom of appeal she had in her into her gaze and after a while Mildred looked away. 'I don't see what I can do,' she said at length. 'Or even why I should.'

'To help me. To help Momma – ' Jessie said and then looked very deliberately at Poppy. 'To help everyone who is a member of his family. Hmmm?'

'Jessie, I don't want to hear another word about – '

Jessie held up one hand. 'Give me some credit, do. If you think I'm going to say anything meant for your ears alone to anyone but you, then you do me down. You know me better than that. I'm just pointing out that you got responsibilities in this, just like I have. I got Momma to worry about – You – you got other worries.'

Again there was a silence and then Mildred said angrily, 'But what can I *do*, for heaven's sake? If he's gone, he's gone – '

'Tomorrow – he said tomorrow – ' Jessie began to scrabble in her reticule and then swore under her breath. 'I left the letter on the table, I was in such a state – but I remember it, every word. Tomorrow, from Southampton he's going. With General Buller – ' She gave a little crack of laughter. 'Just like Lizah, puttin' on the dog. The way he wrote it, you'd think he was going to be Buller's right-hand man, that he couldn't do without him, they'd lose the whole war if he wasn't there – but thank God he likes to show off that way. If he didn't we wouldn't know where to begin.'

'And where do we begin?' Mildred asked sardonically.

'At Southampton, of course.' Jessie sounded almost scornful that she had to explain anything that was so obvious. 'We go first thing to Southampton, find the ship this General Buller's on and go and find Lizah and make him get off.'

Mildred stared at her and then threw back her head and laughed with real hilarity. 'Jessie, you're mad! Do you know how many people go on these ships? They're enormous, big enough for hundreds and hundreds of passengers. And I've seen the pictures in the papers – they're packing these soldiers in like sardines in a tin! You'll never find Lizah just like that – '

'Why not? He's only just gone! He's not a soldier in uniform or anything – just our Lizah – he'll stick out like anything in the middle of all that brown stuff they wear – '

Mildred shook her head. 'This won't be some spur of the moment thing. He's planned it. If he knows he's going with General Buller that means he's already joined up and got his uniform and everything organized. Has he got the money to buy a ticket on a ship? No, of course not. You said that was his problem – money. So someone else is paying, and it has to be the army. He's a soldier already, Jessie, and in uniform. He just didn't tell you till tonight – obviously he knew you'd try to stop him. The way Mama is trying to stop Wilfred.' She looked bleak for a moment. 'No, Jessie, believe me, there isn't a thing you can do about it – you'll just have to accept that he's gone and – '

Jessie jumped to her feet. 'I won't,' she cried passionately. 'I have to get him back, for Momma – for – ' Again she glanced at Poppy. 'If he goes and gets himself killed and I hadn't tried to prevent him I'd never forgive myself. You've got to help me – '

'How can I help you, Jessie? Be reasonable, do! There's nothing I can do – or indeed have any right to do – '

'Never mind rights. Do it to please me. Come with me to Southampton and help me. You can do that. I may look like a strutter, but believe me, inside I'm a jelly, a real jelly. Help me, Millie!' And she held out her hands imploringly.

Mildred opened her mouth and then closed it and then opened it again. 'But Jessie, it isn't that easy! I can't just walk out of here the way you can. I have orders to fill tomorrow – there's a wedding cake to deliver, and I promised cherry pies and heaven knows what else besides – '

'Can't Nellie help? Can't she come tomorrow and – '

Mildred shook her head decisively. 'Of course not. It all has to be ready before eleven. I was going to get up at four o'clock anyway to do the work – the cake has to be iced and decorated and the pies baked and there's a whole lot of other things besides – it all has to be ready by eleven – '

'Right!' Jessie pushed her chair back and began to unbutton the cuffs of her great leg of mutton sleeves. 'We'd better get going.'

'What?'

'We've got work to do! I'll help, you just tell me what to do and do it I shall. And then in the morning, we get Nellie over here to see to the deliveries and we get the first train the London Chatham and Dover Railway sends out of Victoria to Southampton. We can get a bit of kip on the train and when we get there, we can get Lizah off and sleep all the way back and be right as ninepence – '

'I'll do no such thing, Jessie!' Mildred began and got to her feet. 'It's the most ridiculous plan I – ' And then she stopped, for Jessie was looking at her with her face so still that she looked carved and yet there was an expression of desolation there that could not be missed. Both women stood in silence looking at each other, the child staring up at them in equal silence for what seemed a very long time.

At last Mildred stirred. 'Poppy, dear,' she said, still not taking her eyes from Jessie. 'Put your book away now and go to bed. Tomorrow Mama and Auntie Jessie must be away but Nellie will look after you and – '

Jessie seemed galvanized at that and spoke at the same time as Poppy began to protest. But it was Jessie's voice that was the loudest.

'Oh, Millie, thank you. Thank you. And let her come with. What harm can it do? Please God we find him and get him off, then it's as good a way of saying hello as any. I mean not so intense and all that – lot of people around, eh? And if we don't find him – ' Her face went still again. 'If we don't, in time to come the child will be glad to know she came with us. That she helped us try.'

'Jessie, you meddle too much. How can you know what she will want in the future? How can anyone know? You take too much on yourself – '

'Maybe I do, but I got the right. I'm her aunt, and I got the right. I have to speak for the rest of her family – let her come with us, Millie. Anyway, maybe Nellie can't stay here all day. And even if she can, you'll get a fever of worry if you leave her here all day, you know you will. She'll have to come with us – '

'If we go.'

'You agreed we would – '

'I didn't say – '

'No, you didn't say a word. But you agreed you'd come. You know you did.'

Again there was a long silence and then Mildred threw up both hands in a defeated little gesture. 'From the day I first met you, Jessie Mendel, you've been more than I can deal with, indeed you have. What can I do?'

'Oh, Millie, Millie, I love you, you know that?' And Jessie hurled herself at Mildred and threw her arms round her and Mildred almost lurched under the impact. 'You'll never regret helping me like this, never. You won't lose by it, believe me you won't – '

'Apart from a night's sleep,' Mildred said and extracted herself and went over to the fire to build it up. 'We'll need to get the oven well up if we're to bake those pies tonight,' she grunted as she riddled energetically at the grate and then began to shovel in the coal. Her face was red and not entirely from her effort or from the heat of the fire. 'I'll need another scuttleful or two before this night's out, so you'd better get your skirts tied up.' She looked over her shoulder then at Jessie's heavily braided and frilled maroon skirts. 'Or better still, take your gown off and work in your petticoats. I can find you an apron.'

At once Jessie began to undo her bodice, which was a major operation, for it was fastened with a double row of heavy small round buttons, as Mildred closed up the range again and pulled out the dampers to ensure that the flames would soon leap high and lift the temperature of her ovens and then went out to the scullery to light her Rippingille stoves.

'Poppy,' she said over her shoulder, not looking at her. 'Do as I said, and put your book away for now. Go to bed and tomorrow we shall go on a train with Auntie Jessie. I can't come up with you tonight, so be sure to wash carefully and brush your teeth and say your prayers. Good night, Poppy – '

And she came back into the kitchen carrying a large bag of flour and her big yellow mixing bowl and wooden spoons and nodded briskly at Poppy.

She got to her feet and pushed her stool back into its corner, glad to escape from the fireside which was already getting too warm for comfort. She was bewildered by all that had happened and all that was promised; to go on a *train*? That was a thought so exciting she could hardly contain it, for she had never been on one before, and to tell the truth was a little sleepy, too, for it was well past her usual bed time. Mama had said she could sit up a little later and read to her, as it was Friday and there was no school tomorrow, and had clearly not noticed the time; and then Auntie Jessie's dramatic arrival had driven away any sense of the clock at all. But sleepy though she was, she was still very well aware of all that was happening and was thinking hard as she moved towards the door, her precious book beneath her arm.

'Mama,' she said as she reached the door and stood there with her hand on the knob. 'Auntie Jessie – why must we go on a train tomorrow? And where is Southampton?'

'It's by the sea.' Auntie Jessie had now climbed out of her gown and was wrapping herself in one of Mama's aprons, which looked a little skimpy on her ample petticoated frame. 'You shall see ships and soldiers and all sorts of lovely things, boobalah, and – '

'Oh.' Poppy stood and thought for a moment, trying to imagine really looking at the sea and at ships and soldiers, for she had only ever seen pictures of such marvels.

'Will you like that?' Auntie Jessie, at a sign from Mildred, had begun to rub down loaf sugar, while Mildred measured flour into her bowl. 'Will it be exciting?'

'I shan't know till I've been there,' Poppy said and opened the door and a draught of cool air came from the passage, fed by the rawness of the night outside. There was a thin fog out of doors and faint tendrils of it came wreathing in through the cracks round the front door.

'Listen to her!' Auntie Jessie said in her usual fond way, all the agitation she had brought in with her quite gone now that she was busy, and had gained her own way. 'Such a head she's got on her! The things she says!'

'Poppy, go to bed,' Mama said again and obediently Poppy went out into the passage and pulled the door behind her. And then had another thought and pushed it open again, and put her head round and looked into the kitchen. 'Mama,' she said. 'Who is Lizah that we are going to Southampton to fetch? Is it someone I know?'

27

They didn't tell her, of course. It really was remarkable how often grown-ups could talk to you and not tell you anything you wanted to know. Last night they had just sent her to bed, scolding her because it was so late, as though that were her fault, and this morning, when they woke her early and helped her dress and gave her bread and milk, they had been in no mood to talk. Both Auntie Jessie and Mama had been tired; she could tell that by the way their faces looked as though they had been stretched. She had considered asking her question again but then adroitly changed it to a request to wear her new hat and muff when she saw Mama's face tighten when she started to speak, and Mama had looked momentarily surprised and then said she could. So that was all right.

Now she sat in the corner seat of the railway carriage with her hands tucked into the delicious warmth of her muff, and the fur on her hat tickling her cheeks agreeably and stared out of the window with her eyes as wide as she could make them, so that she wouldn't miss anything. First there had been the buildings, one after another, piled high and leaning against each other, sooty and steam wreathed, with dirty windows through which she could almost see people in their kitchens and bedrooms, and there had been posters with huge pictures on them and words about buying tea and soap – she especially liked a picture of a monkey wearing an evening suit and sliding down the banisters in a big rich house, watched by two admiring children, and bearing aloft a bar of soap, underneath which was written, 'Monkey Brand. Will not wash clothes', and then more buildings and more posters. But then the buildings had stretched further apart and become little houses, and there had been glimpses of trees, with rich red and brown leaves on them, and grassy gardens and finally no houses at all. That was how it was now; fields and trees and more fields with animals in them – she had identified cows and sheep from her picture books without any trouble at all – and sometimes rivers and ponds and occasionally children on the roads beside the line who waved to the train. She had considered waving back but decided that today she was a Princess, travelling in her kingdom, and princesses didn't wave. They just bowed their heads politely. So she kept her hands in her muff and did that.

At Winchester station Auntie Jessie leaned out, with a considerable display of her petticoats and much to Mama's disapproval, to shout for one of the boys on the platform who were selling chocolate and apples and meat pies from trays, and bought chocolate which Mama refused, but which she allowed Poppy to eat, though only a little, because, as Auntie Jessie said, 'We won't get our dinners till afterwards, will we? We don't know how it's going to be or what we'll find out or how long it'll take – so we got to make sure we're all right. A bit o' chocolate'll tide us over nicely.'

'We had plenty of breakfast,' Mildred said dampeningly. 'And chocolate makes people feel ill sometimes.'

'Not me,' Poppy said fervently.

'Not I,' her mother corrected her and Poppy subsided, pretending she hadn't seen the vast wink that Auntie Jessie threw at her.

But Mama was right, of course. She wasn't really hungry and the chocolate did make her feel a little odd inside. Or perhaps it wasn't the chocolate, but just the rushing around of it all. The train was full of people, mostly women and children like herself and her mother and her aunt, though there were some men too, and all of them seemed to talk of nothing but war and General Sir Redvers Buller and Wicked Old Kruger and Boers who had To Be Taught A Lesson (what sort of lesson? wondered Poppy. Sums or writing or reading? Were they grown-ups and if they were why did they need lessons?) and some of the women cried when they talked of Our Brave Boys. Perhaps it was the crying (crying grown-ups! Awful!) or perhaps it was the smell of soot that the great wreaths of steam sent into their crowded carriage, or maybe it was the chocolate after all; certainly by the time they reached the end of the journey, she felt tired and uncomfortable and not at all as though this were fun. It would be nicer to be at home by the fire with her book, and she felt her eyes ache and fill with tears as she thought of her new story book, alone and lonely in her bureau in her bedroom far away at home.

But no one seemed to notice for the train had stopped at a long crowded platform, and Auntie Jessie seized her by the elbow so that she had to pull one hand out of her muff, and then held on to her, walking fast, with Mama walking equally quickly on the other side, and also holding her hand, so that she had to trot between them with her muff bouncing up and down and hitting her chin as she ran. It was all very disagreeable, especially as the smell of steam and soot was even stronger now and the noise was dreadful; loud whistles and hoots from the great trains that were in the station, and people shouting and talking and carts rattling and jingling. Poppy became more and more miserable.

It became a little better when they got out of the station and into the open air. It was a cold day, blustery and chill, and that made Poppy take a deep breath and it helped. The chocolate, which had taken to hovering somewhere just beneath her chin, seemed to go down a little further to where it ought to be and that helped a lot, and she pulled one hand away from Mama and said, 'Please – I can't run any more –'

'We're going too fast for her,' Jessie said, full of compunction, and bent down and swept her up and settled her against her big shoulder. 'Come on dolly, I'll carry you for a while. All right? But we must be quick. We have to find out where we have to go and there just isn't much time. The sooner we find him, the sooner we can all go home – '

It was nicer not to have to run to keep up with Mama and Auntie Jessie; not nice to be bounced so much, but she held on to her hat with one hand and her muff with the other and shut her mouth tightly to keep the chocolate in its place and stared at all she saw.

People, people everywhere, all running in the same direction. Ahead of her she could see little but high buildings and tall cranes and ropes and carts and horses – a great tangle of things and activities that bewildered her, until Auntie Jessie said breathlessly, 'Isn't that a ship? There – Look – they said to me the station let you right out by the docks – isn't that a big ship?'

'I can see the name, at the side – ' Mama said, and Poppy looked in the same direction Mama was and saw the writing high on the side of what she had thought was one of the buildings. 'Or – ORIENT,' she said and Jessie laughed and said, 'Ain't she a one? Reading it like that, so easy?' And she turned her head and spoke to a man who was walking purposefully alongside them in the same direction.

'Hey, Mister – that ship there – the *Orient* – that the one going to South Africa with the soldiers and General Buller?'

The man was small and rather thin, and next to Auntie Jessie, Poppy thought privately, looked very silly. He was wearing a shiny black suit and a collar so high he could hardly turn his head, and a round billycock hat and he had a clay pipe between his broken teeth. He took the pipe out of his mouth with great deliberation and swivelled his eyes sideways so that he could look at Jessie.

'All the ships is orf to Sarf Africa, lidy, on account there's this 'ere war on. Don't you know nothin?'

'I know well enough not to need to be told by you,' Jessie said smartly. 'All I want to know is whether that is General Buller's ship. If you know say so, if not bite your tongue.'

'Manners, manners!' said the little man loftily. 'That there is not General Sir Redvers Buller's ship, as any idiot well knows. That there is another ship called the *Orient* what sails this morning very soon, wiv some soldiers but mostly wiv ordinary passengers – lot of these 'ere Sarf Africans wot have bin visitin' 'ere scuttlin' back. Not Boers, mind you. We ain't got none o' them 'ere – but Sarf Africans, wot's really English, or was. There's another ship over there, the *Dunottar Castle* what is orf later on wiv the General an' 'is forces. It's a fair walk away, bein' as it's a different dock, but if it's General Buller as you wants to talk to, it's over there you'd better go. I dare say you've got an appointment, like?'

'Of course!' Jessie said loftily and swerved so that Mildred had to change her tack too, and began heading in the direction the little man had indicated.

'Cocky devil – ' Jessie muttered. 'Talkin' to me like that! An' why isn't he in uniform, I want to know, instead of wagging his tongue at the families of those that are?'

'Are you sure we ought to pay any attention to him?' Mildred asked, as they pushed their way through the still thickening crowds. 'Perhaps we should find someone more – someone in a uniform who would be more likely to know.'

'He seemed definite enough – ' Jessie said doubtfully and then shook her head vigorously. 'Look, he was right! There's the other one – can you see? Right over there. And I can see soldiers – look!'

And indeed there were soldiers, a great many of them, marching in serried ranks to the ragged beat of a band that was blowing and beating away industriously on instruments that blinked cheerfully in the fitful morning sunshine; and the two women hurried after it, trying to get in front of the marching men so that they could turn and see their faces.

Poppy, clinging dizzily to Auntie Jessie's shoulders, tried to see what was going on around her as the scene bounced and swayed with each of Auntie Jessie's vigorous steps, and saw the soldiers, men all in brown with big round white hats with what seemed like buttons on the top, and turned down brims, and loads on their backs that seemed to be very heavy and lots of shiny leather straps round them. They wore breeches like the coalman did, only instead of having string tied round below their knees they had gaiters, and looked, as far as Poppy could tell, very pleased to be wearing such strange clothes. Some of them were singing as they marched along, carrying their long rifles over their shoulders and all round them there were people waving and cheering. And crying. All the women Poppy could see were crying, sometimes wiping their eyes with their handkerchiefs and sometimes waving with them, and that made Poppy feel she wanted to cry too. Seeing other people, especially grown-ups, in tears always made her throat and chest feel very tight.

The chocolate reminded her again that it was still inside her and for a moment she wanted to cry out to Auntie Jessie to set her down, because she felt sick, but she was now running with Mama alongside her and it would have been impossible to make her hear in all the hubbub that was going on around them, so Poppy bit her lips and held on more tightly than ever.

The music got louder and more cacophonous as they came closer to the ship, for there was another band on the other side of the dock playing a totally different tune as more soldiers came marching towards the SS *Dunottar Castle* from their side of the dock. Somewhere high above them some men had climbed up a crane and were unfurling a banner on which they had scrawled in uneven black letters, 'Pull old Kroojer's whiskers!' and there were other people clinging to the same crane, as well as to several others, waving Union Jacks in a frenzy of excited patriotism as up the gangplanks of the great ship brown snakes of marching soldiers moved sluggishly.

By this time Jessie and Mildred, with Poppy still perched high on her aunt's shoulder, had reached the centre of the crowd of shouting, waving onlookers and could get no closer. Jessie was craning her head in an effort to see the faces of the men now marching towards the gangplanks in ever increasing numbers, and Mildred was doing the same, but for all that she had the advantage of greater height, she could see little, for they were surrounded by a forest of waving arms and flags and handkerchiefs and banners.

'This is crazy – ' Mildred shouted in Jessie's ear. 'We can't hope to see him or anyone else in this. We ought to try to find someone who is in charge, give his name, see if anyone knows of him. Someone must have such information somewhere – '

'If you can get any closer, then do – ' Jessie roared back. 'I'll stick here – hey, lady, move that great head of yours – you're not the only one, you know – ' And she pushed hard against the woman in front of her, who was wearing a vast plate of a hat with so many feathers and fruits on it that it was impossible to see space between them, and the woman shouted back at her and shoved with her shoulder, and Poppy, now thoroughly frightened, began to wail.

'Out,' Mildred said with determination and pulled on Jessie's arm and they began to inch away sideways, and for some reason that was much easier, for people seemed willing to let them through that way, and gradually, with Mildred leading, the three of them moved crabwise along the dock, going by slow degrees further and further forwards. Jessie, once she realized what was happening, co-operated enthusiastically, and soon, though buffeted by noise and people, they were a great deal closer to the sides of the ship and one of the gangplanks than would have seemed possible just fifteen minutes before.

Poppy had stopped crying and was holding on as hard as ever, and still feeling queasy, but knew she had no hope of attracting the attention of her mother or her aunt, close as they were there below her. They seemed to have been swept up by the tide of excitement that swirled round the great ship and to be pushing and shoving their way towards it as though reaching it were a goal in its own right, and not merely a means to an end. But now they were there and could look up at the ship and actually see faces, some of the excitement that had buoyed them both up seemed to diminish and Poppy felt Jessie's shoulders sag a little beneath her.

'It's absurd,' Mildred said, and she no longer had to shout so loudly, now they were a greater distance from both the sweating, thumping bands. 'How can you think to recognize one man in such a hubbub of men? And all dressed alike – it's ridiculous – '

'At least we're trying,' Jessie said. 'Not to try is the worst thing in the world – and anyway – listen, I'm going to try to get on.'

'On the ship? They'll never let you – '

'Well, like I said, it's worth a try. Here, take Poppy – ' And she reached up and heaved at Poppy and brought her down to the ground.

The great swooping movement was too much for Poppy. She had been trying manfully for a very long time to hold on to herself, had kept pushing the intrusive chocolate down inside her every time it threatened to raise itself too high, but now, all around her dazzled as she stood on the dock and the chocolate, with what seemed like a cry of triumph, leapt into her throat. And suddenly she was copiously and explosively sick.

At once both Mildred and Jessie bent to help her, and Mama held her head as Jessie lifted her and held her horizontal so that she was at no risk of soiling herself, and the people who were around them pushed away and scattered, as people always do in such circumstances, so that the three of them were there in a tiny space of their own, and Poppy, her head swimming and her eyes pouring helpless tears, went on and on miserably retching, feeling as though now it had started it would never stop.

As the two women went on tending to the child the music of the bands changed their rhythm and became more determinedly cheerful with the latest rag tune, and the tails of the snakes on the gangplanks disappeared into the gaping maws on the sides of the ship and the gangplanks were slowly and noisily drawn up and away. The maws closed as crewmen inside the ship clanged the great metal plates into position and there was a renewed burst of cheering and waving from the crowds on the dock.

'It's too late,' Mildred was holding Poppy now, well mopped and lying against her mother with her head on her shoulder and Jessie looked back as they moved away from the unfortunate evidence of Poppy's indisposition and stared upwards.

The ship was now sealed, and above them at the rails faces peered down and arms waved as the soldiers returned the greetings being offered to them from the shore. There was a great deal of activity at the bow of the ship as men scurried with ropes and cables and slowly, slowly, the great mass of metal and humanity moved away from the side of the dock, turning ponderously, as another wave of sound went up from the people below.

'Yes,' Jessie said. 'Too late.' And she stood there and watched as with infinite slowness the gap between the ship and the shore widened.

He'd found a place on the port side, up near the forward section and had held on to it in spite of a good deal of pushing from other blokes, eager to see their wives and families below, standing there with his shoulders braced against the pressure and staring downwards. So what that he had no one to wave to? Why shouldn't he stay there? Hadn't he got there first? In this world no one else would look after you if you didn't, he told himself, and in this army it's going to be the bloody same. And he pushed away the thought that had been clamouring at him more and more this past week; that he had made a dreadful, dreadful mistake. However boracic he was, however much in trouble with Jack Long's lot and whatever debts he had to deal with, nothing was worth giving up his freedom for, and it was obvious that that was what he had done. Ever since he'd arrived late last night at the embarkation barracks and drawn his kit and been given his orders he'd known that. And now he stood morosely at the rail on this stinking troopship with nothing but three weeks of sea sickness and hard tack to look forward too, and Gawd alone knew what after that. Joining the army might seem like a good idea to some, but once you'd done it, you knew what a shlemiel you'd been.

Far below in the crowd, quite near the gangplank up which the last stragglers were now marching, he saw a little flurry of activity and he leaned forwards to see more clearly, not because it mattered but for want of something better to look at. It was impossible to see any details of the people down there, for at this distance their faces were blurred, but he could see a woman in a dark red gown and a great hat, and a child wearing a white hat thrown back onto her shoulders and as he watched he saw the people around them move back quickly and raggedly as though they had been pushed, leaving the little group in the middle of a clear space, and then he laughed. The child seemed to be casting up its accounts good and proper. That's put some of those old trouts down there in a good two and eight, he thought. Honestly, it's as good as being in the gallery at the old Britannia and watching the idiots right at the bottom getting upset over someone who can't hold his drink – and at the thought of the old Brit and the dear old days there he became even more morose and shoved his shoulder more roughly at the man behind him who was pushing so hard to see over his head that his rifle was digging into his back.

'Here,' he growled, looking over his shoulder at him. 'You want to start something? Just remember if you do as I'm a champion boxer, all right? And I don't like being shoved.' And he returned his attention to the dockside, which was now moving slowly away from them as the engines deep below his feet churned and thumped and gouts of black smoke began to appear in the huge funnels behind him. He could hardly see the little group he'd been watching any more, they had become so small. And it didn't matter anyway, for what were they to him, after all? Nothing at all to Private Lazarus Harris, of the London Volunteer Rifles, on his way to war and already heartily sick of it.

28

It started with a dream, or so Poppy thought. She was walking in a big wood with lots of very tall trees, just like the pictures in her *The Wonders of God's Beautiful World* book except that she knew the wood was a real one, because a train was going through the middle of it, and at first it was nice there. The sun was warm on her back and the ground felt soft under her feet and the train bounced her along cheerfully; which was odd because she was walking on the ground and wasn't on the train at all – but then it stopped being so nice. The ground got so soft she couldn't walk on it fast enough and she had to drag her feet out of the softness and pull herself along by holding on to the trees and then it got hotter and hotter as the sun beat down on her back. Only it couldn't be the sun because it was getting dark and the trees were getting very tall and threatening and leaning down and talking to her and telling her to eat up her chocolate and be sick at once – and she opened her mouth to shout at them to stop it, and felt the hot water pour in over her and woke up.

It was dreadful. She couldn't remember ever having felt so hot or hurting so much. Her hair was wet, the hotness was so bad, and she had been sick again. Not a lot, because she had eaten nothing when they had got home but been put straight to bed, which had been exactly where she wanted to be, but now she didn't want to be there. Bed was hot and sticky and nasty from being sick and her head hurt dreadfully – quite dreadfully –

She got out of bed and pulled off the spoiled sheet and then wanted to be in bed again, and crawled back, but now the blankets tickled and tormented her and she had to get out again, and pull off her bottom sheet so that she could lie beneath it and stop the tickling; and then the mattress felt hard and scratched her and all she could do was cry, and that made her head hurt more than ever, as her nose filled up and her eyes began to smart.

She did fall asleep sometimes, in between pulling so on her sheets and blankets, but only for a little while, for each time she slept the dreams came again and they were dreadful and frightening as all the pictures in her books began to wake up and move about and shout at her, and every time she tried to shout back and that made her head hurt more and woke her up again; and then she had to pull at her bed again to try to make it comfortable and that made her cry, and it went on for ever and ever, amen, just like in the prayers she said. For ever and ever and ever and ever –

She must have shouted aloud in her dream because suddenly there was Mama beside her, her face long and white and her voice very loud.

'What is it, Poppy? Now, hush, do, and tell me, what is it? Do you hurt? Where do you hurt? Show Mama – '

But all she could do was shout some more and Mama's face went away and that made her cry more loudly. Until Mama came back, and that was better for she had a wet cloth and a bowl and she put the wet cloth on Poppy's hot face and that was wonderful, quite wonderful. She slept again then, and the dream got better. The darkness had gone from the trees and they had stopped leaning over her, and then they went away and all that was left was brown men marching, and marching – and she and Mama and Auntie Jessie ran ahead of the

soldiers and turned round to look in their faces and then Poppy
had to scream again for they had no faces, no faces at all.

And once more there was Mama's long white face above her
and the cold wet cloth on her head and it was better again –

On the third day Mildred sent a message round by Nellie's
youngest brother, the sensible one, to Jessie. She had thought
she could manage well enough; had she not looked after
Wilfred when he had the croup and then Samuel and Thomas
when they had the chicken pox and had been so irritable? She
had sat up with them often enough making sure they did not
scratch and so infect their spots, so she should have been able
to look after one small girl.

But what Poppy had was worse than croup and it was worse
than chicken pox. She had sent for the doctor on the second
day – which had amazed the neighbours considerably, for who
ever spent money on such a thing in Leather Lane? – and he
had shaken his head and told her that this year the measles
were especially bad and there was some scarlet fever at the
school too, and it was very possible she had one of them.

'I cannot say at this stage,' he had said portentously, looking
down on the flushed little face on the pillow. 'I dare say it's the
measles and the child will be like this till the spots appear.
There are several cases at Baldwin's Gardens School – she is a
pupil there? Yes – and I dare say she may well have it. There
are those that say they can tell if it's measles from spots inside
the mouth – some new nonsense from America, where all such
nonsense comes from – but you must pay no attention to that.
When she has the spots on her face is soon enough to be sure.'
He shook his head then, even more ponderously. 'If, of course,
it is the measles she has and not the scarlet fever. If she gets
the white strawberry tongue then we can be sure. At present it
is but a fevered tongue. So keep her cool and keep her dark,
and we shall pray. There have been many deaths from the
measles this summer, to be sure –' And he had gone away,

pocketing his half-crown fee and leaving Mildred feeling so cold with fear she could hardly breathe.

So, by the morning of the third day she could manage alone no longer. The sleepless nights and the long days of trying to maintain her work and fill her orders, while running up and down the stairs to lay cooling cloths on Poppy's hot forehead, added to the terror which the doctor's words had dripped into her mind, took their toll, and when she dropped a fresh boiled meat pudding on the floor because she had fumbled as she took it from the copper and it burst and sent its scalding contents all over her legs, she admitted defeat. She needed help.

Jessie came almost at once and the first thing she did was send Mildred to bed. 'You can't look after her if you're exhausted,' she said practically. 'Tell me what I have to do and then go. I promise I'll be as careful as you would yourself, so – '

'I can't go to bed,' Mildred said. 'I'll sleep in a chair – '

'Bed,' Jessie said firmly. 'What good can you do sitting there? If you're asleep? Believe me, I'll be there. I'll watch and if there's anything you should know about, know about it you shall. I'll call you – '

'You promise? Whatever happens, you'll call me?'

'What's to happen? The boobalah'll get hot. I'll cool her with the cloths, she'll sleep, she'll get hot, I'll cool her. And she'll get better, please God, a day or two and she'll get better – '

So Mildred went to bed and slept with the heavy stillness of total exhaustion and Jessie sat and watched Poppy and went through the ritual of wetting the cloths and setting them on her head and then, after a while, sponged her down with cool water to bring down her fever which was clearly raging. But Poppy became more and more ill, and more and more hot.

At six on the morning of the fourth day Mildred woke suddenly from her deep sleep and went padding at once into Poppy's room, not stopping to put on her wrap or her slippers, and with her hair tangled on her shoulders, for she had not even stopped to plait it yesterday after Jessie had come and sent her to bed. And her terror and fury rose, for Jessie was sitting in the armchair beside the bed, her head back on the cushion and her mouth half open in an unlovely gape as she snored gently and Poppy was lying sprawled on her bed with the blankets thrown back to expose her bare legs.

She pushed past the chair, waking Jessie abruptly and leaned over Poppy and touched her, for the child was lying ominously still but after a moment Poppy moaned and half opened her eyes and then closed them again and pushed feebly at Mildred's hands as she tried to cover her again.

'Leave her, leave her – ' Jessie said. 'Poor little dolly, she's so hot the blankets upset her – I let her lie that way and she slept, for the first time she slept. Better to leave her – '

'What do you know? The first night you're here and you can't stay awake!' Mildred said and her voice rang with ice. 'She could have died, lying there with no one to care, and you snoring and me – ' And she choked on the words and turned back to the bed where once again Poppy was trying to push away the blankets with irritable little movements of her hands.

'Die? Who's talking of dying? You shouldn't even think of such things, let alone say them!' Jessie cried and turned her head and spat twice. 'D'you want to bring an evil eye on her? Such talk – '

'Evil eye!' Mildred said, and the contempt in her voice was even colder. 'That sort of ignorant talk is even worse – there have been children dying already from this – and we still don't know what it is – measles, scarlet fever – we still don't know – ' And she turned back to the bed and bent over and pushed the sweat-damp hair back from Poppy's forehead and peered at her in the thin morning light, looking for the signs of the rash that would announce a diagnosis.

Poppy moaned and half opened her eyes and began to gabble and Mildred leaned even closer and said softly, 'What is it, darling? What do you want?' But there were no sentences there, no sense at all; just a string of disconnected syllables, and Jessie came to the other side of the bed and said loudly, 'Hush you, now, boobalah, go to sleep – '

And amazingly Poppy did, opening her eyes again at the sound of Jessie's voice and looking at her with what seemed like puzzled enquiry and then closing them and seeming to sleep, and after a while Mildred straightened her back and looked across the bed at Jessie.

'I'm sorry,' she said dully. 'I didn't mean to be – I'm glad you're here. I need your help.'

'Not to worry,' Jessie said gruffly. 'Listen, go get washed and dressed and then come here. I go make some breakfast – no, don't argue. Much good you'll be if you get ill on account you ain't been eating. Go already – '

The day wore on with no change in Poppy, and Mildred agreed, though very unwillingly, to go and spend a couple of hours in the kitchen dealing with her urgent orders while Jessie sat and kept watch.

'No sense in you losing money,' she said with great practicality. 'Sick little girls, they need a lot of good food when they get to convalescence, got to be built up, and that costs money. Go, you make the cakes, make sure the business runs. I'll call you – and I won't sleep – ' She stopped and said awkwardly, 'Believe me, this morning, it hadn't been more'n a second or two – '

'I know,' Mildred said. 'I know. It's just that – ' She took a deep breath. 'I'm so frightened. The doctor said, they're dying – if Poppy – ' And she closed her eyes, refusing to contemplate the horror of it.

'I told you, you don't want to talk of such things.' Jessie sounded gruff. 'You got to think positive – she'll be fine. Go make cakes. I'm here, use me, already – ' And she gave a sudden little lunge and leaned over and hugged Mildred awkwardly and then pulled away, pink with embarrassment, for that was the sort of thing that Mildred so disliked –

So Mildred baked and Jessie watched and then, at around nine o'clock when Mildred had set a bowl of soup and some freshly made toast on the table ready for some supper for Jessie, before going up to take over her vigil by Poppy's bedside, she heard Jessie calling urgently from the top of the stairs, her voice tight and shrill with anxiety, and she ran, almost unable to move her legs because of the way fear had lurched into her and turned her muscles to quivering jellies.

'It's the way she's breathing suddenly,' Jessie's face was white and strained. 'Come and listen – what is it? I don't know – '

As soon as she was in the room Mildred knew. Croup, that dreadful laboured whooping breathing that made it sound as though the child was fighting for every breath, the sound that she had become so used to when she had nursed Wilfred, and at once she whirled and went hurrying downstairs to the kitchen again. Knowing what to do was the only comfort she had, and also her strength, for the jelly left her legs now, and she could move purposefully, even economically. The kettle was, as usual, on the boil and she seized it and went running back upstairs as fast as she could.

'Get me the Friar's Balsam,' she snapped at Jessie who was standing beside the bed and leaning over it watching Poppy with her eyes wide and terrified in her pale face. 'Move, woman! We have to be quick – '

With swift assured movements Mildred took the small green bottle Jessie fetched her and poured some of its contents into the wash bowl from the stand in the corner and then poured the hot water from the kettle over it and the room filled with the thick fragrance of the resinous stuff and seemed to get even warmer.

'Fetch up the small oil stove from the corner of the scullery,' she said curtly to Jessie. 'And bring the matches with you from the mantel in the kitchen – and a jug of water – and be quick – ' Already she was lifting Poppy, still producing those hoarse struggling sounds, from the bed, wrapping her in a sheet, and bringing her across the room to the wash stand where she had set the bowl full of spicy steaming water. 'Hurry up!' She almost screamed as Jessie hovered by the door, watching her fearfully, and then crouched beside the bowl, and holding Poppy carefully arranged her head so that the steam from it could reach her mouth and nostrils.

By the time Jessie came panting back up the stairs, the small oil stove in one hand and the jug of water slurping in the other, Poppy was breathing a little less noisily as the steam softened her tortured throat, and at a sign from Mildred Jessie tiptoed across the room and set the stove near the bed.

'Light it,' Mildred commanded. 'And fill the kettle and put it on it. As soon as it's boiling, I'll bring her back – '

The two women worked in grim silence, and then, as the steam from the bowl of balsamic water subsided and the kettle began to boil on the oil stove, sending its stream of grey steam into the hot air, Mildred, moving with infinite care, brought Poppy back to the bed and, piling the pillows as high as she could, set her against them and then arranged the kettle so that the steam came and curled its way round Poppy's head. And then she ran to her own room and pulled a sheet from her bed and came back to pin it over the head of Poppy's bed, tying the top of it across the brass railings of the bed frame, and tucking the sides in halfway down the bed to make a sort of open-fronted tent inside which the steam was trapped.

Slowly the noise began to subside, as the harsh croaking breaths eased and at last Poppy slept, her eyes almost closed but with a rim of white showing beneath the lids. Her mother and her aunt sat on each side of the bed and watched and listened, as outside the night thickened and then began to lighten as an unwilling dawn skulked into the sky above the roofs and chimneys of the City away to the East and people and traffic began to stir in the street below.

They had been silent for a long time, listening to the plop and hiss of the gas mantle over the fireplace and the steady bubbling of the kettle on its oil stove and the sounds of breathing from Poppy. They were still difficult, still effortful, but far less so than they had been during that dreadful, terrifying hour when it had started, and as she sat and watched her child sleep Mildred felt rather than thought, watched ideas and words wander around inside her mind rather than gave conscious attention to them, and was almost as surprised as Jessie when suddenly she spoke. She had not known this was how she felt, had given no attention at all to the ideas that had come to her, but as the words came out of her mouth knew beyond doubt that she was right.

'I shall never speak to him again. Ever,' she said in a low voice.

'What?' Jessie had been sitting very still too and was also not actively thinking; she was by no means asleep, but she was not fully conscious either, sitting suspended in a limbo between alertness and lethargy and just letting the time slide over her.

'If we had not gone there, had not dragged her there, it wouldn't have happened – ' Mildred was speaking as much to herself as Jessie. 'If he had not been so stupid as to run off like that, you wouldn't have been so stupid as to follow him, and I wouldn't have been so stupid as to agree to go with you. If she dies it will be the fault of the stupidity of all three of us, but mostly his, for he started it all. Mostly his – '

Jessie stared at her, alarmed by the venom in her voice. 'But Millie – you said the doctor said – there's measles and scarlet fever at the school. She must have got whatever it is there – '

'What's that got to do with it?' Mildred said savagely and now she did look at Jessie. 'So she caught measles? Don't they all get measles? Of course they do. But they don't all get so ill! If she hadn't spent that awful day there in all that noise and – all that nonsense of music and soldiers and people shrieking and crying like demented parrots, she would have been quiet and safe at home here when she started to feel poorly, and I'd have sent her straight to bed and she would have been well by now – but she went to that horrible place because of you, because of him, and now if she dies – '

'She won't die!' Jessie said shrilly. 'She won't die! You know she won't! Don't say such things, you shouldn't speak of such things – '

But Mildred ignored her. 'If she dies it will be at his door that the fault lies. If she dies – I shall hate him for always. And if she lives I shall hate him for always, for all the suffering she has had. And for my own – I shall never speak to him again – '

And that was all she would say. Jessie tried to reason with her, to persuade her that by no stretch of any imagination could anyone be blamed for Poppy's present state and certainly not Lizah. But Mildred sat there rocklike and silent, as the day lifted outside and scrubbed the small window of the bedroom from deep indigo to pallid grey, and refused to listen. Jessie could see that the words she poured out rolled over her unheard, and at length gave up. When Poppy was better, and Mildred less frightened and exhausted, then she'd understand that it was no one's fault that Poppy had been ill and would forgive everyone, including Lizah. And Jessie badly wanted Lizah to be forgiven, for wasn't he now a soldier, nebbish, a poor boy gone to fight for Queen and Country, worthy of attention? And wasn't he, a deep inner voice whispered, her beloved Poppy's own blood father? And if he once could be acknowledged as that, and married Mildred, as Jessie so much wanted him to, wouldn't then Jessie herself be able to see more of Poppy and love her as freely as she wanted to, yearned to and needed to? So did Jessie tell herself as she sat quietly and waited for Poppy to recover, and bided her time.

29

Before the SS *Dunottar Castle* had passed through the Azores to reach the Canaries, Lizah had decided that there had to be a way to get out of the army and back home that did not involve travelling on ships. His knowledge of geography was sketchy in the extreme, but he felt sure that there must be a route from Cape Town that would take him home overland; certainly, he told himself, no power on this earth could get him to suffer again as he had suffered during that first dreadful week of buffeting and juddering. He had been so sick as no man had ever, he told himself fervently, been sick before. He had lain in that godawful hammock swinging helplessly with no one to give him any aid at all, surrounded by countless other men as sick and miserable as he was and making a damned sight more noise about it than he did, and promised himself and any God who might be listening that the moment he got to stinking Cape Town he was walking away from this lousy army and setting off home. And if it took a year to make it on wheels, then so be it. Never again, he whimpered between his bouts of retching, never ever again on a ship –

But then the sickness stopped and together with the rest of the regiment he crept out on deck, blinking like a woodlouse newly freed from its prison under a dark rock, into the sunshine and glittering blue freshness of the sub-tropical sea and began to feel better; and knew how much better when even the army's dull porridge and bread and plum jam tasted good. He would have preferred his mother's salt beef or stuffed chicken neck or gedampte beef laced with carrots and onions and rich gravy, but this would do well enough, and he ate it ravenously and asked for more and even began to enjoy some of the fun the men were organizing for themselves. When they crossed the equator, in particular, they all had a very noisy time of it and General Buller, wise in the ways of soldiers, allowed an extra ration of grog and though that did give Lizah a queasy morning afterwards, for he had little capacity for alcohol even though he liked to drink it, he began to feel life was worth living after all, even in the army.

And then it became even more worth living, for while he was sitting on deck the day after the equatorial crossing, his back to a bulkhead, recovering slowly from his binge, he heard someone shout his name and lifted his chin cautiously to see a group of men leaning over the rail of an upper deck and staring down at him.

'Hey, Kid Harris – you're Kid Harris, ain't yer?'

'What if I am?' Lizah had learned long ago the importance of keeping his guard well up.

' 'Ere, mate, I wants to shake you by the 'and, I do! Won me a sov an' an 'arf, you did once, when I needed it real bad, five or so years back – when you knocked out Jerry the Yank in the third, down the Whitechapel Road. Put on a bob I did, just a bob, on account the Yank was the way out favourite an' you just walked it 'ome and the odds was the best I ever 'ad! Come on up 'ere pal, and let me shake you by the 'and!'

And from then on it was jam all the way. Or almost all the way. Almost within an hour the whole ship knew there was a champion boxer on board, and within half a day, matches had been arranged to be fought in a hastily rigged ring in the stern so that Lizah could show his mettle against all comers, and willing bookmakers came crawling out of every corner to do brisk trade when the officers weren't looking.

Not that they weren't interested. Lizah, after putting on a nice show of unwillingness, agreed to fight only if he could have a few days training time, and found a section on the boat deck when he could skip and jump and shadow box and generally get himself back into some sort of trim, and there he spent his days working hard – but not so hard that he was unaware of his audience.

There were several young officers, very dashing in their crisp newly tailored uniforms, who watched him covertly and then went and watched the other men who had decided to put themselves up against the so-called champion and then came back to watch and whisper before laying their bets; and Lizah, grinning behind his fists as he feinted and jabbed at an imaginary foe, deliberately put on a show of incompetence to mislead them. Think they could tell what he could do just by watching him train? Let 'em think again. He was Kid Harris, and he could outsmart as well as outbox any of 'em –

Not that he was as certain as he might be of his ability to defeat all comers, as he had assured his new-found cronies he could. The first day he spent on his boat deck training area made him realize just how out of condition he was, and just how long it had been since he had been a real top liner. There was no reason to suppose he couldn't get back into good nick, he told himself as he panted rather more heavily than he liked, none at all. But he needed time. And the fight wasn't going to be easy, anyway, using gloves that weren't really his weight, but which were all that were available from the ship's meagre store of entertainment and sports equipment, and on a sloping shifting deck rather than in a properly constructed canvas ring. But he had always been an optimist, had always had a deep conviction of his own ability; as long as he didn't lose his confidence, he told himself sturdily, he would come to no harm. 'Believe you can do it, that's the thing,' he gasped beneath his breath as he made a series of hard jabs with his left, which had always been his weakest. 'Believe you can do it – that's the thing of it – '

The first match had been arranged for a late evening after the men had their evening meal and before being bunked down for the night, and as soon as he heard the four bells that announced the end of the second dog watch he went aft to the roped-off section of the deck where the men waited, smoking and laughing and passing round what was left of their illicit store of booze; they had another week at sea yet and supplies were running low, so there was no heavy drinking going on and Lizah was glad of that. If he lost, so many of them had bets on him that the effect wouldn't bear thinking about. They could get nasty enough sober –

The sky was a vast bowl of rich blue above them and the sea shivered on each side with the barest movement, for there was no breath of wind at all. The air felt thick and hot, for the sun had blazed on the decks pitilessly all day and the wood and metal now began to give back to the air the heat they had collected and he stood for a moment, his hands, already bandaged, dangling at his sides and his gloves looped round his neck on their strings. He was wearing just his drawers, for he had no other fighting kit with him, and the warmth on his suntanned skin made him sweat a little, and he frowned. Sweating already and he hadn't even begun yet –

He took a deep breath to encourage himself and stepped smartly round the bulkhead into the crowd and pushed his way through to the ring, an area marked out with chalk on the deck and enclosed with a few loops of rope, where his second – the man who had won the money for which he had been so grateful five years ago – waited for him, and a cheer went up which made his chest swell with pleasure and regret and fear, all mixed together into an uneasy lump. The pleasure was simple; to be fighting again was a delight. But the regret and fear did spoil it; regret for what he had been and was no longer, for the years which had stolen some of his speed and agility, and the fear which he had always felt when he stepped into the ring, but would never have admitted to anyone. No one seeing him would have known any of it, for he just grinned and ducked under the rope and came into the ring to hold out his hands to his second to have his gloves tied into place.

'Who's the first one?' he asked, his voice low beneath the din made by the audience, now several men strong. 'Got any tips on him?'

'I bin watchin' 'em train – ' the second said, and grinned. He was a carroty-headed man with only one tooth in his upper jaw, which gave him an oddly leering look when he smiled, which was often. 'It's an orficer – a right weed 'n' all – but he's got the science, like. Shifts 'imself around a bit and fast on 'is feet. But 'e don't look to 'ave no real class at all – you should get 'im easy.'

'Right, gentlemen!' the shout went up behind them and Lizah moved forwards to turn and stand with his back to the rope, staring down at his gloves. Let the referee get his chat out of the way, and then he'd be able to get a good dekko at the opposition, size him up, see where his weaker spots were most likely to be –

'This will be a clean fight, a straight fight, an honest fight as befits the British Army, and it will be a fight which General Buller himself approves of. I have it direct from him that he is glad to see his men occupied in such a manly occupation that will fit you all for the coming confrontations with Kruger and his boring Boers! It is understood, of course, that there is to be no gaming involved – just a good clean fight as befits British soldiers!'

A low groan went up and there was some catcalling but the referee, a fresh-faced boy of little more than twenty-five, yet wearing a captain's insignia, ignored it.

'Right then, in this corner the welterweight champion of Whitechapel, boxing at ten stone seven pounds, as far as he knows, seeing we have no scales available – '

' – I'll bet 'e's a good deal lighter on the tack you bin givin' us!' someone roared from the back of the crowd and there was a loud cheer, but still the young captain paid no attention and went on unperturbed.

'Here he is, Ki – i – id – Harris!'

This time the cheer was much less ragged and even louder and someone shouted, 'You show 'em, Jewboy! I got arf a week's pay on you!' at which the referee frowned sharply and shouted, 'There is to be no betting, I said! Just a clean honest fight, no betting, by order of General Buller!' But no one paid any attention at all, and the captain after a moment decided to make no further fuss. With so many men there, it seemed the wiser course of action.

'In this corner,' he bawled instead. 'In this corner, the challenger, ex-City of London School Sixth Form Champion, fighting at ten stone six pounds, though with the advantage in height – '

Lizah lifted his head at last and looked. Now was the time to get his opponent's appearance clear in his eye and he looked and swallowed and stood there, his face as stiff as though it had been frozen.

' – the one and only, your challenger and mine, Lieutenant Ba – a – asil Amberly!'

He was grinning, that was the thing. He was standing there in the corner as the referee fussed with checking his gloves and was grinning over the shorter man's head with such smug complacency that Lizah wanted to go over there and not wait for the bell, to hit him and hit him until his face was a pudding, just as he'd done to him once before –

The bell seemed to come from a long way away. He had hardly been aware of the referee dealing with his gloves or muttering the usual stuff at him about fighting clean; all he knew was that Basil Amberly was there in the middle of the ring with his gloves up and standing in the recommended posture and looking unbearably smug and pleased with himself, and Lizah went in with both hands up and sweat pouring into his eyes and anger boiling up in him as though he were a kettle.

It had been a long time since he had fought like that, with real hate in him. In the early days at Father Jay's gymnasium he had always fought so, for he had known no other way. Hadn't he spent his childhood fighting the jeering boys who shouted after him in the streets because he was a Jew? Hadn't there always been hatred in him for the boys – and later, men – he had fought with? Had there been any other fuel with which to make his muscles do as he bade them?

Father Jay had taught him that there was; that being angry and hate-filled made a man a worse fighter, not a better one. That a cool head that thought about strategy and made plans and carried them out was what won fights, not just fury. And under his tutelage the angry child had become the cool fighting man and been very successful – until recently, at any rate.

But now all that was forgotten. All he knew now, on the SS *Dunottar Castle* in the middle of the Atlantic Ocean, the most unlikely place in which he had ever had to box, was that he had an opponent he hated. He hated him because he loved his sister, and if that was crazy and illogical, Lizah did not care. Right from the start it had been Basil Amberly who had spoiled things for him and his Millie, he told himself as he jabbed and punched and dodged and feinted and jabbed again; the fact that it had been Basil who had brought them together in the first place didn't matter. They would have met anyway, because it was meant that they should. But it had also been meant that they should stay together. Of that Lizah was certain; but they had been kept apart. He conveniently forgot that pressure from his own mother had come into the equation, and that his own doubts about being able to cope with a baby had played their part too; all he knew now, as he bobbed about in the makeshift boxing ring on the deck of the SS *Dunottar Castle*, was that ever since his first meeting with Millie it had been trouble with Basil that had kept them apart. Basil and his hateful stinking family of jumped-up snobs just like himself – and Lizah had to be pulled away by the referee as the bell went to end the round.

' 'Ere, go easy,' the second said reprovingly as he mopped his face with a rag and offered him water to wash his mouth. 'You're layin' in to 'im like there ain't no tomorrow! You got to go fifteen rounds with this 'un, and there's three more fights set up for you. The books are big 'n' all, so go easy, mate – '

'I'll kill the mumser,' Lizah grunted as the bell went for the next round and was up and away so fast that Basil didn't see him coming and for the first time, Lizah managed to knock him down. He was up on the count of five, though, but that was enough to give Lizah a chance to catch his breath and begin to think. The carroty man was right; he had to be less furious and more scientific. Amberly was taller and had a longer reach, but that could be an asset for Lizah, properly used. Get under his guard, that was the thing of it –

And Lizah did. He thumped and punched steadily and more than once his glove made a juddering impact with Amberly's thin frame that sent shock waves up Lizah's arms to his shoulders, but he gloried in the pain and went on glorying in it as round succeeded round and Amberly began very obviously to tire.

In the middle of the sixth round, as the watching men shouted themselves hoarse, Lizah knocked him down again, and as the referee began to count him out, turned away, jubilantly. He'd done it; he knew he had. Amberly had been getting steadily more sweaty, more breathless, and more wild in his blows, and Lizah had been fighting better this past two rounds than he had in all his fighting life and he lifted his chin to acknowledge the cheers and bawls that were coming from all sides.

It was that which defeated him. Somehow Amberly got to his feet before he was counted out, and somehow, moving drunkenly though he was, managed to get round to stand in front of Lizah. And as the officer looking after the bell lifted his hand to strike it, his eyes glued to his watch, Amberly swung out, a great unco-ordinated movement of his right arm that seemed to have little power in it, and yet which had collected enough momentum by the time it ended its arc to be lethal.

Lizah, his chin up and both fists resting dangerously low at chest level just happened to be in the way rather than anything else, for no one else could imagine that Amberly knew what he was doing by this time, but it made no difference to the final effect. He hit the deck with a shuddering blow that made the ship seem to swing directly from daylight into darkness and leave him lying there gasping, and by the time he had come back to the glowing deep blue of the sky it was too late. The referee was shouting 'Ten' at the top of his voice and the crowd of men were shouting and booing, and a few cheering. Lizah had lost and taken a good deal of his fellow soldiers' money into oblivion with him.

'Lousy Jew!' someone bawled and the referee looked up and shouted reprovingly at him but in the hubbub no one noticed, except perhaps Basil and Lizah. Lizah had struggled to his feet, his head spinning, and now stood staring blankly at Basil who was grinning hugely, in spite of the cut lip that was trickling a thin line of blood down his chin, and a bruise that was rapidly appearing on his bony forehead.

'That's one for my sister, you stinking bastard,' Basil said, and laughed at him. 'You hear me? One for my sister! I knew I'd get my own back one day, but I didn't know it'd be here – and now I have, I hope you rot – you hear me? I hope you rot.' And he turned and went back to his corner to be patted and petted by a crowd of officers as the men, disgruntled and still shouting their anger at Lizah, began to drift away to their quarters.

'I knew we shouldn't let an enlisted man fight an officer!' The captain who had been referee was peering into Lizah's face and shaking his head, as the medical officer came into the ring to look at him and prod his eye, which had become spongy and swollen. 'I told the Brigadier I thought it bad for discipline, but he said the General liked the idea, thought it was democratic, good for morale, and so forth, and now look!'

'For God's sake man, don't be so stupid!' The MO started to apply arnica to Lizah's eye, paying no more attention to him than if he had been a side of meat. 'The General is right. It would have been different if the man had beaten Amberly of course – but as it is, it's all turned out excellently as I knew it would. Excellently. Now they know their betters can fight as well as they can, these chaps, and that should give them some sinew when they're in the field. Excellent outcome – excellent – now, you, my man – ' For the first time he looked Lizah in the eye. 'Keep on applying this stuff, and come to my parade in the morning. And next time don't go boasting about how you can beat an officer in this army. They're the salt of the earth, and the sooner you chaps learn to knuckle under the better. You won't be so big for your boots another time, hey?' And he chuckled and went away, followed by the captain-referee, now looking a good deal happier than he had.

'Well, you did go and bloody cock it up, didn't you?' The carroty man said disgustedly. 'After all that bloody talk an' all, and what d'you go and do? Give it away, and all my bleedin' money with it. Don't come to me for help no more, matey! All talk and no do, that's you – '

'Shut up – ' Lizah managed to gasp. 'An' get these gloves off me – ' Sulkily the man obeyed. 'An' don't give me chat about how I let you down. It weren't my idea – it was you lot shouting the odds that made me fight. I told you – I was out o' training – ' He waited as the gloves came off his bruised hands, and then stood there and looked down at his knuckles and his mouth tightened.

'By God, let me get that man alone some time, and I'll show him – I'll show you all what Lizah Harris can do – he won't ever do that to me again. And he won't get away with it ever again, neither, interferin' in my life – I hate the bastard. You hear me? I hate him for all he's done to me and to mine and I'll kill him – '

The carroty man peered at him, puzzled. 'You know 'im, then? I mean, outside the army like?'

'Know him? I know him,' Lizah said grimly. 'An' one of these days I'll show 'im. He'll wish he'd never been born, after what I'll do to him – just you wait and see – '

30

Once the rash appeared, Poppy seemed to recover fast. Her fever fell and with it Mildred's fear, and for a couple of days, as the spots spread and coalesced to create the familiar reddish blue patches that announced that the diagnosis was undoubtedly measles, she was in the highest of spirits in spite of her fatigue. She just had to nurse Poppy back to her old sturdiness with lots of good food and loving care and she could forget the dreadful days of uncertainty when she had been so sure that the child would die.

And she began to be ashamed of herself for the bad thoughts she had entertained about Lizah and think that perhaps it wouldn't be so dreadful to see him again once he came back from the war. And thinking of him at war she had been filled with a sense of such concern and tenderness that she had amazed herself, and vowed to write to him. She would find out his address from Jessie as soon as she was able to obtain it (for in his goodbye note to her he had promised his sister that he would write to her as soon as he reached South Africa) and tell him all about his little girl and perhaps, a little about herself and her own life now –

But, as she was to remind herself grimly afterwards on many occasions, be sure your own wickedness will find you out. She had made a solemn promise to herself and to whoever else was listening – and for all her doubts about established religion, Mildred was not absolutely certain that there was not a divine and vengeful Providence that sat above and watched and recorded all she did – that she would hate Lizah for always, that Poppy's illness and suffering were his fault and she would never forgive him for them. And what had she done? In just a few days from making that promise she had broken it; just because Poppy had seemed better, she had made stupid plans to write him affectionate letters. And she was punished for it, oh, how she was punished!

For on the tenth day of her illness, when the rash was covering most of her body and she had become irritable and clinging and not at all her usual independent and lively small self, Poppy again had a night of horror, of bad dreams and fever and pain, and had woken Mildred with her cries. This time she had one of the more dreaded complications of measles – or so the doctor, called for a second time, told Mildred – infection.

'Otitis media,' he said heavily as he peered into the pathetically weeping Poppy's right ear with a light. 'I can see a nasty red drum – very nasty, bulging badly – better watch out it doesn't turn to a mastoid. Not much you can do if it does, mind you, or to stop it if it fancies spreading that way. So often these mastoids carry off these small ones, no resistance, you see, after the measles. Can only wait and see – ' And off he had gone with another half-crown in his pocket, leaving Mildred almost frantic with fear and self-blame. It had been her fault for forgetting her vow so quickly.

Somewhere deep inside herself Mildred knew that she was being irrational. She, the sensible, cool person who had found the courage to stand up to her tyrant of a father, so that she could live her own life in her own way, she who had found the capacity to earn her own and her baby's living without any previous experience or training for such work, to be so destroyed by a mere superstitious fear? But how can it be superstition, her deepest mind would whisper to her, when

Poppy is so ill again? You vowed and you broke your vow, didn't you? And now look at her.

For Poppy was indeed a piteous sight. Her eyes were reddened and sore and she hated the light, so the room had to be kept constantly shaded, and she could hardly move with the pain she suffered. She lay with her head held rigid and still, turned to the left so that the right ear and the surrounding parts of her neck received no pressure, and screamed in husky agony if any attempt was made to move her. All Mildred could do was give her laudanum drops on sugar lumps to ease her misery and persuade her to sip a little lemon and barley water occasionally, and hate herself for bringing such misery on her own baby.

Jessie came each day, bringing little delicacies to tempt the invalid's appetite, but to small avail. Home-made calves' foot jelly seemed to offer Poppy no inducement to eat, any more than the best beef tea did, and they watched her shrivel into thinness before their eyes as she lay and waited for the infection to run its course, either to resolve, as they both prayed it would, or to spread, a horror neither of them could bear to contemplate.

All the time, whether she was working in the kitchen (for still the business had to be kept running if there was to be any sort of future for Poppy and herself) or whether she sat and watched or dozed uneasily at Poppy's bedside, Mildred castigated herself. Her fatigue and her fear added together to rob her of any commonsense at all in this matter; Poppy's pain and the threat under which she lay was the fault first of her father, for being the man he was, and secondly of her mother for being weak and selfish and breaking a vow. That was the message that thumped and thundered in Mildred's mind and left a mark there that was to be ineradicable.

But there was more in Poppy's favour than her basic good physique and essential good health, for Mildred's careful supervision of her life hitherto had protected her against many of the ills suffered by other children of her age who lived in Holborn and went to her school. Poppy had never been allowed to play in the streets too late, as other children were, to lose their sleep and to eat dubious viands begged or stolen from the stalls thereabouts. Poppy had not been pulled down by an infancy spent fighting off one illness after another, nor had she suffered the chronic infections of ears and sinuses and chests that plagued so many of her schoolmates. Mildred had done her best to give her child the sort of careful middle-class upbringing she had had herself, and with it had given her more strength than she knew.

For Poppy's ear infection did not spread to the mastoid, ultimately to become a cerebral abscess and kill her, as it did to three of the other children of Baldwin's Gardens School who had been caught in the net of the measles epidemic that swept London, and indeed all England, that winter. The swollen tense drum of her ear burst and let out the threatening pus before it could break its bounds in the other direction. Poppy was deaf in that ear for some time and had to have it mopped out gently by her mother at regular intervals, but that did not matter. Her hearing returned well enough as the drum healed over – though for the rest of her life she was to tilt her head to the left to hear anything that was not absolutely clear, an endearing little movement that many people found very attractive and certainly characteristic of her – and she began to sleep more as the pain left her.

She began to eat more too, and as the rash at last faded and left her peeling slightly, she became ravenous and ate everything that was put before her, much to Jessie's delight. She took it upon herself to bring food, vast quantities of it, no matter what Mildred said, or how hard she tried to protest, and after a while Mildred gave in, for there was no doubt that Poppy enjoyed the way Jessie arrived with her basket carefully packed and settled herself at the kitchen table so that Poppy, who spent her convalescent days wrapped in blankets and propped on pillows before the kitchen fire where Mildred could keep an eye on her all day, could watch and clap her hands with delight and nibble all that she was offered.

For the rest of her life she was to have a taste for the exotic Russian and Polish delicacies her aunt brought her when she was recovering from measles in the winter of 1899: miniature blinis of the puffiest yeast pastry filled with cream cheese and slivers of smoked salmon; and tiny balls of the chopped fish mixture called gefilte fish which arrived in little pots of delicate pale amber jelly in which slices of carrot as well as the fish were embedded; and bowls of chicken soup which had to be heated on the fire and served in a bowl in which freshly cooked shreds of fine vermicelli floated. All very different from the sensible nursery food that her mother provided, the boiled eggs with toast fingers and bread and milk with honey and butter, and the little sweet cakes with coconut shreds on top which were her favourites. Different, but so different that she still enjoyed her mother's cooking, and the two women between them settled to seeing her through her convalescence so that she would be fit and ready to return to school. But it would not be till after Christmas, Mildred warned Poppy, for she had already been ill for a month, and it would take her at least as long to get really well again. And now it was raw November, with sulphurous smoke filling the streets with fog as the fires of London burned in the grates and spilled black smoke into the heavy protesting air. Outside was not fit for man nor beast and certainly not her Poppy, Mildred said firmly and she must just be patient. School days would come again – if she was good and ate up all her food and went to bed as soon as she was told –

She took to sitting at the window of the little front room which they so rarely used, for the kitchen was so much warmer and cosier, but there was nothing to see from the windows in the kitchen except the little yard with its tinned iron bath hanging on a hook on the privy wall, and the patch of sad earth where Mama grew her mint and sage and parsley for the pies and puddings. From the front window she could see the market, and that was lovely; so Mildred would light the fire in the parlour for her each day and there she would spend the long daytime hours, perched on the slippery horsehair sofa and staring out between the Nottingham lace curtains to the busy life outside.

There was plenty to see, even in the small area of the street which the window commanded; on the far side there were the stalls which sold boots and antimacassars and blacking and soap and ironmongery of various kinds, and on this side there were the stalls which sold food, potatoes and carrots and turnips and cabbages and parsnips, and sometimes she would sit and stare at the great splashes of colour the vegetables made in the yellowish grey of the wintry days, and pretend to herself that they were really golden treasures piled up for her, the princess who ruled this kingdom. The carrots became gold and the turnips silver and the cabbages piles of emeralds, and she would imagine how it would be if she were to open the window and cry out, 'Take the treasure for yourselves! Take the treasure and be happy!' and what old Solly, who kept the vegetable stall, would say if she did it and all the people came and took away his vegetables and gave him no money. And that would make her laugh.

People started to get used to seeing her there, her small face framed in the frills of the curtains, peering out for hour after hour. Solly would wave to her when he caught her eye and so would many of his customers. The old woman who kept the chicken stall on the other side of Solly, where she sold live chickens (Poppy would not let herself think about what happened to them when they had been bought) and eggs as well as chickens ready to be cooked, waved too, as did Mary who sold coconut ice and humbugs and crackjaw toffee and peanut brittle from a stand next door to her. Sometimes Mary came and tapped on the window and when Poppy opened it, pushing up the heavy sash with some effort, would give her a piece of pink fondant wrapped in paper, or a piece of sticky peppermint rock, and Poppy would take it and whisper thank you and close the window carefully, knowing how much Mama would disapprove if she knew. And she would eat the sweets and feel just naughty enough for it to be interesting and wave her gratitude to Mary whenever she looked up. Oh, there was plenty to watch and see at the window, and she was happy to sit there all day sometimes.

And Mildred was grateful for that, for as the winter bit down harder, more and more people wanted her wares. It seemed that whatever time she got up in the morning and however late she dragged herself to bed each night, she would never catch up. Nellie worked for her full time now, arriving each morning at seven – by which time Mildred had been hard at work for at least two hours – and leaving at seven in the evening, but even she was not enough. Sometimes she brought one of her brothers with her, to help. Not the really silly one, who had been funny since his birth but was biddable enough, but one of the others. There were so many children in Nellie's family that no one ever knew how many there were. Everyone in the district was used to the tumble of dirty ill-kempt half-fed creatures who went in and out of the corner house, like bees in and out of a hive, and no one gave them much thought; except Mildred. She had taken an interest in Nellie from the first, when the girl had shown that under her dirty and unprepossessing surface there was a lively intelligence and a good deal of willingness to work, and above all an affection for Mildred. No one had ever taken any interest in Nellie all her life, until Mildred came along, and in consequence the girl adored her. No matter how much Mildred scolded when she made mistakes or failed to reach her standards of cleanliness, she went on trying to please her, and now was a well turned out, even spruce looking, person of considerable ability and very much part of Mildred's business.

But her brothers, sometimes dragooned as extra hands, were not so useful, a fact which reinforced Mildred's dislike of men coming into her house, even to work. But Nellie persuaded her to let her bring them when the kitchen was particularly busy, and would settle one or other of them at the table to pick over raisins, a tedious and time-consuming task, or to rub down sugar or, in real emergencies, to beat the sponge mixtures which often needed a full hour of thorough beating of eggs and sugar with two forks to make them really light and white.

Late one afternoon in the first week of December, Mildred sent Nellie home. The girl had been struggling to keep up but had obviously been unfit, for she had a severe cold and had quite lost her voice. When she coughed, which was often, it obviously hurt her, for she would cling to the edge of the table and bark until her eyes ran tears, but she had steadfastly refused to go home until Mildred had almost frogmarched her to the door and told her that if she was so anxious, she could send a brother back to help wash up the tins, as long as she herself went to bed with a dose of Balsam on a sugar lump, and slept off her ills.

Poppy watched Nellie go, pressing her cheek against the glass of the window so that she could see her for as long as possible, and was sad for her, for she drooped along the road, picking her way listlessly between the stalls and the fallen rubbish on the greasy pavements with none of her usual bounce. It was horrid to feel ill; no one knew better than Poppy and because she had become attached to Nellie – she was so much a part of her life she was almost like the kitchen range – she wanted to cry for her. That had happened a lot since she had been ill; before that crying was something Poppy didn't do much. Not like some of the other children at school, who cried just because they bumped their knees or hit their heads or someone shouted at them. Poppy thought people who cried a lot were silly; yet since the measles she had cried a lot herself

– and crossly she rubbed her eyes to get rid of the tears and watched Nellie go.

And saw her brother arriving, and shrank back a little from the window. She didn't like Nellie's brother, at least, not this one. Some of them were cheerful enough; there was even a very young one who went to Baldwin's Gardens School, but this one she did not like. She had seen him, often leaning on the wall opposite her window and had hidden as much as possible behind the curtains, for he seemed to stare at her all the time. He was tall and thin – taller than people of seventeen usually were, Poppy thought – and had a drooping lower lip which was always wet; even looking at it made Poppy feel uneasy. Worse than that he had sad eyes with which he would stare at Poppy a lot, and not only outside in the street. She often caught him doing it from the corner of her eye when he was working in the kitchen and if she turned and stared at him he would let his eyes slither away like the eels on the slab of the fishmonger's stall along the market and that was even worse than when he stared at her. It was as though he had stroked her with his wet hands. Horrible –

As he came walking up the market towards the house he saw her at the window, even though she had pulled away into the curtains again, and he stared at her, but he didn't smile. He never did that. Just looked. If he had smiled or spoken she might have liked him better, Poppy thought. It was the strange way he stared and then looked away in silence that made him so nasty. And rather scary, too, though she didn't like to admit that. It was silly, after all, to be scared of someone for no reason.

She heard her mother let him into the house and take him through to the kitchen and by straining her ears she could hear after a while the clatter of pans and knew he was washing up. A big job that, with all the cake tins and the bowls and pots to be scrubbed, and the filling and refilling of the copper to get the hot water, and the scraping at the tins with Borwick's knife powder until they shone like new grey satin. It was not work Poppy would have liked to do; she would have liked to make pastry and cut it out for pies, as Mama did, but she was never allowed to – so she felt a bit sorry for Nellie's brother having to do it. But she still didn't like him.

The lamplighter came down the street outside and Poppy watched him contentedly. He was one of her favourite people and would wave to her as he passed her, just before reaching the lamp that stood almost outside the house next door, where he would pull down the chain with a deft twist of his wrist and then tip the little lever so that the gas plopped into life and glowed and glittered in the smoky air, and then he would wave again and she would wave back. Once that had happened it wasn't daytime any more and Poppy would start to think of ways to persuade Mama to let her stay up late.

There were footsteps outside and Mama came in, tying on her bonnet and wearing her warm winter pelisse over her shoulders.

'Poppy, I have to deliver some cakes myself. I am so put about I hardly know which way to turn – Nellie so ill and this Ted so useless he can't understand half I tell him. I shall have to take the cakes myself. Mercifully, it's just a half-dozen so I can manage them in the omnibus. They are to go to a tea shop in Watling Street, and I can get there in the Shillibeer's that goes to Cheapside and walk through – it will take me no more than half an hour, I do hope. But they say they must have them by five tonight, or they will not take the order, so what can I do? It's now just after four, so come and sit in the kitchen where you will be safe and warm and Ted can keep an eye on you, and be good, now. No running about and getting yourself tired, for you're still not fully well, and I don't wish you to be ill again – '

Poppy knew better than to argue. When Mama chattered and fussed like this it was because she was worried, and when Mama was worried she was all too likely to get cross and then there would be no staying up late at all. So, obediently, she slid off the sofa and waited until Mama had raked down the little fire and set the guard in place and then followed her into the kitchen. It was warm in there, almost too warm, and as Mama pushed her towards the chair beside the fire she pulled off the shawl which Mama insisted she wear and tucked it behind her cushion. Her dress and pinafore were quite warm enough and she hoped Mama wouldn't notice.

Mama did not notice. She was in such a flurry, giving instructions to Ted, still clattering as he stood speechlessly scrubbing in the kitchen, and collecting her parcel of cakes which she was carrying by a carefully knotted string handle. But at last she was ready to go and bent and kissed Poppy and then went to the door where she lingered for a moment, her lower lip caught between her teeth.

'I shan't be any longer than I can help, Poppy,' she said. 'Now, be good. Don't touch the fire – let Ted look after it if it needs attention – and stay there till I return. You hear me? Stay here in this room so that you will be safe – '

'I will, Mama,' she promised. 'I will,' and did not turn her head so that she could see Ted in the scullery. If only she liked him better it would be easier –

The clattering from the scullery went on for some time after Mama had gone, slamming the front door behind her, and Poppy sat curled up in her armchair staring at the flames as they hissed and swirled behind the bars of the range. Watching the flames was almost as pleasant as watching the people outside in the street, and she became a little dreamy as she looked and saw caverns of crimson and scarlet and gold open up amid the piles of coals, and thought of what it might be like to be a princess who lived in such a place; and slowly felt herself getting sleepy and rather liked the feeling.

And then was jerked awake so sharply it made her catch her breath.

333

'Hello, little missy.' She did not turn her head, even though it was so strange a sound. She had never heard Ted speak, but this sound must be him; a thick sort of sound, bubbly and nasty, as nasty as that wet lower lip, and she sat and stared at the fire, her head held still on her rigid neck and said nothing.

'Hello,' he said again. 'Look what I got to show you – just you look – I bet you never seen it before, eh, little missy? Come and look, then – an' I'll let you touch it if you like – '

Still she sat as rigidly as she could, her eyes tight closed, willing him to go away back to the scullery. Her heart was beating thickly in her chest and she didn't know why. All she knew was that she was very very frightened, and very very alone, and wanted her mother desperately, and that there was nothing she could do at all to change the way things were.

And then his hand was on her shoulder and he was pulling her round so that she had to look at him, whether she liked it or not. And she didn't like it at all for he looked so strange with his wet lips and wet eyes too, and his face was so red and excited and his hand was in front of him, low down in front of him and he was trying to make her look at what he was doing with it. And she knew she could not possibly and did the only thing that was possible. She opened her mouth and screamed.

31

By the time Mildred reached High Holborn, her throat was rasping and her eyes were running as though she were breaking her heart with grief. There had been fog about all day, heavy and yellowish, a threatening presence that sat above the chimneys and filled London with a sulphurous glow, but now it had become dark and therefore colder, the fog had been pressed downwards by the rising hot air from the chimneys as people came home from work and lit late fires, so that it had reached pavement level. She could hardly see more than a faint glow of light ahead of her now as she struggled from lamppost to lamppost and people seemed to loom vastly out of the gloom only a couple of feet in front of her, often bumping into her and then going on with either a muttered curse or an apology.

She had told herself that High Holborn would be much better; it was a wider thoroughfare and much better lit, for there were not only the street lamps, but the lights that spilled from the great windows of shops like Gamage's, and there were the buses too with men bearing huge flares walking in front of them. She'd be all right when she got to Holborn –

But she wasn't. She knew she'd reached the end of Leather Lane, because she recognized the broken doorstep of Nellie's home, but all she could see ahead was unremitting gloom and fog, fog, fog. There was traffic and there were people; she could hear wheels rattling, albeit muffled by the thick air and occasional shouts, but she certainly could not see them, nor could she identify whether the buses were those she needed. So she shifted her parcel from one hand to the other, for the string handle was cutting into her flesh cruelly, in spite of her woollen glove, and with her freed right hand began to inch her way along the road by holding on to the wall.

She wasn't the only person to do that; and over and over again she bumped into someone coming in the opposite direction and using the same ploy, and each time there were tiresome moments of shuffling as they decided who should walk around whom. She was no more than a few hundred yards from her home and already she was exhausted.

It was when at last she bumped into a policeman whose bull's-eye lantern looked like little more than a feeble matchhead glow in the murk, that she realized that her expedition was hopeless.

'Buses to St Paul's, lady? Not a hope. They're stranded all the way from 'ere to the Viaduct, and no one can move either way. They're trying to lead people in convoys, and if you can make your way up to the Circus you'll find there's my mate there, leading people over to make sure they gets on the right line. Where d'you live, lady?'

'Leather Lane,' she said distractedly and tried to see the man's face in the gloom, but all there was was the high shape of his helmet dimly outlined against the thick yellowness and only darkness under the brim where his face should be. 'I have to make this delivery to Watling Street, though – it's very important – '

'Oh, don't you try to do that, lady! You'll never get there and back tonight. This 'ere pea souper's in for the night, I reckon. You go 'ome and forget it, best thing you can do – '

'But I promised – ' She was speaking as much to herself as to him, and turned her head to try and stare out along Holborn in the hope of seeing a bus arriving miraculously through the smoky darkness. 'They'll cancel the order if I don't get there tonight – '

'Listen, lady.' The policeman sounded avuncular now, and he reached out and patted her heavily on the shoulder. 'No one won't be expecting any deliveries tonight, not nohow. They'll know as no one can get through. Even if you got there it's my guess you'd find the people've gone. It's a business delivery, I take it? Well, it would be, wouldn't it, being Watling Street. An' all the office and shop people, they went early, I been told. City's almost dead. You go 'ome, lady. Dare say your guv'nor'll forgive you – he should understand – '

'I run my own business,' she said tartly, annoyed with herself for even bothering to say it. What difference did it make to him?

'Better still. Go home, and get out of this. Fit to kill, this one is. There'll be full churchyards if this goes on – good night to you, lady.' And he melted away into the fog, disappearing entirely from view after only three or four paces.

It was all that she could do, and she turned and once again shifted her burden from one hand to the other and coughed to clear her throat of the taste of soot, and started the painful shuffle along the wall that would take her back. At least she'd not be leaving Poppy as long as she would have had to, and she suddenly shivered as she thought of what would have happened if she had managed to get further afield and not been able to get home for long hours. Poppy alone with only that silly boy to watch over her – and she began to shuffle faster, needing to get home as soon as she could, and stopped apologizing to the people she cannoned into.

The silence in Leather Lane was eerie, for even her own footsteps were muffled, and all she could hear was her own rasping and laboured breathing, and as she reached what she estimated to be the halfway mark along the street, just a few score of yards from home, she let her steps slacken, to give herself a chance to catch her breath. And then lifted her chin as she heard what seemed to be a faint mewling sound. A cat perhaps – But it was odd how very strange an effect the sound had on her, for it seemed to sharpen fear in her to a very remarkable degree, and to her own amazement she found herself almost running along the pavement, an extraordinarily difficult thing to do since it was like running head first into cotton wool.

How she knew when she had reached her own front door she was never to understand, but there she was, fumbling with her key in the lock and listening at the same time with her head up; and then she heard it again and now she was terrified. For it was a scream and she knew without any shadow of doubt that the scream came from Poppy's throat and that it was a repeat of the sound she had heard out there in the street. And as at last the door fell open, the key tumbling to the ground with a clatter, and she was inside and plunging along the passageway, almost falling over her parcel of cakes which she had dropped in front of her as she had come in, and not caring what damage she did to them as she trampled them, the sound from the kitchen came again, loud and clear, and filled her with terror.

Once she had started screaming Poppy had gone on and on, taking deep regular breaths and letting them out in a steady shrill sound, and doing it made her feel much better, because it worried Ted so dreadfully. She knew as soon as she looked at his face after her first scream that he was upset, for his blank silly face crumpled and his wet eyes looked even more wet and worried. He went on fiddling with himself in that same way, pushing towards her with little jerks of his hips, yet keeping his feet firmly clamped to the spot, and when she stopped to breathe she heard what he was saying, over and over again.

'It's all right, missy, it's all right. You can touch. I don't mind, it's all right – look, it's all right – ' And then his voice was lost as again she shrieked, sitting there curled in the corner of the armchair by the fire, her mouth opening and filling the air of the kitchen, the hallway, the house, and the whole world with a noise that made her ears ache.

'It's all right –' Ted's face looked so worried now that she wanted to laugh instead of scream. It was as though any minute he would start to cry, and the thought of a great big person like Ted crying was so funny that it was all she could do to keep on screaming. But she knew she had to, because if she didn't he would stop being so worried and instead of crying would come closer to her and make her look and touch. And of all things she didn't want to do it was that. She always turned her head away from the fishmonger's stall as they went by, if there were eels there, all long and twisty and slimy; they were grey and what Ted wanted her to look at and touch wasn't grey but a dull pinkish sort of colour and she wanted nothing to do with it. So even though her throat was beginning to hurt and her head to ache with the noise, she went on screaming, though not so loudly now, because it was quite hard work.

She wasn't at all surprised when the door burst open with a great clatter and there was Mama, her bonnet askew and her eyes wide and frightened and her face so white she looked like a bowl of her own flour. It seemed to Poppy the most natural thing in the world that she should come back now, and she closed her mouth gratefully, for now she could stop screaming. Mama would deal with this now and she turned her head away and put her face into the cushion at the back of her chair and closed her eyes, for she was very tired now. All she really wanted to do was go to sleep.

But she couldn't, for Mama was beside her and lifting her up and holding her and talking, talking, talking –

'Poppy, oh, Poppy, what happened? Did he hurt you? What happened, my poor baby? Tell Mama. Oh, I should never have gone, I should have realized as soon as I went out that it was too thick. Are you all right, Poppy? Are you?' – And then she hugged her so close that even if she had had any answers to all the questions she would have had no breath to make them with.

Behind Mama's back she heard a shuffling and looked over her shoulder and saw Ted scuttling across towards the door, trying to get past the other side of the kitchen table. He had his cap on and his head down so that she could not see his face, and Poppy was glad of that, and his coat and trousers were all buttoned up now and that made her even more glad.

'Ted's going away, Mama – ' she managed to say, in spite of Mildred's bear hug, feeling she ought to know so that she could give him his money. That was what always happened when Nellie or any of her brothers went home; Mama fetched out her purse from her reticule and gave them their shillings and sixpences and said 'Good night and thank you,' politely. Mama would want to know Ted was going, definitely.

Indeed she did. Poppy found herself dropped back into the armchair so suddenly it was almost as though she had been thrown there, as Mama darted to the door to block Ted's way. She was standing there, glaring at him with her face even whiter than it had been, if that were possible.

'What did you do to my baby?' She said it so quietly that Poppy could hardly hear her and she felt her own face get as pink as Mama's was white. It was one thing for Mama to call her her baby when she talked to Poppy herself; it was all wrong to call her that to other people, even horrible Ted, and she opened her mouth to protest that she wasn't a baby, but a person who went to school – when she wasn't ill, of course – and that meant she had to be called a child or a person, not a baby.

But no one was paying any attention to her at all so she closed her mouth again. Ted was whimpering now, a soft watery sound that was quite sad really and Poppy managed to look at him, even though she disliked doing so, because of feeling sorry for him.

He looked dreadful. His face was all twisted and he was crying, for there were tears on his narrow drooping cheeks and his eyes looked red and Poppy for the first time ever thought that perhaps he wasn't so horrible after all. He was just miserable and she wanted to go over and say to him, 'It's all right – ' the way he had kept saying it to her. But she didn't. Mama would not have been at all pleased. That was something Poppy was very certain about.

'What did you do?' Mama said again and her voice was so hard and sharp that it made Poppy want to cry too, and she knew even more certainly that Ted wasn't horrible after all, just sad.

'He didn't do anything, Mama,' she said. She had to say it because it was all so hateful in here with Mama looking at Ted like that. 'He didn't do anything – '

Mama looked at her, letting her eyes shift but keeping her head still and that reminded Poppy of the way Ted used to look at her and that was nasty. 'Then why were you screaming?'

'I was frightened.'

'Why?'

Poppy felt her face begin to get tight and twisted, like Ted's. She was going to cry again; that dreadful crying feeling that came so often now, since she had been ill, was coming back and it made her throat feel as though it were full of sharp pins and needles.

'I don't know,' she wailed and stopped trying not to cry. It was easier to let the tears come and now they were flooding down her cheeks. 'I want to go to bed – '

'All right – ' Mama came away from the door and held her close. 'It's all right, baby, I'll put you to bed. Just be patient – now, you – ' And her voice sharpened and she looked over her shoulder at Ted.

'You. I saw what you were doing, I know what you were going to do, you evil creature, you hateful – ah, you make me sick!' And it really sounded to Poppy as though Mama was going to be sick, just as she herself had been beside the big ship the day she first got ill. 'If Poppy says you did nothing, I'll believe her. I think I got back in time, thank God, and stopped you. Get out, you hear me? Get out. I never want to see you again, ever, nor any of the people to do with you. Tell your sister – tell Nellie the same thing. Never ever will any of you ever come near me and mine – get out – you hear me? Out, out, out!' And now it was Mama who was shouting and the novelty of that made Poppy stop crying and lift her chin to look into her face.

Ted went, half running and half falling out of the kitchen and then down the passageway, and they heard the door slam behind him as they both remained there in silence, and Mildred held Poppy close and stared blankly over her head at the swinging kitchen door.

After a long time Mama spoke, and her voice sounded cracked and tight as though her throat had gone dry. 'Are you sure he did nothing to you?'

Poppy shook her head. 'No, Mama, he just kept saying – "it's all right, look, it's all right and I'll let you touch." I didn't want to touch anything! Why did he want me to touch him?'

Mildred took a sharp little breath and slowly let her knees buckle so that she fell into the armchair rather than sat in it, with Poppy on her lap.

'Oh, how do I explain? Oh, Poppy, my dear child, how do I begin to explain and you, such a baby? Such a thing that would be, to fill your head with such horrors – '

Poppy shook her head irritably. 'It wasn't horrors,' and then stopped. She knew the word and what it meant, of course; Mama had told her all the words she ever saw in her books and she knew Ted wasn't a ghost or anything like that. 'It wasn't,' she said again. 'It was *silly*. Undoing his trousers and wanting me to touch. The boys at school do it sometimes but they don't want you to *touch*.' And she said it witheringly.

'The boys at – ' Mildred took a deep breath and closed her eyes. This was getting worse and worse, and she felt as though she were trying to swim in a sea of mud which was threatening to close over her head and drown her. 'What do you mean, the boys at school?'

'They do it all the time,' Poppy said, and snuggled closer to Mildred. It was nice sitting on Mama's lap. 'They show the girls their peepees and the girls laugh and shout at them and the boys do it again and then the whistle blows and we all go back to lessons. But they never say, "touch me". And it's never like that nasty Ted. He was nasty – ' She shook her head, puzzled. 'It was like school only it wasn't. It was because he was so frightened. Ted was ever so frightened, so I was too.'

'Oh, Poppy, Poppy, what have I done to you?' Mildred was staring down at her with her face just as distressed as Ted's had been. 'What sort of life am I giving you here? I'm a selfish – I can't do this to you. But what else can I do? What possible choices do I have?'

'You didn't do anything, Mama,' Poppy said and wriggled down from her lap to go and sit on her own little stool by the fender. She was tired of being on Mama's lap like a baby. She was big Poppy now that Ted was gone and taken all the fright away with him. And, she suddenly realized, she was staying up late without having had to ask or fuss at all. And she wriggled with pleasure as she sat on her stool, not wanting to go to bed at all now and amazed that she had wanted to before.

'I did.' Mildred was still sitting there, her pelisse on her shoulders and her bonnet hanging by its strings over her shoulders. 'You need a decent clean quiet place, not this – this hateful slum – oh, what shall I do? What shall I do?' And to Poppy's terror she burst into tears and sat there with them coursing down her cheeks and making no effort at all to control or conceal them. It was a dreadful sight and again Poppy felt fear rising in her.

She scrambled to her feet and stood there pulling at her pinafore, trying to unbutton it. 'Mama, I want to go to bed,' she said loudly. 'Please, Mama? I'm ever so tired I want to go to bed – '

And that helped, because Mama stared at her and then rubbed her face with the backs of both hands and got to her feet. And took a few deep breaths, and then tried to smile.

'Of course,' she said as briefly as she could, and to Poppy she sounded almost ordinary, the way she usually was. Almost, but not quite. 'Of course. Now, I'll unbutton you and then you go and take off your things and set them tidy as I showed you and put on your nightdress and wrapper and slippers and come down and I shall wash you and give you some bread and milk for supper – '

'No supper,' Poppy said. 'No supper tonight. Just bed – ' And Mama looked down at her and then suddenly hugged her close and said in a muffled sort of voice. 'Oh, Poppy, you sound so old for your years! Have I made you grow up too fast, keeping you here in this dreadful place?'

'It isn't a dreadful place!' Poppy was indignant. 'It's the nicest kitchen anywhere! Even nicer than Auntie Jessie's – '

'Jessie – ' Mama said and then knelt down to bring her face on a level with Poppy's. 'Poppy, my love, it will be better if you say nothing to anyone about what happened here tonight – '

'Nothing happened,' Poppy said. 'I got frightened and Ted got frightened when he showed me his – '

'I know,' Mama said hastily. 'I know – but all the same, don't tell anyone. Not even Aunt Jessie – especially Aunt Jessie.'

'Why?' Poppy stared at her, her lower lip pouting a little. She was beginning to feel cross now, and wasn't sure whether she wanted to go to bed or not, after all. She felt scratchy and bad inside. 'Why? I like Auntie Jessie – '

'Of course you do – ' Mama swallowed hard and smiled again, but it was a very thin sort of smile. 'Of course you do. So you don't want to upset her, do you? And this will upset her – '

Poppy considered for a moment and then nodded. 'All right,' she said. 'I don't like Auntie Jessie being upset. I don't like being upset. I don't like anyone being upset – ' And she gave a sudden jaw-cracking yawn. 'I think I do want to go to bed – ' she said sleepily.

And when she was there and fast asleep – as she was almost as Mildred pulled the covers up over her shoulders – her mother sat beside her bed thinking and looking at her sleeping face with her own very stiff and tight.

'I have to get her out of here,' she was telling herself over and over again. 'I have to get her out of here – it's bad for her – must get her out – '

But where to? Where could she go where Poppy would be safe from such experiences as tonight's, and where her mother could earn their living? And she remembered her long ago fantasy of the West End flower shop and felt the tears start again, for she could not imagine ever finding enough money to get herself such a shop, however small, and a decent home for the two of them, in a better part of town. It was difficult enough to make a living and save a little against an uncertain future where they were, here on the edge of the slums that threw the human garbage like Ted into her home to pollute it. Where else could she take her precious child and give her the care and the love and above all the surroundings she ought to have and deserved to have? Her Poppy, Mildred knew, was an unusually observant and intelligent child, with a memory as acquisitive as any squirrel's and sharp eyes and ears that missed nothing she could add to the store of information she had already garnered in her short life. There were things she should not know about, ever, if possible. But how could she be protected in such a dreadful part of London?

Mildred sat there for a long time, her bonnet and pelisse still on her, weeping. She knew what she ought to do, but she could see no way to do it, and that was agony.

32

Lizah would have deserted if he'd known how to. It had been his plan to walk off the SS *Dunottar Castle* when it docked at Cape Town and disappear into the crowds and somehow, eventually, find a way to work his way home again. But it wasn't as easy as that.

First of all he had only his uniform, and no mufti at all; all that had been left behind at the recruiting barracks to be reclaimed when he came home, he'd been told; and a man in the uniform of the Queen's army could not wander about the docks of Cape Town without attracting the attention of the great clusters of military police who were everywhere. And there was no way he could just find a shop, walk in, and get clothes; he hadn't the money, for a start.

So he bided his time, certain he would find a chance soon to step back out of sight, as it were, and melt away into his own private life and to the devil with their bloody war; but the right time never came. Two days after disembarkation they had been issued with additional tropical kit and were mustering for a journey North East towards the Tugela River and Ladysmith where, it seemed, a British force was held and in dire need of support.

When Lizah heard from the gossip that went through the ranks like a fire through tinderwood that they were to go to sea again, his heart sank, for how could he hope to get away when he was to be shipped God knew how far away? And there was another cause for trepidation; the fear of actual fighting began to filter through the ranks of men as they sat and stood about on the docks, waiting to be told what to do, smoking and jabbering and playing cards and passing along every snippet of information they could get. There had been a bloody and dreadful defeat at a place called Magersfontein where a thousand British soldiers, the cream of the Highland Brigade, had died and casualty lists had been posted to prove it was true and not just a rumour.

It was difficult for Lizah to get answers to all the questions he wanted to ask, for since the fiasco of his match with Amberly, none of the men had been particularly affable towards him, and he had chosen to be aloof and cold; it was the only way he could salvage what tatters of self-esteem were left to him. So all he could do was listen to the talk while pretending he was uninterested, and think and hope and scheme to escape.

But it got him nowhere. The ship that took them to Durban, on the other side of this great lump of a continent he already hated, was even more uncomfortable than the SS *Dunottar Castle* had been and that had been bad enough; here they slept wherever they could find a patch of deck on to which they could throw their kit to use as a pillow, while from below the stench of cavalry horses, swung in canvas slings two to a stall and whinnying and thrashing about in terror, came up to them to make them toss and moan in their own sleep and wake each other to swearing fury. The low green coast of the Cape slid relentlessly past on the port side, tantalizingly visible to Lizah yet totally unattainable, and frustration built in him as he imagined the people who inhabited these wide open expanses going about their business in tranquillity and freedom, able to make their own choices about what they did and what they ate and when and where they slept, and compared their idyllic existence with his own misery.

It was no better when they reached Durban. The heat was hellish, thick and steamy, and he was sweat-drenched in his heavy uniform and his skin was chafed where the weight of his kit had rubbed the cloth against him. As they marched off the ship and were herded directly to the railway yard, he was almost desperate enough to make a run for it; but not quite, for the military police with their guns held much in evidence were a gimlet-eyed and cruel-looking lot, he decided. The time still had not come.

He had thought the sea journeys bad enough, until he was herded with fifteen hundred other men into the cattle trucks which were to carry them north. The trucks still reeked of their previous occupants and some of them were slippery with ordure as well as stinking and desperately hot and crowded. The train, when at last it started with bone-shaking judders, crept through the night like some sort of weary snail as men snored and woke and swore at each other and would have come to blows if there had been room enough to swing their arms.

And so it went on, hour after hour with his mouth tasting, he told himself sourly, like the bottom of a birdcage, and his head aching and his eyes feeling as though they'd been gouged out of his head and put back with gritty fingers, through places which sounded more attractive than they seemed to be, when he peered out through the wooden slats to see them in the erratic lamplight. Pinetown and Camperdown and Ashbirton and Howick, and some with strange-sounding names like Mooirivier and Pietermaritzburg. And then, it was dawn, and the sky looked like the oleograph his mother had on her parlour wall, all pretty blues and roses and golden glows and quite unreal.

Now he could see the country more clearly and, as he stared with one sore eye through the peephole he'd managed to fashion for himself by digging out the soft wood under one of the slats at the side, he felt a sense of awe. It was so bloody *big*, like a sea, with vast waves of green and dun-coloured land rolling away for ever to the west where a range of mountains reared up like a huge and unimaginably thick wall of living red rock. The Drakensberg, that was it. He'd heard someone call it that, and had rolled the word round his mouth, Drakensberg –

And God, but it was hot. He heard someone say he reckoned it was a hundred in the shade already, and the sun hadn't been up half an hour yet, and sweat poured out of him, and out of all of them, so fast they seemed to steam and certainly smelled chokingly rank. All Lizah wanted was water to drink and lots of it, but all they were issued with were small bottles of soda water which he drank so fast that it felt as though he had none at all; and one of the men deigning to speak to him for once grunted, 'You'll do better if you sip it, you damn fool. That way you'll be bloody ill – ' And so he was, throwing up painfully into the dust of the yard where they had all at last been decanted.

It got a little easier after that. They were mustered in a broad patch of scrubby land not far from a small place called Estcourt and there they pitched their bell tents and the quartermasters broke out supplies and they had their first real food since they had left Cape Town; or what was to be considered as real food for the rest of their time out here. A thick porridge made of corn which the men peered at suspiciously and then ate voraciously, for it had a mild and milky taste to it that was very comforting; and strips of leathery brownish meat, dry as a thistle, which was called biltong and which, the men grumbled, was like eating your boots, though Lizah actually liked it. It reminded him in taste a little of his mother's salt beef. And when he thought that he almost cried with homesickness. But didn't, and managed to sleep that night like a dead thing, freed at last of the rattle of trains and swing of ships, and above all the stink of bodies, human and animal. The open air, even in this heat, was cleaner and fresher than any he had known since they had arrived in this benighted, hateful country, he told himself, and began to think again, tentatively, about how he would make his escape. Except that he couldn't think how he would get back to England from this place, wherever it was, which felt like the outer limits of hell.

They started to march next day, their kit strengthened with their own supplies of biltong and biscuit, the twice-baked rusks that the Boers used and which the British army had learned to respect as useful rations for long forced marches, and bottles of water. Now he knew how to use it, Lizah felt safer; having his own supplies made him feel less tied to this dreadful army, made it possible to believe that one day, somehow, he could get away –

Where he got to was Colenso on the Tugela river, on the far side of which, the men were told, General Botha and his Boers were waiting for them. They had herded the English into the tin-roofed cluster of buildings and scrub that was Ladysmith and there they rotted, starving and fearful, waiting for the army to come and rescue them; an army made up of many as unwilling as Lizah and as ill-equipped to deal with this alien landscape as he was. Even the eager soldiers, thirsting for blood and fed with springs of patriotism, were not up to the standard of the Boers, those despised enemies for whom the regular soldiers had nothing but jeers and sneers. Yet these scornful soldiers were fit only to obey orders and to march steadily forwards to be shot at as easy targets; the Boers had lived in and loved their huge hot country and its eternal veldt for too many years not to be good soldiers in it. They could melt into the landscape and disappear as easily as any snake, and their gunshot fire across the shimmering heat haze was wickedly accurate, where the British marksmen often fired wide, confused by the strange way the light and colours distorted their vision. But there they were, the British Army, ready to throw Botha back where he belonged and relieve the garrison at Ladysmith.

'Before dark,' the officers boasted, and Lizah, keeping as far back in his platoon as he could place himself heard them as they went by on their horses; fresh-faced boys with all the arrogance of their youth and their schoolboy games ideas and brand new uniforms. 'We'll get these damn farmers scuttling away before dark.'

But it was not to be. The orders were that they were to wait, and wait they did, as more and more men came pouring in from the South, until there were fully thirty thousand British soldiers and great masses of heavy artillery clustering close to Colenso. Occasional observation parties made sorties to spy out the land and reported back on available crossing places in the river, and men were disposed at different points, ready for the charge when the order should come. Lizah, by now hopelessly aware that he was not going to be able to escape yet, and even more sickeningly certain that he was going to have to be somewhere where fighting was going on, even if he were to avoid actually doing any of it himself, followed his platoon gloomily to their new tented billets near Tritchard's Drift. It cheered him a little to see that behind them, on the higher slopes on this side of the river, heavy artillery was being brought in; great naval guns that glimmered in the light and sent reassuring flashes of reflection down to the men sitting there hunched in the heat by the riverside. But it did not cheer him a great deal. And there they sat and waited.

Lizah tried to think more about getting away and actually began to hide some of his food supplies in his uniform, instead of in his kit – a forbidden activity though that was – in the hope of slithering away from his tent one night when the other men who shared it were asleep, and making his own way back to the railhead and from there south to Durban and a ship on which he could work his way home. And then suddenly lost his nerve and most of his hope, when he heard one of the men say something about the date.

'My old woman's birthday,' he said. 'January 22nd. Bloody midwinter, trust her! Always went down the music hall, we did, and then had a blowout at the old pie and eel stall on her birthday. She'll 'ave to do it on 'er own this time. An' if I get back and find she did it wiv someone else, I'll kill the bloody pair of 'em – '

They had been sitting outside their tent after nightfall waiting for a can to boil water on the damped down fire to make tea, and Lizah lifted his head at the man's words, so sharply he nearly spilt the can.

'What did you say the date was?'

'January 22nd,' the other man growled. And it's bleedin' 1900 an' all. Flippin' great twentieth century this is, and no mistake.'

'Gawd – how long we been here, then? It don't make sense – so hot and all – I just didn't think – ' And as the men guffawed at his stupidity he stared up at the sky and tried to see familiar patterns there; but the stars were in the wrong places and made the wrong patterns and he was swept with a sudden sense of desolation as he contemplated the size of the world and where he was in it. To get home, to escape this lunatic, alien, eternal high summer and get back to the reality of a normal fog-bound London winter again would take weeks, even months. He had no money, for pay was not being issued on active service, but being allowed, the men were told, to accrue to them for payment on their return, and no real resources apart from his army rations, meagre as they were. He was tied to this hated army as closely as he had been tied to the table leg by his mother long ago in his infancy when she had wanted to keep him under control and out of her way, and he remembered now how furious that had made him and how he had pulled and shouted against her ribbon controls, and felt the same rage rising in him. And he could do nothing about it, any more than he had been able to as a baby. He could have wept.

The battle started at last two hours before dawn, with men running eagerly about as though they were to go to a party and the officers having a glorious time snapping out their orders and herding the men into position. The artillery started first, sending great pounding shells over the river towards their main target, a low hill crowned with ragged trees; it was called, someone said, Spion Kop. There were said to be hordes of Boers dug into trenches there, waiting to attack. So, the English were to attack first and so they did, with deafening effect. Shell after shell whined over Lizah's head and he stopped wincing and ducking after a while. It became as normal as the heat and the stink of cordite and the churning of fear in his guts that never left him. He had lived like this, he felt, all his life. Any other experience was like a long ago dream, and of no real relevance to him at all.

It went on all day as Lizah and his platoon, and many more like them, lay on their bellies in the scrub above the river, their eyes fixed on the target, where plumes of black smoke and pieces of flying shrapnel, looking for all the world like drunken eagles in their erratic flight, starred the enamel sky, with their rifles on the ready and their minds almost numb with fear. And then at sunset the shelling came to a ragged stop and the men were told to stand down, and Lizah almost fell into his tent as other platoons came to relieve him and his fellows. It was easier now with the rest of the men; a day spent under those circumstances had wiped out the memory of the money they had lost when he had failed to box his way to victory on the *Dunottar Castle* and that helped, for they talked to him now and seemed to treat him much like one of themselves. And for the first time since he had come to South Africa Lizah experienced a glimmer of pleasure in being alive.

One of the men in his squad was a chef at a London hotel in civilian life and he had managed somehow to get hold of some vegetables in his travels, for now he dug out from his pack a couple of onions as well as the eternal ears of corn which seemed to be the staple diet in these parts and with some of the biltong issue, and some of his own store of pepper and spice and a good deal of skill, produced a meal which tasted something approaching the sorts of stew they all understood and which filled their bellies very comfortingly.

Above them, as they sat out in front of their tents round a camp fire which was carefully screened to the North so that no marksman from over the river could pick them out, the stars shone like steady lamps as they ate, and Lizah felt the size of the country about him with relief rather than the misery that he had felt last time he had contemplated it. The vast bowl of sky above him, for all its alien stars, was a beautiful sight and he lay on his back after he had cleaned his mess can of every last scrap of food and stared up at it and found himself half remembering, half dreaming as he let his weary gaze wander from glittering clusters to milky dusting and on to great twinkling southerly stars in the great indigo expanse.

Millie, he thought after a while, with a deep sentimentality. Millie. And his eyes filled with tears as he looked at her face in his memory. It was a smiling welcoming face, and she held her hands out to him meltingly and her eyes were large and dark with desire and he was laughing at her, and teasing her, and she was getting even more amorous as she came towards him and then –

And then he was awake suddenly as the voice above him ordered, 'Attention!' and he was scrambling to his feet with the rest of the men in his squad.

'Right!' A tall officer was standing there, just outside the circle of light from their fire so that he could see only his outline and not his face. 'We are to charge over the river, in half an hour, and take Spion Kop. Those are the orders. Get your mess cleaned and get your kit on. At once – '

'But, sir!' Their corporal was a regular soldier, grizzled in army ways and knew to a nicety how far he could go. And also knew his responsibility to his platoon. 'Sir, we've been on the line all day, since before dawn. First break we've had, this is, and – '

'Are you querying orders, Corporal?'

'No, sir. Just pointing out as there's other platoons as has been behind the lines all day and is fresher and less likely to make mistakes sir, and you know how easy tired men do that, sir – '

'You won't make mistakes.' The officer stepped forwards now and revealed himself to be a lieutenant and clearly a very new one; even after these long and dirty and effortful days in South Africa his uniform had the taint of newness about it. 'I'm leading you, and no men I lead ever make mistakes, you hear me?'

Lizah caught his breath sharply, and the officer threw a glance at him and both men stood very still.

'I see,' the lieutenant spoke first. 'It's you, is it, Harris? I might have guessed I'd draw at least one rotten apple in my barrel. Well, if that's the way of it, so be it. You'll still do as you're told and you'll fight to better effect than you did on the *Dunottar Castle*. If not, you'll answer to me, you understand?' He stood and stared sneeringly at him, clearly delighted with the sight of Lizah standing there in silence. 'In fact, we might even make a hero out of you. A dead one, perhaps, but a bloody hero for all that. You understand?'

Lizah said nothing, standing and staring at him with his chin pushed forwards as he bit hard on his tongue to prevent himself saying more than he should.

'Answer me!' Amberly snapped. 'Do you understand?'

'Yes,' Lizah said at last, grinding it out as though it took an enormous effort, as indeed it did.

'Yes, what?'

'Yes, sir.' He managed it. He managed not to attack the bastard, managed not to hit that sneering face right where it should be hit. He was no army man, Lizah Harris, but he had already learned something of the way this crazy private world operated, and one of its most basic rules was the sacrosanct nature of an officer's person. To hit an officer, in temper, at a time of war, was probably a shooting offence. If he did as every atom of his nature was crying out to him to do and ground this hateful bastard's face in the dry red earth at his feet, they'd find time, even in the middle of this stinking battle, to shoot him. And he'd managed to avoid that.

'Right,' Amberly said, in high good humour. 'Half an hour, Corporal, and you are to be ready. The tent cleared, the fire out, and the squad on the ready to he part of the push over the river. We go over wading – hold your rifles and kit well out of the water – at the Drift. And then we take that bloody Kop of theirs. Be sharp about it!' And he was gone into the darkness to rouse three other squads who were to be forced into unwilling heroism that night.

33

The water was cold. Blessedly wonderfully cold and even though he knew he was walking towards unimaginable horrors of gunfire and even, perhaps, hand to hand encounters with enraged Boers, Lizah was able to relish the sensation of water on his skin. Never mind that it reached him through the layers of heavy fabric and leather boots that were his uniform; it was cool and that was bliss.

For a little while. Once they were over the Drift and had obeyed the whispered command to spread out and move as quietly as possible towards the shadow on the near horizon that was Spion Kop, his clothes felt heavy and rough and as they began to dry a little in the hot night air, they chafed agonizingly and he slowed down considerably as he tried to find ways to make himself more comfortable, if he possibly could.

On each side of him he could feel rather than hear the presence of other men; a great many of them, he thought, and all as frightened as he was. He could smell the fear in the air; it prickled in his nose and made the hairs on the back of his neck stand up as it seeped into his very bones and made his legs shake beneath him, and he let himself fall to his knees and remained still, not thinking, not planning, just stopping.

And after a while it seemed to him that he had managed to do a remarkable thing. He felt the rest of the men of his platoon move on ahead of him, and within a matter of minutes knew he was alone. The tide of the war had run on in front of him and left him stranded behind, like a crab on a shingle beach. There was no one to see him, or tell him what to do, or be aware of what he chose to do.

For a little while he contemplated the pleasure of curling up and going to sleep, for God knew he was exhausted. But that road would lead to disaster; he'd wake in the morning to find himself stranded out here in the sight of every marksman in the Boer army. Back to his own lines, then? That wouldn't work either. If he came back without his platoon when no shot had been fired – for ahead of him there was only silent darkness and the shape of that damned Kop against the starlit sky – he would be branded a deserter on the field of battle and shot out of hand. So, it had to be something else – for he was not going to go forward where the Boers were, and worse still, where the rest of his platoon were. And then it hit him, like a sudden ray of purest light; he could, if he thought it out carefully, begin to make his complete escape.

The railhead lay, he knew, to the east and the south of where he was at present. If he could move sideways, to his right, instead of ahead to where the platoon was about to storm the lower, southern slopes of Spion Kop, he could ease back into the lines in a section where no one would know him by sight, and somehow reach the trains. Reinforcements were still coming up from Durban, and clearly the trains had to go back; there might be a train waiting there that he could get on to and sleep his way back to Durban and a ship where a stowaway might be a practical chap who could take care of himself on a journey home to London and the cold and the fog for which his whole body yearned. Whatever happened there, however high his debts, however vindictive his ex-friends and now enemies, the Jack Long lot, it could only be heaven compared with this.

He unhooked his pack from his back, and with fingers shaking slightly with excitement, began to pull out the necessities; the rest of the biltong and rusk and chocolate and bottles of water, all of which he managed to stow in the capacious pockets of his uniform. The rest he left there, lying in the dry stubby grass, and began to crawl, easily and slowly, his head well down, to his right.

He had gone less than half-a-dozen yards when he returned; to leave his rifle would make it clear he had deserted. If anyone found the pack abandoned they would think little of it; a soldier jettisons what he must to be the most effective fighter possible. But he never leaves his rifle, so whatever sort of burden it was, Lizah must take it with him. And so he did, and was not altogether unhappy to feel it bumping on his rear as he crawled steadily onwards. There was a certain comfort in having it, after all.

He seemed to crawl for hours. It would have been heaven to stand up on his two legs like a man, and walk, but he dared not risk that. To have his whole figure outlined against the sky was to ask for trouble. He had to go like an animal on all fours, like a dog or a cat –

– Or a lion or tiger or elephant, he found himself thinking absurdly. I've seen none of 'em here, not one, and everyone thought we would. Supposed to be like a bleedin' zoo, it is, but the only animal here is me, crawling for hours on all fours –

Suddenly, ahead of him, an automatic weapon chattered and then was silent, and at once other guns took up the chorus behind him, and he lifted his head gingerly to see flashes of light as rifles sent their bullets screaming into the night, and his heart jumped directly into his throat and then sank again. They were a hell of a lot closer than he had imagined and on the wrong side of him; and he hurled himself flat on his belly to try to think.

While he had been sitting there in the darkness, planning to run away and then went crawling off to look for a train to Durban, the platoon and several others with it had also gone curving away eastwards, and he was now, heaven help him, in *front* of them. How it had happened, he couldn't imagine. Some peculiarity of the way the land lay was to blame, he told himself feverishly, or perhaps he had been mistaken in his own sense of direction and he had gone due north instead of the way he had meant to go? And again he lifted his head and looked about him.

'Keep down, you bloody idiot!' someone hissed at him and again bullets whined and spat but this time they were hitting the dust around him, sending up spurts of dry mist that he could see clearly, even in this poor light, and he flattened again, his face pressed into the dirt and so sick with terror he could hardly breathe.

'Well done, whoever you are – you've pushed us right up – who is it? You're a good chap – ' The voice that came in a hoarse whisper was a terrified one. An officer's voice but clearly shaking with sick, blue funk. Lizah could hear it in every syllable of his speech, and he lay there with his face down, actually wanting to be dead, just for a moment, rather than pretending to be. Bloody, bloody Amberly! What did a man have to do, where did he have to go, to escape that mumser? The hate that filled him at that moment was a rich pure vein that curled itself all through him, so much so that it washed out the fear that had been lurking there for so long.

'The Kop is right ahead. No more than five hundred yards. I don't think we've been spotted by more than a sniper – can you make it?' The voice came again, still shaking, trying pathetically to sound normal, and totally failing.

Lizah lay there, still silent, thinking, and then knew he had to speak. 'I can make it,' he said as he lifted his head. 'Can you?'

'Who – ' Amberly peered at him in the darkness and Lizah felt the intake of breath shift the air between them. 'You? How did you get this far ahead of the platoon?'

'Like you said. Good chap – ' Lizah said loudly and then ducked his head as again gunfire sprayed them.

'I'm getting out of this – ' Amberly rolled over on to his side and peered ahead at the darkness. 'I'm not staying here with a bastard like you – let me out of here – '

Lizah had heard people talk of men going to pieces. He'd seen some dissolve into tears when pain became more than they could bear, seen others tremble with fear at the sight of him in the opposite corner of the boxing ring, but he'd never seen anyone dissolve as rapidly into liquescence as he saw Basil Amberly do. He had no control over himself at all, no power in him that could make him think, or behave, like an intelligent man. He was, pure and simple, a mass of instinct with every cell of his body clamouring to run away, as fast and as far as possible.

'Don't be any more stupid than you can help,' Lizah said sharply and felt Basil stiffen at the sound of his whisper. It was as though he, Lizah, were now the eager officer and Basil was the totally helpless, unwillingly enlisted soldier under his command. And suddenly, as though he were watching a scene change on a stage, it was all different. They weren't members of an army lying out in the South African veldt trying to take from entrenched Boer soldiers a strategic position. They were Kid Harris, the brave, the successful, the tip-top boxer, in his own gym, in the East End of London half a world away, and Basil Amberly, a weedy youth with more arrogance than sense, trying to beat a man who was twice his value in every way; and Lizah laughed softly in the darkness and thought – I wish Ruby were here – we'd show the bugger – and was puzzled, for he had not thought of Ruby for years. 'You're here and you're lumbered, like me,' he said then. 'All you can do is the best that's possible. You say the Kop's ahead? What's behind? Our chaps? Or – '

'I don't know – ' Basil was almost weeping now, for the rifle fire had continued and was no longer intermittent, but a steady chattering din that was battering at both of them. It was impossible to tell who was firing at whom, for the bullets seemed to be coming from all directions, and what little veneer of command Basil had had now seemed to be completely stripped away. He was a boy of twenty-four, terrified out of his wits in a situation he could no longer either understand or control.

'I'm going back!' Lizah said with decision. 'It can't be worse than goin' forwards. At least behind us we know we've got our own lines. We might get back safe to the tents and – '

'They'll kill me.' Basil almost wailed it. 'We were all given the orders – get to the Kop. If I go trailing back without my men, they'll kill me – I can't go back – '

'Then bloody don't,' Lizah said. 'I'm going. We're more likely to get shot here than there. I'll take my chances the safest way.' And he began, painfully and stiffly – for his uniform had dried now to a board-like hardness and every move was agony – to ease his way back to where he thought their own lines were, keeping low beneath the hail of bullets which had at last begun to ease off a little.

'Don't leave me here!' Basil began to crawl after him but he was so much taller that his humped shape stood out more clearly against the star-filled sky and at once the rifle fire from the direction of the Kop was redoubled.

Lizah saw Amberly duck down and grinned in the darkness. Stupid sod! Well, he'd learn. To see a man go to pieces like that was a disgusting sight, Lizah told himself sanctimoniously, as the stiffness began to ease out of him and he could move more easily, his rifle still banging on his back as he went. He's a sickening piece of work altogether. How he ever came to have my Millie for a sister is beyond me –

He stopped, suddenly, and again flattened himself against the ground as a bigger missile went over his head. Not a rifle bullet; were they bringing in the bigger artillery? He heard the explosion behind him, where whatever it was hit the ground, and lifted his head gingerly. It had exploded harmlessly well to his left and he turned his head and was about to start crawling

again, back to the safety of his lines when he stopped and
realized what he had seen.

Or rather, not seen. Amberly had not got up again after that
last burst of fire. Lizah had seen the humped shape that was
his body lying there in the scrub and he lay flat for a while,
trying to think.

Was it indeed his body? Had he been hit by a bullet and was
he now dead? If he was it bloody served him right, Lizah
thought viciously and then almost at once thought – God
forgive me. For wishing another man dead was tantamount to
wishing yourself dead; he had learned that long ago, when he
had gone to the cheder, the religion and Hebrew classes to
which his father, but above all, his mother, had sent him
hoping he would learn to be a good Jew. He'd never learned
how to be that but he had learned that wishing someone dead
was tempting fate. It'd be you that got walloped if you so much
as thought it –

Maybe he wasn't dead. Maybe he was just too scared to
move any more and was lying there like a great shlemiel,
crapping himself with terror. In which case he'd be dead soon,
on account of come daylight they'd see him there, these lousy
Boers, and shoot him just to be on the safe side, in case he was
alive.

So, do I go back and get him? That'd be a crazy thing to do,
Lizah told himself. Bleedin' crazy. What chance have I got to
make the man crawl back safely if he hasn't the wit to do it for
himself? The stupid bugger could kill the pair of us, making a
fuss and drawing fire, if I go back.

And if I don't, then, it's the same as if I wished him dead
and I'll get walloped – and Lizah's mind spun and twisted as
he lay there with his head to one side and his cheek pressed
into the dirt, with gunfire going on all around him, caught as
much in a trap by his attempt to behave as a man should, as
Basil Amberly had been caught in a trap by his own terror.

After a while the gunfire eased and then stopped and the night, as black and inky now as a velvet curtain with holes through which the stars glittered with an almost vulgar intensity, became silent. He lay and listened hard, but heard nothing more than the rustle of grass as the occasional breeze moved over it, and the distant cry of an animal somewhere. No soldiers, no fighting, nothing.

Except that he thought he could hear breathing after a while. Stertorous, thick, but definitely human breathing and he lifted his head again to listen more easily, and now there was no doubt. There behind him Basil Amberly was lying still and bloody well snoring –

If he left him there, he'd be in real stooch when the man brought himself back to the lines. He'd come back like some tiger full of lies and complaints and say that he'd been deliberately left there by one of his own men, a man with a grudge against him for beating him in the boxing ring, one Lizah Harris, who would be fit then only for court martial and the chop, no question of it –

Lizah knew he was thinking stupidly. Even as his thoughts chased themselves absurdly through the labyrinth of his mind, he knew that he was no longer behaving like the sensible man he was, at heart. He was exhausted and frightened and confused and in a wilderness of a world that made no sense to him. That was why he was being stupid – but even though he knew it, it did not stop him from continuing to behave stupidly.

He stood up. There was no sense in crawling any more. If there was a bullet out there with his name on it, it would find him whatever he did, he told himself, and that would happen whether he stood on his head or on his heels. So he stood up and went stumping back over the intervening yards of dry rough scrub to where Amberly lay snoring in the darkness.

It wasn't a snore, actually. The man had been hit by one of those bloody bullets and was lying there with his eyes half open, just the whites showing, a horrible way to look, and with his head back, and Lizah leaned over, feeling something very like irritation rather than any stronger emotion, and hauled him up to lift him and shove him over his shoulder in the sort of fireman's hold he had so often used to fetch knocked-out boxers from the ring to their dressing rooms.

It was still silent as he stumbled forwards, with not a shot fired, and he began to be hopeful. He could get there, get to the lines and get rid of this great lump of bleeding meat – for he could feel warm blood sticky on his hands, and knew it was coming from Basil – and lie down and go to sleep. No one could say he'd behaved badly if he brought the man in. They'd see he'd not run away from the fight for Spion Kop once he got back to the lines and made them look at Basil, and under his burden, he managed to grin, seeing himself tell them; 'Found my officer, sir. Thought I ought to – ' and trying to salute and collapsing elegantly into the MO's arms – a lovely picture, that was.

There was a sudden sound ahead of him, and he stopped, frozen, and then it came again, a hiss of a voice.

' 'Oo's that? Friend or bloody foe? I got a gun 'ere, so don't you try nothin' – ' The words were difficult to hear as they came through chattering teeth, and Lizah thought disgustedly – another frightened sod – and said loudly, 'Friend, you stupid bugger. Take this from me, will you? Lieutenant Amberly needs the MO. Where is he?'

'Where the rest of the flamin' brass are, mate – back over there behind the lines, safe and easy. 'Ere, I've got 'im – '

Lizah frowned and opened his mouth to protest. These were the lines which he'd just reached, surely? The man had seemed to indicate the lines were behind him, that he'd gone in the wrong direction – and that couldn't possibly have happened. He had to tell them that, explain. But there was a shuffling sound and then more voices and someone reached towards the burden on Lizah's back and he began to ease open his fingers which had become twisted with cramp and pins and needles, for they had been so tightly clamped round Amberly's wrist that he had lost the full use of his muscles. They'll explain soon, he thought. Just get rid of the weight first, then he'd sort it all out; but suddenly the rifle fire began again, spitting and clattering so loudly that it seemed to be coming from just a few feet away and at once the other men around him, mere shadowy figures in the dimness which he could not count at all, disappeared and he tried to do as he assumed they had, which was to fall flat on the ground. But the dead weight of Amberly on his back made that almost impossible and he stood there swaying, wanting to unlock his hands, to let go and pull both of them down to safety.

But he was too slow. He felt the bullet hit Amberly, for it almost whirled him round with the force of the impact, and then felt the pain in his arm as he swayed and fell and at last hit the ground, with Amberly's dead weight on top of him. And he lay there trying to breathe and escape from the pressure on his aching chest, and the cold numbness that was spreading through his arm.

He felt himself sliding into a different sort of blackness. It was no darker than it had been when he had been stumbling across the scrub with Amberly on his back, but he knew it was different and was inside his own head, and a small inner voice screamed at him, 'No – no, no, no! I'm not dead, I'm not, I won't be, I won't – '

And then he felt the blackness recede and become the real blackness again, the blackness of the night, as a hand was clasped over his mouth and a voice hissed in his ear, 'Shut up, for Christ's sake, shut up – they'll get a bead on us if you don't shut up.' And he knew it was he who had been screaming aloud, not any inner voice.

And he stopped screaming and turned his head pettishly, so that he could breathe more easily and closed his eyes. He was now deeply, exquisitely, tired and wanted only to sleep, and he lay there, his lids clamped tightly over his eyes and he heard them whispering around him.

'Stretcher-bearers,' someone said. 'See if they can get both of 'em up the protected side to the ridge. We'll get reinforcements there by morning and we'll be sure to be able to get the wounded away then – '

'Lieutenant's dead, sir, no point shifting him,' someone said. 'The other chap's breathing though. He's got a nasty one, upper arm, left side. Bleeding a lot – '

'Then stretcher-bearers and tourniquets,' the other voice said brusquely, and Lizah sighed softly behind his sleeping eyes. Soon he'd be asleep, comfortably asleep and then they could talk as much as they liked about these people, whoever they were. Soon he'd be asleep –

'It could be worse,' the brusque voice was saying. 'We've lost a good number and there's a deal of wounded. But we've taken Spion Kop. That'll show Kruger we mean what we say – '

And then Lizah did go to sleep, sliding contentedly away into a world where there was no pain and no heat and no cold and no Basil Amberly. Only peace and quiet.

34

'Nineteen hundred,' Poppy said. 'It sounds so funny. Nineteen hundred – ' And she went on saying it, thinking that might make it sound less strange. But it didn't; it just sounded funnier and funnier.

'Poppy, for heaven's sake be quiet!' Mildred said sharply and Poppy subsided but she didn't stop saying the words inside her head.

She said a lot of words inside her head these days. She had to, because Mama had become so silent and so unwilling to talk and so cross and snappy when Poppy talked that it was all she could do. She couldn't go out to the park any more to play with the other children after school, and she couldn't go and walk through the market any more and look at the stalls and the people, because Mama wouldn't let her. So all there was was sitting at home and reading and talking to herself inside her head, which was getting very dull and miserable.

At first Poppy thought it was because she had been ill; for a long time after that Mama had been very careful about everything she did and where she went and made her wrap up every time she so much as went out into the yard to the lavvy, but now she was quite well again, it seemed to Poppy to be almost as silly as the fact that the year was now called nineteen hundred instead of eighteen-ninety-nine. She had tried to say that to Mama and been roundly scolded for being saucy and sent to bed early; which had made Poppy very quiet all the next day.

Mama had been a bit easier then. She had made Poppy come and sit on her knee before bedtime that day and talked to her.

'Dear one, I don't want to make you miserable, truly I don't. I would very much like to be able to let you go out and play as you used to, but now I know that it isn't safe for you – '

'Why not?' Poppy stared at her unblinking. 'It used to be safe enough when I was still only four, and now I've had a birthday and that means I'm getting on for six, so it ought to be more safe now. I'm a *big* girl – '

'Yes, I know. And it ought to be safe, but it isn't.' Mama said. 'And anyway, I don't think it was so safe before. I think we were just lucky.' And she suddenly held Poppy in a close grip, so tight that it made her breathless, so she pulled away.

'I'm ever so careful when I go out,' Poppy said. 'I always look out for puddles so I don't get splashed, and I only cross the road after looking ever so carefully, or I ask someone to take me over and – '

'That isn't what I mean,' Mama said. 'If it were only dirt and traffic – ' and she shook her head, looking so worried and confused that Poppy almost wanted to cry. But she didn't.

'The thing of it is – ' Mama said and then suddenly stopped and looked so strange that Poppy leaned forwards and stared into her face.

'What's the matter, Mama?'

'Mmm? Oh, nothing. It's just that – I meant to say, the problem is that we're living in the wrong place.'

Poppy laughed. 'Oh, Mama, of course not! We've always lived here. This is our house!'

'But it shouldn't be,' Mama said grimly. 'I knew I couldn't make you understand. Why should you, after all? A baby like you – ' And she hugged Poppy and looked over her head into the fire.

'I'm not a baby!' Poppy said, indignantly and scrambled down to stand on the floor, her hands deep in the pockets of her pinafore and her face scowling. 'I'm a big girl – and I want to go out like a big girl – '

'Well, you can't,' Mama snapped. 'Not while we live here. And that's an end to it.' And she leaned forwards and began to riddle the fire with the poker so violently that the sparks began to fly and the embers rattled in the grate.

'But when I go to school again – ' Poppy began but Mama shook her head almost as violently as she was poking the fire.

'I'm not sure what to do about that. If I could make arrangements soon enough you wouldn't have to go there at all – but I just don't know – it's all so difficult – ' And she dropped the poker and leaned back in the armchair and rested her head on the back and lay there with her eyes closed, looking so miserable that Poppy couldn't talk to her any more. All she could do was sit on her own small stool by the fender and stare at the flames and try to understand. Were they going to live somewhere else? That seemed to be what Mama was saying, and yet where could they live except here? She had a bright thought then; perhaps with Auntie Jessie in Jubilee Street? Now that would be lovely – and she let her mind wander off into imagining how it would be to live in that house with its red, red kitchen and its red, red bedrooms, and to come home from school (which school? It couldn't be Baldwin's Gardens, for that was too far away. Well, another school, then. Any school) and find Auntie Jessie waiting with delicious things to eat. And she liked the thought so much that she turned her head to talk to Mama about it. And then, seeing that she was still lying back in her chair with that same bleak expression on her face, thought better of it. She didn't know how she knew, but she was very certain that Mama would not want to talk about Auntie Jessie just at present.

And so it had gone on day after day, as the winter weather outside became colder and colder and the market outside the front room window looked gloomy and wet and dull with none of its usual liveliness, for once Christmas was over no one seemed to have much money to spend and that made the stallholders morose and far from interested in waving to her through her net curtained window, even old Solly from the vegetable stall. Weeks and weeks of it, it seemed to Poppy. Weeks of dullness and quietness and a cross, silent, worried Mama, and she spent more and more time dreaming and imagining and being a princess. But even that was beginning to get dull now.

But then something happened to change everything. She woke up one morning to find her bedroom had gone a strange colour, all light and yet grey and she got out of bed – and the lino under her bare feet was so cold it made her toes curl up – and ran to the window and looked out to see the rooftops across the street covered in snow. Even the street below had some, though already it was mostly grey slush because so many people had walked on it.

She ran downstairs, full of excitement; surely Mama would let her go out now, to play in the park? She had only ever played in snow once before, years and years ago – or so it felt – and she could only just remember it. There had been that wonderful whiteness that filled her hands and then gently and slowly disappeared like magic and she had made a slide and slipped along on it on her bottom and that had made everyone laugh, Mama as well. It would be good to make Mama laugh again, and she burst into the kitchen to find Mama and explain to her how important it was that they go together to the park this morning at once.

Mama was standing by the fire, a letter in her hand, and staring down at it. The kitchen was rather nice this morning; Mama had been baking apple pies, Poppy decided, for the smell was there, all spicy and warm in her nose. Mama had told her once that the smell was cinnamon and cloves and she had liked the words, and now she said them out loud.

'Cinnamon and cloves! Can we have a pie as well, Mama?'

'I've made us a small one,' Mama said absently, and then looked at Poppy and frowned. 'Silly child! Where are your slippers? You'll catch your death!'

'I'll go and put them on,' Poppy said, full of compunction. How silly to make Mama cross when she wanted to coax her to come to the park! And she turned to run upstairs again, but Mama called her back.

'No, wait here, by the fire. I'll fetch what you need – ' And she went upstairs and Poppy went and curled up in the big armchair, listening to her footsteps overhead and wondering why it was taking her so long to find her slippers. Surely she'd left them at the side of her bed where they were supposed to be?

But Mama was not carrying her slippers when she came down. She had her best dress and a clean white pinafore and her best polished boots, though usually in the mornings she wore yesterday's pinafore, putting on a clean one after dinner. And she also had her coat and her black straw hat and gloves.

'Where are we going?' Poppy leapt to her feet and began to jump on the chair, up and down, up and down, so that her nightie flew around her legs, loving the movement and almost delirious with excitement. Going out? Oh, to be going out at last, after so long! 'Where are we going? Oh, Mama, where – '

'Not so much noise now,' Mama said and piled the clothes on the table. 'First a wash, and then dressed as far as your chemise and stockings and then some breakfast. Afterwards I must dress and then you may put on your frock and – '

'It's my best dress,' Poppy discovered, staring at the clothes on the table and stopped jumping. Best blue serge was not the sort of thing people wore to play in snowy parks, and she stared at the clothes and was so disappointed that she felt the crying begin and that made her feel so angry and cross with herself that she couldn't stop it happening and the tears spilled over the edges of her eyes and ran down her face and made it itch so that she had to rub it hard.

Mama didn't seem to notice. She had gone out to the scullery to fetch the bowl of warm water for Poppy to be washed. 'Now, Poppy, I have a great deal to do, so you must be quiet and sensible and let me get on without any fuss. Then we shall go at eleven. It will give us just enough time – '

'Time for what?' Poppy managed to say without Mama hearing she was crying. It was hard to make her voice sound ordinary but she could do it if she tried hard. This morning she tried very hard.

'I – I'll explain on the way,' Mama said and came back with the bowl of water. 'Just let me get on now and I promise I shall explain on the way.'

And that was all she would say. So Poppy was washed and half dressed and ate her bread and milk and then finished dressing and at last stood with Mama in the street outside as she carefully locked the door and tucked the key back in her reticule. Inside the house it was all quiet with the freshly baked pies standing in rows on the table cooling, for Mama had worked very fast and very hard to make sure they were all ready in time, and it was strange to think of the house quite empty of people. Usually there was someone there – Nellie, mostly – to look after things and Poppy said, as Mama took her hand and started to walk down the road towards Holborn, 'Why isn't Nellie coming any more? Shouldn't she be at home now?'

'You know she isn't coming to us any more,' Mama said and didn't look at her. 'Not since – I told you. We are never to speak to any of those people ever again.' She looked down at Poppy then for a moment and then looked away. 'That is why I won't let you out on your own. I did explain, you know I did. They are bad people – '

'Nellie isn't bad,' Poppy said a little breathlessly, for Mama was walking so fast she had to run to keep up. 'And Ted wasn't bad really. Just – '

'We won't speak of it,' Mama said. 'Not ever. Now, we are to take an omnibus – '

Poppy stopped running then, dragging back on Mama's hand as hard as she could.

'An omnibus? Where are we going? Is it to that horrible house like last time?'

'I – ' Mama looked at her and it was as though, Poppy thought, she was asking me for something, for her face looked so hopeful and yet worried. And she stood still and wouldn't move even though Mama tugged on her hand.

'Poppy, I told you, I shall explain on the way,' Mama said. 'Please don't be a silly girl and just come along – '

Oh, Poppy, please, Mildred was beseeching her child silently, the words framing themselves behind her lips. Please, don't make it more difficult than it is. It's going to be dreadful, dreadful. Please, darling Poppy, don't make it worse –

'Tell me what we're doing and where we're going,' Poppy said, almost, it seemed to Mildred, in answer to her unspoken plea and Mildred bit her lip and then looked at the watch pinned to the bosom of her heavy braided serge coat by a short chain and made a sudden decision. They would go straight there; she had planned to go to the house and travel to the cemetery with the family, as was seemly, but sometimes things did not work out as you had planned, so there it was; she would explain when she saw them.

'Poppy, we shall go and have some refreshment,' she said firmly. 'And you shall hear all there is to be told. It is absurd of me not to tell you. There is, after all, only you and me. We only have each other, and if I can't talk to you, who can I talk to? Come along – we shall go to that tea shop and you shall choose whatever you like to eat and drink – '

Immediately beguiled, Poppy came along. She had seen the shops' fronts often with their big signs 'Aerated Bread Company' and been fascinated by them, for there were two of them in Holborn, one at each end, and they had big windows that were often half steamed over through which you could see people sitting at little tables, eating and drinking, and she had always wanted to go into one. That Mama should take her now was amazing, and not a matter over which to argue.

It was all she had ever hoped it would be; warm and steamy and smelling almost as nice as Mama's baking and full of people who smiled at her, and she chose a large red jam tart to eat – Mama didn't often bake jam tarts – and a glass of lemonade which she was to drink through a straw. Suddenly it didn't matter she hadn't been out of the house for so long and had been so dull and miserable; this more than made up for it.

'Now, Poppy,' Mama said when the waitress, dressed in a very frilly cap which Poppy thought would look nice on her, as well, had brought Mama's coffee and gone away. 'I shall explain all to you. You remember the last time we went on an omnibus?'

Poppy's mouth was full of jam tart, so she couldn't speak. She just nodded her head and stared at Mama, hoping she would see by looking at her how much she remembered it as having been a nasty day.

'I know you didn't like that day,' Mama said and Poppy swallowed her bite of tart and felt better. As long as Mama remembered that, it would be all right. 'And I know I said you wouldn't have to go back there. But sometimes things change.'

'How?' Poppy said and took another big bite. Some of the jam got on to her chin and she managed to put out her tongue far enough to lick it back in again, and Mama leaned forwards and used her handkerchief to wipe her clean again. It seemed to help Mama to do that, as though having a jammy chin to clean was so important it made it easier to say the words she had to say, and obviously didn't want to.

'People change,' Mama said. 'They get ill. And sometimes – '
she swallowed. 'You remember the old man there, the one you
did not like?'

Poppy nodded vigorously. How could she forget someone
who had been so nasty about her hat and muff? And suddenly
she remembered that she wasn't wearing them and wondered
if Mama would go back and fetch them. It was cold enough
outside today to wear them. But she didn't say anything.

'Well, Poppy, darling, he got ill and – and went to heaven.'

Poppy stared at her and frowned. 'He couldn't have,' she
said firmly. 'Miss Rushmore says only good people go to
heaven. He wasn't good.'

Mildred stared at her and then at first quietly, and then more
and more loudly began to laugh, until tears ran down her
cheeks and other people turned and stared at her curiously, but
no more curiously than Poppy was looking at her.

'Oh, Poppy,' she managed to gasp as at last she regained her
self control, and was wiping her eyes on her handkerchief. 'Oh,
my dear, you are so right! He wasn't good at all – ' She stopped
then and took a deep breath and again wiped her eyes. But
they remained very bright as though tears were still there.

'It is better to be direct, isn't it? Even with children – ' It was
as though she had asked a question, but Poppy did not answer
it. Instead she ate the last piece of her jam tart and then started
on her lemonade, drinking it in lovely long slow sucks through
the big yellow straw.

'Well, then,' Mama said and leaned forwards and put her
hand over Poppy's as she was holding her tall glass. Poppy
went on drinking but she did not take her eyes from her
mother's face.

'He died, you see. My father. Your grandfather. He took ill
one night at a City banquet – an apoplexy the letter said – and
died three days ago. The funeral is today, and my Mama – my
stepmother wrote to tell me of that fact and to ask me to come
to the funeral and to bring you.' She stopped then and let go of

Poppy's hand and sat up more strongly. 'Indeed, she begged me to come. And I feel I must. God knows he was a hard man and there were many times I hated him, but he was my father – ' And suddenly she bent her head and began to hunt through her reticule for a dry handkerchief, for the one she was holding was little more than a wet rag now.

'A funeral,' Poppy said after a while. She had finished her lemonade now, having made several satisfactory sucking-up noises with the last drops. 'I've never been to funerals. What do they do? Do they put the dead people in a blanket and go one, two, three and throw them up to heaven? Or do they make a big fire and put them in to go to hell?'

'Oh, Poppy,' Mama said. 'Oh dear, oh Poppy!' and again she began to laugh, but it wasn't quite so noisy this time, nor so unhappy. 'Where do you get your ideas from? All that happens at funerals is that there are prayers said and – and the dead person is in a large and beautiful special box, covered with flowers and it is put in the ground and then covered up, and a special stone is put over it, with words on it explaining who the person was and how much everyone is sad they are dead.' She stopped and stared silently at Poppy for a moment and then with an almost visible effort went on, 'And then everyone goes to the person's home and they all have something to eat and drink and talk of their nice memories of the dead person.'

'No one will be able to do that for that man,' Poppy said dispassionately and then frowned. 'But the person in the box? What happens to them?'

'Nothing. They just stay there.'

'Oh,' Poppy said consideringly. 'That sounds dull. Like it's been at home all this time. Never going anywhere, and never seeing anyone but us.'

'Oh, no!' Mama said and her face was blank with dismay. 'It hasn't been that bad, surely! I just want you to be safe – '

'It's been very dull,' Poppy said. 'And miserable, and you're so cross a lot and – ' She stopped. 'Anyway, we're not at home now, are we? And the jam tart was lovely and the lemonade was better. Will you make some lemonade sometimes for the orders, Mama, and some jam tarts like those?'

'Oh, yes, Poppy if you want me to.' Mama got to her feet. 'And I shall find a way to make being at home with me less – less funereal. I dare say it has been misery for you – Come along then. Let's go and get it over and done with – '

And Poppy decided that after all it wasn't worth nagging Mama about going back to fetch her fur hat and muff and instead took her hand obediently and went to catch the omnibus.

35

Generally speaking, Poppy liked colours, and the stronger they were the better she liked them. That was one of the reasons she so loved Auntie Jessie, for Auntie Jessie was one of the most colourful people she had ever seen. She knew more kinds of red than anyone in the world, Poppy thought. But even though there was no colour in the place to which Mama took her when they got off the omnibus – and it was the second one they had been on that morning, a remarkable thing! – Poppy thought it very beautiful.

It was all black and white. White ground and white branches on black trunked trees. White leaves on black stemmed shrubs. Crisp white edging on tilted black stones and models of angels and crosses and crying people wearing only sheets which stood in white tipped black earth. And over all a heavy sky which was a rich mixture of both colours, a thick bright grey that seemed to press down on her head and bite the tips of her ears and the end of her nose with the cold. Even the few people there were to be seen were black and white; black clothes, white faces with black shadows on them, and Poppy stared at them as Mama hurried her along one of the white paths, liking the look of their long sad faces and bent heads. It seemed right to look so sad in a place like this, even though its black and whiteness was so beautiful.

'Where is this, Mama?' Poppy asked and she said it quietly, because this was not a place in which people shouted, she was sure.

'This is the cemetery,' Mama said and held her hand more tightly. 'Now hold on to me, and don't ask questions. You can ask me all you like when we are going home, but please Poppy, be quiet now. People mustn't talk at funerals.'

Which was a pity, Poppy thought, because she had a lot of questions to ask. She suddenly remembered one she meant to ask before but had forgotten; what was it Mama said happened to the nasty man? It had been a beautiful word that Poppy had liked and she had meant to ask more about it, but there had been so many interesting things to talk about she had forgotten. She tried to remember now as she almost ran along the path to keep up with Mama, who was walking purposefully towards a large group of very black figures clustered further along the path and moving slowly forwards, but she couldn't. It was something like her own name and lex as well, and she tried to make the word inside her head; poppylex, poppylex; but it wasn't right and that irritated her. It was dreadful not being allowed to ask questions.

They had reached the group of people now and Mama put one finger to her lips warningly as Poppy lifted her head to look up at her and then stood quietly and Poppy stood still too, trying to look up at the people around them to see who they were.

There were tall men on each side of her, so tall she could see nothing of their faces; only chins over white shirt fronts, so that was dull and she began to peep between the gaps in front of her to see what it was they were all looking at.

Enthralling, she thought. There was the box Mama had told her about, all covered with flowers and for the first time there was colour. Reds and yellows and blues and greens, and she stared at them, because they looked so very much brighter than colours usually did, after all the black and white, and she liked that. Beyond the box there were ladies in black gowns and pelisses and most dramatic of all, with black veils falling from their hats over their faces. One lady in particular was wearing a very thick and voluminous veil and she was leaning on the arms of the men on each side of her. Next to the men were three boys all in the same sort of black overcoat and hat. One looked, Poppy thought, about as old as some of the biggest boys at school, and the other two were much bigger, about as big as Nellie's brother Ted. They looked sad, but the other one, the smallest, didn't. He looked bored and Poppy looked at him and wondered what he was thinking.

He seemed to hear her thinking, because suddenly he looked across the box towards her and saw her staring and at once stuck out his tongue and Poppy blinked, startled, and at once stuck hers out too. And then there was a rustle as the people standing around moved a little and a faint voice, coming from somewhere in the crowd that Poppy couldn't see, began to speak in a sing-song sort of voice.

'I am the Resurrection and the Life, saith the Lord. He that believeth in Me, though he were dead, yet shall live, and whoever liveth and believeth in Me shall never die – '

Which, Poppy decided, was silly. People who are dead aren't alive. So she stopped listening and let the words just roll past her ears and started to stare again, instead.

It went on and on, it seemed, with the man talking and talking in the same singing sort of voice – it wasn't like talking at all – and the people standing there and saying nothing back. Very boring. So she tried to catch the eye of the boy on the other side again and as soon as she did, poked out her tongue. But this time he just looked at her as though she wasn't there and then looked away, which made Poppy feel dreadful. She felt her face go red as she thought about how awful it was to be looked at as though you weren't there when all you were trying to do was be friendly.

It stopped at last, the singing talk, and there was a little rustle of movement as though the wind had blown over all the people and made them bend, and they were closer together now so that she couldn't see. There were sounds, though, and she craned to stare at the box from which they seemed to be coming, but Mama held her back and whispered, 'Be still, Poppy!' So she had to. And could see nothing of what was happening.

People moved again and now she could see that the box had gone. There was just a hole in the ground and the box had vanished and Poppy longed to get closer so that she could peer down inside the hole and see what had happened to the box, but she couldn't. The flowers hadn't gone though; they were all in a row on the ground in bunches and rings and some shaped into crosses and she looked at them instead.

And then people were walking, moving away to the path and Mama took her hand and tugged her forwards and she had to walk round the hole in the ground – too far round to be able to see in – and towards the woman in the thick veil. People were standing in front of her and the three boys and shaking their hands and then moving away, and after a while Mama was there, with Poppy beside her.

'Oh, Mildred,' the woman in the veil said and Poppy wanted to laugh for when she spoke the veil puffed out in front. It looked very comical. 'Oh, Mildred, you came! You were not at the house when the carriages came and the hearse – oh, Mildred!' And she began to cry as one of the boys leaned across and patted her shoulder.

Poppy knew who she was now. The woman who had sat on the sofa in the big house and talked with a voice that sounded like a kettle that whined to itself when it wasn't quite boiling. Somewhere under the black veil was the yellow hair like fluffy cotton wool and the red patches that had been painted on to a melted face. Poppy hadn't liked her much when she met her at the big house, and she liked her even less now she was covered all over in black cloth. Except for the way the veil blew out when she spoke; that was funny, and Poppy liked it.

'I am sorry, Mama, I tried to reach you in time, but sadly the journey is long and made it impossible. I wish you well, Mama, and am saddened for you and your grief.' And she bent over and kissed the black veil.

'And I for you, dear Mildred, for he was your dear Papa, was he not? And he is such a loss to us all – ' The kettle was whining at top pitch now and Poppy looked at Mama, and saw her face stiff and hard, like a board, and thought – she doesn't like the sound much either.

'Indeed, Mama,' Mildred said after a moment and then stepped aside as a man in what looked to Poppy like a long white dress came to join them. She hardly stared at him at all, even though he looked rather strange, for she had seen so many strange things already this morning that one more really made no difference.

'My dear Mrs Amberly, we share your grief, and wish you comfort in your distress. God will be good to you, if you turn to him. Be of good heart – '

'Thank you, Vicar. It was good in you, indeed it was, to agree to come so far for the funeral. Edward would have so much preferred to lie in the churchyard at St Mary's, of course – '

'Ah, indeed, indeed. So sorry there was no room – but this is an excellent resting place, excellent. We are indeed fortunate to be so near Kensal Green – well, I must return to my duties – '

'You will return to the house with us, perhaps, on your way?' The voice came from behind Poppy and she turned to stare up at the source, a tall young man with a bright face that was not at all sad, and wearing a soldier's uniform. Poppy thought he looked very beautiful. 'My mother would welcome you, I know, and we – my brothers and I – would also. It was an excellent service and encomium – we much appreciated it.'

'Indeed, Mr Amberly – or perhaps I should say Lieutenant Amberly – it is good in you to say so. I do my poor best, you know, my poor best. And indeed your late father was a very special man, a very special man – '

The woman in the veil gave a little yelp and then began to cry and the lieutenant put out his arm and set it round her shoulders.

'Come along, Mama! We shall return home. The carriage is ready, and you need some brandy to get the chill out of your bones – I'm sure Mildred will come with – and here's the little one, too! Poppy, isn't it? Yes, Poppy – here you are then, Vicar, my niece, don't you know. Papa managed to be a grandfather before he snuffed it – sorry, Mama – ' the whine having grown louder. 'Before he passed on – though he didn't relish it as much as he might have done, eh, Mildred? M'sister, Vicar – '

'How do you do,' the Vicar nodded a little frostily. 'But if you will forgive me I will not return to the house with you. So many pressing duties – again my sympathy – ' And he went away along the path, his white surplice flapping behind him.

'That's down to you, Mildred!' the lieutenant laughed softly. 'Did you see how sour he looked? Someone's told him of your naughty ways – eh, Poppy?' And he tapped the top of Poppy's hat and then chucked her under the chin in a way that Poppy particularly disliked and which made her pull away.

'I hardly think this is the time or place for your silly witticisms, Wilfred,' Mama said frostily and Poppy held her hand tightly in approval. He was being horrid which was particularly naughty, when usually he was so nice, and it was right of Mama to tell him so. 'Come, Mama, let me help you to the carriage. And when we get back you shall have some hot tea and feel better – '

'She'd rather have the brandy,' Wilfred said softly, behind Poppy, so that only she and Mama could hear, but Mama took no notice of him and they all went back along the path, the lady in the black veil and another tall man – one of those

Poppy seemed to remember seeing at the house that day she had visited it so long ago – and the three boys. Poppy carefully didn't look at the youngest one. She had decided he was not a person she wanted to know at all.

At the far end of the path there were many other people waiting for them, some of them stamping their feet up and down to warm themselves in the cold and Poppy looked at the clouds of mist they made when they breathed and the bigger clouds of mist that the horses made, as they stood waiting patiently in the shafts of the carriage, and then blew softly with her own breath to make a private cloud and watched it as it rose against the thick grey sky and disappeared.

It was getting colder now and she felt hungry and thirsty and was beginning to think it might be quite a good idea to find a lavvy and she pulled on Mama's hand to whisper to her; but Mama was too busy talking to the veil and Poppy decided it was better not to think about the matter at all and hope to get wherever they were going in plenty of time.

The journey back in the carriage was interesting, but not because of what was happening inside it. Mama talked softly to her own Mama, who now looked a little better, for she had pushed back the veil as soon as she had settled into her seat in the corner, and she whined back, but Poppy didn't listen, just as she hadn't bothered to listen to the man who had talked about people who were dead being alive. If it wasn't interesting, why bother? Especially when outside there was so much to look at: tall handsome houses with steps that led up to them from the pavement, and white pillars beside the front doors and railings and balconies and high windows with lots of curtains to be seen through the glittering clean glass. The houses ran away on each side as the horses went trotting along the road between them and looked as grey and black and white as the cemetery had looked, and just as beautiful.

And when they arrived at the house she had visited before, Poppy had to say it also looked beautiful. She didn't much like the people who lived in it – especially not the veiled lady and Wilfred and the horrid boy – but it was still very handsome and as she climbed the big steps behind Mama, who was helping her Mama to get up them (and every time Poppy thought of her Mama having a Mama of her own it seemed very strange) she wished she lived in such a house. What would be really nice, she decided as they stood at the top and waited for the people in the other carriages – of whom there were a great many – would be if a giant could come along and pluck up this house in his great hand and carry it away to Leather Lane, and push aside the little houses already there and tuck this one in the middle of them. And that was such a delightful thought that it made her smile widely.

The boys who had been in the carriage behind which had also just arrived came up the steps just at that point and the youngest one stood in front of her and put both hands in his trouser pockets so that his coat bunched over his arms on each side, and stood and stared down at her, for he was considerably taller than she was. He must, she decided, be at least eight or nine. Very old. He had a dark suit just like the men, and a black tie and a black bowler hat which was now pushed back so that his fair hair flopped out in front over his forehead.

'And what might you be grinning at?' he said, as the other people, including Mama and her Mama went into the house after the man in the uniform, from last time, opened the door. 'You look like a great stupid monkey, grinning like that.'

'I was not grinning!' Poppy said indignantly.

'Yes you were. I saw you. Like this – ' And he bared his teeth in a ferocious grimace.

'I did not!' Poppy wanted to cry, she was so angry. 'I only smiled because I thought of something funny.'

'What?'

'I shan't tell you.'

'You must tell me. If you don't I shall pinch you – like this – ' And his hand snaked out of his pocket and reached for her face and pinched her cheek hard and then went back to his pocket so fast she hardly saw it move. The pain of the pinch made her eyes water, but she was certain now that no matter what happened he wasn't going to make her cry.

'I shan't, because you are a very rude and nasty boy,' she said as loftily as she could and turned and went stomping into the house, going as fast as she could without looking as though she were running away. She wouldn't let that horrid boy think she was afraid of him for anything; although of course, she was, very much.

'Don't you dare say I pinched you. If you do I shall tell them what a liar you are. You hear me? If you do, I shall say you're a liar – ' He was immediately behind her and hissing in her ear.

She ignored him and caught up with Mama, who had now reached the big room to which they had gone on their last visit and she stood beside her as she helped remove the veil and hat from the yellow curls and then helped her Mama to settle on her sofa.

'Tea – ' Mama said to a servant who was standing behind the sofa and 'Brandy,' said Mrs Amberly at the same moment and the servant looked wooden and went away and came back with a tray on which a glass of brandy stood in solitary splendour.

'Poppy, dear, go and – ' Mama looked at her a little distractedly. 'There are some picture books in the nursery, upstairs. Go and look at them. And there will, I dare say, be a nursery lunch – I shall find you when it is time to leave.'

'But, Mama – ' Poppy began but Mama frowned and shook her head.

'Please, Poppy don't argue. I really must talk to – you must leave me be. And there are so many people here that truly, you will not be comfortable. Go upstairs – ah! Harold! There you are – you can take Poppy upstairs to play, can you not? There, that will be nice. Off you go then. And be good – '

Poppy stood there and looked at her and then at the boy identified as Harold. He was now standing with his hands still in his trouser pockets and his hair sleeked down, having taken off his hat and coat, and was looking at her with his brows a little raised, daring her to say anything to Mama, who was now fussing over her, taking off her hat and smoothing her hair and removing her coat. Her face was tingling still where he had pinched it and she wanted to rub it, but she wouldn't, knowing that would make him look even more pleased with himself than he already was.

'I'm not hungry, Mama,' she managed at last. 'I really don't want any.'

'Then don't have any.' Mama sounded thoroughly exasperated now. 'You may eat when we reach home afterwards. But do go *away*. This is not the place for you at present. I would not have brought you here if I didn't have to, and I will leave as soon as possible. But I must talk to Mama – ' And indeed the yellow curls were bobbing anxiously as their owner beckoned eagerly – 'and as soon as I can, I promise we shall go. Now, upstairs, Poppy. At once. Take her away, Harold, and look after her. Carefully, you understand me?'

'Yes, Mildred,' Harold said with great politeness, and held out his hand to Poppy. 'Come along then,' he said with a bright voice and even brighter smile. 'We'll go and play, shall we?'

So, she had to go with him. She couldn't do anything else.

36

'But, Mama – ' Mildred said and then stopped. She had meant to protest, to say it was out of the question, but even as the words had begun to frame themselves on her tongue, she had known she could not. Was it not precisely the remedy she had been seeking? It might not be what she wanted but it was undoubtedly what she needed, and although it might not be an answer that would make her happy, her own happiness was, she had felt, beside the point. And anyway, how happy was she in her present situation? Yes, she was independent, yes, she had the control of her own life and her own child, but at what cost? And she remembered how she had felt standing there at the kitchen door on that foggy night staring in at Ted and his flustered excited face, and at Poppy, sitting wide-eyed in her armchair – and she took a deep breath and said nothing.

'You must see that it is your duty, anyway, my dear Mildred. I know you behaved badly leaving us as you did, but I do not bear grudges and it is your duty – ' And she peered at Mildred over the rim of her glass – the third she had had, a detail Mildred had not been able to ignore – and blinked her red-rimmed eyes. 'Your dear Papa would have wished it – '

'Mama, if we are to talk sensibly, we must be honest with each other. I cannot subscribe to any myth about how good Papa was. He was monstrous. He treated me badly enough, but you little better. I left this house because I had little choice. I had no real home here and certainly no contentment. And I doubt you did either. His treatment of you made you ill.' And she flicked a glance at the glass in Maud's hand. 'So let us have no inventions about his goodness.'

The red-rimmed eyes filled up with tears again. 'Oh, do not speak so, Mildred. He is dead, and he was your father. It is wicked to speak so.'

'And it's wicked to tell lies,' Mildred said brusquely. 'So we will not, if you please. Now, if that is understood, we may talk of your suggestion. If not, we must forget it.'

'I would not tell lies for the world, Mildred, you know that. I try so hard to be good,' Maud said and sniffed and looked about her for a servant. The room was still full of people, all eating cake and drinking brandy, and servants were moving among them with decanters but Mildred caught the eye of the one at whom Maud was signalling and shook her head, and the maid's eyes slid away and she ignored Maud. That is another reason for agreeing, I suppose, Mildred thought and looked at Maud's disappointed face and leaned over and took the glass from her fingers.

'We shall get some tea for you, Mama, and then you must go and lie down and rest,' she said firmly. 'Perhaps we should not talk of this now – '

'Oh, but we must, we must!' Maud clutched at her hands tightly. Her fingers were hot and moist and Mildred gently withdrew her hand and patted her shoulder.

'As long as you do not excite yourself, then,' she said.

'I shan't. I promise,' Maud said and tried to smile but it was a pathetic little grimace which made Mildred's own eyes smart for a moment.

'Very well. Now, listen, Mama. I have been my own mistress for some years now.'

'Of course you have,' Maud said eagerly. 'Of course you have. And you are an excellent housekeeper, my dear. Why, when you were with us, I never had a moment's anxiety about our situation. We were fed and warmed and all went well, but as soon as you went – ' She shook her head and looked about her, her eyes flickering as she sought to see someone with a glass of brandy she could have. 'It was quite dreadful. Edward became so angry and the servants so insolent and the cook, oh, so hateful! Edward did not eat a meal in his own house for so long a time because it was so bad, and the boys complained and – and I was so afraid to speak to her – oh, Mildred, please do come back! I will do all I can to make you happy. You shall have your legacy – I told your Papa he was wrong to withhold it, indeed I did. I told him roundly, and was very definite. "It is not right, Edward," I said, "that Mildred should not have her mother's money," but he paid me no attention at all for you know how very strong a man he was – '

'He was not strong. He was a mean and greedy bully,' Mildred said and once more Maud's face crumpled.

'Oh, Mildred, you must not say so!'

'I must and I will. I needed that money quite desperately at the time and he withheld it on the merest whim of the law. There was no moral weight in his argument at all. I was a grown woman with a child of my own – '

Maud shook her head dolorously. 'It was a great disgrace you brought on us, Mildred. A great disgrace.'

'Stuff and nonsense. It is no disgrace to you in the least. I went away and had my child on my own, with no support – or affection – from anyone here. That being so, there can be no disgrace on you. For you to share in what happened to me in any way, there had to be continued intercourse between us. As it was, we were strangers to each other. We still would be if it were not for Basil.'

The tears began afresh. 'Oh, dear Basil! He knew how anxious I was, and how despairing and it was so good in him to come and find you to bring you here to talk to Wilfred. Not that it made any difference – ' She lifted her head and then looked across the room to where Wilfred was standing with one highly polished boot on the fender and his uniform glittering with pressing and polish, talking to a group of admiring women. 'But I am much less fearful now, for he agreed to apply for a posting here at home as long as I agreed to his joining, and dear Edward said he was able to arrange matters so that my darling boy would be safe and have a good job at the War Office, and indeed so it has been. And he does look so handsome in his uniform. It is such a comfort to me that he did not have to go to South Africa – '

'He may have to go yet,' Mildred said. 'The news is not good and every man they can get is required, with Ladysmith still held, and Mafeking – '

'But not my Wilfred,' Maud said quickly. 'He must never go. They promised me he should not. That he should stay here and work at the War Office – '

'That's as may be,' Mildred said. 'You say that Basil has gone – '

Maud nodded. 'He went in October last, on the *Dunottar Castle*, you know, with Sir Redvers Buller. I had one letter from him which he wrote in Durban but nothing since. But as long as my Wilfred does not have to go – ' She shifted her eyes to Mildred's face again. 'You see how it is with me? I am so nervous and so fearful that I am quite prostrate. I am a widow now and I cannot be alone, with my dear son at risk of leaving me at any moment and the little ones to care for – oh, dearest Mildred, please do as I ask! It is a small thing, after all! I wish you only to leave that nasty little poky house you live in – Basil told me, you see, and it is in the middle of a slum he says, and you work so dreadfully hard and it is quite wrong for a lady like you – you have to leave so little to come and be with me! This house is much more agreeable, you must admit, than a slum house and you must surely prefer to be here.'

'My home is clean and well cared for – ' Mildred began hotly and then subsided. How could she argue? The house she lived in might be clean and well cared for, but it *was* in a slum. Not as bad a slum as some that London boasted, but for all that, a dubious area. Here amid the Portland stone and white stucco, the big rooms and the turkey carpets and big mirrors and costly furniture with which she had grown up she felt much more comfortable. To deny that would not only be dishonest but stupid.

'I'm sure it is,' Maud said. 'You have such a gift for housekeeping, the mending you used to do so exquisitely – the boys were never so well furnished with their linen after you went away. And the cook was so much better and – '

Mildred laughed aloud then. 'Oh, Mama, really! I recall the sort of cook we had when I lived here and she was quite dreadful! The food she ruined was quite disgusting – I am better fed now that I have the cooking of my own victuals than I ever was in this house.'

'There you are, then, another reason to return!' Maud cried triumphantly. 'For we are now even worse fed! Ask Wilfred if you do not believe me!' And she lifted her head and called him eagerly, and he looked across the crowded room and smiled and said something to the women he was still with and made them laugh, and then turned to come towards where his mother sat, her face as pink with pleasure as a girl's, waiting for him.

'Does he not look quite wonderful?' Maud demanded. 'He is turning all the girls' heads quite shamelessly.'

'Do they know you have not yet had your eighteenth birthday?' Mildred was unable to resist the barb, and Wilfred frowned sharply.

'Now, hush! Papa, rest his wicked old soul, told them I was fully twenty for he was as eager to be rid of me as I was to go, and they, looking at my manly frame, believed him! So I won't have you spoiling my fun with your tales – '

'If they tried to send you to South Africa, you might be glad of such fun-spoiling,' Mildred said and he grinned, easily.

'Well, that is as may be. I won't deny that the tales we are getting back from such battles as Magersfontein and so forth do not fill me with the desire to march into the veldt which I had when I joined. I was all for rushing off to the land of lions and tigers and striking noble attitudes, but I have a little more caution about me now – and I am having a splendid time, Mildred, at the War Office! The parties and the balls, you know and all the girls bowled over by my uniform and just a bit of clerical work to deal with – it has its compensations.'

'I'm sure it has,' Mildred said dryly and could not help smiling back. A villainous child always, Wilfred, but a likeable one for all that, and he was clearly still as much of a scamp as he had ever been.

'Wilfred, dear, do you not agree it would be best if Mildred returned home now to live with me, now I am a widow? I need to have someone to care for me now your dear Papa has left us – ' And she wiped her eyes again ' – and who better than my own dear daughter, which is how I have always regarded her?'

'Who better indeed,' Wilfred said heartily and grinned at Mildred. 'But does she want to? It's a pretty dull house, Ma, you must agree. And Mildred perhaps has a better time where she is.'

'Oh, no.' Maud waved one hand in airy dismissal. 'She lives in a slum house, do you not, Mildred? Poor dear Basil said so – '

'I wish you would not speak of him so,' Mildred said with sudden sharpness. 'He is in South Africa fighting, perhaps, but you do not have to speak of him as though he were – as though – ' And she shook her head, furious with herself for not being able to say the words that had formed in her mind.

'Of course he isn't!' Wilfred said cheerfully. 'Old Bas knows better than to get himself wounded or killed. Good and scared he is, so he'll take care of himself. I can't imagine how he came to join in the first place. No sense of adventure in him at all! And here's me, who only joined for the fun of a good scrap who's learned the good sense of staying snug at home and fighting the war from behind the lines. Rum, ain't it?'

'Very,' Mildred said and then sat and looked down at her hands linked in her lap. What was she to do? Here was the exact answer to her dilemma about how to protect Poppy. A home where the child would be not merely safe from dangerous influences but living in great comfort. Her small room at Leather Lane was as elegant as Mildred had been able to make it, but it had cold lino on the floor, and not a thick warm carpet as had the bedrooms here. There was no bathroom in Leather Lane and Poppy had to wash and dress before the kitchen fire like some servant, whereas here there was a vast enamelled iron bath and a beautifully warm tiled bathroom, fully equipped with brass hot water cans and basins galore. And when she was out of the house – and Mildred shivered as there rose in her mind's eye a picture of the dilapidated building on the corner of the street where Ted and his family lived. Poppy could not be allowed to be out of her home without her, Mildred, to watch over her, and that meant her life would be that of a virtual prisoner if they stayed there. But here – and she lifted her head and looked round the room.

The room stared back at her, displaying its comfort so vividly that it was almost as though someone were holding out the items and crying their value to her. The velvet curtains and upholstered furniture. The richly decorated and lavishly polished chairs and tables. The fireplace with its winking brass fire irons and elegant pink tiled surround; it was all so rich and good and desirable and she sighed softly and looked again at Maud and Wilfred.

'I see what you mean,' she said. 'I would be a fool if I did not. And now that *he* is dead this house could indeed be a happy and comfortable place for me and Poppy – '

'Poppy,' Maud said and it was not a question. It was more a wondering sort of statement, as though she had quite forgotten her.

Mildred looked at her sharply. 'You are prepared to have another child in the house? After all, she is only five. Still very young, though a well-behaved child. I credit myself that she has been carefully reared and knows her manners.'

'Of course,' Maud said heartily. Too heartily. 'Wherever your home is, there must be the home of your child. But we must make some sort of arrangement that – '

'How do you mean?' Mildred was sitting very upright now and staring at her stepmother with her eyes very bright and dark. 'What sort of arrangement?'

'My dear!' Maud spread her hands wide. 'If you return here as Miss Amberly, how are we to explain a little one? Our neighbours are very superior people, you know, and – '

'Let us be quite clear on this, Mama,' Mildred said strongly. 'If I return here, it is as Miss Amberly. And my daughter, who is Poppy Amberly, returns with me. I shall not tell lies about myself nor about her.'

'Why not?' Maud said and looked at her with her red eyes wide and enquiring. 'Would you have every servant know she was a – a – '

'Bastard, Mama,' Wilfred said helpfully and grinned at Mildred. 'That is what you are saying, is it not, Mildred?'

She ignored him. 'I care nothing for servants' gossip,' she said with all the hauteur she could muster.

'You will when they talk to other servants who will talk to their employers who will then shun us,' Maud said and she drooped, her head down. 'I had such hopes of us all being happy and content again, and you having your own money and living here and being comfortable. I should make you a handsome allowance too. You could – ' She looked up then, brightening. 'You could send Poppy away to school! Now, that would suit well enough, would it not? Let her go to school to be educated and give her her father's name and – '

'She carries my name,' Mildred said. 'And she will indeed go to school. If we come here, there's an excellent school, or always used to be, in Bayswater Road, near Orme Lane. I saw many children there when I walked in the park in – in the old days. If we come here, Poppy goes to that school – '

'And has a dreadful time at the hands of the other children as soon as they discover she is Miss Amberly, the daughter of Miss Amberly,' Wilfred said and grinned that wicked little grin of his. 'Do be sensible, Mildred! Come back, make this house fit for civilized people to live in again, and take care of the Mater. She needs someone to watch over her and her brandy – oh, Ma, don't make such faces – ' for Maud was flapping her hands about and grimacing furiously at him ' – you know it is true. It is why you want her here. To run the house while you settle down to serious toping. Well, I want you here, Mildred, to make sure she does not kill herself with drink, and to take decent care of us all. And it will be better for you, for you will have the full running of the place and no more misery, with the old devil dead, and good riddance to him – oh, Mama, do hush! – and your little Poppy, who looks like a jolly enough little sprig, will be better off as well. It can't be right rearing her in that gutter place you're in now. When she talks you can hear it, you know. Got the accent of the kitchen, undoubtedly. Certainly not the drawing room. But you cannot label her with a bastard's ticket as well, just to please your own stubbornness.'

There was a long silence and then, as people began to come to the sofa to bid the grieving – if now somewhat preoccupied – widow farewell, Mildred could sit and think.

It was difficult to think clearly with so much going on around her. She needed more time, she told herself desperately, more time and quiet in which to plan it all right. My business – and her heart sank as she thought of that. For how much longer could she go on as she had been this past five years, putting in those long hard days and short exhausted nights of constant bone-grinding effort? And she seemed to see those five years as a procession of pies and cakes and puddings and tarts, marching across her with leaden feet, and wearing her out. And suppose I should die of it all – what then? Suppose I were not alive to care for Poppy, who would look after her? She closed her eyes as she imagined the sort of person she would grow up to be if Jessie – the obvious person – took care of her. An over-dressed, over-noisy, over-painted East Ender; and she opened her eyes quickly to banish the vision of such a Poppy. Her Poppy was to be a new woman, a brave, upright and well-spoken, well-educated, well-reared woman. Not a guttersnipe. Yet that was what she would become if she remained where she was –

'Come on, Mildred, there can't be a choice to make!' Wilfred was saying and slapping her on the back. 'Here we are, a vast family for you to take care of, and you greatly in need of some new clothes and a little fun for yourself. Come here, banish the old devil's ghost for good and all, and we'll all be happy again. Including your little one. Just tack her father's name on, whatever it is, and she can go to school with her head up, the dear child of a sad widow.'

He lifted his chin then and laughed. 'It'll be quite suitable really! This will be the house of a brace of widows – mother and daughter. All very apt. Well, whatever you decide, I must go. Mama, I shall be back late tonight, I want no dinner – invited to the Stanhopes, don't you know. All very jolly – their younger son just invalided back and I intend to get all the gossip – goodbye, Mildred. Hope to see you here soon!' And he was gone, following the last of the visiting mourners out of the house and leaving his mother sitting staring imploringly at her stepdaughter, who stared back, her head in a whirl.

Upstairs in the nursery, Poppy sat in the corner, trying not to cry. They had teased her dreadfully, all three of them, and not only Harold. Samuel and Thomas, big as they were – and they had told her loftily that they were eleven and thirteen – had been just as nasty and tugged her hair because it was curly and laughed at the way she spoke, mimicking her very words, and jeered when she had to whisper to the housemaid because she wanted to go to the lavvy and she didn't know where it was. Altogether, she had had a very miserable time of it and was aching to go home. All she wanted in the whole world was the safety and joy and beauty of the kitchen at home with its lovely black range and glowing fire inside the big oven, and the table full of cooling apple pies, while outside in Leather Lane the market stall men shouted their wares. 'Please, Mama,' she whispered inside her head. 'Please, Mama, come soon and take me home. I never want to be in this house ever again.'

37

The train moved slowly and majestically into Victoria Station, sending great gouts of steam up into the vaulted roof and even before it had stopped, he had the leather strap of the window down and the door open and was half hanging out in his eagerness to set foot on London stones again. To be back in the Smoke, at last; all through these past months of misery, of pain and fever and loneliness, it had been his homesickness that had been the hardest to bear. And now he was home, at last, and he teetered awkwardly on the step, waiting for the right moment to jump down, still doubtful about his balance and afraid of falling. It was going to take a long time to get used to the way his weight was distributed now, for clearly he'd lost more than his career as a boxer – but that was not to be thought of and as usual he pushed down all his fears and doubts about the future and thought of only one thing. He was home.

A porter, seeing him awkwardly manhandling his battered old Gladstone bag out of the carriage came running to help, but he almost snarled at him; he wanted no help, for help implied pity and that was an insult and the porter backed away, startled. He had been impelled only by an eagerness to talk to someone who was obviously an ex-soldier home from South Africa, going by the sunburn on his face, and a heroic one to boot, going by the empty sleeve pinned across his chest, but if the bugger wanted to be a bad tempered bugger, so be it, and he went off in a huff to look for more cheerful passengers who would be generous with tuppences.

And Lizah, hating himself for being so surly – for it wasn't in his nature to be anything but cheerful and full of bonhomie – picked up his bag and, leaning heavily to his left to balance himself, began the long walk down the platform to the crowded booking hall and the way out to the London air he had been craving for so long.

It was just dark; the day had been a dull cold one for the time of year, and there had even been white caps in Southampton Water as the ship had come slowly home at last, and he had shivered a good deal as he waited on deck to disembark. The long weeks of fever and the hot sun of a South African summer and autumn had thinned his blood, making fifty degrees above zero fahrenheit feel as cold as fifty below, but that hadn't dispirited him. Nor was he dispirited now as he came out of the Chatham line exit and stood breathing deeply, with his head up, taking it all in.

And thank God, it was still all there. The stink of smoke from a myriad coal fires still being burned in this, the coldest May there had been for some time, the oil and horses and human sweat and an indefinable something else that was unmistakeably London, a sort of essence of the place, and his eyes filled with the ready tears of the recently ill as he stood there looking at cabs and the buses and the drays and the lights, and knew he was home.

'Where to, Guv?' A hansom cab pulled over to the side of the kerb where he was standing and the driver leaned over, touching his hat with his whip at the same time. 'My ride, it'll be, an' my pleasure to serve a soldier of the Queen the way 'e's served us.'

Lizah stared up at him in the dim light and for a moment he wanted to treat him to the same peremptory dismissal he had given the porter, but bit his tongue. He'd have to get used to this, clearly; in the hospital at Durban and afterwards in the barracks where they'd sent him to convalesce there'd been plenty more like him and no one had paid them much attention. But, inevitably, now he was home, people were going to notice and respond to what they noticed. And he was more obviously a wounded soldier than most of the other people he had been with as he recovered. For every man in the hospital because of a Boer inflicted injury there had been four others there because of sickness. Cholera, typhoid, dysenteries of various kinds had gone through the army like scythes through ripe corn and sent thousands of men scattering to uselessness in hospital beds where they lay burning with fever and scouring their guts day after day as they got thinner and thinner. He had come home on the ship with some of them, and most of them had improved in their weeks at sea, with plenty of good food and nothing to do but sun themselves but he, he would always be recognizable and he lifted his chin so that he would not have to see the evidence of his crippledom pinned across him and said gruffly, 'Not sure, mate. Just thought I'd mooch around the town, you know, see what's changed since I was last home – '

'In you get, Guv!' the cab driver said heartily and bent forwards to flip open the hansom's front with his whip. 'Hoick your bag up here an' I'll stow it and you settle in. I'll take you all over the place. I was on my way home anyway, an' a half-hour spent with a hero is a real pleasure!'

Perhaps, Lizah thought, as he obeyed and settled himself against the dusty leather squabs of the cab and fastened the fronts over his legs, perhaps being a hero won't be that bad, at that. Free cabs have got to be good, and Gawd knows I've little enough cash to spend on them. Or on anything else for that matter. And for a moment he was thrown back into the gloom that was always hanging over him, waiting to pounce.

But not for long, for the cabbie took him at a spanking pace through the traffic along Victoria Street and then across Parliament Square to Bridge Street before wheeling left into

Victoria Embankment. There he slowed down a little and Lizah sat swaying and staring out at the river and the buildings of Southwark and Lambeth over on the South Bank, winking their early evening lights at him, and was grateful to the cabbie for being so aware of where to bring him.

Although he had grown up in the wilderness of streets around Spitalfields and had made the East End his stamping ground, he was a true Londoner and that meant the river; the stretches he knew best were further along, at Tower Bridge, both on the North and on the Bermondsey sides, where as a child he had mudlarked along the edges and found treasures he could flog in the markets, and had on hot days swum and splashed, caring nothing for the foulness of the water. Here it was all much cleaner and brighter – though the river was still foul. He could feel it sour and thick in his nostrils, for it was still London's river and the recipient of much of her ordure and as he thought of that tears of nostalgia did fill his eyes and would not so easily be staunched.

'Fancy goin' West now, Guv?' the cabbie called down. 'I could get up rahnd the back doubles to the Strand and then go back up West if that's what yer fancies – '

'No. No, I think I'd as soon head for home after all,' Lizah called back. 'It's been a long time – but go down the Strand anyway. Only go east to Aldgate Pump – '

'Thought as much,' the cabbie said, highly satisfied. 'Reckon I can place a London voice to a few streets, I can. Not from over the water like me, I thought – me, I'm a Lambeth man – and not from the City neither. Got to be the East End. So, bin a long time away, 'ave you?'

'Yes,' Lizah said. 'Long time.' And caught his breath. 'Six bloody months, that's all – '

'Blimey,' the cabbie said. 'That *is* a long time without the missus. She'll be main glad to see you, I'll be bound.'

'There isn't a missus,' Lizah said shortly.

'Ah, just as well,' the cabbie said adroitly. 'An' you with such a nasty injury an' all. Women make a big fuss over things like that, don't they? Where'd it happen, Guv?'

'Spion Kop – ' Lizah was beginning to relax. Being deferred to, treated as someone special like this was what he was used to, after all. In the good old days in the gym and in the restaurants as well as at the old Britannia they'd all hung on his words. He was entitled to it –

The cabbie whistled. 'Heard about that. Nasty do, that was. The way them Boers run you off the hill after you took it. A lot killed, I'm told – '

'A lot. Including my own officer.' Lizah leaned even further back and flexed his back muscles to ease the pain that was coming into his left shoulder again. 'I did what I could. Carried him out of the fire to the foot of the Kop and thought I'd got him through, but the bastards fired on us again, and him a wounded man, and this time they killed him and hit me into the bargain.' And with his right hand he reached across and began to massage his aching shoulder. 'So here I am. Me, a boxer! I ask you – '

The cabbie was clearly enchanted and leaned forwards, allowing his horse to slow to little more than a walk as he plied Lizah with eager questions about all he'd seen and done and heard and being lavish with his praise and admiration and, slowly, Lizah began to thaw. He had been frightened to come home, that was the thing of it; eager, indeed desperate, to get here, but deeply frightened too. How would it be? How would people treat him? What was the good of a boxer with only one arm? But here he was, not set foot in the Smoke above a minute and already getting the attention he needed. And with it, the beginnings of an idea about how he would deal in the future. Perhaps it wouldn't be that bad after all –

The Strand was busy as the cab went easily along it, but not as busy as it would be later; the theatres were all in and the restaurants were sparsely populated, waiting for the rush that would come when the curtains finally fell at the Strand Theatre and the Gaiety, the Lyceum and the Tivoli. Lizah stopped talking for a while to lean out eagerly to see what was on where. Always an avid theatre-goer, he had prided himself on knowing what plays were running where and now he needed to pick up information again so that he could feel he was really at home; at the Strand an original farce in three acts, *Facing the Music*; at the Gaiety another of their musical comedies, *The Messenger Boy*; at the Tivoli Music Hall, George Robey, and Vesta Tilley, Bransby Williams, Minnie Palmer and the great Dan Leno – he'd certainly have to see that bill if he could – and at the Lyceum, Signora Eleanora Duse in repertory with *Magda*, *The Second Mrs Tanqueray*, *Madame Georges*, *Gioconda* and *Fedora*. A busy season, but he'd give that one a miss. He liked a bit of fun and laughing and real feeling, not that fancy West End stuff – and he sank back, contented. Oh, but it's good to be home, he thought, as the cabbie again started to question him about his adventures. *Good* to be home.

The cab began to thread its way through the tangle of streets where houses and shops and banks were being demolished to make way for the new road that was to link the Strand with Holborn and Lizah stared out, amazed at how much had changed since he had last been here. Wych Street and New-castle Street were almost gone, now being little more than piles of rubble, and it was a dispiriting sight. He was indeed glad when at last the horses went clopping past the Law Courts, on their way to Temple Bar and Fleet Street and thence the City and Aldgate Pump. And home – and he closed his eyes, trying to imagine how his mother would behave when she saw him. And couldn't, for this was not like coming home with a few cut lips and black eyes after a tough fight in the ring –

He opened his eyes as a ragged cheering began somewhere further along the street, and stared out. It was quite dark now, for it was nine o'clock. The sun had set over an hour before, leaving the sky a rich indigo, and the lights of the shops and the street lamps glittered softly in the chill air. A group of men were cheering and a bus was coming towards them with the conductor hanging on the outside rail of the staircase, halfway up, and waving his cap and shouting even more loudly.

'What's the matter with him?' he called up to his cabbie. 'Drunk, d'you reckon?' But then the bus passed him and they could hear what the driver was shouting.

'Relieved, relieved!' he bawled and the men on the pavement came abreast and they were shouting it too. 'Relieved, relieved, Mafeking relieved!'

'Stow the flippin' bleedin' crows!' the cabbie cried and whipped his startled horse into a trot. 'They must ha' heard something down the newspaper offices – come on.' And come on they did, careering along the Strand and into Fleet Street, together, it seemed, with every other vehicle on the road, at a breakneck pace.

It really was amazing; when they reached the *Daily Express* office, halfway down, there were already people on the buses waving Union Jacks, and someone had put up a string of them across a building on the other side of the street. Outside the newspaper office there was even more of a crowd, pushing and shouting and cheering and hats were being thrown in the air.

'Is it true?' the cabbie bawled down over Lizah's head and someone in the mob raised a flushed face and bawled back, 'True as you're asking, squire, true as heaven! Baden-Powell's done it, God bless him. He's done it! He's got 'em safe too – ain't it a marvel?'

'A bleedin' marvel!' shouted the cabbie and Lizah, fumbling for the catch of the apron so that he could free himself, echoed it. A bleedin' marvel. It had been bad enough lifting the sieges at Ladysmith and Kimberley; this one had looked to be set for ever. He and the rest of the wounded men had sat in their convalescent home and waited for this news as eagerly as anyone here, and the knowledge that at last that ramshackle town of corrugated roofs and meagre buildings was free – and fed – again was well worth celebrating.

He pushed into the crowd, leading with his good shoulder, and when someone saw his sunbrowned face and empty sleeve, he slapped him on the back, and then others and still more joined in until he was aching with it. And then a young man in a natty suit bent to grab him round the middle and another took his legs and they heaved him high and perched him on their shoulders to carry him triumphantly away back towards the Strand, and he let it happen, laughing and cheering with the best of them; not noticing or caring that his first friend, the cabbie, was shouting after him and waving his battered bag in the air. He had forgotten the cabbie, forgotten the bag, forgotten everything in the infectious fever of excitement that filled everyone about him.

He was never quite to remember the details of the next few hours. All round him London burst into human flames; shrieking, weeping, laughing people waved and shouted and threw hats about. Flags and portraits of the Queen appeared as if by magic and flowered everywhere. Men carrying black bottles of beer and porter offered a swig to anyone who wanted one and girls with their bonnets askew and their hair tumbling down their backs kissed as indiscriminately as bees in a clover patch, and by no means all of them were ladies of the night; even respectable people seemed to have caught the hysteria and were as out of their minds with it as any of the usual denizens of London's night-time streets.

Wherever Lizah went he was fêted. No sooner had one group of men tired under his weight and set him down but another took him up, and everywhere he was hailed as a hero. If he had been in uniform and covered in bandages his status could not have been more obvious and there were so few like him around that he was treated with as much adoration and respect as if he had been the victorious Baden-Powell himself.

He rode in state in a human convoy all along the Strand and into Trafalgar Square, and all the way people threw him kisses and girls tossed flowers and several, much to his delight, passed up bottles. By the time he got to the Square his vision was dazzled and his head was spinning with all he had swallowed as well as the general excitement and he let someone perch him high on the neck of one of the lions at the foot of Nelson's Column and sat there happily, a bottle of beer in his hand, and alternately drank from it and waved with it as the crowds eddied and milled about beneath him.

It must have been close on midnight when the more exciting beer effects began to wear off. He had suddenly become very dozy despite the noise and the lights and he leaned forwards on the neck of the lion and fell asleep; but not before thinking muzzily that this was the nearest he'd ever got to a lion in all his life, in spite of having spent damn near half a year in their own horrible country; and there he lay as hour after hour the din went on.

It began to lessen at about half-past four in the morning. He woke suddenly, stiff and very cold, and managed to drag himself upright with an effort to peer blearily down into the Square below him. It was littered with people as weary as he was; couples clutching each other lay snoring against the plinths of the lions and round Nelson's Column and those who couldn't find such protection lay out in the middle of the Square on the paving stones. The fountains had long since given up trying to work, or someone had turned them off, and in the empty basin, which had been swept clear of water by splashing revellers, some people lay with their heads propped up on the parapet while a few were moving desultorily about making their way out of the Square towards home.

Home, Lizah thought, still bleary. Home, I was going home. And he managed to reach in his pocket with his cold hand to fumble out his watch. And blinked when he managed to see what the time was.

There was no traffic anywhere about and he longed suddenly for his friendly cab driver, and then remembered his bag which contained what little he possessed – a change of socks and underwear, a clean shirt, his razor and little else – and cursed, and then fumbled in his pocket, twisting awkwardly to reach it, seeking for his wallet.

He should, he told himself bitterly, as he slid down the side of the lion with what care he could, he should have guessed it. Even bloody heroes are worth robbing. No money, no gear, and no one to help him; and again he found himself weeping and hated his own weakness.

Above his head the sky was beginning to lighten and he lifted his chin and sniffed the air, trying to recognize the change in it that he had learned about in his days in the veldt, but this wasn't Natal and all he could smell was oil and dirt and spewed-up beer and he spat to rid his mouth of the foul taste that had been left in it and began to trudge eastwards out of the Square, up to the Strand and on towards home.

Ahead of him the sky went on lightening slowly as he picked his way over the detritus of the night. Torn paper, empty bottles, muddied flags and battered portraits of the Queen filled the gutters, and everywhere there was unpleasant evidence of just how unbridled Londoners had been last night, and he marvelled as he remembered it. And then felt depression settle over him again as fog settles on the city on a cold night; thick and stifling. He was penniless, and his only skill had been rendered useless by the loss of his arm. He was thin, and hungry, and had nothing in the world to look forward to – except going home to his mother. And for a moment there was a rent in the thick gloom that enveloped him as he conjured up an image of the bright kitchen and the warm fire and his mother in her chair beside it. She'd look after him, give him some food and a soft bed and the courage to sort something out. Of course she would. And he pulled up his collar awkwardly with his one hand and then, pushing it into his pocket, set out to trudge the miles home.

38

'You should have let me know,' Lizah said again, and he knew he sounded sulky and childish and didn't care. 'I had a right to know.'

'Well, of course you did,' Jessie said. 'But put yourself in my shoes. There you was, wounded – Momma had had this letter all the way from South Africa saying you was wounded and she'd shown it to me to read to her, and I didn't know how bad you were! I wrote and asked, but you never answered, and for all I knew you could have been dead yourself. Only no one wrote and said you were, so I thought, well, he's alive at any rate. But you never wrote so when it happened I didn't know what to do. I didn't want to go sending you nasty letters if you was badly ill yourself, now did I? Believe me, bad news keeps well enough. It gets no worse and no better for waiting.'

'You should have let me know,' he said again and drank his cup of tea to the dregs and then held it out for a refill. 'Even if I never wrote to you, I'm no hand at letters, anyway, and I was all right. There wasn't much to say, so I thought – when I get home, then I can explain it all. I can't be doing with letters. But this – it was wicked of you not to let me know.'

'And you was wicked to go off and enlist and only leave me a letter. For one who says he can't be doing with 'em, you use 'em well enough when it suits you!' Jessie retorted, and poured the tea and then got up heavily to go to the fire and refill the pot from the kettle which sat on the range, softly chattering to itself. 'You sent us running down to Southampton like crazy things to get you back and the poor little boobalah got so ill after that and – and what about Momma? Did you think about her when you took off like some crazy thing? She did nothing but cry and cry for weeks – '

'And if I'd told you, what then? You'd have said don't go, wailed and carried on and made a great megillah and tried to stop me – '

'And maybe we'd have done just that and you wouldn't be sitting there a bleedin' cripple with only one arm – ' she shouted back and then caught her breath and sat down with a little thud. 'Oh, Gawd, I'm sorry, Lizah. I should have bitten my tongue out before I said such a thing, God forgive me – '

'It's all right,' he said dully, and put down his cup again. Somehow it wasn't so important any more to slake his thirst. 'I suppose you're right at that – '

They sat in silence for a while as he stared down at his hand on the table. A square hand with stubby fingers and a dusting of dark hair between the knuckles, the nails rather chipped and dirty, and as he stared he tried to remember what it felt like to have two such hands; and closed his eyes to shut out the pain of not being able to remember at all. It was as though he had always been what he now was, little more than half a man.

'So, tell me what happened,' he said at length. 'Was it my fault? Was she pining for me or anything like that?'

'No,' she said firmly. 'Never think that. Not Momma. You've forgotten – there was three of her children died, and she didn't pine away then, did she?'

'No,' he said and looked at her appealingly. 'No. But all the same – you're sure it wasn't because I was away?'

'Don't be so full of yourself,' she said sharply and leaned over to pat his hand to take the sting from her voice. It was dreadful to see him looking so drawn and anxious. 'She got the pneumonia, for Gawd's sake. It was a bad winter. How can that be your fault?'

'I dunno,' he mumbled. 'You 'ear of people don't want to live no more because they lose someone – '

'Stubbornness, that was what it was. She'd been ill – all bronchial – three days and never let on to anybody, not to me, not the people downstairs, not the next doors, no one. I was away in Southend with Nate and his sister, and of course I went to see her as soon as I got back, and there she was, looking – well – believe me, *I* blamed myself. I thought, if I hadn't gone away – but it's silly to think that way. I ain't God no more than you are. If Momma had called Mrs Levy upstairs or the people next door, who knows how it would have turned out? As it is, four days more it was, and she died peaceful and easy. Please God by me, Lizah, I tell you. No lingering, no pain and tuckah, she was seventy-five already! Not a bad age, rest her dear soul.'

'It don't sound so old no more. It did when I was younger; it sounded like for always. But now – ' He shook his head. 'Now it seems she was no age.' And suddenly he bent his head and let the tears run down his cheeks, making no effort to dry them.

'Oh, Lizah – ' Jessie was on her feet at once and came and crouched beside him, mopping his face with her handkerchief and then pulling his head down to let it rest on her shoulder so that he could cry more easily. And there she stayed, rocking him gently as the sound of his weeping filled the dark little kitchen and echoed back from the bare walls, for the room was half stripped of furniture and packing cases filled with china and glass lay scattered around.

He lifted his head at last and sniffed lusciously and took the handkerchief from her and rubbed his damp red face.

'Sorry,' he said huskily.

'God forbid you should apologize for crying for your mother,' she said piously. 'Listen, dolly, let me get you something to eat, eh? And you look like you need some sleep. I'll fix a bed for you, and you can have a little shloof and feel better for it. And then after, we'll go down to Plashet Grove, you can see where Momma is – '

He shook his head vigorously. 'I'm not going down to no cemetery. Wherever she is, she ain't there. Listen, just give me time. I'll get over it. It was just so – I mean, getting there to the house and there's a stranger there. I never had such a shock. I knock on the door and they come and it's strangers! I thought I'd gone mad, seeing this man open the door, thought I'd come to the wrong house.' He shook his head again, but in reproof this time. 'You should have told me.'

Wisely she bit her tongue and stood up and went to one of the packing cases and began to riffle through its contents, collecting bedlinen. He watched her for a moment and then frowned and rubbed his red-rimmed eyes.

'Listen, what's going on here? What's happened?' He looked round the room as though he were seeing it for the first time, even though he had been sitting there for over an hour. 'What's happening? You having the place papered or something, or what?'

She straightened her back and stood there with the little bundle of sheets and blankets across her arm and looked at him and then bit her lip.

'I'm going away, Lizah,' she said and then couldn't look at him any more and shifted her gaze so that she was staring out of the window, now looking sadly naked without its swathe of red curtains.

'Going away? How do you mean, going away?' He frowned then, sharply, and shook his head as if to clear it. 'I don't understand – and there was something else you said before that I didn't understand and you got to explain – but what do you mean, going away?'

'What I said.' She seemed irritable now and began to bustle, setting the sheets and blankets on the table and then returning to the packing case to fiddle with its contents, folding and refolding towels busily, so that she did not have to look at him. 'Away. A W A Y.'

'I can spell,' he growled. 'You don't have to give me lip. Just tell me what the hell you're on about – '

She whirled then, dropping the carefully folded linen. 'Listen, Lizah. I ain't a kid no more, all right? I'm past thirty, getting on, you know? It's time I settled. I tried to make a life without Barney, God rest his wicked soul, but what sort of life is it with no one to work for, to care about, eh? I thought maybe the little one – but Millie – ' She shook her head. 'Well, that wasn't meant neither, so I thought, all right, I'll marry Nate Braham. He wants me, he's a real mensch, got lots of blood in him, know what I mean? I'll have my own kids, maybe. It's time – and he wants us to go to America so there it is – I'm also a person, you know that? I've got a life to live, an' all. So I'm going to live it.'

He was staring at her, his mouth half open and his face blank.

'And what about me? Where am I to live? And – what was it you said? Millie? That was what you said before I wanted to ask about – who was ill? What happened when you went to Southampton? What was it you said about being ill?'

She sat down and rested her elbows on the table and stared at him from between her hands on which she had propped her chin and he stared back and thought for a moment – she's got thinner. A lot thinner. She has got a man, at that, she must have – and blinked, trying to clear his head which was muzzy still with last night's beer and excitement and with lack of sleep and general upheaval. There was just too much going on, too much to take in altogether.

'Listen,' Jessie said and her voice was harsh. 'And listen good. I ain't going to go on about this. I can't – it's just that – well, Millie went down to Southampton with me to find you, to stop you going to South Africa. You left this letter, so I got upset – so Millie came with me. And we took the boobalah – '

Her voice seemed to crack a little. 'I tell you, that child, Lizah! She's – you can't know how much I love that kid. She's the cleverest, the sweetest, the – well, we went. And the little one got the measles and was so ill we was terrified. Terrified. But God se dank, she came through all right. But Millie – she was never the same after. Always a hard one, your Millie. Got ideas in her head she never talks about, got these notions about what's the good way for a kid to be and the bad way – she's not wrong, of course. She's got her rights, she's a mother, she's got her rights – but she kept me away, see? No one could love that child more'n I do, but Millie – well, let it be. She's got her own notions. So she took Poppy away – '

'What do you mean took her away?'

'What I say. She sent me a letter. Didn't even have the decency to come and see me, say it to my face, let me even say goodbye properly. Sent me this letter, she's sold the business, she's going away. I shouldn't try to find them on account I won't be able, she's gone so far. Here, I can show you the letter – ' And she got to her feet and went heavily across to the dresser and began to fumble in the big cooking pot that stood on the main shelf.

'I don't want to see no letters,' he said harshly. 'I told you. I'm not good with letters. Just tell me. Where did she go?'

'Do you think I didn't try to find out? As soon as I got the letter, I went straight there, to Leather Lane, and there she was, gone. The house empty, nothing left there at all. The neighbours said she'd sold all the furniture, the lot, and gone. I found the woman she'd sold the business to – not that there was much to sell. Only a list of her customers and how she dealt with 'em – and that was it. It was like she'd melted, phht! Nothing else – and the boobalah gone too – '

Lizah stared at her, his forehead creased into its familiar pattern. He looked frightened now, and his upper lip was pearled with sweat.

'And now you're going too.' It wasn't a question.

She shrugged. 'What's to stay for? I got nothing and nobody. For all I knew, you wouldn't be back. You know what you are, Lizah! You do what you want, when you want, how you want. What do you care about anyone else, except when you need 'em? You can't say different. You didn't write to Momma or me from South Africa – yeah, yeah, I know. You're no hand with letters. But for Gawd's sake, three lines, hoping to find you as it leaves me, or something of the sort! All I had was Momma, after poor old Poppa died, and that boobalah. I lived for her, you know that? To see her, to listen to her chatter – I tell you that kid's got such a head on her, such a tongue – she's so clever, it'd scare you. It was all right when I knew I could see her sometimes. Not as often as I liked – Millie was funny, but what could I do? If I wanted to see her at all, I had to do what Millie said. And I understood, you know. I really did. She had a bad time, Millie, what with that stinking family of hers, and you. Oh, don't look like that! You treated her bad and you know it! She should have had a home, someone she could trust to lean on, to look after her when she had that baby! If you'd done the right thing she'd be living here yet, and the baby with her. As it is, what have I got? Nothing and no one. So I'm marrying Nate Braham. He at least wants me – ' And she began to weep, but not as noisily as he had. She just sat there with tears sliding silently down her face.

'Christ almighty!' he shouted and jumped to his feet, almost toppling sideways as he did, for he had forgotten for a moment to watch his new balance. But he recovered his posture and shouted it again. 'Christ almighty, what could I do? I was boracic, right on my uppers and up to my neck in trouble, and she gets herself in the club! What could I do? Another few months'd have made all the difference – '

'What difference?' she jeered. 'What difference? Look how long it was before you came back to me, and no better off than when you went away – you treated her bad, Lizah. You should have packed in all that boxing lark, got a job, worked while you got straight – but not you. You just ran off.' She straightened her back and shook her head. 'Ah, what's the use of talking. It's over now, dead water. All I know is she's gone, and I don't know where. So I'm going too – '

He sat there silently staring at her, and then she got to her feet and smoothed her dress over her hips. It was as red as all her dresses were, but somehow it seemed to lack lustre. It wasn't the glowing crimson it usually was; or perhaps she wasn't glowing as she usually did and it was that which detracted from her. She looked tired and ageing and far from happy.

'So,' she said after a minute. 'Aren't you going to wish me a mazel tov? I told you. I'm getting married again.'

'Mazel tov,' he said mechanically. 'I wish you every joy – ' And then his blank gaze cleared and he looked at her sharply. 'America, you said? Why America?'

She shrugged. 'Why not? He's got people there. A sister married into a big delicatessen family. They got openings for him, they say, in Baltimore. So we're going. Why not? It's a good place to bring up kids, they say. You should know – you've lived there, haven't you? And please God, I'll have kids. My own kids. Then no one can take 'em away from me – ' And she looked fierce and bereft at the same time and again her eyes filled with tears.

But he didn't seem to notice. He was staring round the kitchen with eyes dark with anxiety.

'And where shall I go? What shall I do?'

She gazed at him and now her expression changed. There was affection there and concern, but even more there was exasperation and a sort of contempt. 'What do you want to do?'

He stared back at her and then shrugged, and looked down at his empty sleeve. 'What can I do?' he asked piteously. 'You tell me, what does a boxer do with only one arm?'

'He thinks,' she said tartly. 'He thinks sensibly, he don't sit and feel sorry for himself, and cry nebbish, the world owes me a living. So, you were a soldier? It was your idea, be a soldier. And you paid for it. It's a terrible thing to lose a limb – ' And she carefully didn't look at the empty sleeve, for she knew if she did she would weep even more than she had. And knew deep inside that would be a disaster for him. The last thing he needed was pity. 'But the end of the world it ain't. Think – what do you want to do?'

He lifted his brows. 'Do you think I haven't? Do you think I didn't lie awake night after night thinking and listening to the bloody insects sawing away, and in the fever with my arm hurting like it was the devil with pincers working on it? Do you think I didn't think?'

She managed a grin then. 'I doubt it. You was never famous for thinking, Lizah. Talking and noshing and shmoozing round the girls, this you was famous for. But not for thinking.'

Amazingly, he managed to grin too, a thin and uncertain grimace, but a grin for all that. 'All right, so I'm not a big brain. It's no crime. But I *have* been thinking. A gym, I thought for a while. Maybe I ain't a fighter no more, but I know how fighting is. I can still teach – '

She shook her head. 'It won't work. I may not be a great maven when it comes to boxing but I know about men. And they won't show you the respect – '

'Do you think I don't know that? I tell you, I *thought*, that was all. I didn't decide. I thought a lot of other things as well – but then only yesterday – ' He stopped then and blinked. Only yesterday? It seemed a hundred years ago. 'I thought yesterday that people like to talk, to hear of things that have happened, they like a drink, a nosh or two – I'll get a pub. Yesterday, the way people wanted to talk to me about the war and all – it made me realize. A pub. I'll stand there behind the bar and they'll come and talk to me and I'll make a nice living and – '

She shook her head dubiously. 'And how long do you think they'll go on being interested? Right now everyone cares about the war and battles – no one's talked of anything else round here for weeks. You should have seen last night, Whitechapel Road – they went crazy! But that was last night, maybe tomorrow night – but every night?'

'You're a misery, you know that?' He had flushed up sharply. 'You ask me what I'm going to do, and I tell you and all you can do is throw cold water.'

'I don't mean to do that,' she protested. 'Believe me, I'm delighted you're trying to make good plans. But I don't want you to catch a cold and be no better off than you are – and what about money? It takes money, don't it, to start a pub?'

'The brewers – they'll arrange it all!' He sounded lofty. 'From where should you know? Tomorrow I'll go down to Truman's and maybe Whitbread's, and see what's what. They'll see me, a man like me, back from the war – you'll see, they'll grab at me. I'm quick to learn, you know that. I'll get it all worked out in no time – I can do it – '

'I wish you all the luck in the world, dolly,' she said and came round the table to hug him and kiss him. 'All I ever wish for you is the best of everything. I wish I could stay here and look after you – to make you a home, it'd be a pleasure. But I got to think of the future. You, you'll settle down, find a wife, and then what about me? Just the old sister, and who wants to know? Nate wants me and I'm not getting any younger – '

'I'll manage,' he said and glowered a little as he stared down at his sleeve again and the very obvious pin that was holding it in place. 'I'll manage, I'll get lodgings for a while, look round, see what I can do – '

'You want me to help? I know people round here, in Jubilee Street – '

He shook his head violently. 'No! No, I don't want to live here. I want – oh, I don't know what I want. I mean, I do – but

– well, you'll see. Listen, get on with your packing. I don't want to get in your way. When do you go?'

'The people who've taken this place, they move in next Friday. I'm going over to Nate's sister Lizzie, just till the ship goes. We're getting married at the synagogue in Commercial Road, first Sunday in June. You'll be there?'

'Of course! Who else have you got to stand up for you?'

'Rae and Joe'll be there, of course – '

'Rae!' He dismissed his older sister with a wave of his hand. 'Her, the misery! Much she cares about you or me. She's all Vinosky now, got more love for her bloody misbocher than she's got for us – '

Jessie lifted her brows and shrugged. 'So? She's got to live with her in-laws, ain't she? Her and Joe, they owe them money, getting the business set on its feet. You can't blame her. But she's standing up for me, under the wedding canopy. I'd like to see you there too.'

'I'll be there,' he said gruffly. 'And listen, Jessie. I wish you all you wish yourself. You got a right, I suppose. Nate's not a bad fella – '

'No,' she said. 'Not bad.'

'And me, I'll manage well enough. Don't you worry about me. I'll *manage.*' And he went and kissed her and then went up to bed, taking the blankets and sheets with him. He had a lot to do, but first he needed a day and a night's sleep. And then – then he had to put his whole plan into action. And it involved more than persuading a brewer to give him a pub to run.

39

'Well, well,' Ruby said and leaned back in his chair. 'After all these years, Kid! It's good to see you.' But the look on his face wasn't entirely of welcome; there was pity there too and Lizah felt a dull flush lift in his cheeks as he recognized it. For two pins, he told himself wrathfully, for two pins I'd walk out of here and never see the bastard again. Who did he think he was, for God's sake, sitting there like some bloody duke behind that desk and looking at me, Lizah Harris, with pity? But he needed him and that meant he had to bite his tongue.

'So tell me,' Ruby went on. 'How's the world been treating you? I heard a long time ago you'd had a bit of a problem with Jack Long's lot and gone off for a bit of a holiday, like, and then I heard no more – '

'Army,' Lizah said briefly and lifted his left shoulder so that his chest moved and the pin on his folded black sleeve winked in the light. 'But that's not important. Listen, Ruby, I want you to do something for me. For old time's sake, you know?'

'For you, Kid, anything,' Ruby said heartily. 'Believe me, I owe you a lot. I learned a lot round you in the old days when I was a lad. Thought the sun shone out of your toochus, you know that? When you sat down the light went out for me.' And he laughed fatly, pleased with his joke.

'It wasn't that long ago,' Lizah said tartly. 'You're not much more'n a lad now. How old are you – nineteen, twenty?'

'What's age got to do with it?' Ruby said and grinned. 'Yeah, I ain't doin' bad. You must've known I'd be all right, though. You knew me well enough in them days when you was winning all your fights.'

'I'd be winning them now if it hadn't been for going to fight for Queen and Country – ' Lizah began.

'Sure, sure, you would,' Ruby said soothingly. 'Sure you would. An' I dare say you'll get on top again, one way or another. You're a goer, Kid Harris, you always was.' He leaned forwards across his desk. 'I admired you, you'll never know how much. I saw you as what I wanted to be. A big one, a success, right? Well, okay, maybe I got on a bit faster than some might have thought and maybe I've sort of overtaken you. You've had some bad luck, after all. But I swear I owe it to you. You was my model in those days and that's why I'm where I am now. Not bad, eh?' And he leaned back and waved his hand expansively to take in the room they were sitting in.

It was indeed a room worth looking at. Everywhere there was an aura of money lavishly spent. The desk and the chair behind it on which Ruby sat were of mahogany, heavily polished and inset with the best green leather, and against one wall was a heavily decorated mahogany sideboard on which several crystal decanters stood winking in the morning sunlight which came pouring in through the long window past green velvet curtains. There were several other well-upholstered chairs dotted about on the thick green carpet and every inch of the flower-papered walls were covered with posters for theatrical productions, each and almost every one of them proudly headed 'Reuben Green presents!' and then bearing the names of some of the best known variety acts in the music hall business.

'Who'd have thought it, eh?' Ruby said. 'There was I, all set to make a living like you, a boxer, but then you had a couple of not so good fights – remember, when the Welsh boy got you in the fourth round? – what was his name, Beaver Bevan, that was it. Remember that? Well, that was when I thought – there's no percentage in this, not in the long term. Better to promote than to do. And then you went off and me, I had to do something and I tried to set up a few fights but it never got me nowhere. No one'd take me serious, you see. Thought I was just a kid. Well, I was, o' course, but only on the outside. In here – ' And he tapped his beautiful moleskin waistcoat, with the gold chain looped across it, with one well manicured finger. 'In here, I was already a mensch, a real doer, you know? So I looked around and I thought – everyone likes to eat and drink and laugh. That's where I'll make a place for myself. So I got me a coffee stall, took a bit of villainy, you know how it is, but I managed. And I set it up by the old Britannia theatre stage door, and made a few bob. But better still I got to know the performers – they all loved my hot pies and the eels and mash I did – Harry Randall, he was crazy about 'em. And then there was R G Knowles – remember the way he used to sing that number of his – "Brighton"? – and Eugene Stratton and Albert Chevalier – oh, they was all my customers. So I sort of drifted into that business. Put on my first night at the Britannia for charity – a Sunday night show it was, for Father Jay's place, and they all turned out, all the stars, for their hot eels and mash boy! And it was a great evening, great. And out of that I raised a bit o' cash – ' He laughed then. 'Father Jay got his share, believe me, but me, I didn't do so bad out of it either. And there I was, all set to go. Been getting bigger and bigger ever since. Three girls I got out there working for me.' And he jerked his thumb towards his outer office. 'I won't take fellas. They get fancy ideas, trying to cut in on you, wanting to be the guv'nor themselves. Girls you can keep where they belong. So here I am! Not bad for a street arab, eh?'

'Not bad at all,' Lizah said and wished he could feel better about his protégé's success. It shouldn't have made him feel so sick, but it did. 'So you'll be too busy to help me, then?'

'It all depends,' Ruby said and made his face look businesslike. It was a thinner face than it had been, and now that it was faintly blue-shadowed across the jaws and had a thin moustache on the upper lip had taken on a sharpness that was much less attractive than the boy's face had been. But his eyes were still large and dark and lustrous and he looked now at Lizah with a watchfulness that made him move uneasily in his chair.

'Remember Millie?' Lizah said at length. 'That girl from – '

'From up West,' Ruby said at once. 'Yeah, I remember her. You took a lot to her, didn't you? You used to hang around with her. I remember seeing you with her at the old Brit sometimes. Whatever happened to her?'

'That's what I want to know,' Lizah said. 'She lived with my sister for a while, when she had her kid – '

Ruby whistled. 'You a father, then? There's a turn up for the book!'

'And why shouldn't I be? Is it so terrible?'

'Not at all!' Ruby sounded hearty. 'Just a bit – I supposed I reckoned you was cleverer than that.'

'I wanted it,' Lizah growled. 'So don't you go thinking I was caught or anything. I wanted it.' And he stared Ruby straight in the eyes, to prove to him – and to himself – how truthful he was being.

'I believe you!' Ruby said soothingly. 'Thousands wouldn't, but I believe you. So, all right. What about Millie?'

'She's sloped off,' Lizah said. 'There I was, away in the army and I come back and she's hopped it.' He let his eyes slide away from Ruby's now; whatever else he'd been, he'd always been a tolerably truthful man. It wasn't easy to lie like this. 'I mean, I hadn't seen her for a while before I went. You know how it is with women. They get notions. And she got one – well sort of. The thing of it is, though, now I want to find her. I'm changing my style, Ruby, and that's the truth of it. A man gives all he can for his country, and then he has to sort out his life as best

426

he can. I gave up a lot – but I ain't finished yet. Want to make a new start, you understand? I'm getting a pub to run, and I need a family. A man needs a family, right? 'Course he does. So I want to find Millie. She went off with the kid and never said where. My sister don't know. My mother, rest her dear soul, I can't ask, so how can I find out? I didn't know what to do, and then I remembered you. If anyone can find her, I thought, Ruby will. So I asked around for Ruby Grühner and got told you was now Reuben Green. Very fancy!' And he managed a laugh.

'It's easier to deal with West End managements when you got a West End name,' Ruby said. 'So, you want me to find her? Listen, Kid, I ain't a Street arab no more. The old days, when I executed commissions for you – that was a long time ago.'

'If it's too much trouble,' Lizah said tartly, 'forget it!' And got to his feet. He wanted to find Millie badly. He'd spent several days making the same enquiries Jessie had and getting precisely the same answers and ending in the same blind alley. But he wasn't going to let this jumped up little squirt make him grovel. Either he helped willingly or not at all.

'But that don't mean I can't help,' Ruby said soothingly. 'For Gawd's sake, Kid, get off your high horse and sit down. We'll talk. Tell me what you know about what she was doing and all that, and I'll get one of the boys I know to look into it. I may not go out myself on these things any more but that don't mean I can't get 'em done.' He leaned forwards confidentially. 'So tell me. What has she been up to these last few years? What do you know about her and her kid? Then we'll see what we can do for you.'

Poppy had made her humbug last all morning and no one had noticed she was sucking it. That was a very considerable achievement because Miss Peach was the most gimlet-eyed of all the teachers and everyone said she'd notice if you were just sitting with a tiny violet cachou under your tongue. But Poppy had sucked a humbug right from its sharpest four-pointed hugeness down to a mere sliver of peppermint without once chewing it up and no one at all had noticed. The underside of her tongue was numb with it and she felt a little queasy at the thought of having to eat a luncheon after walking back to the house, but never mind. She had won today's battle.

That was the only way she could make the days go by. Each morning she would make herself a promise about what she would do today that she shouldn't. Sometimes it was crossing the traffic-clotted Bayswater Road on her own on her way to school and then crossing back, without anyone trying to stop her or escort her. She could only do that on the days when it was Queenie, the under-housemaid, who was supposed to take her to school for she was a lazy girl at the best of times and also had an understanding with the milkman. So all she ever did was come to the corner of Leinster Terrace and watch Poppy as she went the rest of her way alone, so that she could stand and talk to her lover over his churns.

Sometimes Poppy would promise herself that she would make all the teachers, one after the other, tell her she was a good girl – and sometimes she would do the opposite and set out to make them all tell her she was naughty. Whatever it was she had to have something to make the days pass, for they were really dreadfully dull otherwise. All that the other little girls did was whisper and giggle and cry because they found the reading hard and couldn't do their sums. Poppy had no trouble with the reading for she had been reading harder books than the ones the school gave her for years and years and *years* – and as for the sums – they were so easy they were silly. So what else was there but her own private games?

Private games were important at the house too. Poppy never talked of home; when she heard the word she thought of Mama's warm kitchen in Leather Lane and would see herself standing there in the doorway looking in at its bright warmth and the pink china clock and the purple and blue vases full of paper spills and the dresser with its arrangement of blue and white china, and smelling the delicious cakes and pies as the fire crackled in the range and the kettle hissed a welcome.

The house she lived in now wasn't like that. It was big and cold and full of people who watched her and teased her and laughed at her and that made it hateful. The only good thing about it was that it also had a lot of secret places where a person could hide; the little cubbyhole under the stairs, and the place behind the wardrobe in her bedroom and the cupboards that lined the long passageway on the other side of the green baize door that led to the kitchen. In the last few months she had been very clever, finding ends of candles and vestas to hide in each of her special places, so that she could creep away and sit there and read and no one would know where she was or what she was doing.

Not that anyone cared; she knew that. If anyone thought about where she was, they always thought she was with someone else. Mama would say vaguely, 'Playing with the boys then, m'dear?' when she appeared in the drawing room and the boys would look up and sneer if she came into the nursery or the schoolroom and think she'd been with her mother. So she had lots of time for reading – and happily, lots of books to read. That was another good thing about the house; there were books galore, in the room they called the study where no one ever went. Some of them were dull and some of them were stupid but they were all full of words, and that was what made them important. For Poppy words in a row were what made life in that horrid house possible.

She had tried very hard at first to make Mama understand how much she hated the house. She had begged to go home to be just happy again and to return to Baldwin's Gardens School with Miss Rushmore and the other girls and boys, but Mama had suddenly become dreadfully angry; so angry that she had frightened Poppy who had sat and stared at her as she talked and talked and talked.

'We're never going back there, never, never, never, do you understand me, Poppy? I never want to hear another word about – about where we used to live and what we used to do. It was a bad time and it must be forgotten. It was a bad school for there were boys there and boys are bad and – '

'Why, Mama?' Poppy had ventured, but Mama had just rushed on.

' – they do bad things to little girls. You must never talk to boys except for those you know, here at home. Do you understand me, Poppy? Say yes, you do.'

'Yes,' Poppy said obediently, but she didn't. The boys here at the house were horrible, much more horrible than she could ever have imagined. They pinched her and pulled her hair and laughed at her and made faces at her and took away any of her things that she did not hide and keep safe. The boys she had talked to at Baldwin's Gardens School hadn't been like that. They had made her laugh and made jokes and been nice. But she knew better than to argue with Mama when she was as white as she was now and her eyes looked so bright and glittery.

'And you must not talk to people about how we used to be or – or anything except here and now. And – ' She had swallowed. 'There are things you cannot understand but you must and I don't know how to – your name, Poppy. You only know a little of your name. You don't know all of it.'

Poppy had stared. 'Of course I know my name! I am Poppy Amberly.'

'There is another part of your name which – which I did not tell you for it was a lot for a little girl like you to learn. Your name is Poppy Amberly Harris. Say it – '

'Why?'

'Because I say so!' Mildred had flared and then bit her lip and looked anxiously at the door. They were sitting in the small boudoir that Mama had chosen to be her very own private room and it was the only room in the house Poppy liked, for only she and Mama ever came in here, except for Queenie who came each morning to clear and lay the fire and dust and sweep. It was quite a pretty room and it had some of the things from the kitchen at home – the pink china clock and the blue and purple vases, though not the blue and white dishes – and though they looked as miserable as Poppy felt in this house, at least they were there.

'Poppy, darling, please try not to argue with me. I promise when you are a big girl I shall explain it all, but now – I just cannot. Just practise it as I say. Poppy Amberly Harris.'

'Poppy Amberly Harris,' Poppy said obediently and made a face. 'It sounds silly.'

'It isn't silly. It is your name. It is what they will call you at your new school. Don't forget.'

'Why is it Harris?'

There had been a little silence and then Mama had got to her feet and gone to the fire to poke it and stir up the flames, though it had been burning quite merrily before. 'It is – it is your name. Your father's name.'

Poppy stared back at her and tried to think. Her father's name. 'But I don't have a father,' she said.

'Of course you do. Everyone has a father.'

'Who – '

'Poppy, don't ask so many questions! Just remember you are now Poppy Amberly Harris and go to the nursery and play with the boys. And remember not a word about anything – about the other place we lived in, about anything – ' And now Mama turned and looked at her, and she had one eyebrow raised in a way that made Poppy shake inside. She only did that when she was very, very angry.

But there was another question she had to ask, and she stopped at the door, her hands twisted in front of her in her pinafore and looked at the floor, instead of looking at Mama, and said, 'Is he dead?'

'What?'

'My father. Is he dead?'

'Oh, Poppy, please do as you are told! Just go to the nursery and stop asking so many questions! It is very naughty to keep on doing so, and you must stop it. When you go to your new school, they will soon tell you that you must not be impertinent! Now do as you are told and go to the nursery.'

So Poppy went, and she asked no more questions. But that did not mean she did not think the questions. Sometimes they got mixed up with her stories and her father became a king, which was after all what he ought to be, for was she not a princess in the stories inside her head? Sometimes, though, he was a hero, especially when everyone talked so much about the war and the soldiers. It would have been quite nice if he had been Colonel Baden-Powell, she decided. She saw pictures of him in the newspapers that she sometimes managed to pick up in the kitchen when Queenie and the cook weren't looking. There were lovely pictures of him in the *Daily Express* and the *Daily Mirror* with his nice moustache. It wasn't as good a moustache as Lord Kitchener's, though, and sometimes she thought she would rather he was her father. And then decided that she didn't want him to be a soldier at all, but to be a king, after all. At least for the present.

This morning, walking home along the Bayswater Road as the last thin glassy sliver of humbug dissolved on her tongue, she wasn't thinking about her father at all, whoever he was. She was thinking instead of what to do this afternoon, when she went back to school after eating her luncheon. She only went back in the afternoons on Mondays and Thursdays. On the other days they only had school in the mornings so on those days she did not have to think of a second promise to make herself, but today was Thursday. So what should it be? She could, perhaps, pretend to be sick; that was something she was getting quite good at, for she'd done it three or four times in the past few weeks. But it wasn't as much fun as it might be, for the last time Miss Peach had taken her back to the house early and told Mama who had put her to bed and given her Gregory's Powders which tasted horrible and gave her a stomach ache. So perhaps it ought to be something different today.

At the corner of Leinster Terrace Queenie was waiting, her hands tucked into her apron bib and the strings on her frilled cap blowing in the breeze, but she wasn't scowling as she usually was when her milkman wasn't there. She had another man with her, a tall one with a floppy hat on and a long coat that was rather dirty.

They had their heads together and were talking busily as she came up and Poppy tried to walk past Queenie, whom she did not like at all, to go to the house, but she reached out and tugged on her coat.

'Hey, Miss Stuck Up, you wait for me!' she said.

'I have to go and have my luncheon,' Poppy said and didn't look at her. She didn't like her teeth, which stuck out in front. 'If I am late Mama will be angry.'

'This is it, is it then?' the man said and Poppy lifted her head and looked at him. He talked like the people in Leather Lane, and she liked that. It was a much friendlier sound than the way the people talked here in Leinster Terrace. 'Looks a nice enough little kid to me.'

'You ought to have the care of her,' Queenie said. 'Too sharp by half, this one. Cut herself she will, if she isn't careful.'

'Bet you're not, eh?' the man said to Poppy. 'You look a nice little girl. What's your name?'

Poppy stared at him and opened her mouth to answer and then remembered and pulled sharply away from Queenie's restraining hand and began to run along the Terrace. 'I'm not allowed to talk to strange men,' she called over her shoulder and then ran even faster. But the man didn't follow her. He just grinned at Queenie and tipped his hat to her and turned to go.

'That's the one I been looking for,' he said. 'Ta for your help, ducks. And remember, not a word to no one.'

433

And Queenie immediately followed Poppy back to the house and ran to the kitchen to tell everyone there of the common sort of chap who'd come looking for Madam upstairs and her kid and what did they all think was behind it? And none of them knew, but they had plenty of ideas between them.

40

'I'd never have thought you'd come back here,' he said and stood there, his shoulders well back so that she could clearly see the empty sleeve, and smiled. 'It's good to see you, Millie. But what are you doing here, of all places?'

She stood just inside the drawing room door and stared at him and he actually saw the colour leave her face so that she was white and pinched. 'How did you get here?' she said at length and her voice was harsh and dry. 'How did you know I was here?'

He grinned and his forehead made the familiar corrugations she knew so well and her belly tightened at the sight. 'You'll never guess,' he said and chuckled. 'Remember Ruby? The boy who used to run for me? He's doing very nicely for himself these days, and when I couldn't work out where you were – it never entered my head you'd come back here – why, it seemed to be the best thing to do, to ask him to look. And here I am.'

'Yes,' she said and closed the door behind her. 'I would have preferred you were not. Why are you here?'

'We've got a lot to talk about, Millie! I mean a lot. Look at me – can't you see we got a lot to talk about?'

'No,' she said baldly. 'There is nothing for us to discuss. I would prefer it if you left now.'

She moved away from the door and went to stand beside the fireplace, where the flames were crackling busily and trying to compete with the June sunlight that was clothing the floor

435

from the tall windows which looked out over the street to the tall houses on the other side. She was not looking at him now, but standing with her head slightly bent and her eyes downcast and he could study her properly.

She looked, he decided, quite old. Only in her thirties, but looking more like forty; her hair was pulled back hard from her forehead so that her nose, that long wandering nose he had always found rather endearing, seemed to jut from her face even more pugnaciously, and her skin was sallow and beginning to be lined about the mouth and nostrils. She was still thin, though not as thin as she had been when he first met her, and there remained that straightness about her body that offered a man nothing interesting to look at; the bodice of her black shirtwaist was flat, and her waist, above the black skirt, for all the belt that surrounded it, seemed to make small effort to reveal any curves. But for all that it was good to see her, for the fascination she had always had for him was still there, and he moved a little closer and said as winningly as he could, 'Now, come on, Millie! Let's be friends again! We used to have a lot of fun, for God's sake! Don't stand there looking like a wet weekend. Say you're glad to see me, say you're sorry I got myself cut about like this, say something!'

She looked up then and this time her face seemed a little less hard. 'I am, of course, very sorry to see you are wounded. I would not wish such a loss on any man.'

'Well, that's handsome of you, very handsome,' he said savagely and threw himself into one of the chairs that stood by the far side of the fireplace. 'I get the fishy eye from the man at the door and I'm left to kick my heels for ten minutes while you decides if you'll see me or not, and no one offers me so much as a glass of water and the best you can do is say you wouldn't wish such a loss on any man? I'm not any man, I'm Lizah Harris, remember? I'm the father of your kid, remember? We were friends, for God's sake! Whatever else has happened, do you have to treat me like a piece of dirt? I'm not dirt! I've been away fighting for this bloody country. I've lost an arm. I tried to save your brother's life and the best you can do is – '

She had gone white again and now she said sharply, 'My brother?'

He bit his lip and subsided again, furious with himself. He had not meant to say anything at all about Basil. Indeed he had done all he could to forget all that had happened between them. There had been enough long and anguished nights of fury and tears when he had lain in that Durban hospital, eaten up with the pain that came from the ghost of his left arm, cursing Basil Amberly for ever having lived, and cursing him even more for having died. If he had kept out of his way, he, Lizah, would have got away unscathed from that bloody battlefield. If he had not had to carry the man across that patch of bullet-spattered scrub he would have his good left arm still instead of this stupid ugly stump and a bleak future as half a man. He had decided long before he left South Africa that life would only be supportable if he never thought about Basil Amberly again. He could boast about 'saving his officer' if he got the chance and it seemed a good tale to tell for business purposes – indeed, he had devised an excellent version of it for use behind the pub bar counters, once he got there – but real thought about the real man; that was never to happen. And here he was already breaking his promise to himself.

'What about my brother?' Mildred said. 'He – he died at Spion Kop.'

'I know,' Lizah mumbled.

'How do you know? Did you see the casualty list? Was that it? And what do you mean about trying to save his life?'

'I was there, God damn it!' he shouted and then turned his head away and pushed himself back further into his chair as though by doing so he could get away from the sharpness of her stare.

'You were with him?' She was still standing very straight, her head up and her eyes fixed on him and he could not keep his own gaze away and he looked back at her. Her eyes looked as dark as the darkest amber, and as hard, and he blinked as she said again more loudly, 'You were with him?'

'What if I was?' He tried to bluster, knowing how important it was that he should not talk more to her about Basil than he had to. He knew perfectly well that he was bad at lying; he could tell a well-embroidered story when it suited him, but that wasn't lying, it was just talking, and he knew that if she pressed him he'd end up telling her how her brother had behaved there in that battlefield, of his tears and his terror and his total uselessness as a soldier let alone as an officer, and he didn't want to do that. The man was dead and clearly she was sad about that. Let her just stay sad, and not be sickened as surely she would be if he told her how it had really been.

'I have a right to know,' she said in a low voice. 'We had a letter from his commanding officer saying that he died under fire. That was all. It – my stepmother has been prostrate ever since and my – Wilfred, my brother Wilfred, has gone to South Africa. After Basil died he said he had to. It has caused so much – I need to know what happened. To say he died under fire – it is so little. What do you know? How is it you tried to save his life? What does that mean?'

'Nothing,' he mumbled again, but this time he saw the look of contempt on her face and it made him redden. 'Dammit, nothing you need to know!' he snapped, and again cursed his own loose tongue.

'And what does that mean?'

'Oh, for God's sake, Millie! I came here to talk about us, not the damned war. I want to see my child. Jessie tells me she's a wonderful child, clever and pretty and all – clever we are, you and me, always was, but no one could call us beauties, eh? Interesting and that – but us, with a pretty kid? What do you say to that, eh? Can I see her? I got such plans, Millie. We're going to have a great time, a really great time – '

'What happened to Basil? I am not interested in speaking of anything else.'

'You don't want to go on about things like that, Millie. Bad enough the poor devil got his chips, isn't it? Let him rest easy. Just say he did his best, like I did. We was altogether, trying to help each other get through – soldiers and officers together.' He was doing his best, trying to mend the harm his own stupid loquacity had caused. 'Listen, the thing of it is, it's morbid going on about what happened. Let's talk of better things – like us getting married. Eh? I was wrong, Millie, I was dead wrong and I'm here to say it. We should have got married as soon as you got in the club – I know that now. I've thought a lot about us, all this time, a lot. We ought to be together, us and our kid, have more maybe. I've got it all worked out, the whole thing. I got Truman's to agree I should be licensee of this lovely little pub they've got in Hoxton, a nice part, not rough at all, and when I've learned the business properly, they say they'll send me to a better place and I can do really well. There's a nice little flat over and plenty of room for the kid as well and there's plenty of trade for us. Jessie tells me you're a great cook now, that you made a nice thing out of baking, so we can do food at the pub, eh? A little restaurant in the back – we could be sitting pretty, you and me. Really pretty. So let's let bygones be bygones and start again, Millie. What do you say? You don't want to live here in this apology for a cemetery! It's like walking into misery to come into this house. You feel it as you walk up the steps – what do you say, Millie, eh? I took you away from here once before, remember. Now let me take you away again – '

'You took me away?' She was blazing with anger and had it barely under her control. He could feel it coming at him like waves of heat from a banked down fire. 'I left here of my own free will – and I've come back here in the same way. You dare to come here and speak so to me? You want me now because you're crippled and for no better reason! You want to be looked

439

after and coddled and – and – well, find someone else! Ask
your sister to take care of you, ask your mother – leave me
alone and – '

'My mother's dead and Jessie's getting married again.' He
meant to sound dignified but he sounded merely sulky, even in
his own ears. 'She's going to live in America.'

'I'm delighted to hear it!' Mildred flared. 'It's time she had
her own life. I wish her joy. But you – you can get out of this
house and never come near it or me again! What do you think
I am? A street drab that will sit willingly waiting for you to pick
her up and set her down again as it pleases you? I am a woman
of better worth than that! I am well able to care for myself and
for my child, and need no part of you, and never will! Find
someone else to look after you and cater to your selfishness
and high opinion of yourself. I have no opinion of you and do
not care whether you live or die. You understand me? Whether
you live or die!'

He stared at her and blinked and then shook his head.
'What's happened to you?' he said wonderingly. 'You used to
be – I mean, you was always spirited. It was the first thing
about you I ever saw, that spirit in you, but you weren't hard
like this. Now you've turned into a – whatever did I ever do to
you to get such a tongue-lashing as that?'

'What did you do to me?' She threw both hands up in the
air in an oddly quaint little gesture. 'What did you do to me?
You ruined my life! You seduced me, you left me to do as best
I could when my baby was born, and you ask me that?'

'The life I was supposed to have ruined wasn't all that
wonderful as I recall. And as for seducing you – you were as
eager as I was. I remember that too,' he said, and again tried to
be dignified, and this time almost succeeded. 'It was your idea
to leave this house, sure it was – because you hated it so much.
Have you forgotten? I haven't. That was why I never thought
to look for you here, though Ruby did. I couldn't believe you'd

ever willingly come back to your father, you hated him so much.'

'He's dead,' she said, and turned her back on him. 'Just as my brother is, and for all I know my other brother too. I have to look after my stepmother and my younger brothers. Someone has to be responsible. That is why I am here. And I wish to stay here unmolested. Go away. Just leave me alone and go *away*. All I want to hear from you is news of what happened to my brother Basil. If you have anything to tell me of him, then say it. If not, go away. I never want to see you again. I never want to see any man again – ever – ' And she stood there beside the fire with her head down staring into the flames.

He got to his feet and stood very still, watching her, and there was a long silence as he tried to untangle the confusion in his head.

Tell her he had lost his arm trying to save the life of her coward of a brother? What good would that do? Would it make her lose all her anger, make her hatred of him melt away? Would she even believe him? He had a dim picture in his mind of how it would be, how she would sneer at him and accuse him of speaking ill of the dead to make himself look good, and he closed his eyes, trying to see a way out of the trap into which he had fallen. And could not.

'I never meant you any harm, Millie,' he managed at last. But she ignored him, not moving from her place beside the fire. 'I loved you, you know that? I still do. You've got class, Millie, you always did have, and you still have it. I thought, the past is the past. I didn't behave all that well, I dare say, but then neither did you. And it's no fault in us. We do what we have to do, and when we have to do it, don't we? You do the best with what you are and what you've got. You had to live in this house with money and a father you hated who made your life a misery and you got out. I lived in the East End with

441

good people but no money and no hope of getting any except with my own fists, and I did the best I could to get out. And together I thought we could make an even better best – and we still could, if you'd just try.'

She shook her head. 'You're mad to think it, just as I was once. It's over. The past is indeed the past, and I have no intention of repeating any of the mistakes I made. I want no part of it.'

'But you've got your kid,' he said. 'Jessie says she's quite a kid – '

For the first time her face softened. 'Yes. I have my daughter. And I'm going to see to it she has a good life, a better life than I did. She'll have the best I can get for her. That's the reason why I'm back here. I don't pretend this is a happy house for me. It never was, and I doubt it ever will be. But it's good for Poppy and it will be happy for her. Here she can be cared for and educated and become the sort of woman she should be. Not one who can be bullied and put upon and – and used as I was, but one who has her own life in her own hands and is free of men like my father, and like – you – Go away, please. There is nothing more for us to discuss. Go away.'

'She is my daughter too – ' he began but now she turned a look of such fury on him that he actually took a step back.

'Don't you ever dare to come near her, do you hear me? You are – you have no rights at all. She is my daughter, mine, mine, *mine*. What do you know of her? What care have you ever had of her? She nearly died because of you – if you had not gone running off to South Africa and made Jessie so fearful I would never have taken the child to – oh, go away!' And she stamped her foot and then almost ran across the room to the door to fling it open. 'Get out! I never want to see you ever again, and if you ever come near this house again I shall fetch the police to you. And they will look at you and at me, and who will they believe? Be warned. I have no wish to talk to you ever again.

If you have anything now to tell me of my brother Basil, then say it. Otherwise, go!'

Poppy had been sitting all afternoon at the nursery window, peering down into the street. It had worked out very well, after all, pretending to be sick. She had been fetched back to the house by Miss Peach and put to bed by Mama, who always put her to bed at the least hint of any illness, for she worried about it so, and the boys had all been out for they were at school and she could lie there and read and be as happy as if she were a real princess, all on her own. But it got a little boring after a while so she crept out of bed and listened at the door. Mama was in the drawing-room; the door was shut and she had heard someone go in there a while ago. Visitors, she thought, and was glad she wasn't there. Visitors were always so tedious; old ladies from the other houses in the Terrace who sat and spoke in long sad voices about the war and people dying and being ill; Poppy didn't like them at all. But there might be something to look at in the street below so she went and curled up on the window seat and stared out through the bars.

It had been raining and the paving stones which she could see through the green leaves of the plane tree just below her were shiny and bright; and she could see the reflection of the people in them as they walked by and she giggled inside her head as she thought what fun it would be to open the window and lean out and spit on them. Spitting was a dreadful thing to do but great fun, and she pushed on the window to see if it would open. It did and she could lean out and it was lovely. She pulled her wrapper closer and leaned over the sill, staring down below at the wet leaves and the pavement and the people and began to collect spit in her mouth, wondering if she would dare to do it when the time came. This was the best game she had thought of for a long time, for it made her chest feel tight and excited and that was a lovely feeling.

Somewhere far below the font door opened and she leaned out even further, a little precariously, to see who it was. No one she knew. A man in a brown suit but no hat and with an empty sleeve pinned across his chest. She had seen other such men in the streets lately, and when she'd asked about them, been told they were brave soldiers. So this was a brave soldier, and she decided that perhaps it would be better not to spit on him, but to wait for someone else. Besides, he looked, as far as she could see, quite nice. He had dark curly hair and she wondered what sort of face he had to go with it, and almost as though he had heard her thinking it, he lifted his head – to look up and she pulled back, scared she would be seen, and the spit she had collected in her mouth disappeared as she swallowed without thinking.

It was a very nice face, she decided, with big eyes and a lot of lines on the forehead, just like the lines she had seen when she had looked out of the train window when they had all gone to see the ships in Southampton before she got ill, only there were more of them, and she stared at the man as the leaves below her shifted and murmured in the breeze that had sharpened now as a little rush of rain swept across the street.

In the drawing-room Millie heard the front door slam shut and lifted her head and listened as silence filled the house again. The tears rose in her chest like a tide and she hated herself for her own weakness. There is no reason to weep, she told herself fiercely, none at all. He is as he has always been, a disaster for her. His chatter, his charm, his ridiculous plans – what good had they ever brought her? Nothing but trouble, nothing but pain.

And Poppy, her treacherous inner voice whispered. And Poppy? Is she a disaster, is she pain and trouble? He gave you Poppy – and now you are robbing him of her. And she of him. Perhaps Poppy would like to live with her father as well as her mother in a flat over a little public house and help her mother cook for the customers and –

And now she had no trouble in suppressing the tide of tears. Poppy deserved better than that. If all he could offer his child was that sort of slum life, then he wasn't fit to be her father. Poppy was to be a lady, an educated lady, a person who could earn her own living if the need arose, and not be dependent on any man. Poppy was to be a Twentieth-Century woman of the best kind, not a weak and useless creature like her mother. She may be pretty and therefore in less need of the equipment that would make her independent, Millie told herself, still fiercely, but that made no matter. She is to be a strong woman who owns herself. She won't ever suffer as I do, eaten with a need that is so shameful, so – so – and now the tears did come as she stood beside the handsome fireplace in the big drawing room of her stepmother's house in Leinster Terrace, literally holding on to the edge of the mantel to prevent herself from doing what her body so desperately wanted her to do. Which was to run after the man now walking away from her down the rainy street outside.

Why he stopped and looked up he didn't know. The flood of hate and anger Millie had hurled at him had almost literally taken his breath away, and there had been only one answer in him – to turn and go and leave her there with her glittering eyes and her bitter stare and never think about her again. He could do it. Whatever he had felt for her before, he could do it. No man could go on caring about a bitch like that. Why should he? He had done all he could for her, had never tried to pretend to be anything other than he was, yet she treated him so villainously – and he had whipped up his thoughts like horses, making himself boil with enough anger to fuel his escape.

And then had found himself stopping and turning and looking upwards, without knowing why. Until he saw her. A small white face peering over the edge of a window sill, high up behind the leaves of a tall plane tree, and he knew at once who it was. And it wasn't just the way she looked, the dark curly hair that was so like his own, and the wide dark eyes. There was more to it than that, a sort of shock of recognition. Even though he had never seen her before, he knew at once who she was.

And he lifted his chin even higher and smiled, and half lifted his right hand and for a moment she stared back at him, her face quite blank, and even at this distance he could see that clearly, and then she disappeared. He stood there and waited for a long time, just standing and waiting for her to appear at the door of the house, there at the top of the steps just behind him.

But the seconds became minutes and there was no sign of her and the rain increased, soaking his thin suit and making the stump of his left arm ache abominably and at last he knew he was being ridiculous, making a damned fool of himself, waiting here in the windswept street for a child who was just such a one as her mother. She wasn't coming down, had never had any intention of coming down. She had just stared and sneered and gone away, and he sniffed hard to clear his nose and upper lip of the rain and turned to go, hunching his cold shoulders against the chill.

It took so long to get dressed again, that was the trouble. Usually there were people there to help with the buttons on the back of her dresses and with the even worse buttons on her boots, so she wasn't very good at it, and all the time as she struggled she knew he was down there waiting and that made her fingers even more awkward and slow. But she managed it at last and opened the nursery door and slipped out on to the landing and down the back stairs.

The servants were in the kitchen; she could hear their voices murmuring and the occasional crack of laughter from behind the closed door, and she crept through the passageway to the back door and managed somehow to open it, even though the handle stuck as it always did. It didn't rattle too much though, and, with a scared glance over her shoulder, she slipped through as quickly as she could and ran across the area and up the steps and out into the street.

He wasn't there and for a moment she stood still, wanting to cry and not knowing why. She didn't know who the man was, didn't even know why she was running after him. All she knew was that he had looked up at her through the wet leaves of the plane tree and waved and his face had been a face she liked, with its crinkled forehead and its dark eyes and she wanted – no, *had* to talk to him. And now he was gone.

But then she lifted her head and stood on tiptoe so that she could see further down the street and at once her chest seemed to burst with excitement again, because he wasn't gone at all. He was walking along the street, with a funny sort of walk, as though he were bouncing from one foot to the other, and she could see the way his shoulder on one side was the wrong shape, because of the empty sleeve in front.

And she began to run after him, her half-buttoned boots slapping on the wet pavements and splashing into the puddles, and the distance between them narrowed slowly, and she ran even faster so that she could hardly breathe. But that didn't matter, because she knew now she could catch him. And she knew, too, that it was very important that she should.

CLAIRE RAYNER

FLANDERS

(BOOK TWO OF *THE POPPY CHRONICLES*)

It is 1911 and at sixteen Poppy can appreciate the courage of the suffragettes as they demand a fairer future for women. Then the First World War breaks out bringing devastating loss and suffering. As the old certainties are swept away, Poppy's life changes forever. She bravely volunteers to work as an ambulance driver at the front in Flanders. There, amongst danger and death, she discovers an unexpected liberation. She also meets a handsome war correspondent...

FLAPPER

(BOOK THREE OF *THE POPPY CHRONICLES*)

During the First World War, Poppy finds freedom and also love. She marries, only to be widowed after a brief but idyllically happy marriage. Despite her grief she makes every effort to cope with Chloe, her determined and strong-willed stepdaughter. To complicate matters she must also take care of her mother. *Flapper* powerfully illustrates how Poppy, like so many women, struggles to provide unwavering support for her family, in the process denying many of her own needs and desires.

Claire Rayner

Blitz

(Book Four of *The Poppy Chronicles*)

As the Blitz brings a reign of terror to London, Poppy, now a mature and capable woman, struggles to ensure her family lead as normal lives as possible. The problems with which she must cope are problems known to all mothers. Poppy's own daughter is torn between two men. Her headstrong stepdaughter is persistently difficult. It is a time of fear and uncertainty; however, love and passion grow amidst the devastation.

Festival

(Book Five of *The Poppy Chronicles*)

In 1951 shortages caused by the war are beginning to come to an end and the Festival of Britain announces a time of optimism. Once again people have hope in the future. Poppy is having a degree of success running her own business and is thoroughly enjoying her independence. However, she continues to be the anchor for her family, the unfailing support for their dreams and aspirations. Then one day the steadfast Poppy meets Peter Chantry...

CLAIRE RAYNER

SIXTIES

(BOOK SIX OF *THE POPPY CHRONICLES*)

It is the Sixties and Poppy is devastated by the loss of her
mother. However, with typical resolve she faces the future with
courage and determination. Poppy has steered herself and her
family to great achievements. Her own business is flourishing,
as is her daughter's Carnaby Street boutique. Her son is in the
music business and stepdaughter Chloe is in America. As a
new era of liberation and rebellion begins, Poppy's story ends
on a note of optimism.

OTHER TITLES BY CLAIRE RAYNER AVAILABLE DIRECT
FROM HOUSE OF STRATUS

Quantity	£	$(US)	$(CAN)	€
THE POPPY CHRONICLES				
FLANDERS	6.99	12.95	19.95	13.50
FLAPPER	6.99	12.95	19.95	13.50
BLITZ	6.99	12.95	19.95	13.50
FESTIVAL	6.99	12.95	19.95	13.50
SIXTIES	6.99	12.95	19.95	13.50
THE PERFORMERS SERIES				
GOWER STREET	6.99	12.95	19.95	13.50
THE HAYMARKET	6.99	12.95	19.95	13.50
PADDINGTON GREEN	6.99	12.95	19.95	13.50
SOHO SQUARE	6.99	12.95	19.95	13.50
BEDFORD ROW	6.99	12.95	19.95	13.50
LONG ACRE	6.99	12.95	19.95	13.50
CHARING CROSS	6.99	12.95	19.95	13.50
THE STRAND	6.99	12.95	19.95	13.50
CHELSEA REACH	6.99	12.95	19.95	13.50
SHAFTESBURY AVENUE	6.99	12.95	19.95	13.50
PICCADILLY	6.99	12.95	19.95	13.50
SEVEN DIALS	6.99	12.95	19.95	13.50

ALL HOUSE OF STRATUS BOOKS ARE AVAILABLE FROM GOOD BOOKSHOPS
OR DIRECT FROM THE PUBLISHER:

Internet: www.houseofstratus.com including synopses and features.

Email: sales@houseofstratus.com
info@houseofstratus.com
(please quote author, title and credit card details.)

Tel: **Order Line**
0800 169 1780 (UK)
International
+44 (0) 1845 527700 (UK)

Fax: **+44 (0) 1845 527711 (UK)**
(please quote author, title and credit card details.)

Send to: **House of Stratus Sales Department**
Thirsk Industrial Park
York Road, Thirsk
North Yorkshire, YO7 3BX
UK

PAYMENT

Please tick currency you wish to use:

☐ £ (Sterling)　☐ $ (US)　☐ $ (CAN)　☐ € (Euros)

Allow for shipping costs charged per order plus an amount per book as set out in the tables below:

CURRENCY/DESTINATION

	£(Sterling)	$(US)	$(CAN)	€ (Euros)
Cost per order				
UK	1.50	2.25	3.50	2.50
Europe	3.00	4.50	6.75	5.00
North America	3.00	3.50	5.25	5.00
Rest of World	3.00	4.50	6.75	5.00
Additional cost per book				
UK	0.50	0.75	1.15	0.85
Europe	1.00	1.50	2.25	1.70
North America	1.00	1.00	1.50	1.70
Rest of World	1.50	2.25	3.50	3.00

PLEASE SEND CHEQUE OR INTERNATIONAL MONEY ORDER payable to: HOUSE OF STRATUS LTD or card payment as indicated

STERLING EXAMPLE

Cost of book(s):.................... Example: 3 x books at £6.99 each: £20.97

Cost of order:..................... Example: £1.50 (Delivery to UK address)

Additional cost per book:.............. Example: 3 x £0.50: £1.50

Order total including shipping:.......... Example: £23.97

VISA, MASTERCARD, SWITCH, AMEX:

☐☐☐☐☐☐☐☐☐☐☐☐☐☐☐☐☐☐☐

Issue number (Switch only):

☐☐☐

Start Date:　　　　**Expiry Date:**

☐☐/☐☐　　　☐☐/☐☐

Signature:

NAME:

ADDRESS:

COUNTRY:

ZIP/POSTCODE:

Please allow 28 days for delivery. Despatch normally within 48 hours.

Prices subject to change without notice.
Please tick box if you do not wish to receive any additional information. ☐

House of Stratus publishes many other titles in this genre; please check our website (**www.houseofstratus.com**) for more details.